Caroline Anderson is a matriarch, writer, armchair gardener, unofficial tearoom researcher and eater of lovely cakes. Not necessarily in that order! What Caroline loves: her family. Her friends. Reading. Writing contemporary love stories. Hearing from readers. Walks by the sea with coffee/ice cream/cake thrown in! Torrential rain. Sunshine in spring/autumn. What Caroline hates: losing her pets. Fighting with her family. Cold weather. Hot weather. Computers. Clothes shopping. Caroline's plans: keep smiling and writing!

Allie Kincheloe has been writing stories for as long as she can remember, and somehow they always become romances. A Kentucky girl at heart, she now lives in Tennessee, with her husband, children, and a growing menagerie of pets. Visit her on Twitter: @AllieKAuthor.

Also by Caroline Anderson

One Night, One Unexpected Miracle

Yoxburgh Park Hospital miniseries

Their Meant-to-Be Baby
The Midwife's Longed-For Baby
Bound by Their Babies
Their Own Little Miracle
A Single Dad to Heal Her Heart
From Heartache to Forever
Tempted by the Single Mum

Heart Surgeon's Second Chance

is **Allie Kincheloe**'s debut title

Look out for more books from Allie Kincheloe

Coming soon

Discover more at millsandboon.co.uk.

TEMPTED BY THE SINGLE MUM

CAROLINE ANDERSON

HEART SURGEON'S SECOND CHANCE

ALLIE KINCHELOE

MILLS & BOON

First Published in Great Britain 2020
by Mills & Boon, an imprint of HarperCollins*Publishers*
1 London Bridge Street, London, SE1 9GF

ISBN: 978-0-263-27966-5

MIX
Paper from
responsible sources
FSC™ C007454

This book is produced from independently certified FSC™ paper
to ensure responsible forest management.
For more information visit www.harpercollins.co.uk/green.

Printed and bound in Spain
by CPI, Barcelona

TEMPTED BY THE SINGLE MUM

CAROLINE ANDERSON

MILLS & BOON

I have many people to thank, not least my editor
for her endless patience. Sheila, you are a star.

Also Juno, who's looked after us for very many years,
through many trials and tribulations.
Thank you for your kindness and support.

And, last but not least, thanks also to
my long-suffering husband John, who must
surely be sick of me saying, 'We can't do that,
I have to write my book…'

CHAPTER ONE

WHY? WHY TODAY, when she was already running late before she'd even started, did someone have to make it even worse?

She glared at the car reversing neatly into the one remaining doctors' space—a car she didn't recognise, and she'd never seen the driver, either. He certainly wasn't one of their doctors, so whoever he was he had no business parking there.

Didn't seem to bother him. He either didn't know, or didn't care, but he flashed her a smile as he got out of the car, then locked it and headed for the surgery without a backward glance.

Who did he think he was? Cocky, arrogant—argh! There weren't words for what she felt. The expensive car, the confident stride, the easy charm—not to mention the insanely good looks. Clearly a man for whom everything had always gone his way. Well, not now. Whoever he was—probably a drug rep—he was about to get his comeuppance.

Still fuming, she reversed into the last available space in the car park, not really wide enough but doable—or it would have been, if she hadn't been so cross.

She heard the scrape, closed her eyes and breathed, then shuffled the car slightly further from the offending wall, squeezed out of the ridiculously narrow gap she'd left herself, slammed the door and headed across the car park.

Seriously, could today *get* any worse? Well, his could. If he was still in Reception—

He was. He was chatting to the receptionist, leaning forward engagingly as he spoke, and that easy charm was obviously working on Katie, which just infuriated her more. His hands were shoved casually into the pockets of immaculately cut trousers that fitted his neat, strong hips to perfection. Of course they did. They wouldn't dare do anything else.

She eyed his shoulders, broad and yet not heavy, the legs strong and straight below firm, taut buttocks. He probably worked out in a fancy gym somewhere. You didn't get a neat, sexy bottom like that by accident.

She dragged her eyes up to head height.

'You've parked in a doctor's space,' she said crisply to his back, keeping a lid on her temper with difficulty, and he straightened up and turned towards her, that infuriating smile still on his face.

'Yes, I—'

'I know parking's tight, but that is just not on. There was another space, so why not park there yourself? Or anywhere else, frankly! Or was that the only space big enough for your ego? Thanks to you I've scraped my car, I'm now ten minutes late and I've got patients waiting!'

An eyebrow rose a fraction. Over his shoulder she could see Katie gesturing wildly, but she ignored her and stood her ground, and he shook his head slowly.

'Maybe you need to get up earlier,' he murmured, and she stifled the urge to growl at him.

'And maybe you need to learn to read!'

'Ellie! Dr Kendal!' Katie chipped in, getting to her

feet and looking even more flustered, and his eyebrow went up a little further, a lazy smile now playing around his aggravatingly beautiful mouth.

'I think we'd better start again,' he said, holding out his hand, the smile tugging at his lips. 'It's a pleasure to meet you, Dr Kendal. I'm Nick Cooper. *Dr* Nick Cooper.'

The new—and desperately needed—member of their team.

Brilliant.

Why didn't the ground just open up and swallow her?

He had to stifle his laugh.

Her jaw sagged, and for a second she was speechless. Then she shook her head, mumbled what could have been an apology and fled through the staff door as Katie opened it, her face flaming.

He dropped his hand back to his side, shrugged and smiled at the receptionist who was looking horrified and fascinated all at once.

'So, that's Dr Kendal,' he murmured, vaguely intrigued.

'Yes. Ellie. I'm so sorry, she's normally lovely. I don't know what's got into her.'

He pulled a face and walked through the door into the back of Reception, closing it behind himself. 'I do. I took the last doctor's space, and now she's scraped her car. Oops. If I'd known who she was I would have moved, but I didn't have a clue.'

'She's only part-time, so if she wasn't on duty when you came for your interviews you wouldn't have met her—and she does normally walk. You weren't to know.'

He nodded. 'No. Ah, well. I have no doubt we'll have time to catch up later.'

Katie gestured towards the other doorway, still looking flustered. 'Come in and I'll introduce you to the admin team, and I'm sure Dr Gallagher will be out in a minute to talk to you. I've let her know you're here.'

She led the way, and he followed her into the office and scanned it for any sign of his fiery new colleague, but she'd gone.

Pity. Never mind. He was here all day, there was time, and he could look forward to what was bound to be an interesting conversation…

Why had she done that?

Torn him to pieces without even giving him a chance to speak? And if he'd been a patient, he would have been well within his rights to complain. No, it was even better than that. He was a colleague, her senior, and she'd just hurled abuse at him in their first interaction.

Marvellous. Just marvellous.

Not that he'd been exactly polite himself, telling her to get up earlier. She'd been up before half five as it was to do the laundry, and if Maisie hadn't been a diva and Evie hadn't needed her nappy changed again and Oscar hadn't lost one of his shoes and then had a meltdown, she wouldn't have been late and then none of this would have happened.

She felt her eyes prickle, and clamped her jaw shut hard, blinking furiously as she closed her consulting room door behind her and leant against it. It could have been worse. There could have been a whole bunch of patients in Reception, so at least she hadn't had an audience while she'd made a total fool of herself.

'Breathe,' she said softly, and closed her eyes, sucking in a long, slow breath through her nose and out through her mouth. In…and out… In…and out—

The quiet tap on the door made her jump, and she

leapt away from it and wrenched it open, to find herself face to face with her worst nightmare, no doubt coming to tear her apart in private. Well, it was certainly justified, and he probably hated her already.

Or maybe not…

'Katie thought you'd want this,' he said quietly, holding out a mug of tea without a trace of a smile, and she stared at it suspiciously.

Beware of strangers bearing gifts...

'Why are you bringing me a peace offering? I'm the one who should be apologising—or have you slipped something into it?'

His mouth twitched. 'Don't tempt me,' he murmured, and gave her a wry smile. 'It's not a peace offering. Katie was about to bring it to you, and I suggested I do it. I thought we could do with clearing the air.'

She took it from him with fingers that weren't quite steady, then made herself meet his eyes. He held her gaze, his searching, thoughtful, the smile gone now. She was quite glad she didn't know what he was thinking…

She felt her shoulders drop in defeat. 'Look, I'm sorry, I didn't know who you were, which is no excuse whatsoever, I know that, but—' She broke off, still mortified and wondering if there was any way she could rescue the situation. 'I hadn't realised you were coming in today, I thought you'd be starting on Monday, so I wasn't expecting you, I didn't recognise you, and then you took the last reserved space, and as if that wasn't enough I scraped my car parking by the wall, which was just the icing on the cake—'

'Ellie, breathe! It's OK. Forget it. You're right, I *am* starting on Monday, I'm just having an induction today, learning the ropes a bit, finding my feet before I start. I guess nobody told you. And I'm sorry I took your parking place, but Lucy told me to park there because you usually walk to work. Obviously not today.'

'No. I should have been, I nearly always do, but I got—held up,' she said, for want of a better way of putting it.

'So it seems. Parking's tight, isn't it? Lucy said it's a regular occurrence with the building work going on.'

She nodded, sighing with relief because he had every right to be unreasonable about this. 'It is, but they should be finished soon and the builders' vans will be gone, and not a moment too soon. Look, I'm sorry, can we do this later? I don't mean to be rude—again—but I do have patients waiting and I'm already on the drag.'

'Of course. And I'm sorry about the parking—and your car.'

'Don't be sorry. You had every right to park there, as it turns out, and I massively overreacted. And thank you for the tea. I haven't had time for one today.'

His eyes softened at the corners, that flickering smile sending strange little shivers through her body. 'My pleasure,' he murmured. 'We'll catch up later.' His lips twitched again. 'You can teach me to read, and I can teach you to tell the time.'

She rolled her eyes. He might have forgiven her, but he clearly wasn't going to let it drop.

'Oh, I can tell the time,' she told him wryly. 'I was up at five twenty-seven, for what it's worth.'

A silent ah, and he backed out, fingers waggling. 'Better not hold you up any more, then. I'll see you later.'

She nodded, and the door closed softly behind him.

Shaking her head and wishing she could wind the clock back, she put the tea down, washed her hands and fired up her computer, her mind refusing to let go of that lazy, sexy, fleeting smile.

Stupid. She was nearly twenty minutes late now, and it

would have a knock-on effect on the rest of the day. She didn't have time to daydream, and particularly not about a man who probably practised his smile in the mirror!

'Get a grip, Ellie,' she told herself, took a gulp of her tea and pressed the button to call her first patient.

Predictably she finished her morning surgery late, checked some results and wrote two referral letters and then, just because why not, when she went upstairs to their temporary staff room to make herself a coffee and eat the lunch she'd hastily thrown together at crazy o'clock, Nick was in there alone.

Time to eat humble pie again…

He looked up from the paperwork scattered on the table in front of him, and his unbelievably blue, improbably beautiful eyes locked on hers with that clear, steady gaze that she was beginning to find unnerving.

'OK?'

She laughed. Was she? Probably. 'I'll live. People don't normally die of embarrassment. Have they abandoned you?'

'They're all busy. I'm fine. I'm reading through a pile of stuff they gave me and I was sort of hoping you'd come in so we could start again.'

'No need, Nick, it's fine, and I think I've probably said enough to last a lifetime. Can we just drop it? I'm not normally so inexcusably rude.'

'I'm sure you're not, but you were hassled and I was in your space. And you'd just trashed your car.'

She shrugged and headed for the kettle. 'It's hardly trashed, it barely shows, and I still shouldn't have been so rude. You could have been anyone.'

Though how anyone else would have been worse than the new partner it was hard to imagine.

He got to his feet and headed over to where she was standing, moving with a lithe, easy grace—and a slight wince? 'Let's start again. I'm Nick.'

'And I'm Ellie.'

She took the hand he was holding out to her, and as his fingers wrapped around her hand she felt warmth and reassurance and strength. And about a million volts. She dropped it like a hot potato, and he switched on the kettle and settled back against the worktop edge, legs crossed at the ankle, arms folded, sex appeal pouring off his perfectly honed body in waves.

Why did he have to be so darned sexy?

'I'll get you a drink, you eat your lunch,' he said, that smile flickering again. 'And while you do that, you can tell me why you were up at five twenty-seven.'

She rolled her eyes, handed him her empty mug and ripped the lid off her lunch box, retreating to the other side of the table for a bit of much-needed distance.

'Coffee, please, white, no sugar. And since you asked, it was nothing unusual, I'm often up that early. I put the washing on, hung out the load which had done overnight, showered, dressed, hung out the second load, got the kids up, finally got them dressed after the usual arguments, we had breakfast, then Maisie had another strop because her best dress was on the line, Oscar lost a shoe and then had a meltdown and wouldn't put his other shoes on, and Evie did a poo so I had to change her nappy, by which time Oscar had taken his shoes off again and hidden them, and Maisie was changing her dress for the third time. So, just another day at the office, really.'

He put the coffee down in front of her, his eyes wide and brimming with something that could have been sympathy if it hadn't been for the laughter fighting its way to the top.

'Ouch,' he said softly, sitting down again and propping his elbows on the table as he held her eyes with that gorgeously blue and now sympathetic gaze. 'That's not a great way to start the day!'

She tried to smile but it was a wan effort and she abandoned it, making him frown. He leant slightly towards her, his eyes searching.

'Are you OK, Ellie?' he asked softly, and she shrugged.

'Of course. I'm just tired. And it could have been worse,' she said, forking up another mouthful of salad and trying not to think about the gorgeous eyes. 'At least none them had thrown up in the night or had a temperature, but I pity the people at nursery. Oscar was still screaming by the time we got there because I'd put him in the car without his shoes on, and Maisie was mutinous and grumpy for England.'

'And Evie? You did say Evie, didn't you?'

She felt her face soften into an involuntary smile at the thought of her baby girl and put her fork down, the salad forgotten. 'Yes, it's Evie. She was her usual sweet, sunny little self, bless her heart.'

He grinned, his eyes crinkling and making him suddenly even more approachable. 'Small mercies?' he murmured, and she laughed.

'Absolutely. I live for them, and I'm sure it won't be long before she gets the terrible twos and it all falls apart. I'm enjoying it while it lasts.'

He sat back, his eyes still searching hers thoughtfully. 'So, where's your husband while all this is going on?' he murmured.

The urge to smile evaporated, along with any trace of humour she'd been feeling, and she sat up straighter and dropped her eyes to her salad, prodding it around for something to do before she looked up again. 'No husband,' she said crisply. 'I'm divorced.'

'Ah. Join the club. I tell you what, let's not go there, shall we? It'll take all day and we've got much better things to discuss.'

It was his turn to look away, but not until she'd seen a subtle change in those fascinating eyes, a flicker of something like regret or disappointment or—grief? No matter. She was happy to let the subject drop and sip her coffee. Divorce was always a bit messy, and some were messier than others. Clearly not everything in life *had* gone his way…

'So, how long have you been working here?' he asked lightly, moving the subject on, and she was happy to pick it up and run with it.

'Since after Maisie, so a little over three years? We had a flat in London, but David's parents live in Yoxburgh and we'd bought a holiday home just round the corner from them, but he was away all the time working abroad so after we had Maisie we moved up here to our house and kept the flat on for when he was doing a fast turnaround, and I started work here when she was ten months old. And then two months in I realised I was pregnant with Oscar, which wasn't planned, and then Evie came along.'

Although she wasn't going into that, because David's reaction had devastated her. It still hurt now, nearly two years later, and probably always would, but she was fine without him. Better, really, no matter how tough it might be sometimes.

'So, how old are they now?' Nick asked softly.

'Maisie's just four, Oscar's two and a half, and Evie's nearly fifteen months.'

His eyes widened. 'That's…'

'Three in thirty-four months. I know. It's ridiculous.'

He let out a long, slow breath. 'I don't know about ridiculous, but that's pretty hardcore, for a single parent. For any parent, come to that, especially if you're working. It must be a nightmare.'

She shook her head. 'They're a joy, really, when I have time to draw breath and think about it. Today was just one of those days, but I wouldn't change it for the world, tantrums and all.'

'No, of course not. I'm sure you love them all dearly.'

'I do.' She eyed him steadily, wondering if she'd heard something odd in his voice. 'So, your turn. Why here?'

He shrugged. 'Why not? I wanted a total change, I don't have any ties, and it's the sort of job I've always wanted. I was ready for it, it was there—it seemed sort of meant.'

'What about your kids?' she asked, blatantly fishing, but he just shook his head, his eyes steady but expressionless now.

'No kids. If we'd had kids, I'd still be there. Children are a lifetime commitment. You don't walk away. It's not negotiable.'

She gave a little snort. 'Tell it to the fairies. My ex walked out when I was eight weeks pregnant with Evie.'

He blinked, his eyes startled. 'Seriously? He left when you were pregnant? Did he know?'

He sounded appalled, and she couldn't help the bitter little laugh. Oh, yes, he'd known. It was why he'd gone.

'I thought we weren't going into this?' she said, trying to keep it light and move on, but he didn't let it drop.

'Does he see them?'

'Oh, yes. He comes up every fortnight and stays with his parents, who think it's dreadful that he walked out on his marriage, and they're not thrilled with me, either, because I won't have him back, but they're sticking by us because they want a decent relationship with their grandchildren, and the kids adore them. His loss.'

'And the children's. Idiot.' He held up a hand. 'Sorry, not my place.'

'Oh, no, feel free. Nobody's going to argue with you except him, and he's not here, thank goodness.' She gave him a wry smile. 'Just as well, or he'd be ranting at me for scraping my car on the wall this morning.'

He pulled a face, his mouth tipping ruefully up at one side. 'Sorry—again. I ought to pay for it to be fixed.'

'Why? You weren't driving it.'

'No, but it was my fault and I didn't exactly make your morning any better, did I? And I really am sorry about that. You obviously have enough on your plate.'

She answered his smile, wondering why that little tilt of his lips was having such a weird effect on her. Crazy—

'Yes, well, I think we need to forget all about it, and I think I need to do something a bit proactive or my afternoon's going to go down the tubes as well. I'm duty doctor this afternoon so I've got all sorts of patients slotted in. I need to go.'

She got to her feet, hesitated a second and then leant across the table, holding out her hand, telling herself it wasn't to find out if she felt that electric tingle again. 'Friends?' she asked, and he smiled and took her hand.

Yup, still there, fizzing all the way through her body.

'Friends,' he murmured, and she smiled and dropped his hand and straightened up, resisting the urge to rub her tingling palm on her trousers.

'Good. I'll see you on Monday, then,' she said, as the door opened and Lucy Gallagher came in.

'You'll see him tonight at ours for dinner, I hope?'

Lucy said, and she turned to her friend and colleague, her jaw dropping.

'Dinner?' she said blankly.

'Yes—Nick's welcome dinner?'

Oh, no. 'Isn't it next Friday?'

'No, it's tonight, at seven. Ah…' Lucy tilted her head to one side. 'No babysitter?'

She closed her eyes and counted to ten. Could Liz help out? Maybe. Another favour—oh, lord.

'No. I didn't need one, but David changed his weekend, and I didn't join the dots. Idiot me. I'm so, so sorry, Lucy. I'll ask my mother-in-law, and I'll let you know. I'll come if I possibly can, but it might just be for a short while.'

Lucy smiled and shook her head. 'Don't worry, I quite understand. Give her a ring, do what you can.'

'I will. I need to go; I've got a stack of patients. I'm sorry.'

She threw a vague smile in their direction, scooped up her coffee and headed for her room, her salad forgotten, but her hand was still tingling from his touch, scrambling her brain even further.

Liz said yes, bless her heart, and even volunteered to pick the children up from nursery for a sleepover, so after her surgery was finished she drove home, packed their things and dropped them round, then went back, threw the breakfast things in the dishwasher, brought in the washing off the line and then went to change. But into what?

She studied the contents of her wardrobe blankly, but nothing was right. Ridiculous. She was going for an informal supper with the rest of the doctors and their partners and the practice manager and her husband, just to welcome Nick. It didn't matter what she wore. Anything would do.

Except it wouldn't, somehow, because she'd already made a disastrous impression, and she wanted a chance to remedy that. If it wasn't already way too late…

So, the blue dress? No, too dressy. Pink? No. Too casual. Black? Too formal. OK, not a dress, then. Trousers and a top and pretty pumps?

Better—but which top?

She tried all of them, in the end, and went for the one that hung well, disguised her flabby bits and made her feel good about herself. That alone was quite an ask, but hey. Not that it mattered, she reminded herself crossly. The only thing that really mattered was getting there on time, because if she knew Lucy's husband, he would have been in the kitchen all day cooking up a storm, and the last thing she needed was to upset anyone else!

She touched up the makeup she'd hurled on hastily at six thirty this morning, slipped on her shoes and coat, grabbed the bottle of wine she'd bought for them and walked out without checking herself in the mirror again because it *just didn't matter.*

The Gallaghers only lived round the corner, and the drive would be full, so she walked, timing it so she'd be there just after seven so that hopefully some of the others would have arrived and she could melt into the background without having to talk to him. Not that she wanted to be rude to Nick, she'd done enough of that today to last a lifetime, but she didn't want to look over-keen either.

And heaven knows why she was letting it worry her! He was a work colleague, nothing more, and never would be. She'd be polite, friendly enough, and stop thinking about his cute behind and that lazy, oh-so-sexy smile. Surely she could manage that?

She arrived at five past seven, just as Dev and Reeta got there. Perfect.

Brian's car was there, and she could hear the others talking as Dev opened the door, but there was no sign of Nick's car on the drive. Had he walked? Or was he late? No. He didn't seem like the type to be late—or totally forget that he'd been invited for dinner.

Thank God for her mother-in-law. She would have been sunk without Liz in so many ways. The woman was a saint.

She plastered on a smile and followed Dev and Reeta in.

He was sitting in between Julia Wade, the practice manager, and Sarah Baines, another part-time doctor whose husband was at home with their children, and on the other side of Julia was Brian Rowlings, the practice principal. He'd met him and Julia before at his interviews, and also Dev Patel, the only other full-time doctor apart from him and Brian.

Dev was seated on the other side of the table, his wife Reeta, another part-time doctor, on one side and Ellie on his other, with Julia's husband next to Ellie on her other side, which put her right opposite him and gave him a perfect opportunity to study her. It was threatening to become a habit…

He dragged his eyes off her and looked up at their hosts. Lucy Gallagher, the most senior doctor after Brian, and her husband Andy, who he gathered was a part-time ED consultant at Yoxburgh Park Hospital, were busy piling food on dishes and setting them down along the length of the table, watched longingly by their black Labrador, Stanley.

'Just dig in, folks,' Andy said, so they did, passing

things around, spoons waving in the air and not a trace of inhibition. It felt like a noisy, cheerful family Sunday lunch, he thought, not a formal introduction to the practice, and he liked it. He liked all of them, but he wanted to know more about them, most particularly Ellie.

He didn't get a chance to talk to her, though, because not surprisingly everyone wanted to ask him questions or tell him interesting and useful things about the practice, and he had to force himself to pay attention, but he was still aware of every breath she took.

After the main course they swapped places, and he ended up next to Ellie, which would have been fine if it hadn't been for the unmistakeable current of something seriously tempting that ran between them.

She wanted trifle but she couldn't reach it, so he stood up and leant across her, feeling the brush of her arm against his thigh as he picked it up, and he nearly dropped the dish.

'Here,' he said, sitting down again and holding it for her, then passing it across to Brian when she was done. And then Brian started to tell him things about the practice, things he probably needed to know, and at any other time would have been interested in, so he still didn't get to talk to her. Didn't mean he wasn't still utterly aware of her, of her scent, the sound of her laugh, the hitch in her breath and slight shift of her leg away from his as his thigh accidentally brushed hers—

'Coffee, anybody?' Lucy asked when they'd all ground to a halt, and Ellie shook her head.

'No, it's been lovely, Lucy, but I need to make a move. Sorry. I had a very early start and I'm running out of steam.'

'Yes, me, too,' he said, getting to his feet with a rueful smile. 'It's been great to meet you all, and I'm looking forward to working with you and getting to know you all much better, but I've got a lot to do over the weekend before I start on Monday. My house is in chaos and I need to be able to find my clothes, at the very least.'

'Give us a shout if you need a hand,' Andy offered, which produced a chorus of other offers, and he nodded and thanked them all, thanked Lucy and Andy for the meal and ended up on the drive at the same time as Ellie.

'Did you walk or are you driving?' he asked her.

'I walked—why?'

'So did I. I'll walk you home.'

'You don't need to do that—'

'Yes, I do. I don't want you on my conscience.'

She laughed at that. 'Nick, this is Yoxburgh! Nothing's going to happen to me.'

'Nevertheless,' he said with a smile, with no intention of backing down. 'And anyway, I want to talk to you. I have questions.'

She looked up at him, her face illuminated by the porch light, her expression sceptical as if she could see right through him. 'Such as?'

'Oh, practice stuff. Well, people stuff, really,' he added, improvising like crazy, but she nodded as if that seemed reasonable, and then turned away and set off, and he fell in beside her.

'So, ask away,' she prompted.

'Brian,' he said, because he genuinely was interested in what she had to say about him, so it seemed a good place to start.

She glanced at him. 'What about him?'

'He was on his own, and I understand he's had some time off recently. Anything I should know?'

'Yes. His wife had early onset Alzheimer's, and he

took time off and looked after her. She was only fifty-eight when she died last year, and she didn't know him for the last few months.'

He felt the weight of a familiar burden settle over him. 'That must have been difficult.'

'It was difficult. I covered what I could, but I was pregnant with Evie so we all picked up a bit and we got a locum for one day a week, and then she died and he came back a couple of months later. I think he was glad to get back to normal, to be honest. He'd been very isolated.'

He knew how that felt, when he'd been coping with his brother after Rachel had left him. He'd been hanging by a thread by the time Sam died. Still was, in a way.

'So, what else do you want to know?'

Nothing, really, but he drummed up a few questions to take his mind off Sam as much as anything, and then she came to a halt outside a surprisingly modest and fairly boring little eighties house—or at least it would have been, if it wasn't for the fact that it overlooked the sea.

'Well, this is me,' she said with a smile. 'See, no muggers or rapists or roving gangs.'

'No,' he said. 'Well, I'll say goodnight, then.'

She said nothing for a moment, and then looked up at him. 'Coffee?'

He tried to read her eyes, but it was too dark to see them properly. 'I thought you needed an early night?'

'I do, but I'm going to sit down first and chill for a while. It's been a hectic day. And we can talk more about the practice if you like. Up to you.'

The practice was the last thing on his mind. Getting to know her better, though…

'No, I don't fancy coffee.'

Did her face fall? Maybe, and he tipped his head on one side and smiled slowly. 'Tea, on the other hand…'

She let out a soft huff of laughter and turned away. 'You'd better come in, then.'

CHAPTER TWO

IT WAS A MESS. Why had she invited him in? She must have been nuts.

'Come on through. I'm sorry, it's a bit of a tip. I left in a hurry this morning and I haven't had time to tidy it.'

He gave a quiet chuckle that did something weird to her nerve endings. 'Don't worry about it. I've seen much worse.'

'Very likely, but that doesn't mean I'm proud of it.'

He chuckled again, the sound soft and rich and oddly disturbing. She busied herself with the kettle, ridiculously aware of him behind her. What was he making of the house? And what did it matter what he thought of her *or* her house?

'Are these the kids' drawings?'

'Well, they're not mine,' she said with a laugh, turning back to him. He was studying the fridge, plastered with Oscar's little doodles and scrawlings, Maisie's almost recognisable pictures of a house and a bunch of flowers, and in the middle Evie's small messy handprints in pink and green and orange. He reached out a finger and traced a little handprint, and there was a wistful smile on his face that touched her heart.

Why doesn't he have children?

'How do you take your tea?'

He turned back to her, the smile becoming suddenly more generic as he hid whatever feelings they'd been that she'd had that little glimpse of. 'Oh, white, no sugar, as it comes.' He glanced around, frowning slightly. 'So how do you get to the garden? I take it there is a garden?'

'Oh, yes, it's a nice garden once you get to it, but you have to go through the sitting room—or out of the front and round the side.'

His eyebrow twitched. 'That's handy for the bin.'

She laughed again, this time with real irony. 'You don't say. The layout's ridiculous. Someone blocked up the kitchen door that led to the garden, and yes, it's handy to have more cupboard and worktop space, but a back door would be handy, too. If you can stand the mess, I'll give you a guided tour while the kettle boils.'

He chuckled again. 'I can stand the mess,' he said, and followed her, eyeing the house curiously as she pointed out the interesting features, like where the back door should have been, the lack of a utility room, the dining room with the wasted sea view, the three cramped bedrooms and tiny bathroom.

'It's not what I expected.'

'What did you expect? Pristine tidiness?'

He laughed and looked down at her, his eyes gentle. 'No, I didn't mean that at all. This is just normal family mess. I wasn't expecting a sea view. You were lucky to get it. They're always at a premium.'

'Absolutely. That's why we bought it. David never did anything by accident—well, not a lot,' she added economically, and headed down the stairs. 'And the sea view would be fine if I ever had time to look at it, but even if I did, you can hardly see it because of the stupid layout. The house isn't big enough for three children, but I can't afford to extend it or move house, and David's attitude is if I want to do things to it, or move to something better, then all I have to do is have him back.'

'I take it that's not an option,' he ventured cautiously.

She laughed at that, a brittle little tinkle of sound, and led him back to the kitchen. 'I don't think it's a serious suggestion anyway, so even if I thought it was a good idea, which I definitely don't, I'm still stuck here.'

'So what were you planning to do?'

'Move the sitting room to the front and the dining room to the back because it's as far from the kitchen as you can get at the moment, and extend it out into the garden to make a family area and put another bedroom and bathroom on. That way at least there would be a sea view from a room that would be used, rather than just the dining room, which I hardly use, and my bedroom, where I sleep with the curtains shut. As I said, wasted.'

'That's not wasted! You could lie in bed with a cup of tea in the mornings and look at the sea. Bliss.'

'With three small children crawling all over me? That's not bliss, that's asking for trouble.'

His face softened into a wry grin. 'Yeah, maybe. But the downstairs layout is crazy, I'll give you that. I'd probably just open it all up if you didn't want to spend a lot.'

'But then there'd be nowhere where I could just retreat and know it's going to be tidy and not covered in toys. Here, your tea,' she said, handing it to him, and led him back into the sitting room, sweeping little wooden blocks out of the way with her feet, and behind him she heard that chuckle again.

'You need a fairy, Ellie. Someone to come in while everyone's sleeping and tidy it all up.'

She rolled her eyes and curled up on the sofa. 'Er—that would be me? Nice idea, though. I wonder if the tooth fairy has a cousin who's looking for work?' she added with a grin, and he gave a soft huff of laughter and sat down opposite her, stretching his legs out with that little wince she'd noticed earlier.

'Are you OK?' she asked, and he tilted his head slightly.

'OK?'

'You winced.'

'Oh, that. No, it's an old fracture. It plays up a bit if I've overdone it. It's nothing.'

'Overdone it? You sat in the staff room or the office for a lot of the day, and you've been sitting down at dinner.'

'That's today. Yesterday I moved all my stuff up here into my new house. There was a lot of lifting and lugging.'

'Didn't you have a removal company?'

He smiled. 'Yes. There's still a lot of lugging around to be done. My fault. I should have been more specific about where I wanted things. Anyway, it's all in the right place now, more or less. All I have to do is unpack.'

She wondered where the house was, but it seemed rude to ask—except he'd seen every inch of her chaotic and overcrowded little house, so the location of his could hardly be a state secret. Even if it was none of her business…

'Where is it?' she asked, finally giving in to her curiosity.

'Just round the corner, on a little private road with half a dozen or so houses on it near the steps to the beach.'

'Jacob's Lane. Wow. I know it well. There are some lovely houses there. Which one is it?' she asked, totally forgetting that she wasn't supposed to be being nosy.

'Split-level timber thing on the right, built in the seventies, with a weird mono-pitch roof?'

'I know the one, it's been empty for a while. I really like it.'

'Yeah, me, too. It's nothing from the front but it's quite interesting inside, and it's got a lovely courtyard style walled garden—and all the rooms open onto it. The only thing lacking is the sea view, but I've got legs and it's hardly far away.'

That quirky grin again, which seemed to have some magic power over her.

Why? Why him, her new colleague? Although he seemed to have forgiven her for her tirade this morning, so she should be grateful for that, and she could live with a bit of unrequited lust in the interests of a peaceful and amicable working relationship.

'So does it need a lot of work?'

'Not really. Just an injection of my taste and a bit of tweaking.'

'Not a project like this was meant to be, then?'

He gave a soft laugh and shook his head. 'No. I didn't want that, not now, not at this point in my life. I've had enough challenges. I'm ready for a quiet life.'

She chuckled softly. 'Me, too, but there's not much chance of that with three small people. Frankly I'd settle for six hours' sleep a night. That would help.'

Just the thought made her want to cry with longing, and she was running out of steam. She stifled a little yawn, and apologised, but he gave her a wry smile.

'I need to go. You've had a long day and I'm keeping you up, so I'll leave you to what's left of that early night you wanted. Maybe you'll get more than six hours.'

'Oh, bliss. I might even take a cup of tea up in the morning and look at my sea view. That would be a novelty.'

He chuckled and got to his feet—that wince, again—

and headed into the kitchen with his mug, setting it down on the worktop before he walked to the front door. Then he turned and smiled down at her, his eyes gentle, and her stomach flipped over.

'Thanks for the tea and the guided tour, and for filling me in on the practice.'

'You're welcome. Thank you for walking me home, even if it wasn't strictly necessary. I'll see you on Monday.'

'I'll look forward to it.'

He hesitated for a moment, then cupped her shoulders in his hands and touched a kiss to her cheek, then dropped his hands, turned away and headed off in the direction of his house.

She watched him go from the open doorway, her fingers tracing the tingle on her cheek. She'd felt the slight graze of stubble on her skin as he'd kissed her, breathed in the scent of his skin against hers, and her breath caught.

Crazy. Her mind was scrambled by a mixture of tiredness, the two glasses of wine she'd had with dinner, and her unexpected reaction to a man she'd been convinced she'd dislike.

And she didn't dislike him at all, she realised. She liked him. Liked him a lot, and wanted to know more—such as why he didn't have children, why his marriage had gone wrong, and why he'd moved here on what seemed like a whim. For the quiet life he'd talked about?

Too many questions, and none of those things were anything to do with her. Just a colleague. Nothing more.

'Get a grip, Ellie,' she told herself, and closed the door firmly.

Damn.

Why was she so nice?

Stupid, really, but he hadn't wanted her to be. Not a

woman with three children. A woman with three children definitely wasn't on his agenda, and there was no way on earth he was going there.

So what was with the pang of regret?

He missed his footing slightly in the dark, and his ankle wrenched a little, taking his mind off her.

Not before time. They had to work together, and the last thing he needed in a new job that he hoped would be a long-term, settled future for him was an inappropriate reaction to an inappropriate woman.

He crunched over the gravel drive, slid his key into the lock and closed the front door behind him with a sigh. Boxes everywhere, stacked up in every room. Boxes containing his life—and some of Samuel's. Not that he was ready to unpack those yet. Might never be.

Navigating his way to the kitchen, he put the kettle on, made himself a cup of chamomile tea and turned up the heating. Not that it was particularly cold, but the house had been empty for months, and it needed warmth and life injected back into it.

A fridge smothered in multicoloured handprints and colourful scrawls? Blocks and cars and jigsaw pieces all over the floor?

Hardly. He'd leave that to Ellie.

Not that he had a choice. His own stupidity had taken care of that, but at least his sisters had provided their parents with grandchildren, so that box was ticked. One small thing that he didn't have to feel guilty about.

He went up the few steps to the sitting room, dropped onto the sofa, went to reach for the TV remote and changed his mind. Instead he leant back with a sigh, cradling his tea and letting his mind run back over the evening and all he'd learnt.

Brian was a widower, working part-time but for how

long Ellie didn't seem to know, and as for the others, they were a cheerful, friendly bunch of people he'd be happy to work with. It would be nice to be part of a team again, after four years of patchy locum work as his brother had grown steadily more dependent. He'd taken time out to help his parents, but he'd missed it, missed the camaraderie, the belonging.

He wanted to belong again, and from what he'd seen so far, he'd be welcomed with open arms by the other practice members.

And then there was Ellie.

Ellie, with her long dark hair, grey-green eyes that showed every emotion, and that wickedly dry sense of humour. Not to mention a curvy, womanly body that made him ache to wrap her up in his arms and kiss her senseless.

No, that would be him who'd be senseless, because it wasn't just her eyes and her wit and her lush, beautiful body. It was her three very small children, all part of the same package, and he wanted nothing to do with it.

Liar.

He sighed again, sipped the chamomile tea and pulled a face. The tea was the last thing he wanted, but he had no idea where he'd put the bottle of single malt he kept for the times when he wanted to drown his sorrows and wallow in self-pity, and maybe that was just as well.

He had a lot to do tomorrow, and he needed to spend Sunday resting or his hip and ankle were going to give him hell.

He got to his feet, went back down to the kitchen, poured the tea down the sink and went to bed.

Just because the damage was already done, the children were saints on Monday morning, and she dropped them off at nursery and walked into the practice at ten past eight with plenty of time to prepare for her morning surgery.

She'd vowed not to drive so that Nick could have the parking space, this time without argument, and there was no sign of his car as she arrived. How gratifying—

'Morning!'

He appeared at the top of the stairs as she put her foot on the bottom step, and she couldn't help the wry smile.

'Your car isn't here. I thought I'd beaten you to it.'

His mouth kicked up, and she felt a strange sensation in her chest, a weird flutter that brought a tiny glow with it. What *was* it about that smile that it seemed to light up the corners of her heart?

'Sorry to disappoint. I've been here since half seven. Lucy and Julia came in early so they could talk me through my day. It's looking busy already.'

'It will be. It's always busy. Have you had a cup of tea?'

'No, I've had coffee, but the kettle's hot. I'll be up again in a minute.'

She nodded and headed up, passing him on the stairs. Wasn't that supposed to be unlucky? Except that the stairs were wide and she'd hardly felt the brush of his arm against hers.

Even so, it had left a little tingle in its wake—or was that the fresh scent of soap or shower gel that lingered in the air? She recognised it from Friday, when they'd been seated side by side at Andy and Lucy's table, and again when he'd kissed her as he'd left. Not aftershave or cologne, more subtle than that, but it had made her want to rest her head against his chest and breathe him in—

Pull yourself together! You've got work to do. Enough of the daydreaming and fantasy. He's just a colleague.

And if she told herself that often enough, maybe it'd sink in. She made a cup of tea, took it down to her consulting room and logged into her computer, and there was a tap on the door.

'Come in!'

It was Nick, sticking his head round the door with a serious look on his face. 'Have you got two minutes? One of your patients is down to see me and he'd rather see you, apparently, only your list is full. James Golding?'

'Oh, Jim. Yes, of course I can see him. He's a dear old boy and he never makes a fuss. He's had a triple bypass but he still gets angina from time to time, so it might be that. I'll get Katie to swap it over.'

'OK. I think he might be here already, actually.'

'Sounds likely. I'll see him now. You could take my first patient, if you like. I have no idea who they are so there's no continuity of care issue.'

'Done. I'll see Katie. Thanks.'

'Don't thank me. I'd rather see Mr Golding myself because there must be something going on. He doesn't like to make a fuss, so I'll check him over thoroughly.'

'Good. Thanks. See you later, maybe.'

They shared a smile, and she went out into the waiting room and spotted Jim Golding, tucked into the corner with his hands knotted round the handle of his walking stick. She went over and perched beside him.

'Morning, Jim. I gather you wanted to see me?' she murmured, and he looked up and gave her a weary smile.

'They said you were busy,' he said, his voice distressed.

'No. We've swapped. You're with me. Do you want to come now?'

Not that she really had time, because there was always a ton of admin to do before she could start and it was going to put her behind, but there was something about the cautious way he stood up that set alarm bells ringing.

'No rush,' she said gently, and ushered the frail, elderly man into her consulting room and settled him in the chair. 'So, Jim, tell me what's going on.'

'How was he?'

Ellie put her cup down with a plonk next to the kettle, not sure where to start, and he got up and went over to her.

'Ellie? What's up?'

She pulled a face. 'I'm not sure. He said he was OK but he'd had a twinge or two, so I've sent him to see Megan for a twelve-lead ECG and a raft of bloods. Just to be on the safe side. He also wanted me to draw up a DNAR.'

'Really?'

She nodded. 'Yes, and I don't like it. I think there's something going on that he hasn't told me. Gut instinct?'

He gave a soft huff of laughter. 'Yeah, I know the feeling. Sometimes I hate my gut.'

'Don't hate it. Trust it. I trust mine and it's giving me grief right now.'

His mouth kicked up into a fleeting smile. 'You could be being overcautious.'

Or not, as it turned out, because when she was back in her consulting room wading through test results, she heard a yell and went out to find Nick on his knees in the corridor, bent over Mr Golding.

'What's happened?'

'I don't know. An MI, maybe? We need to move him and repeat the ECG. Oh, hang on. No, no, no, no, don't do this!'

She turned back to find Nick had the elderly man's shirt open and was listening to his chest.

'Anything?'

He shook his head and started doing chest compressions. 'No. He's arrested. Can you call an ambulance?'

'No. Nick, stop.' She dropped to her knees beside him and covered his hands with her own, stilling them. 'He's got a DNAR, remember? He signed it before he went in with Megan. We can't resuscitate him and I wouldn't want to. His wife died last year, he's really struggled without her. He doesn't want this.'

'Is it in his notes?'

'Yes. I put it on the computer, and we have the physical document on file. He signed it in front of witnesses.'

His hands slowly lifted, and he stared down at the man for a long moment before he shut his eyes and sat back on his heels.

'We need to close off the corridor and move him somewhere until they get here to take him away. I'll do that, you call the office and get an ambulance.'

She nodded, went back into her surgery and asked Katie to call an ambulance, and then left a message on Jim's daughter's voicemail asking her to call. She ought to call in her next patient, there was no time to grieve for the patient she'd grown very fond of over the past few months, but somehow her heart was heavy and she just needed a moment…

Something splashed on her hand and she swiped it away, and then she heard her door open and she turned, as Nick's arms closed around her.

'I'm sorry I couldn't save him,' he murmured, the sound echoing through his chest under her ear.

She shook her head and eased away a little, feeling suddenly awkward. 'Don't be. It's what he wanted. I just wish I could have done more to help him.'

He let go of her, one hand coming up to wipe a tear

gently from her cheek. 'You helped him get what he wanted in the end, Ellie. He went very quickly, and he wasn't distressed. I think he knew what was happening.'

She nodded, hauled in a breath and straightened up, blew her nose and tried to smile. 'We aren't supposed to get involved.'

'No. We're not.' But his smile said it all, and with a quick check to make sure she was really OK, he went back to his patients and left her to deal with Mr Golding's daughter.

'I'm sorry you lost a patient on your first day. Are you OK?'

He looked up into Ellie's concerned eyes, closed the file he was working on, shut the lid of his laptop and stood up. 'I'm fine, Ellie. It happens, people reach the end of the road, and anyway he wasn't my patient. How about you? Are you OK?'

'Yes, I'm fine,' she said, but he wasn't convinced.

'You're working late tonight.'

She shook her head. 'No. I always do an evening surgery on Mondays. It's a busy day but I'm done now. I'm glad I caught you, though. I spoke to Mr Golding's daughter and broke the news, and she rang back later after she'd been to see him to thank us for looking after him and for letting him go when we did. Apparently he'd rung her and said I was making him have all sorts of silly tests, but I'd been really kind so he was indulging me.'

'Do you know what he said to me, when I found him on the floor? "Oh, dear, I'm making such a fuss."'

She swallowed, as if she had a lump in her throat, and let out a soft laugh—to diffuse her emotions, maybe?

'That's so typical. He was such a gentleman,' she murmured, and her wistful smile warmed something deep inside him and made him want to hold her again, because frankly that tiny hug this morning for a sad colleague had been nothing like enough.

'Do you have to collect the children?'

'No. Liz takes them back to mine and gets them ready for bed.'

'I'll walk you home then. I'm done now.'

She hesitated, then nodded and gave him a weary smile.

'OK. But just to the end of your road. I'll walk the rest of the way on my own.'

'Because you don't want your mother-in-law getting ideas?'

She laughed, probably because he'd hit the nail right on the head. 'Something like that. And anyway, you don't need to be exposed to the monsters at the end of the day. They can be pretty grim when they're tired.'

He smiled and shook his head, not in the least concerned about the children, or the mother-in-law, come to that. And anyway, he had to get home.

'Don't worry about it. I need to get back to the dog anyway.'

'Dog?' Her eyes widened in surprise. 'I didn't know you had a dog. You said you didn't have any commitments.'

His smile felt a little off kilter. 'I didn't, not until yesterday when my parents delivered him. He's my brother's dog.'

'Your brother's? So how come you've got him?'

He looked away so she couldn't read his eyes. 'He died last year,' he said economically, and felt the usual sick feeling in the pit of his stomach.

'Oh, Nick, I'm so sorry. I had no idea.'

Her voice was filled with compassion and it choked

him for a moment so he picked up his bag and slung it over his shoulder as they headed down the stairs.

'No reason why you should have known,' he said. 'Anyway, Rufus kind of adopted me while it was all going on, and he's been pining for me since I left last week, apparently, so I said I'd have him. They've been in Kettering with my sister, so they just popped over for the afternoon and dropped him off.'

He held the door for her, and then fell into step beside her.

'So what is Rufus?' she asked.

'Cavalier King Charles spaniel. He's a nice little thing, and very placid. He spent most of his life on Samuel's bed, and he used to let us know when he was about to have a seizure, which was totally unexpected and incredibly useful.'

'Was he a trained seizure alert dog, then?'

He shook his head. 'No. He had no training at all, and he was chronically disobedient, but he just latched onto Sam and he was amazing with him. He really calmed him, and even when Sam didn't recognise us any more he knew Rufus.'

'Poor dog. He must have been gutted when your brother died.'

He swallowed and drew in a long breath. 'Yeah,' he said, and left it at that, mainly because he couldn't say any more. How could it still feel so raw, over a year later?

'What had happened to him? To Samuel?'

He shrugged. 'He was born with very complex needs. Nobody could say why, but he was very compromised in all sorts of ways, and my parents' lives revolved around him for thirty-eight years.' And not just their lives. His, too, but that was another matter.

And there was that lump in his throat again, which

didn't get any better when she rested her hand lightly on his arm.

'I'm so sorry.'

He nodded, and kept walking, and then they were at the end of his road and he slowed to a halt and smiled at her.

'Right, this is me. I take it you can find the way from here?'

She rolled her eyes at him, then cocked her head on one side and studied him thoughtfully. 'Are you OK?'

'Yes, of course I am. Why shouldn't I be?'

Her smile was tender and nearly pushed him over the edge. 'Because you're sad?'

He was. Sad, and guilty, because there'd been an element of relief when Sam had finally slipped away and he'd been free of the burden, and he was filled with shame about that.

He found a smile and pinned it on. 'I'm fine, Ellie. Will I see you tomorrow?'

She nodded. 'I work Monday, Tuesday and Friday.'

'I'll have the kettle on for you,' he promised, and her mouth curved into a grin, and she went up on tiptoe and brushed a kiss on his cheek.

'You do that. Take care, Nick. I'll see you tomorrow,' she murmured, and turned and walked away, leaving him feeling oddly—lonely? He watched her till she was out of sight, and then let himself into his house and went to find Rufus.

He wasn't hard to find. The little dog was curled up in his bed in the hall beside the boxes of Samuel's possessions, and he lifted his head and wagged his tail in greeting, his eyes huge and sad as ever.

'Hi, little guy,' he said gently, his voice gruff and scratchy, and as he crouched down Rufus got to his feet, put his paws on his chest, whined softly and licked his face.

'I'm sorry, mate. I'm a pretty poor substitute, aren't I?' he murmured gruffly, but Rufus wagged his tail and sat down, looking hopeful.

He gave the little dog another stroke, straightened up and went into the kitchen, hauling in a long breath. 'Come on, then, little man. Let's find some supper, and then you need a walk, and we'll see if we can find something nice on the telly later, shall we?' he murmured, and Rufus followed him, tail wafting gently, his mournful eyes fixed on Nick's every move.

CHAPTER THREE

SHE HARDLY SAW Nick the next day, but as promised the kettle had just boiled when she got in, which made her smile. They passed on the stairs, and she asked him fleetingly if he was OK.

'Of course I am. Why wouldn't I be?' he asked.

But she wasn't bringing his brother up again, especially not at work, so she just smiled and said, 'Good,' and moved on.

She saw him later at the other end of the corridor outside the consulting rooms and he flashed her a smile, but that was all they had time for and she left at the end of the day without seeing him again.

Oddly, though, just knowing he was in the building made her feel different about it, that little tingle of anticipation that if she turned the corner he might be there. Which was ridiculous, because he was *just a colleague.* If she told herself that often enough, maybe it would sink in.

She spent Wednesday with the children, playing in the garden, and on Thursday they wanted to go the beach with buckets and spades. She'd been trying not to think about Nick, except of course they walked past his house on the way and she couldn't help but study it and think about him.

She'd love to see inside it, but it probably wasn't a good idea, not the way she reacted to him. She chivvied the children past it, but then it started to rain as they got to the top of the steps so they ran back and she took them to a soft play centre instead and spent the time lecturing herself for being so obsessed by him.

It was still raining on Friday morning, but it didn't matter as she had the car with her. She'd dropped the children's things off at Liz and Steven's on the way to the nursery because it was David's rescheduled weekend with them, and as she turned into the car park she crossed her fingers that Nick hadn't driven, too.

He hadn't, or at least he hadn't arrived yet, which seemed unlikely. He'd always been there before her even when she'd made good time, and today of course she'd been on the drag again after another emotional meltdown from Oscar over the missing shoe, which still hadn't turned up.

Still, summer was coming, and she'd buy him some sandals next week.

She went up to the staff room, and the kettle was still fairly hot, but there was no sign of him and she felt a strange sense of anti-climax. Stupid. She made a coffee, headed downstairs and waded through a pile of prescription requests and results before seeing her first patient, and she didn't see Nick until after she'd finished her lunch.

'Are you hiding from me?' she asked jokingly as they passed on the stairs, and he stopped and grinned.

'Now, why would I do that? Actually I've been hoping to see you. Am I right in thinking you're child-free this weekend?'

She nodded, puzzled that he should ask. 'Why?'

'I just wondered if you'd like to be my first guest? If you haven't got anything better to do, that is, which you probably have.'

She felt a smile edging in, and tried to moderate it so she didn't look too ridiculously keen. 'Well, now, let me see. There's sorting the washing, or cleaning the house from top to bottom, or weeding the garden…'

'Is that a no?'

'Absolutely not,' she told him, letting the smile out. 'When were you thinking?'

'I don't know. Whenever you like. Dinner tonight, or tomorrow, or lunch tomorrow, or Sunday—whatever. I'm easy.'

She mentally scanned her fridge and came up with not a lot, or nothing that wouldn't keep. 'Tonight would be nice, but that's a bit short notice for you, isn't it, unless you're planning on getting a takeaway?'

He shook his head. 'I've got an internet order coming at seven. Tonight would be fine.'

'Can you cook?'

He chuckled. 'What if I say no?'

'I'll eat first,' she said, unable to stop the little laugh, and he joined in, shaking his head again slowly, that lazy, sexy smile doing strange things to her pulse.

'You don't need to eat first. I can cook. Any special dietary requirements?'

She shook her head, and he grinned.

'Well, that's a relief, since I've already done the order. So—seven thirty?'

She felt a little bubble of excitement burst in her chest. 'Seven thirty sounds fine. Can I bring anything?'

'No. I have everything covered. Just bring yourself and an appetite.'

* * *

He felt nervous.

Why, for heaven's sake? It wasn't as if it was a date, not in that sense. He'd just invited a colleague around for a meal, a sort of impromptu housewarming, and he wasn't going to do anything elaborate.

The entrance hall doubled as a dining room, so the first thing he had to do was find the table under the pile of boxes he'd dumped on it, so he shifted them into one of the bedrooms, hesitated over the pile of Sam's boxes on the floor and then moved them, too. It might worry Rufus, but he dug out Sam's old blanket and put it in his bed, tucked in the corner under the stairs. Maybe that would be enough.

Right. The table was clear, the floor was clear bar the dog bed, the kitchen was clean anyway because he'd been using it for a week, and the moment the delivery came he turned on the oven and started to prep the salmon parcels.

By the time Ellie arrived the fish was ready to go in the oven, he'd made the avocado and sweet chilli salad starter, the rice was cooked, the melting middle chocolate puddings, his one concession to laziness, were unwrapped and ready to go, and the wine was nicely chilled.

He heard the crunch of gravel and opened the door as she stepped onto the porch, a pot plant in her hand and a smile on her face, and he felt an odd sensation in his chest.

'Here. A little housewarming present,' she said, and he took it with a smile, kissed her cheek and ushered her in, trying to ignore the weird thing going on with his heart.

By the time he'd put the plant down she was on the floor, making a fuss of Rufus, who was rolling on his back for a tummy-rub.

'Oh, he's really sweet,' she murmured, smiling tenderly at the shameless little flirt, and he chuckled.

'He is. He's a nice little dog, and he'll stand any amount of that, but he's normally quite shy, probably because he's had a sheltered life.'

'Well, he doesn't seem shy now,' Ellie said with a laugh, getting to her feet, and then she looked around curiously, glancing up the short flight of stairs on her left. 'So what's up there?'

'The sitting room. Let's get a drink and take it up there. It overlooks the garden and it's still light, so you'll be able to see it—unless you want a guided tour first?'

She laughed, the sound rippling through him and reactivating that heart nonsense, and her eyes were twinkling.

'Absolutely. I'm insanely curious. I've walked past this house so many times on our way to the beach, and I've always wanted to know what it was like inside because it's so unusual and it fascinates me. Can we?'

'Sure. We can take our drinks with us. It won't take long to look at it and it'll probably be a dreadful anticlimax.' He headed into the kitchen and glanced back at her. 'Are you OK with white wine or do you want something else?'

'White's fine. Thanks. Wow, it's a good-sized kitchen.'

'Good-sized everything, really. The bedrooms aren't huge, but they're big enough and there are four of them, so if either of my sisters wants a seaside holiday I can accommodate them and their families, so it sort of makes sense even though it's just me. Come and see. We'll do the bedroom wing first, then go up to the sitting room.'

'Wing? That sounds very grand.'

He chuckled. 'No. It's not grand at all, it's pretty basic, really. Very simple, but that suits me. I'm a simple man.'

* * *

There was nothing simple about him, she thought as she followed him. A single man who had no ties and responsibilities, buying a family-sized house so his sisters could come for a seaside holiday with their children? A dog who'd belonged to his late brother and had been pining for him, so he'd adopted it? And yet he'd left them all to move to Yoxburgh. Why?

He led her through a little dogleg and down the narrow hall that ran away from the front of the house, opening doors and gesturing as he went.

'So the bedrooms are on this side, all overlooking the garden, and the service rooms like the bathrooms and utility room are across the corridor because they don't need a view. It's not fancy but it seems to work.'

'I'm sure it does,' she said, peering into the first bedroom. It was long and narrow, with a window at the far end, but she couldn't see a lot more than that. 'You've got a lot of boxes.' Surely more than one man could need in a lifetime.

He glanced at them and nodded. 'Yes. I have. My life's been in boxes since Rachel left and we sold the house.'

'Rachel's your wife, I assume?'

'My ex-wife. Yes. She—uh—she walked.'

Like David…

'So, anyway, some of the boxes are from that, and my parents packed up all Samuel's stuff and had no idea what to do with it, so I've got all that here, too. Heaven knows what I'll do with it all, but it seemed wrong to throw his life away and I'm not short of space. I guess I'll sort it sometime.'

She turned to look at him keenly, concerned, and he looked away as if he didn't want her reading him.

'You think about him a lot, don't you?' she said softly,

and he gave a little huff of laughter but didn't answer, just led her back out of the room and down the corridor, pushing the doors open so she could see the other rooms. The next two were the same as the first, and then he pushed open the last door and stood back.

'This is mine. It's bigger than the others, obviously, and it's got a dressing room and en suite, and a door to the garden, which is nice.'

She looked around, taking in the space, the simple lines of the furniture, the bed made up with crisp white linen without a single mucky handprint on it, and sighed. 'Oh, I'm so jealous of all your space,' she said with a wry laugh, and turned back to him, catching a glimpse of something curiously like guilt.

Why on earth would he feel guilty?

'Seen enough?' he asked, and turned and walked away anyway, because he'd suddenly seen it with her eyes and he wished he'd never shown it to her, because although it was never going to be anything that special, this house would be ideal for her and her children, unlike the one she'd got, for which she'd had had such grand plans until her husband had walked.

He wondered why, but it didn't seem right to ask and he didn't want to bring it up because once they started on that conversation there was a world of stuff on his side that she might want to know, and he really, really didn't want to talk about it.

'Come on, let's go and put the fish in the oven—are you OK with teriyaki salmon parcels and rice?'

'Oh, no, it sounds awful,' she said, but her eyes were giving her away so he stifled a laugh and went back to the kitchen and put the fish in the oven, then topped up their glasses and led her up to the sitting room.

'Oh, this is a lovely room! I love the sloping ceiling—it brings in so much light! And what a fabulous sunset! Look at it!'

'I know. I could sit and watch the sky changing all day long.' He lifted down a dish of nuts and raisins from the bookcase, and offered it to her. 'Just keep Rufus out of them because of the raisins.'

'Would he steal food?'

He looked down at Rufus, sitting at her feet and begging shamelessly, and laughed.

'What do you think?'

The food was wonderful. Simple, fresh, perfectly cooked and utterly delicious.

Rather like her host. Well, not simple. There was nothing simple about Nick Cooper, as she'd already thought, but now, after spending the last hour or so with him, lingering over their dinner, she'd seen more of that other side of him. There was a whole world of stuff going on behind his eyes, and she had no idea who or what had hurt him most, but he'd certainly been affected badly by his brother's death.

Survivor guilt? Maybe. Or maybe just plain grief.

They were back in the sitting room, with her curled up in the corner of a sofa, him sprawled on an adjacent one at right angles and a box of after-dinner mints between them, and she turned her head and searched his eyes in the lamp light.

'Tell me about your brother,' she said softly.

He looked away, his body utterly still, and she wished she hadn't asked, but it was too late now and maybe he needed to talk.

'What do you want to know?'

'Not the medical stuff. The other stuff. What was he like, what could he do, what was your role?'

He met her eyes again. 'My role?'

She nodded, searching his eyes, but they weren't giving anything away. 'Every family with a disabled child has altered priorities. It's inevitable. I guess you found that.'

He held her eyes, and for a fleeting second the shutters opened and she saw raw pain and regret, then he looked away again.

'Yeah, I guess you could say that. So, my role.' He shrugged. 'I was his brother. You know the song "He Ain't Heavy, He's My Brother"? It's not that simple. He was a lead weight in my life, but he was also an anchor, someone to listen, someone who loved me unconditionally.'

'Could he communicate?'

'Oh, yes. He could talk, sort of. I could understand him, and we used to have fun before he got too ill. It was OK when we were kids, it was just normal for me, what life was, but then when I was twelve and he was eleven, my mother got accidentally pregnant with twins. And everything changed.'

'Everything?'

He nodded. 'My father gave up his job and started working from home, so he could be there to support my mother, and more and more of Samuel's care fell on me. Obviously I was going to school and so was he, when he was well enough. He went to a special school and they'd come and pick him up in their adapted minibus, but in the evenings and at weekends and in the holidays, more and more it was me hanging out with him so Mum could be with the girls and Dad could work. And we stopped going out, really, because Samuel was getting heavier and it was harder to move four kids with the wheelchair, too, and it was a special chair, a bit reclined, so getting a vehicle that would take us all was impossibly hard. I think it just got too difficult, to be honest, so we stopped doing it.'

'So your family life revolved around your home and your brother?'

He nodded. 'Yes. Totally. And because my father needed to earn a living it ended up with me being asked to look after the girls or Samuel, so Mum could do the other stuff. I was nearly seventeen by then, wanted my own life, and the girls were five and wanted to do things I hated, so I was spending my life either shut in a room with Sam while I did my homework or revision, or hanging out in playgrounds and supervising the girls in the garden and trying to keep them out of trouble, and all I got from them was, "You're not our daddy, you can't tell us what to do." So I decided it was my turn.'

She frowned at that, because there was something in his voice that made her blood run cold. 'Your turn?'

He swallowed. 'Yeah. For some reason I thought it would be a good idea to ride my bike off the garage roof.'

She felt her eyes widen. 'What? How? Why?'

His chuckle held a world of pain. 'To get attention? I knew I'd hurt myself, but I was past caring. It was the summer holidays, I was sick of being used, and our garden was on a slope, with the garage cut into the bank. It stuck up about three feet at the back, so I found a plank, propped it up against the back wall to make a ramp, rode my bike down the hill, up the plank, straight across the garage roof and onto the drive.' He gave her a slightly twisted little grin and put another mint chocolate in his mouth. 'Needless to say it didn't end well.'

She felt sick. 'What happened?'

'My left pedal broke as I landed, so I trashed my ankle,

crashed down onto the crossbar and shattered my pelvis.' He paused for a moment, then added with a wry smile, 'There was a bit of other collateral damage in the area, too.'

Her eyes widened. 'Collateral damage?'

His smile was wry and hid a world of pain. 'Let's just say that's why Rachel and I never had children—well, one of the reasons.'

Good grief. She could only imagine what he might have done, and none of it was good. 'Did you pass out?'

He laughed again, that hollow chuckle she was getting used to, and shook his head. 'Sadly not, not for a single second. Well, not until the paramedics arrived and straightened out my ankle. That wasn't fun. None of it was fun, to be fair, and my parents were distraught, my sisters were in floods of tears, I could hear Samuel calling because he'd realised something was going on, and I just felt sick. That could have been pain, of course, but whatever. I had their attention, at least.'

'And did it help you?'

That laugh again. 'No. No, of course not, not in any way. Well, it did, eventually, I suppose. I realised a little better what Samuel went through on a daily basis if nothing else. There's nothing like being a teenage boy and having someone else wipe your—well, whatever, independence with personal care is something I now prize very highly.'

'I bet you do. Poor you.'

'Poor me? I was an idiot. It was a stupid thing to do, and I got exactly what I deserved. My parents, though, didn't deserve any of it, and all it did was stress and upset them even more, so on top of the resentment was a whole world of guilt. I pulled myself together after that, once I got out of hospital, and so did they a bit, in that they'd ask me how I felt about doing things to help out, and I learned to tell them. It was a revelation for all of us.'

She frowned at that. 'I don't understand.'

'I'd never complained. Anything they asked me to do, I just did it, and the resentment got bigger and bigger until I couldn't cope with it.'

'Hence the crazy stunt?'

'Hence the crazy stunt. My father called me an idiot, and he was absolutely spot-on. I'll live with the consequences of it for ever. That's what happens with self-inflicted life-changing injuries. You get the rest of your life to remind yourself you were an idiot—and if that comes over as self-pitying, it's not meant to. I know it was my fault, I've accepted that, and I've come to terms with the consequences and learned to live with it.'

She wasn't convinced. 'How long were you in hospital? You must have had some horrendous damage,' she said contemplating the extensive microsurgery he must have had.

'Weeks. I don't know how many. I missed the start of the autumn term, I know that. Plenty of time to feel sorry for myself while I was having all sorts of surgery on my most personal places,' he said with a slightly awkward laugh.

And yet he'd been married, so… 'You must have had a good surgeon,' she said, and he nodded.

'Yeah, I did. An excellent surgeon, but even he couldn't rescue me entirely. You could say I discovered the concept of self-preservation the hard way.'

Her mind pictured a young man on the brink of adulthood facing weeks or months of rehabilitation and the news that his life would be changed for ever just because of a foolish stunt that had gone horribly wrong. 'That's a tough lesson to learn,' she said, watching the laughter fading from his face.

'It was, but it could have been a lot worse. My surgeon's one of the reasons I went into medicine. I contemplated a career in urology for a bit.'

'And then you went into general practice.'

'Yes. Because it offers variety and a more flexible career path, and I wanted to be there for Samuel. I owed it to him, and to my parents, and I could be closer to them that way. And I'm OK. Well, apart from the kids, but I've come to terms with that. I thought Rachel had, too, but she left me when Samuel was getting worse and I was on call to my parents more and more often, because she'd met someone else.'

'She left you *then*? When you really needed support? Nick, that's awful!'

'It happens, though. Your husband left you when you were pregnant.'

'Yes, well, we won't talk about him,' she said, dismissing him and picking up another chocolate. 'So, did Rachel have children with this new man?'

'Yes. She was pregnant when she left me, and of course there was no way it could be mine, not without IVF.'

'IVF? So that's still an option?'

'Yeah. There was a chance they could aspirate some viable sperm cells from the undamaged tissue if we'd really wanted to try for children, but it meant IVF with all the drugs and stuff, so it wouldn't be easy and there were no guarantees, and she wasn't interested in doing that. She'd had a friend who'd had a horrendous experience, and it freaked her out so she wouldn't consider it.'

'And that's the only way?'

'Oh, yes. The tubes were shredded beyond repair, so I am well and truly firing blanks.'

Her brain was still processing what he'd told her when she opened her mouth.

'So I guess that means it all still works otherwise?' she asked without thinking, and he started to laugh as she felt her face burn up. She buried it in her hands and met his eyes over her fingertips. 'I can't believe I said that. Oh, I'm so sorry—'

He shook his head slowly, his eyes laughing. 'Oh, no, don't be, it's worth it just to see your face. And, yes, it does all still work, thank you for your concern.'

He grinned, his eyes alight with mischief now. 'My mother found that out. She came into the bathroom and caught me doing what teenage boys do a lot, and she went pink, said, "Well, that answers that question," and shut the door behind her. I thought I was going to die of embarrassment, and I didn't leave the bathroom for well over an hour.'

She bit her lip, but the laugh wouldn't stay inside and they ended up in stitches.

'Sorry. I know it isn't really funny, but…'

'It sort of is. Didn't feel it at the time, but I can laugh about it now.'

'So. you must have been very lucky—either that or the surgeon was particularly brilliant. I can't believe you got away with it. That's amazing.'

'It is. Want to check it out?'

She met his eyes, startled, and for a breathless moment neither of them said anything, but then he grinned and leant back with another chocolate, and she saw the twinkle in his eyes.

'I think I'll pass, if that's OK,' she said with a smile, but her heart was pounding and all she could see was that crisp white linen at the far end of the house and she wanted him like she'd never wanted anyone before.

* * *

Why had he said that?

Just when it was all going well and everything seemed fine and comfortable between them, he went and messed it up.

That weird thing with his heart again, and although he'd only been joking, he kind of hadn't been. Not really.

Not that he'd have expected her to say yes, but he certainly wouldn't have turned her down. He'd probably put her off with all the gory stuff.

He swung his legs off the sofa and got to his feet. 'I'm sure I'll get over it. Fancy another coffee?'

She shook her head and stood up, still looking a little flustered. 'No, I—I ought to go home. Things to do.'

'At eleven o'clock on a Friday night?'

She looked at her watch, more for something to do than to tell the time, he thought, and then looked back up at him.

'Nick, I…' She let out a shaky breath and walked past him down the stairs and stopped at the door. 'I need to go.'

He followed her down and stopped an arm's length away from her, just for safety's sake, and met her eyes. They were filled with all sorts of things he couldn't begin to analyse, but rejection wasn't one of them.

'You don't, not if you don't want to. I wasn't hitting on you, Ellie, but I'd be more than happy if you wanted to stay. Truly.'

Their eyes locked, and for what felt like hours but was probably only seconds, neither of them breathed. And then she took a tiny step towards him, then another one.

'It's really not a good idea,' she said, her voice thready, her breath soft against his face.

'No, it probably isn't.' He lifted a hand and stroked

his knuckles down her cheek, then turned his hand and dragged his thumb slowly over her dry lips. She flicked her tongue out to moisten them, and his breath hitched in his throat and he swallowed.

'Stay with me, Ellie,' he said gruffly, and with a broken little sigh she stepped into his arms and lifted her face up to his.

CHAPTER FOUR

HIS STRONG HANDS cradled her face gently as his head came down to meet hers, his mouth warm and supple.

His touch was delicate, but it seemed to reach every nerve cell in her body. She felt the tender caress of his fingertips against her cheeks, the heat of his tongue as he stroked her lips, tracing the tiny gap between them, and she parted them and felt his breath fill her mouth before his tongue claimed it.

He tasted of coffee and chocolate with a hint of mint, and his kiss was sure and slow, searching, tempting. She heard a tiny sound—hers?—and he let go of her face and eased her body up against his, letting out a low groan as they came into contact from top to toe.

'You feel so good,' he whispered, rocking his hips against hers, and she squeezed her legs together to soothe the raging need as one hand slid round and cradled her breast, the other pressing her closer, lifting her hard against him so she felt the unmistakable jut of his erection against her body.

'OK, you didn't lie,' she said breathlessly, to defuse the tension, and she felt the soft huff of his laughter in her mouth.

'I think it probably needs a more thorough examination,' he murmured, and the smile in his voice made her laugh.

'Oh, definitely, but maybe standing by a glass door with the light on isn't the best place for it,' she mumbled, and he laughed again and eased away from her, his eyes oddly intense as the smile faded and the heat ramped up again.

'Come to bed,' he murmured, and she nodded and watched him swallow, the tension like a tight cord between them as he took her hand and led her down the corridor to his bedroom. He closed the door and turned back the covers, but he didn't put on the light. He didn't need to, because the room was flooded with moonlight, slanting across the floor and highlighting every plane of his face, leaving his eyes in shadow.

He held out his hand and led her to the bed, then cupped her face again in gentle fingers that weren't quite steady.

'I want you so much,' he said quietly. 'I've wanted to touch you, to hold you, since you let rip at me in Reception.'

'I have no idea why, I was horribly rude,' she said, feeling another wash of shame about the way she'd behaved, but he just smiled, and as he tipped his head on one side there was a twinkle in his eyes that could have been the moonlight, but she didn't think so.

'You were, but you were outrageously beautiful with it.' His fingers traced her face, the touch making her nerve endings dance as his hands moved slowly lower, his fingers finding the hem of her top and sliding up under it.

She sucked in her breath, pulling her post-baby tummy in, and she saw him frown as he stroked the skin with his warm hand.

'Why are you doing that? Relax. You're beautiful, Ellie.'

'I'm flabby.'

'No. You've had three children. Be proud of your body and what it's achieved. It's amazing. Such a gift. Don't ever feel ashamed of that.'

And just like that, he took away her worries, the niggle of fear that he wouldn't want her when he'd seen her, and freed her to be herself.

'I think you're wearing too much,' she said to him, suddenly braver, and he laughed again and took a step back.

'I think we're both wearing too much,' he said with a smile, and pulled his sweater over his head, hooked his thumbs in his waistband and shucked off his jeans and underwear in one.

'Better?' he asked, and she just stared at him, at the fit, honed body that clearly wanted hers, the strong, straight legs, the board-flat abs, the deep chest and powerful shoulders, and felt another wave of doubt.

'Hey,' he murmured, a little frown pleating his brow again, and he stepped closer again and touched her face. 'Do you want me to close the curtains?'

She shook her head. 'No. I'm just being a coward.'

'Then let me help you,' he said quietly, and took hold of the hem of her top and lifted it up and over her head, dropping it on the floor with his clothes. He undid the button on her jeans and tugged them down inch by inch, his mouth tracing down over her ribs, her stomach—sucked in again—and then pausing.

'Lacy knickers,' he said with a smile, and left them there while he stripped off her jeans, impatient now. 'Lift up,' he instructed, and eased them off one foot at a time, then straightened and pulled her up against him. 'That's better,' he murmured, and his mouth found hers again in a gentle kiss.

Except it wasn't gentle, not for long. She felt his fractured sigh in her mouth and gave a tiny whimper in response, and that was enough. With a ragged groan he cradled the back of her head with one hand, hauled her hard up against him and plundered her mouth, his tongue delving, searching, duelling with hers as they rocked against each other, their bodies striving for more.

'I need you,' he breathed, the air shuddering from his body, and she felt her legs turn to jelly.

'I need you, too,' she told him, and then they were on the bed in a tangle of arms and legs and desperate, seeking hands, their mouths locked together as their bodies found each other. Her underwear was gone, his hands on every inch of her, so clever, so knowing.

'Now, Nick, please…'

She gasped as he entered her, caught his groan in her mouth and they stilled, letting sensation wash over them.

'Ah, that feels so good,' he said after the longest moment, and then he kissed her again and started to move. She met him thrust for thrust, her body arching into his, touching him everywhere she could reach while his hands sought out all her sweet spots as if he knew her better than she knew herself.

She felt the tension building, her hands clawing at him now, begging, pleading, and then she was there, wave after wave of sensation crashing over her as his body stiffened and he surged into her one last time.

Then the tension drained from them both, and he sagged against her, a soft huff of laughter teasing her skin as he rolled to his side and took her with him, his chest rising and falling as his breathing slowed and returned to normal. He lifted a hand and smoothed the hair off her face and then kissed her, a lingering brush of his lips before he let out a long, heartfelt sigh and smiled, his eyes tender.

'That was amazing,' he murmured, sifting her hair with his fingers, his smile contented.

She smiled back and lifted her hand to cradle his jaw, the slight graze of stubble prickling her palm.

'It was. I think I love your surgeon.'

He chuckled, a deep rumble in his chest, and rolled onto his back with a long, drawn-out sigh.

She propped herself up on one elbow and studied his body, stretched out in the moonlight in all its glory. 'You had an ex-fix on your pelvis,' she said, tracing the little silver scars on his hipbones with a fingertip.

'Mmm. I had one on my ankle, as well, until they were able to rebuild it.'

'Is that why you limp sometimes? Your ankle?'

He nodded. 'It doesn't like the cold. I tried an ice bath once just to see what it was like, and it was excruciating. There's a ton of scaffolding in it, but hey. At least I still have my foot. I nearly didn't.'

She felt her eyes widen. 'It was that bad? You really did trash yourself, didn't you?'

'Oh, yeah.' His smile was wry. 'I don't think my parents have ever got over it.'

'Do they know why you did it?'

He nodded again, his smile fading. 'I don't remember telling them, but they gave me some pretty fancy drugs in hospital and apparently I blurted it all out and gave them a massive guilt trip. I just thought—I don't know what I thought. Maybe I'd fall off my bike as it landed and I'd break my arm, or scrape myself on the ground and get a load of bruises. I never in a million years imagined just how badly I'd hurt myself, but as I lay there getting all that attention, there was a moment when I thought it had been worth it.'

'But not now.'

'Oh, no. Absolutely not, and the feeling didn't last long. I was an idiot, and I suppose I got what I deserved, but you know, I was a kid, and my judgement was flawed. We all make mistakes, but most of them don't hurt that much. Not just me, but everyone, and most particularly Samuel. That was what really hurt me, more than anything else.'

She stared at him, horrified. 'Did they tell him why you did it?'

'No. He guessed. He cried when he saw me, and told me I didn't want to be like him, but while I lay there helpless for weeks I got a taste of what he went through all the time, and it changed me for the better. I suppose in a way it was worth it, just for that, to make me a better person. And there was plenty of room for improvement.'

She felt her eyes prickle for the boy he'd been, so desperate for someone to notice he was struggling, too kind to say so until it all got too much. She lay down again beside him, wrapping her arm around his waist, his arm around her shoulders as she laid her head on his chest and listened to the slow, steady beat of his heart. She felt the touch of his lips on her hair, the warm drift of his breath against her cheek.

'I'm OK, Ellie. Truly. It was more than half my life ago. I've made my peace with it and it's over now.'

Was it? Was it really? She wasn't sure. She tilted her head back and tried to read his eyes, but the moon had gone behind a thin wisp of cloud and she couldn't see him clearly any more.

He kissed her briefly, then pulled away and swung his legs over the side of the bed. 'I need to take Rufus out for a minute and then settle him in his bed. Mind your eyes,' he murmured, and reached out and turned on the bedside lamp and started to pull on his clothes.

She watched him, seeing the scars now in the lamp light, his left leg a mishmash of fine lines, the ankle slightly thicker.

At least I've still got my foot.

'Are you taking him for a walk?'

'Yes. Not far, just out onto the lane and down to the top of the steps so he can have a bit of a sniff around before he goes to bed. I won't be long.'

'I should go home,' she said, not really wanting to but not wanting to outstay her welcome.

He turned back to her. 'Really?'

She shrugged. 'I haven't got my toothbrush,' she said, which sounded pathetic as it came out of her mouth, but it was the only thing she could come up with, and he gave a soft huff of laughter and sat back down on the edge of the bed, dropping a kiss on her lips.

'I'm sure we can get round that. Please stay.'

It was the 'please' that did it, that and the look in his eyes which told her clearly that he meant it.

'OK,' she said softly, and he kissed her again.

'Keep the bed warm for me,' he said, and went out, leaving the door open.

She heard him walking briskly down the corridor, calling Rufus, heard the jingle of his collar and the sound of the front door closing, and she slipped out of bed to investigate the bathroom.

Did she have time for a shower before he got back? Maybe. She turned on the shower, stepped into the stream of hot water and reached for the shower gel. It smelt of him, the smell that had tantalised her all week, and as she smoothed it over her body she felt the caress of his hands, the touch of his mouth, the warmth of his arms around her.

Fantasy was a wonderful thing.

He heard water running, and settling Rufus with a biscuit he went back to his bedroom, closing the door in case the dog got any ideas.

She was in the shower, and he stripped off his clothes and went into the bathroom to join her.

'That seems like a good idea,' he said, sliding his arms around her from behind.

'Oh! You made me jump,' she said, turning and smiling up at him, and he smoothed the damp hair away from her face and found her mouth with his.

'Sorry,' he murmured. 'I just couldn't resist it.'

'You're too late, I'm done,' she said sadly, and he smiled.

'That's a shame, but I'm not,' he told her, then held his arms out to the side, his smile mischievous. 'Well, go on, then. You know you want to.'

So she did. She explored every inch of his body with soapy hands, driving him crazy with every touch and leaving the best till last. Her hand closed around him and he shut his eyes, his breath hissing out as she stroked him firmly but annoyingly slowly.

'You're killing me.'

'Mmm. Maybe it's time to move this somewhere more comfortable,' she said, and reached for a towel, leaving him to rinse.

He wasn't far behind her…

She went home after breakfast, but only long enough to do some laundry and tidy up a bit, and then she went back to his house with a change of clothes and her toothbrush, and they spent the weekend doing nothing.

Well, not nothing. They walked Rufus along the beach and had lunch in the Harbour Inn down by the river, and then went back to his house and made love lazily all afternoon until, as he put it, she'd checked out all his scars and satisfied herself that everything worked. And then checked again…

He threw together a tasty pasta dish for supper, and they ate it on their knees in front of the television, then walked Rufus again before going back to bed, and the next day they got in the car and drove to Dunwich Heath and took Rufus for a longer walk with lots of things to sniff, then had lunch in the café and got back in the car to drive back to Yoxburgh.

Back to reality, she thought, and realised that for the first time ever, she hadn't thought about the children all day, and that made her feel sick with guilt.

She was quiet in the car, a little unresponsive, the light-hearted banter of their weekend suddenly absent.

'What's wrong?' he asked, when she'd been silent for a while.

She shrugged. 'Nothing.'

'Yeah, there is. Come on, talk to me. Don't bottle things up. We need to be honest with each other, Ellie. If my stupidity taught me nothing else, it taught me that.'

She shrugged again. 'I just feel guilty.'

'Because of David? Tell me not, please.'

She stared at him for a second as if he was mad, and shook her head with a quiet laugh. 'No. Absolutely not because of David. I have no guilt where he's concerned.'

'Good.' He searched her eyes for a moment, then he slowed the car and pulled over to the side of the road in a little layby on the edge of some woods and cut the engine, undoing his seat belt and shifting so he was facing her.

'What happened, Ellie? Why did he leave you when you were pregnant?'

She sighed and looked away, staring blankly out of the windscreen. He had no idea what she was seeing in her head, but it didn't seem to be making her very happy.

'He didn't believe the baby was his,' she said softly after a pause so long he wondered if it would ever end. 'He was away a lot—an awful lot, and he came back after being gone for nearly three months and of course as usual the first thing he wanted was to go to bed, but we didn't have any condoms, and I wasn't using oral contraception because I was still breastfeeding Oscar, so I said no, and he said it was fine anyway, while he'd been away he'd had the vasectomy he'd been talking about so I couldn't get pregnant.'

'But you did.'

She nodded. 'Yes. I did. And when he came back six weeks later I'd done a test because I'd missed a period and it was positive, so I told him we were having another baby and he said it couldn't possibly be his.'

He frowned, because it didn't add up. 'But—surely he'd been tested? Didn't it occur to him to go back to the clinic and get them to check their results?'

'There were no results,' she said flat, her voice oddly flat. 'He hadn't been back for the tests—too busy, apparently. But he still didn't believe it could be his, because they'd told him he'd be fine. Or so he said. So he told me he wanted me to have a termination, and I refused. I hadn't really wanted him to have a vasectomy anyway, but he didn't want any more children, and he said he certainly didn't want someone else's. I said he could hardly blame me if I *had* found someone else, as he left me alone so much. So he walked out.'

'That's what happened with me and Rachel. I was never there, so she found someone who was. It's not unheard of.'

She shrugged. 'I know, but I didn't do that. Anyway, he took it as an admission of guilt and walked out. His parting shot was that he said he wasn't supporting another man's child. Then I got his mother on the phone, begging me to get a DNA test to prove the child's paternity, and I refused, because I knew perfectly well who the father was, so he divorced me on grounds of adultery.'

'And you didn't contest it?'

'I couldn't be bothered, and anyway life was easier without him. So he divorced me, put the house in my name and he pays me maintenance, and when Evie was born she was the spitting image of the other two, of course. None of them look like me, so they're either all his or none of them are, but he wouldn't hear it.'

'Couldn't he see the resemblance?' he asked, deciding the man was an idiot and hoping he never got to meet him, and she turned and gave him a tired smile.

'Probably, but I think pride got in his way. Anyway, his mother had the test done without telling me, which made me furious, but of course then he had proof that he was wrong, and he wanted to come back.'

'And you said no.'

'I did. He didn't trust me at the time, he didn't believe me, he accused me of committing adultery and he's never apologised because that would mean he'd have to admit he was in the wrong, and he'll never do that. He says I misled him, implied I'd had an affair, which I hadn't, I'd just said that he could hardly blame me if I had. Anyway, he now accepts Evie's his, and he has all of them at the weekends, and he does his best to be a good father but we don't always agree on how he does that.'

'Does he spoil them?'

'Always. They have what they want, which isn't good for them, but hey. He has them, he maintains contact, and they need that so I just deal with the fallout and mitigate it where I can.'

'What about his parents? What do they think?'

'Oh, they're furious with him for walking away from his family without establishing the facts, but they support him and they've always known Evie's his. Liz just wanted to prove it to him, which she's done, and although I was cross it was probably the right thing to do and at least he now acknowledges her.'

He nodded slowly. 'OK, so that's David out of the way, so why are you feeling guilty? Why now, today? Because of us?'

She shrugged again, her shoulders shifting a fraction in defeat. 'Because of us doing this. Having fun. I haven't thought about them once all day, Nick. What kind of a mother does that make me?'

'A perfectly normal one. Your children are safe, you know that. You're just having me time, and you're entitled to do that, surely?'

'It just seems wrong.'

'Why? You have a right to be you.'

'But I'm not being me. *Me* is the mother of three children, not…'

'Not the warm, generous, vibrant woman who's spent the last two nights in my bed making love with me? Making me laugh, making me smile? You can be both, Ellie. Sure, you're a mother, but you're also a woman, and you're entitled to feelings that don't revolve around your children. Time to be yourself, to do the other things that make you who you are. We can still do that.'

She shook her head. 'How? I have every other weekend, that's all, at best, and sometimes not even that. My time without them is so short, but I don't really want them to form a relationship with you, because when it goes wrong they'll be hurt and I don't want that for them, and anyway that's not what this is about, and it's not like they need a father figure, so that cuts out any other time.'

'So we'll have every other weekend when we can, and we'll make it special, and that's fine. It's fine with me, at least. I'm not a hormonal teenager, Ellie. I can do deferred gratification without getting all stroppy and demanding. It's about quality, not quantity. I'm not going to behave like a spoilt brat if I don't get to see you one weekend, either.'

Unlike David, who'd apparently wanted every second of her attention every time he'd seen fit to come back into her life for a few days before jetting off back to his real world. He didn't say that, though, just left her to fill in the gaps.

'I know you're not like that, but you deserve more,' she said, her voice oddly choked all of a sudden, but he shook his head.

'I don't *want* more than that, Ellie. I don't need you twenty-four seven. And wonderful though I'm sure they are, I don't need to be part of your children's lives. They've got a father, as you've pointed out, and I've done standing in for the real father with my own sisters and it didn't go well. Really, I'm fine with it. It suits me. I'm pretty self-sufficient. I don't mind being alone. I like it. It makes a refreshing change after a lifetime of caring, believe me.'

She turned her head and searched his face, and he held her eyes and smiled.

'Are you sure?' she asked, and he nodded.

'Yes, Ellie. I'm sure. We'll get together when we can, and it'll be fine.'

'But—what if it's not enough?'

'It will be.'

'But what if it's *not*? What if we want more?'

'Then we'll cross that bridge if we get to it,' he said, and leant over and cupped her chin in his hand and kissed her gently. 'Don't worry, Ellie. We'll make it work. Maybe not always, but as often as we can.'

'Are you sure? Sometimes he's away for four or five weeks at a time.'

He smiled and kissed her again. 'Then we'll have to find another way. And anyhow, we'll see each other every day at work.'

'Three days. I only work three days.'

'Even so. Don't worry, Ellie. It'll be fine.'

He gave her a reassuring smile, restarted the engine and drove back to his house.

'Tea?'

She shook her head. 'No, Nick, I need to go home. I'm not sure what time Liz will bring them back. It varies between four thirty and well after their bedtime, and they never tell me. I think he must imagine I hang myself up on a hook in the hall cupboard and wait for them to come home.'

He chuckled and drew her into his arms. 'Go on, then. You go home to your hook, and I'll see you in the morning. I'll walk so you can have the parking place, just in case they're on the drag tomorrow. I think the forecast is rain anyway and you don't all need to get drenched.'

'You're such a star,' she said, looking up into his eyes, and they creased with his smile.

'I aim to please,' he murmured, and kissed her lingeringly, then lifted his head and stared down at her. 'Go home, Ellie, before I cart you off to bed and make you late.'

Oh, she was so tempted to let him. 'I wish,' she said with a tired huff of laughter, and then she laid her palm against his cheek. 'Thank you, Nick—for everything. It's been such a lovely weekend. I don't remember when I last laughed so much.'

His smile touched her heart. 'No. Nor do I. It's been amazing.' He kissed her again, and let her go with a reluctant smile. 'Go on, go home. I'll call you later.'

'Don't call. Text me, just in case they're late. I might be putting them to bed still.'

He nodded, and she picked up the bag with her change of clothes in it and made her way home, the warmth of his smile wrapped around her heart.

'Mummy, Mummy, look what Daddy got us!'

She frowned at the two tablets in their childproof, supposedly indestructible cases, and met Liz's eyes over their heads.

'I thought we had an agreement about this stuff?' she said under her breath, trying to keep a lid on her frustration. 'They're too young for electronic devices, David knows that. It's not good for their developmental skills. If he wants to entertain them, he needs to try talking to them.'

'But you know what they're like, Ellie. All Maisie talks about is unicorns and mermaids, and Oscar just wants to run about pretending to be an aeroplane. He doesn't know where to start.'

'So get him to talk about unicorns and aeroplanes! Or take them to the park, or soft play or something, instead of buying them expensive electronic babysitters so he can spend the whole weekend on his phone checking on his investments!'

'He doesn't do that,' Liz protested weakly, but she knew better and said so.

'I lived with him for five years, Liz. I *know* what he's like.' She shifted the sleepy baby to her other hip and eyed her mother-in-law steadily over Evie's head. 'What did he get Evie?'

She looked awkward. 'He didn't. Even he agrees she's too young for a tablet. And I did ask, Ellie, but he's not easy to reason with and he doesn't really understand babies.'

She stifled a growl of anger and called the children. 'Come and say goodbye to Grandma, please. And say thank you for your presents and having you for the weekend.'

It took a minute more before she could close the door behind her and let out the sigh of frustration. There was a scream locked up behind it, but she kept that under control and took them into the sitting room and put Evie down on the floor with a box of her toys.

'Mummy, I can't do this unicorn game!' Maisie wailed, but the wail only increased when she took the machines away from her and Oscar and told them they'd be rationed to half an hour a day maximum, and only at the weekends.

She asked them what they'd done with their father, and from what she could glean it was not a lot apart from the wretched electronic devices, which he'd *known* she didn't want them to have. By the time she got them all to sleep that night it was almost ten o'clock, and she was exhausted and even crosser, if that was possible.

She was sitting down with a coffee wondering how the judge might react if she killed him when she heard the message tone on her phone.

Nick, as promised.

How are things?

She snorted softly and wrote, He got them tablets. Not pharma, obvs. I might have to kill him.

Oh, dear. Best not. Not great for your career... Want to talk?

She rang him, and just the sound of his voice was enough to calm her fury.

'Why did he do it?' she asked, frustrated. 'He knows what I think. We've had this conversation several times. He just ignores me and goes over my head.'

'So take them away and tell them they can only have them when they're with him. Simple.'

That made her laugh. 'I can tell you haven't met my children,' she said. 'And anyway, that's not the worst of it. The thing I'm most angry about is that he didn't get Evie anything at all. It's like she doesn't exist.'

'How old is she?'

'Fifteen months—and I know she doesn't know what she's missing, but it won't be long. She's his, too, for heaven's sake, and he knows that now. Why can't he treat them equally? I just wish...'

'What? That he was a reasonable human being? That you were a better judge of character? Don't go there. I've been through all of this with Rachel, all the "what ifs", and if you let it, it'll eat you alive. Deal with the tablets, ration the screen time, put up with the protests. They'll get over it, although it'll probably take a while. And buy something nice for Evie.'

She could hear the smile in his voice, and the sympathy, and she sighed and settled back against the sofa.

'You're such a reasonable human being.'

'I wasn't always. Maybe he just needs to learn the hard way, whatever that is.'

'If only. I'm sorry, it's not fair of me to unload on you, especially after such a lovely weekend,' she said wistfully. 'Thank you so much for going to so much trouble for me. It was like living out a fantasy. Just idyllic.'

'Hey,' he murmured, his voice soft. 'Don't sound so sad. We can do it again in two weeks. And anyway, it was no trouble, I seem to remember I wasn't exactly left out of the fun.'

'I just wish it wasn't over. Don't get me wrong, I love my babies to bits, but it was just so nice to be the other me for a while.'

'I know. So what are you doing now?' he asked.

'Lying on the sofa, drinking coffee.'

'Decaf?'

She smiled wearily. 'Don't worry, it won't keep me awake. For some reason I don't seem to have had very much sleep this weekend.'

'I wonder why that could be?' he asked, and she could picture his lazy, sexy smile.

'I can't imagine,' she murmured back, and then yawned hugely. 'Oh, sorry, I really am pooped. I need to go to bed.'

'Me, too. Rufus is out for the count. I think that walk at Dunwich was a bit long for him. It was lovely, though. We ought to do it again when the heather's out.'

'We should.'

She yawned again, and he laughed and said goodnight and she put her phone on charge and headed up to bed, still frustrated about the tablets but wrapped around now by the sound of Nick's voice and the warmth of his smile.

And in two weeks' time, they could do it all over again…

CHAPTER FIVE

'MORNING! KETTLE'S HOT.'

And not just the kettle. His voice was bright and breezy, but his eyes across the busy staff room held a different and far more personal message, and she felt her breath hitch. This was going to be much harder than she'd thought.

'Morning!'

She'd conjured up her best cheery voice, to match his, and she picked up her mug and gave him what she hoped would look like a friendly and professional smile as she reached for the teabags. 'Thank you for leaving me the parking space. The thought of trying to frog-march the children to nursery in the pouring rain is enough to bring me out in hives. I hope you didn't get soaked?'

'Only a bit. Don't worry, I'm pretty waterproof. So, how were the little darlings today?'

She rolled her eyes, and he grinned.

'*That* good.'

'Oh, yeah. They were overtired, overstimulated by the electronics and properly grumpy last night, and they're not much better today. I don't envy nursery.'

He lowered his voice a fraction. 'Sounds like you haven't forgiven him yet.'

'Absolutely not. I swear he does it just to annoy me.'

She turned round with her tea in her hand and smiled at the others. 'So, how's the day looking? Has the entire population of Yoxburgh gone down with the plague?'

Lucy chuckled and got to her feet. 'Maybe not the whole population, but the phone hasn't stopped ringing so we'll all be pretty busy, I think. Better go and make a start if I want to get home tonight.'

'Yeah, me, too,' Nick said from behind her, and touched her back discreetly. 'See you later.'

Much later, as it turned out, because the phone didn't stop ringing and while they didn't have the plague, what seemed like half their patient list apparently needed urgent appointments, and her surgery list was huge.

Please let them be nice, simple, straightforward cases.

Or not. The first was fine, but her second patient of the day was an asthmatic who was disturbingly short of breath. She gave him oxygen and medication and got Megan, one of the nursing team, to monitor him, but three patients later she had a call from her to say he was deteriorating, so she checked on him again and phoned the hospital, spoke to Lucy's husband Andy in the ED at Yoxburgh Park Hospital, and the patient's wife took him straight over there. It was the easiest and quickest thing to do, as the hospital was just across the park from the practice and it would save waiting for an ambulance and get him seen quicker.

She went back to her patients, only to be interrupted again by a call about a deteriorating terminally ill patient who urgently needed end-of-life medication. She said she'd authorise it and visit him as soon as she could get away, then called the pharmacist. It only took five minutes to sort out, but it was yet another interruption, and it was after twelve before she had time to review her pharmacy queries, deal with the sick note requests and make calls to patients who'd requested phone consultations.

She went up to the staff room at five past one and found them all gathered round having their daily catch-up and signing repeat prescriptions. Lucy handed her a stack for her own patients, and she sat down and worked her way through them as fast as she could.

A coffee appeared in front of her, and she glanced up and met Nick's sympathetic eyes.

'Oh, you're a star. Thank you.'

'My pleasure,' he murmured, and hooked out the chair opposite her and sat down. 'Can I have ten seconds?'

Really? She put her pen down and met his eyes again. 'Sure. Fire away.'

'I've just seen one of your patients—Judith Granger. She's seen you a couple of times with query irritable bowel, but it's flared up over the weekend and she's feeling very tired and a bit breathless, and I'm a bit worried there's something more going on. She's lost weight, and she says it's probably because she's been too busy to eat as much and she hasn't been that hungry, but she seemed quite happy about it.'

'And you're not?'

He shook his head. 'She's lost several pounds in the last two months, but it's the tiredness that brought her in, and she looks tired, too. Tired and drained and a bit anaemic.'

'You're thinking bowel cancer?'

'Maybe. I've sent her off to the lab for blood tests and a faecal sample, and we'll see what comes back, but I think she needs an urgent referral to the colorectal team for further investigation. I just thought I should give you a heads-up.'

She nodded slowly. 'Yes. Thank you. So when did I see her last? Did I miss this?'

'No, I don't think so. You saw her four months ago, and the weight loss has all happened since then, and she said she wasn't too bad until the weekend.'

'Any blood?'

'Not that she noticed, apparently. Anyway, I told her I'd fill you in.'

'OK. Thanks. I'll look out for the results.'

He nodded and went back to his pile of prescriptions, and she put Judith out of her mind and went back to her own, eating the odd bite of her lunch as she worked, but then just as she was about to leave she had a call from the nurse with her terminal patient to say that he'd died quite suddenly.

She was gutted. She'd wanted to see him, to be there for his wife as much as him, and now it was too late. Damn, damn, damn. 'OK, I'll come now,' she said, and stifled a sigh.

'House call?' he murmured, and she met his eyes and nodded.

'Yes, I've got to certify a death.'

'Want me to go?'

She shook her head. 'No. Thank you, but no. He was my patient and I've built a relationship with him and his wife. It's the last thing I can do for him.'

He nodded, gave her an understanding smile and went back to his admin, and she put her lunch back in the fridge. Maybe she'd get time to finish it later.

'Hi.'

'Hi, you.' He could hear the smile in her voice, a quiet murmur over the phone, and he felt it warm him.

'It sounds very peaceful your end,' he said softly. 'Are you good to talk? Are they in bed?'

'Oh, yes. They were ready for an early night, thank goodness, because the last thing I needed after today was another fight about bedtime.'

'So no fight over the tablets?'

He heard a little chuckle. 'No. I'd hidden them, and I told Liz they couldn't have them except at the weekends for a very limited time, so I don't know if they said anything about them to her but they didn't even mention them to me. I think they were too tired, to be honest. Nursery drains them. They keep them very busy.'

'So how was your widow? Did you ever finish your lunch?'

'No. Well, not till four. And as expected she was sad, resigned, glad it was over for him, a bit numb. She'll be OK, but you know how it is. Even when you know it's coming, it's always so final, and we're never ready for that.'

He thought instantly of Samuel, of how he'd thought he was ready and yet wasn't, when the time came. 'Yeah. Yeah, I know. So how was the rest of your day?'

'Oh, busy, too much to do, not enough time. Yours?'

'Mine?' He stretched out on the sofa, one hand idly fondling the dog's ears, and gave a quiet sigh. 'Much the same as yours, I guess. Busy, not enough time. Your car had gone by the time I left, and I still hadn't finished all the admin, so I'll need to get in early tomorrow and nail it before I start. That'll be a rude awakening for poor old Rufus.'

'So what does he do while you're at work all day? Does someone let him out?'

He glanced at the sleeping dog on his lap, and smiled. 'No, he's got a little dog-flap into the area of garden behind the utility room. There's a bit of grass there and he seems quite happy to pop out when he needs to. He's got toys, and he's used to lying around all day, and he gets plenty of games and cuddles when I'm home. He gets a walk morning and evening, regardless of the weather, and he seems happy enough with that unless it's pouring.'

'I bet he wasn't happy this morning, then,' she said, and he heard the smile in her voice and chuckled.

'Not especially. He has a coat I put on him if I have to walk him in the rain, but he did look at me as if I was mad this morning when I opened the door, and he was more than happy to go back to his blanket when we got home.'

'Poor Rufus,' she murmured, her voice rich with sympathy, and he laughed.

'Poor Rufus nothing. He's on my lap right now and I swear if he could purr he'd be doing it.'

'I know the feeling,' she murmured, and he groaned, the flashback to his bedroom so vivid he felt his heart pound.

'Don't. That's torture, Ellie. I'm trying so hard not to think about our weekend and that *really* doesn't help.'

He heard the rueful chuckle. 'Sorry. I've been doing the same, and I'm not having any joy with it either. I didn't mean to torture you.'

'Good, because our next weekend seems an awfully long way away.'

'Tell me about it, and it's only Monday. We've got another eleven days to wait,' she said in a wry and slightly despairing voice, and it was his turn to laugh.

'We might have to get creative at work. Lock ourselves in a cupboard or something.'

'Like we have time.'

'Yeah. Ah, well. We'll have to make do with phone sex.'

He heard a splutter of laughter, and he grinned.

'I thought you said you weren't a hormonal teenager?' she said, still laughing, and he chuckled.

'Did I? I might have to retract that.' His smile faded, because it was true, he had said it—said it, and believed it, and it seemed he'd been wrong, because all he could think about was being with her and it was killing him.

'I tell you what,' she said. 'I'll make your life easier and get off the phone. I've got laundry to sort before I can go to bed, and I'm shattered.'

'Yeah, me, too. It was a long day. See you tomorrow. Sweet dreams.'

'You, too.' There was a tiny pause, and for a second he thought she was going to say something else. Something on the lines of 'I love you'? But then the line went dead as she hung up and he felt a curious sensation.

Relief? Or disappointment?

He had no idea, but it was oddly disturbing, whatever it was, and he went to bed wondering exactly what it was she hadn't said.

Judith Granger's results came back, and there was blood in the faecal sample and she was quite severely anaemic.

Nick was in the staff room when she went up there at lunchtime on Friday, and he frowned at her, instantly picking up on something, as he always did.

'You OK?' he asked softly.

'Judith Granger. You were right. I've put in an urgent referral request to the colorectal team. She's got an iron deficiency and they found blood.'

He nodded slowly. 'Doesn't surprise me. Have you told her yet?'

'No. I got Katie to call her and ask her to come in and see me again, and she's got an appointment this afternoon. I don't want her wondering what they've found all weekend. She needs to know—but then of course she'll spend the next couple of weeks until she sees them wondering what they'll find.'

He smiled understandingly and turned on the kettle. 'It's always the way. There's no easy way to break bad news, or even to hint at it, but she struck me as someone who'd want answers.'

She nodded. 'Yes, she is. Thank you for picking it up. I'm kicking myself for not chasing it earlier.'

'Hey, you didn't miss anything. I read your notes. They were thorough, and she didn't have any symptoms severe enough to indicate cancer. You haven't let her down, Ellie, and she might not have it. There are all sorts of other things it could be.'

She wasn't convinced, though, and it took Judith herself to point out later that day that things had changed quite rapidly in the past week or so, which made her feel a little better.

'I'm sorry it's not better news, though, Judith,' she told her, but the woman just smiled.

'That's OK, Dr Kendal. I thought you might find something, and in a way I'm glad. At least now I know I wasn't imagining it and I'm not wasting your time.'

'No,' she said vehemently, shaking her head. 'It's never wasting our time if you think something's wrong. You know your body better than anyone. If it's telling you something, there's a reason, and it's far better to get it checked out than to wait until it's too late, and very often it turns out to be something much less significant, as it might well do now. That's why I've referred you. You should see someone within a week or so.'

'So what will they do?'

She ignored the time pressure and talked Judith through all the possible diagnostic tests she might have, the imaging techniques they could use, and assured her she could come back at any time if she needed to talk about it. It put her behind, of course, but that was the story of her life, and she ended up running to nursery and collecting the children five minutes late.

And then, because it was the weekend, all Maisie and Oscar wanted to do was play games on their tablets, even though Oscar could hardly understand what he was meant to do and Maisie was getting increasingly frustrated.

Not as frustrated as she was, and if it wasn't for the ensuing row it would cause, she would have put the wretched things in the bin on Saturday morning.

David had a lot to answer for.

She got to her feet. 'Come on, guys. It's a lovely day. Let's go for a walk along the beach.'

'I don't want to go for a walk. I want to play the unicorn game!'

'No. You've done enough, Maisie. It's time for some fresh air and sunshine.'

She rounded them up, put Evie in the backpack and chivvied Oscar and Maisie into shoes and jumpers, then headed out of the door. And of course once they were out it was fine, the children running along the pavement towards Jacob's Lane because that was the way they *always* went to the beach, with her following.

Would they bump into Nick and Rufus?

Maybe. She wasn't sure if that was a good idea or not. Probably not, but although her mind was telling her that, her heart and her body seemed to have a different view.

They passed the beach huts under the trees at the top of the cliff, then the houses beyond them set back from the road towards the cliff edge, and then they were there, turning onto the small gravelled road that led past his house and round the corner to the top of the steps.

There was no sign of him at the house, although she looked up at his sitting room windows on the way past just in case, and she felt a twinge of disappointment.

Stupid. Why did she want to see him when she was smothered in children? Unless she wanted to put him off her completely, of course. Not that she wanted a relationship with him that included the children because, as he'd pointed out, they had a father, and even if he was an idiot, he was still their father and they didn't need another one.

Oh, why's it so complicated?

And then she turned round to see where the children were, and he was there, rounding the corner, Rufus trotting happily beside him, his ears and undercarriage sopping wet, his tongue lolling. He caught sight of her and came running, ears flying, lead trailing, and she bent down and made a fuss of him.

'Morning.'

She looked up—past sodden trainers, up long legs clad in dripping jeans, to a smiling face.

'You got them away from the tablets, then,' he murmured, and she straightened up and smiled at him a little self-consciously.

'Yes. I thought I'd drag them out for some fresh air.' She glanced down at his wet legs. 'It looks like you got caught in the surf,' she added, and he gave her a rueful grin.

'Yeah, that wasn't planned. I saw a wave coming and grabbed Rufus before he got washed away. He doesn't mind wet feet, but he panics if he's out of his depth and it's a bit rough today, but it was quite chilly. So this must be Evie. Hi, Evie,' he said, smiling over her shoulder at the baby in the backpack, and she turned and scanned the lane for the others.

'Kids, where are you?' she said, feeling a moment of

panic, but then she heard a giggle and there they were, tucked behind a shrub in the entrance to his drive, hiding, and the breath left her lungs in a rush.

'Monkeys. Come here!' She turned back to him. 'Sorry about that. They don't understand the laws of trespass.'

He chuckled and looked round as the children emerged from the undergrowth and ran up to them.

'Who are you?' Maisie asked, looking up at him curiously, and Ellie's heart sank. This was not meant to happen!

'I'm Nick. Who are you?'

'I'm Maisie, and this is Oscar. Why are you talking to Mummy?'

She dived in fast. 'Nick's a doctor, too, and he's just started working in Yoxburgh, so I know him.'

'Are you at Mummy's work?' Maisie asked, studying him intently, and he nodded.

'Yes, I am.'

'Is she your friend?' Oscar asked him.

She saw his mouth twitch. 'Well, sort of. We see each other at work a lot and I suppose you could say we were friends. We're colleagues, really.'

'Collies? Like the dogs?'

She rescued him before it got any worse. 'Not collies, Maisie. Colleagues. That means people you work with. It's like I work with Lucy and Dev and the others,' she explained. Except of course it wasn't, not anything like it…

'Can you fly a plane?' Oscar asked out of the blue, and Nick laughed and shook his head.

'No, I'm afraid not.'

'My daddy can,' Maisie said proudly, and Ellie frowned.

'I don't think he can.'

'He says he can. He's got a friend with a plane and she

lets him fly it. What's your dog called?' she asked, moving on abruptly as children did and leaving Ellie wondering who the friend with the plane was. And…*she*?

Not that David's friendships or private life were any of her business, any more than hers were his business, and besides, coming from Maisie it was as likely as not all a work of fiction.

'His name's Rufus,' Nick told Maisie, and met her eyes over the children's heads. 'Fancy a quick coffee?'

'Oh. Um—we were heading to the beach—'

'Can we have a snack?' Oscar asked, looking remarkably like Rufus when he was begging, and Nick's lips twitched again.

'That's up to your mother, but I'm sure I could find you something if she says it's OK.'

''Nack,' Evie said from behind her ear, and before she knew it they were all inside his house and the children were clustered round him as he investigated the contents of a cupboard.

'For a doctor, you have an astonishing collection of unwholesome rubbish,' she said drily, and he grinned at her.

'Don't I just?' he said unrepentantly, and pulled out a giant packet of crisps.

Not that unwholesome, though, she realised when he handed them to her and went to change, because they were lightly salted and oven baked, and he'd also dug out a punnet of blueberries and put them on the table.

Two minutes later he was back in dry clothes and they were kneeling up on his dining chairs with a little bowl of crisps, a handful of blueberries and a drink of water each, and Rufus, who obviously had a great understanding of small people, had stationed himself between Oscar and Evie, as if he knew they were the most likely to drop things.

'He's not stupid,' Nick said drily, noticing what she was looking at, and she laughed.

'No, I can see that. He's definitely an opportunist.'

'He's also on a diet, but he's nearly down to what he ought to weigh. Mum and Dad were spoiling him a bit.'

'I can imagine. It must have been hard for them, the last year or so.'

He gave a soft snort and poured hot water into the cafetière. 'Try thirty-nine years. They don't quite know what to do with themselves now, but the grandchildren keep them busy.'

'Little people have a way of doing that.'

'Tell me about it.' He pressed the plunger and handed her a coffee, and they stood side by side leaning against the worktop and watching the children eat while they munched on the left-over crisps.

'Where are your parents?' he asked quietly. 'You haven't mentioned them.'

'Oxfordshire—well, my father is. I don't see him very often. My mother died when I was fifteen, and since he got married again it just doesn't feel like home any more.'

'When was that?'

'When I was nineteen? I was away at uni, and I came home for the summer and the whole house was redecorated and all trace of my mother was gone. The only room left untouched was mine, but he'd let her do everything else.'

And it had hurt. Hurt so much that she hadn't gone home again for three years, and then only very occasionally since.

She glanced up at Nick, and he was studying her thoughtfully, his eyes concerned.

'I'm sorry,' he murmured. 'That must have been horrible.'

She swallowed. 'It's fine. I'm over it,' she said, not

quite truthfully. 'And I'm a grown-up. I have my own home now, and even if it's inadequate in many ways it's still mine, my sanctuary, the place I can relax and be myself, and it might not be perfect, it might not be immaculate or particularly restful, but it's still home, or the closest thing we have to one, and in the grand scheme of things we're really very lucky. We could be a great deal worse off.'

Maisie pushed her bowl away and looked across at them.

'Mummy, can we go in the garden?'

'That's up to Nick. He might be busy—'

'No, you're fine,' he said, and before she could say any more, he slid open the door in the hall and let them out.

They stayed for an hour, the two older children exploring every inch of the garden with Rufus running around with them and wagging his tail furiously while he and Ellie sat on a bench with Evie close by and kept an eye on them, and then she took them away and he watched them go with mixed feelings.

They were lovely kids, but like all small people they were a challenge, and she was right, he did have things he should be doing. Things like sorting through the boxes in the first bedroom—although maybe not today.

Instead he gravitated back to the kitchen, staring out of the window and trying to process what she'd said about her mother, and her father's new wife.

How had it felt, going back to her home and finding all trace of her mother had been eradicated from it by her replacement? Dreadful, even if it had been four years later. And although she'd said she was over it, he didn't believe it, not in the slightest bit. Losing her mother at fifteen must have been devastating for her, and he thought back to her words on—when? Monday?—when he'd asked after the widow of her patient who'd died.

You know how it is. Even when you know it's coming, it's always so final, and we're never ready for that.

He'd thought she was talking professionally, but she hadn't been, of course. She'd been talking about the loss of her mother.

Poor Ellie. And her words about her house, or at least her home, being her sanctuary. He could understand that, too, because he'd lost his home when he and Rachel had split up and he'd moved back home to help his parents with his dying brother, and although this house wasn't yet as he wanted it, it was definitely his home, his sanctuary, the place he could go and be himself, to borrow her words.

Although at least he liked his house. He got the distinct feeling she didn't like hers at all, but maybe he'd misunderstood because she'd certainly described it as home.

Home is where the heart is?

Not that she'd said that, not in so many words, but it was where she was bringing up her family and, with the possible exception of Maisie, it was the only home they'd ever known.

He poured himself another coffee and sat down at the kitchen table with the last of the crisps and watched Rufus, who was sitting at attention by the front door and looking hopeful.

'Rufus, they've gone, go and lie down, mate,' he said gently, but Rufus didn't move, and every now and then he gave a little whine.

He knew just how the dog felt. Even though he'd wanted to be alone with his thoughts, suddenly he didn't, and the house seemed huge and empty and soulless without them all.

Although that was what he wanted, wasn't it? To be alone? But perhaps not quite this much. Not that he wanted the children, lovely though they were. He didn't need that in his life, didn't want any more responsibility or involvement, didn't need anyone else depending on him or coming to rely on him in any way. He was done with that.

But Ellie—Ellie was a different matter altogether. She didn't want that sort of relationship from him either, and this time next week the children would be with their father and he'd have her to himself again. He could hardly wait.

He pulled out his phone and started looking for things that they could do, and then gave up, because he realised it didn't matter what they did as long as they were together. Maybe a stroll around the town, to help him get to know it, or a trip across the river on the ferry—whatever. He didn't care. He just wanted to be with her.

And if he had a grain of sense or any instinct of self-preservation, he'd be worried about that, but he wasn't, because he was having way too much fun and it had been a long time coming. This was his time, and he was going to enjoy it if it killed him.

CHAPTER SIX

THE WEEK CRAWLED BY, but finally it was Friday and she dropped the children's bags off with Liz and Steven, took the children to nursery and bounced into the staff room with a smile.

'Someone's happy,' Dev said with a grin, and she beamed at him.

'Because it's the weekend, and David has the children, so I'm going to crawl into bed when I get home and stay there until Sunday,' she said blithely. Well, it wasn't a lie—

'Sounds like an excellent plan. I might do that myself.'

Nick's voice came from over her shoulder, and she felt a startled laugh bubble up and caught it just in time.

'Coffee?' he asked her, walking over to the kettle, his face deadpan, and she couldn't look at him because she just *knew* his eyes would finish her off.

'Um—thanks. That would be lovely,' she mumbled, and sat down at the table, pretending interest in her phone. He put her mug down in front of her with a decisive plonk and she looked up and met his mischievous eyes and nearly lost it. 'Thank you,' she croaked, and he just gave her a wicked grin.

'My pleasure,' he murmured innocently, and walked out, leaving her to gather herself together in peace. She gave him two minutes to get out of the corridor, then put her phone away, picked up her coffee and went down to her consulting room. Instantly there was a tap on the door, and she opened it to find him there.

'What can I do for you?' she said with a smile, and his mouth twitched.

'Well, there's an interesting question,' he said, so softly she could hardly hear it, and he propelled her gently back into the room, pushed the door shut with his foot and kissed her thoroughly.

She pulled away with a laugh. 'Stop it! I have to concentrate.'

'Well, so do I, but you just blew that out of the water by announcing your weekend plans,' he said with a grin. 'I was going to do an internet order, assuming those plans include me?'

'Absolutely! Well, unless you don't—'

'Oh, I do. I definitely do. So, any special requests?'

'Whatever. I'll try anything.'

His mouth kicked up at the side. 'I've found that out already. I was talking about food.'

She bit her lip and pushed him towards the door, trying hard not to laugh. 'Go away, Nick. I've got twenty patients to see this morning, a lot of admin to get through and a chronic conditions clinic before I can go home. Order whatever you want. When do you finish?

'Six thirty, if I'm lucky.'

She nodded. 'Call me when you're done, and I'll walk round. I don't want David seeing my car on your drive.'

'Is he likely to?'

'Maybe. They'll walk that way to the beach if the weather's nice enough to play on the sand. I hope they don't, because they'll tell him all about going to your house if they walk past it.'

He cocked his head on one side and frowned a little. 'Would that matter? Is that really such an issue?'

She nodded, not sure why it was but just feeling uneasy about it. 'Yes. I think it would. I don't really want him to know about us. I don't want him speculating, or asking me questions, or interrogating the children. It's none of his business what I do.'

'Would he, though? Interrogate them?'

'I don't know. Possibly. It's just—I want this for us, Nick. I don't want to share it. It feels too private.' Too new, if she was honest, although she wasn't saying that to him, but she could see from his eyes that he understood.

'Yeah, you're right, and it's not far—and you won't need much luggage, not if you get your way,' he added, and he gave her a smiling peck on the lips and let himself out, leaving her to ponder on exactly why it was she didn't want David to know.

Because it was none of his business?

Or because the way Nick made her feel was so unlike her, so alien to the person she'd thought she was, that she didn't dare to believe in it?

After all, what did they have, apart from a shared interest in medicine, and hot sex? Very hot sex, hot enough to melt the paint, a side of herself she'd never known existed—but what kind of a basis was that for a relationship?

That wasn't all they had, though. There was also tenderness, on both sides, and respect, and something that seemed very like affection. Not love. Not yet. But… maybe?

No, she definitely wasn't ready to go public, least of all to her ex-husband and probably not even to Nick, not about that, because there were still three very important little reasons why this wasn't going anywhere. Except his bed…

She turned on her computer, dragged her mind back to business and buzzed in her first patient.

He called at a quarter to seven to say he was home, and she set off on foot with a change of clothes and her toothbrush tucked into her bag. The door swung open as she reached for the bell, and Rufus ran to her, tail wagging furiously, tongue lolling.

'Hello, poppet,' she murmured, giving him a little stroke. 'Are you pleased to see me, by any chance?'

She straightened up, and Nick drew her in with a warm and welcoming smile and closed the door behind her.

'OK?'

'I am now,' she said, smiling up at him, and he laughed softly, slid his arms round her and hugged her.

She rested her head on his chest and breathed in the scent of him, and felt peace steal over her. Such a simple thing, a hug, but there was no one in her life now to do it apart from the children, and although she cherished their hugs, Nick's warm, solid, affectionate embrace gave her a curious feeling of emotional security that had been missing for at least two years, or maybe even longer.

Maybe since she'd lost her mother twenty years ago.

No. She was being silly and sentimental. It was nothing like that.

She tilted her head back and his mouth found hers in a searching kiss that was filled with promise, but it was rudely interrupted by the sound of a car pulling up outside.

'Ah. I forgot about that. I hope you're hungry,' he said as he lifted his head, and she smiled ruefully.

'Ravenous, actually. I didn't get my lunch again. Is that your delivery?'

'No. The internet order won't be here until tomorrow because all the slots were gone, so I ordered a Chinese takeaway. I hope that's OK?'

She grinned. 'Absolutely. Bring it on!'

After they'd finished, Nick took Rufus for a walk and she tidied up in the kitchen, wiped the table, loaded the dishwasher and put it on, then filled the kettle in case he wanted coffee. He probably would, so she found clean mugs and the cafetière and put them by the kettle. It gave her a weird feeling, a sensation of unreality, as if she was caught up in some cosily domestic little bubble that was all make-believe.

What was she doing? It didn't seem real, and yet here she was…

The front door opened and Rufus came in, wagging his tail, and she put away her odd thoughts and busied herself with the kettle.

'Wine or coffee?' she asked over her shoulder, and Nick slid his arms around her from behind and nuzzled her neck, making her fizz all over at his touch.

'That would be lovely,' he murmured against her skin, and she tilted her head out of the way to give him better access.

'So which do you want?' she asked, a touch breathlessly.

'You,' he murmured, and nipped her skin gently, then straightened up. 'Failing that, wine, but we should probably let our food slide down a bit and keep the dog company for a while. He's been alone all day and it would be mean to sneak off to bed and leave him just yet, tempting though it is.'

She turned and looked up at him, wanting him even more for the fact that he'd put the dog first. That would never have occurred to David.

'You're an utter softy, do you know that?' she murmured with a smile, and looked down at the dog. 'Come on, then, Rufus. Let's go and have a snuggle on the sofa before I steal your master.'

'Sounds like an excellent plan,' Nick said, and they headed up to the sitting room. He turned on some music, settled down next to her with his arm along the back of the sofa and handed her a glass of wine.

'Oh, this is nice,' she said, resting her head back against his arm.

'The music or the wine?'

'All of it. Everything. It just doesn't feel quite real.' She turned and looked up at him, and he dropped a tender kiss on her lips and rested his head against hers.

'It's real, Ellie.'

'Is it? It doesn't feel it. I feel a bit like Alice in Wonderland, you know? I'm just waiting for someone to chop off my head.'

He chuckled, the huff of his breath teasing her cheek, and his arm hugged her closer. 'Nobody's going to chop off your head. You're safe with me.'

Was she? She wasn't at all sure about that, but one thing she did know, she didn't want to be anywhere else.

She rested her head against his and let the music wash over her, carrying her niggling worries away.

Bliss…

She woke up with a stiff neck, the snoring dog on her lap and Nick's arm draped heavily around her shoulders.

'Hey,' she said, and poked him gently in the ribs,

and his eyes fluttered open and he smiled down at her, yawned hugely and stretched, then glanced at his watch.

'It's eleven o'clock. How did that happen?' he asked, looking confused, and she chuckled.

'Search me, I've been asleep, too.'

He yawned again, and Rufus lifted his head and yawned, too, then shut his eyes and settled down again with a sigh.

'I think that's our cue to go to bed,' he said with a chuckle, and he lifted the little dog off her lap and put him on the floor, pulled her to her feet and headed down to the hall. 'I'll take him out for a quick wander, if you want the bathroom first?'

She was in bed waiting for him when he'd settled Rufus, and he bent over and dropped a kiss on her lips.

'Give me two minutes, I need a shower.'

It was nearer three, but when he got into bed and his body came into contact with hers he let out a long, slow groan.

'Oh, that feels so good…'

'You're damp,' she murmured, and he could feel her smile against his mouth.

'Mmm. Sorry. I didn't want to keep you waiting any longer.'

She gave a soft chuckle, her breath cooling his damp shoulder as she wriggled closer. 'I'm not complaining. You smell gorgeous. I love your shower gel.'

She propped herself up on one elbow and traced her finger over his chest, blowing on his nipples and teasing them with her fingertip before running it down over his ribs and sliding the flat of her hand over his hip.

He reached for her, but she pushed his arms out of the way and straddled him, and he sucked in his breath and met her eyes in the soft lamplight as she rocked gently against him, a naughty smile flickering around her soft, full mouth.

'You're evil, do you know that?' he growled through gritted teeth, and her smile widened.

'Mmm. Fun, isn't it?'

'It's torture,' he corrected, and groaned as she rocked her hips again.

'Want me to put you out of your misery?'

He let out a soft huff of what started as laughter and ended as a gasp, and the chuckle echoed through her body straight into his.

'Ellie…'

She lifted up a fraction, and he closed his eyes and reached for her, but she batted him away again, pinning his arms down above his head.

'Stay there,' she told him, and he stayed, although it almost killed him, while she teased and tormented him until he was ready to howl with frustration.

And then she lowered herself down onto him slowly, taking him into her body inch by torturous inch.

He nearly lost it, and he gripped her hips and held her still, his eyes closed, not daring to look at her until the moment passed, but then he tilted his hips and she gasped, and he opened his eyes and watched her as she rose and fell in a slow, steady rhythm that threatened to kill him.

God, she was beautiful, her body strong and yet soft, full and lush and, oh, so tempting. He wanted to roll her over and drive into her, but she'd threaded her fingers through his and was pinning his hands above his head, holding him down.

He could so easily have overwhelmed her, but he

didn't want to. He just wanted her in reach, and right now she wasn't.

He stretched his arms out to the side, her fingers still locked with his, and it brought her breasts into reach. 'That's better,' he muttered, and he lifted his head and drew a nipple into his mouth, making her whimper. She let him go then, sitting up a little and gripping his shoulders, and he reached up and cupped the weight of her breasts in his palms, feeling the soft fullness of them fill his hands.

'You're so lovely,' he murmured. 'Come here. I need to kiss you and you're too far away.'

She smiled and lowered her head, her mouth finding his in a sweet, tender kiss that blew him away because it was so unexpected, so gentle, so filled with warmth and emotion as well as sensual promise.

He cradled her head in his hands and kissed her back, and the sensation spiralled as she rocked harder against him and shattered his self-control.

Done with patience, he held her tightly and rolled them over, their bodies locked together, his mouth still on hers but urgent now, too close for subtlety, too needy to wait.

'Come with me,' he growled raggedly, and he felt her body tighten, her hands clawing at him, her breath locked in her throat. And then she bucked against him, sobbing, her body contracting around him, and they tumbled together headlong into oblivion.

They didn't spend the entire weekend in bed, mostly because of Rufus but also because the weather was gorgeous and they wanted to get out into the fresh spring air.

'I don't know the area. Where would you like to go?' he asked, and she replied without hesitation.

'Can we go to Walberswick? I loved it when we went there last summer. Maisie and Oscar pottered about on the sand for ages, and I sat with Evie on my lap and tried to stop her eating sand. Rufus would love it, and it's beautiful. Fabulous sandy beach, sea stretching out to the horizon in front of you, sand dunes behind you—just lovely. It was a bit of a trek, though, and Oscar got carsick, so we haven't been since, but I'd love to go again.'

'We'll do that, then,' he said with a smile, and they drove up the coast to Walberswick, parked the car and made their way to the beach.

'Wow, it's lovely,' he said as the vista opened up in front of them, and they headed through the dunes and down to the sand.

The tide was almost out, the sand damp and firm underfoot, so they took off their shoes, rolled up their jeans and strolled along hand in hand while Rufus tore in and out of the gently lapping waves and had a wonderful time.

Then the tide turned and they headed back from the beach and found a pub serving food outside, then after lunch they drove back to his house, went to bed and made love again.

There was no urgency. They took their time, exploring each other slowly and lazily until the end, and then when it was over curling up together for a nap before pulling on their clothes and heading to the kitchen.

'Crayfish and linguine with a touch of chilli?' he said, his head in the fridge.

'Ooh, that sounds nice,' she murmured, peering over his shoulder. 'And we can have the leftovers from last night as a midnight feast later.'

He straightened up and turned to look at her. 'Are you planning on working up an appetite?' he asked, his eyes speaking volumes, and she bit her lips and tried not to smile.

'Might be.'

He laughed softly, shook his head and turned back to the fridge.

'Anything I can do?' she asked, but he shook his head again and said no, and she settled down at the little breakfast bar and watched him as he worked.

'You would have been a good surgeon.'

'Nah. I can't stand for hours, my ankle doesn't like it. That was another reason for going into general practice, and then I found I liked it better, anyway. How about you? Why are you a GP?'

'Work/life balance,' she said without hesitation. 'That was why I chose it. I loved hospital medicine, but it wasn't practical if I wanted to be a mother, so I trained as a GP and discovered a whole new world, and I can't imagine doing anything else now. I love it. Love the continuity, the ability to see a patient through a course of treatment and watch them improve, be there for them if it all goes wrong and there's nothing more we can do, watching babies turn into children with distinct personalities—it's great. So varied, so interesting, so full of human emotion and—I don't know. I just feel I can really make a difference to people's lives, and that's important to me.'

He nodded thoughtfully, and flashed her a little smile.

'Exactly,' he said, the single word carrying a wealth of meaning, and then went back to preparing their meal while she watched him and wondered if she was falling in love.

No. She couldn't be. She just liked him, and they had a lot in common. That was all. It wasn't love.

Was it?

* * *

'Hi, Liz,' she said, expecting to be told when her mother-in-law was going to return the children, but then she felt a chill run over her as Liz spoke, her voice urgent.

'Ellie, can you come? Steven's had a fall and I'm going to have to take him to hospital. I think he's broken his arm—it's all right, darlings, Mummy's coming soon. Ellie, please…'

'Of course. I'm on my way. Are you at home?'

'Yes—yes, we are. Please be quick.'

Liz hung up, and she turned to Nick.

'My father-in-law's had a fall and Liz thinks he's broken his arm and she needs to take him to hospital. I've got to go.'

'I'll drive you home, you'll need your car,' he said without hesitation, and then as they pulled up outside he put a hand on her arm. 'Do you want me to come? I know you wanted to keep us all separate, but this is an emergency and he's bound to be in pain. I can have a look at him, maybe immobilise it, give him some pain relief. Then you can get the children out of the way so they're not distressed by it.'

She dithered for a moment, then nodded. 'If you could.'

'Of course. I'll follow you. I've got my bag in the car.'

It was a Colles' fracture. He could tell that much as he got out of the car, and he could see at a glance that it was going to need surgery.

Ellie was busy comforting Evie, who was crying in Liz's arms, and Oscar and Maisie were sitting on the edge of the drive looking a little shocked.

'Take them home, I'll deal with this,' he said gently,

and she nodded, put them in the car, collected their bags from the hall and left him to sort it out, so he headed over to the man sitting on the front step, guarding his arm.

He crouched down and smiled at him, noticing that he was pale and sweaty and clearly in shock.

'Hi. Steven, isn't it? I'm Nick Cooper, I'm a new colleague of Ellie's. She asked me if I could come and lend a hand. Do you mind if I have a look?'

'No, that's fine,' he said, but he was very reluctant to move his fingers, and the fracture was clearly displaced.

'Can you feel your fingers?' he asked, touching them gently in turn.

'Yes, but they feel weird. It's broken, isn't it?' Steven said, and he nodded.

'Yes. Yes, it's definitely broken, and you'll have to go to hospital. I think you could do with an ambulance, or at least a paramedic with a decent sling before we try and move you. I'll give them a call—unless you've already done it?' he asked Liz, but she shook her head.

'No. No, I just rang Ellie and sat with them. I thought she might be able to help me get him in the car. Thank you so much for coming. It's such a help. The little ones were getting upset—'

She bit her lip and turned away, and he laid a hand on her arm and squeezed it gently.

'It's OK, I'll call an ambulance.' He pulled out his phone, passed on the information and crouched down again.

'Steven, can you remember how you fell?'

'Oh—no, not really. I was feeling a bit odd—hot, sweaty—and then I was on the floor and my arm was killing me. No idea how I got here.'

'Mmm. Sounds like you might have had a little blackout. Have you ever fainted before, or felt as if you might?'

'Not exactly, but I've felt close to it once or twice.'

'Recently?'

He nodded. 'Yes, I—I've been feeling a bit weird, but I didn't think it was anything to worry about.'

'I can't believe that!' Liz said, sitting down abruptly beside him on the step. 'What were you thinking, not telling me? Is that why you haven't wanted to drive?'

He let out a little sigh and nodded. 'I didn't want to make a fuss.'

Nick grunted. Jim Golding had been the last person to tell him that and he'd died a couple of minutes later. He gave Steven a firm look.

'You need to make a fuss when things don't feel right. I'm not saying there's necessarily anything drastic wrong, but it's really important that you get things like that investigated, because falls are dangerous and they don't tend to happen spontaneously. Let me get my bag and have a listen to your chest, and then I'll give you some pain relief while we wait for the ambulance.'

His heart sounded steady, if a little fast, so Nick drew up ten mg of morphine and delivered it slowly over five minutes into a vein in his other arm. By the time he'd done that the ambulance had arrived, so he ignored his ringing phone for the third time in as many minutes and turned his attention to the crew.

'We were just round the corner having an ice cream and thinking it was a bit too quiet,' the paramedic said cheerfully, so Nick introduced himself, gave him the details of what he'd found and the drugs he'd given, handed over his patient, made sure Liz was OK, got back in his car and pulled out his phone.

Four missed calls now. She must be worrying. He'd go round to hers and put her out of her misery.

What on earth was going on?

The moment she opened the door she could hear running water, and as she stepped into the hall and felt the carpet squelch under her shoes, the sinking feeling in her stomach got a whole lot worse.

The dishwasher. She'd put it on as they'd left the house on Friday morning, and it must be leaking. Damn.

'Stay here,' she told the children, sitting them on the stairs, and she opened the kitchen door and gasped at the devastation.

Part of the ceiling was down, water streaming steadily through the joists from upstairs and splashing on the ruined kitchen units, and the light fitting was dangling at a crazy angle. Starting to panic, she ran up and opened the door of Maisie and Oscar's bedroom and found a repeat of the scene downstairs.

Sagging plasterboard, loft insulation hanging down and funnelling water straight onto a huge slab of sodden plasterboard on Maisie's bed—and above, in the loft, she could see the underside of the water tank.

Why was it leaking? How?

And she didn't even have a loft ladder so she couldn't get up there to see what was happening. Not that she'd know what to look for.

She stared around in disbelief, totally overwhelmed by the level of damage, paralysed by the shock.

What do I do? The children. Get the children out...

She ran back down to the children, scooped up Evie, grabbed Oscar's hand and towed him down the hall, Maisie on her heels, and as she opened the front door she heard a crash and a shudder ran through her. Another ceiling somewhere?

She ushered them out of the door before anything else happened, and rang Nick. He didn't answer, not then and not the next three times she phoned him, and then reaction set in and she started to shake.

What if it had happened while the children were asleep? They could have been killed in their beds!

She had to take them somewhere else—somewhere safe, but where? She couldn't go back to Liz and Steven's, because they wouldn't be there, but she could go to Lucy and Andy. At least there they'd be safe. Except they were away for the weekend and might not be back yet.

Nick, where are you? I need you...

She put them in the car out of harm's way and was about to call him again when his car pulled onto the drive.

She'd never been so glad to see anyone in her life.

CHAPTER SEVEN

SHE LOOKED AWFUL.

Damn. He should have called her back. He might have realised she'd be worried. He got out of his car and strode towards her.

'Hey, Ellie, he's OK—'

She shook her head. 'No. No, it's not Steven,' she said, her voice sounding really weird, and the bottom dropped out of his stomach.

'Ellie? What on earth's happened?' he said, and she fell into his arms and burst into tears. He gathered her up against his chest and held her tight, swamped with guilt for ignoring her calls. What if something dreadful had happened?

'Ellie, talk to me. What is it? Is it one of the children? What's wrong?'

She shook her head. 'No. It's my house. There's a leak—there's water everywhere and everything's ruined…'

He looked past her, past the children sitting in the car, on through the open door, but he couldn't see anything. He gave her another quick hug, let her go and put his head inside, and he could hear water running still. Not a good sign.

'Any idea where it's leaking?'

She nodded. 'The tank in the loft. At least, that's where the ceiling's down, under the tank. I've never been in there but I imagine that's what's leaking.'

'Where's your stopcock?'

'Um—under the sink, but the kitchen's trashed, so's their bedroom, and the water's running off the wires, too. I just had to get them out—'

Her face crumpled again, and he reached out and rubbed her arm gently. 'Of course you did. Stay here, I'll make sure it's safe. Where's the mains switch for the electricity?'

'Under-stairs cupboard, right in front of you.'

'OK. Back in a minute.'

She nodded, and he went in and glanced through the kitchen door and winced. She was right, it was trashed, but he wasn't going in there until he'd checked the power was off because the water was streaming down the dangling cable of the light fitting and the floor was awash, but at least the ceiling was already down and nothing else was going to happen.

He found the electricity supply under the stairs and discovered it had already tripped out, so at least it was safe and she hadn't been in any danger. Good. He turned off the mains switch and picked his way through the sodden plasterboard, turned off the stopcock under the sink and listened.

The trickle of water slowed to a steady drip. Good. That was that solved. Now for the cause. He went upstairs, squelched across the landing and looked in the bedroom above the kitchen.

Poor Ellie. No wonder she was in bits. He could hardly see the beds for the sodden plasterboard, the wet loft insulation hanging from the rafters had water dripping steadily off it, and he could see the tank through the gaping hole. Almost definitely the culprit.

He went back to the landing and looked up at the loft hatch. It wasn't hinged, which meant it wouldn't have a ladder. Great. It just got better. He dragged a chair out of her bedroom, stood on it and stretched up, tipping the hatch cover out of the way, then hauled himself up and made his way across the loft using his phone as a torch.

As he'd suspected, the float had sheared off the arm so there'd been nothing to stop the cold tank endlessly filling, but the overflow which should have stopped the flood was still submerged, so it must be blocked. Spiders' webs? Very likely. It had happened in his parents' house, although they'd found it before it could do any harm.

Unlike Ellie. Her house was going to be out of action for weeks, maybe months. They'd be homeless.

Except they wouldn't, he realised, the inevitability of it settling in him like a familiar weight. He couldn't allow that.

He found a bit of wood lying around and wedged the arm up in case the stopcock leaked, then lowered himself down and went back to her.

She was sitting in the car with the children, and she turned her face up to him, her eyes red-rimmed but dry now.

'Well?'

'It was the tank overfilling, and the overflow must be blocked. I've turned off the water, wedged up the arm so it can't refill the tank, and the power's off so it's safe to go in, so you'd better go and find what you need for the night. You're coming back to mine.'

'Yours?'

'Well, there's no way you can stay here, not without power or water. It isn't practical. You've got no beds for the children, no kitchen, no bathroom facilities you can use—nothing.'

She stared at him blankly. 'Nor have you—well, not beds, anyway. Um—I'll try Lucy, see if she's back—'

'No, you won't,' he said firmly. 'And before you say it, you can't go to Liz, she's got enough on her plate with Steven. And I have got beds. You're coming back to mine.'

She shook her head. 'But—we can't! You don't want us all there!'

'Don't be ridiculous, Ellie, of course I want you! And I've got three spare bedrooms. Why on earth not use them?'

She kept staring, searching his eyes, and then finally her shoulders drooped and she nodded. 'OK, if you're sure—but just for tonight, and I'll sort something out tomorrow. And I don't need to go back in. They've got overnight things in my car.'

'And you? What about yours?'

'I hadn't packed when Liz rang. I didn't have time to think about it.'

He nodded. 'OK. Well, lock it up and we'll sort it out in the morning.'

'How? We're at work.'

Her eyes were desperate, the situation overwhelming her again, so he took charge, took the responsibility off her shoulders without even thinking because that was what he did, what he'd always done all his life.

'You're not,' he said firmly. 'Not now. You need to deal with this, Ellie. I'll cover you.'

'How? We're all stretched. I'll have to work. I'll make a few calls in between. I'll be fine—'

'Don't think about it now,' he said, quietly but firmly. 'Come on, let's get you back to my house and settled in, find the children something to eat and then we can talk about it. OK?'

She nodded, to his relief, and he leant in and smiled at the children. 'Hey, guess what? You're all going to come back to my house for a sleepover. That'll be fun, won't it? Do you remember coming to my house?'

They nodded, their little faces brightening.

'Is Rufus there?' Maisie asked, and he grinned.

'Yeah, and he'll be really pleased to see you all. Come on, then. Let's go!'

It was still warm enough to be outside, the late afternoon sun slanting down into his garden, but Ellie felt chilled to the bone. She sat huddled on a bench while the children played on the grass with the delighted dog, seemingly oblivious to the turmoil going on inside her.

Not that she minded that at all. She'd rather they had no idea, because the more she thought about it, the worse their situation got.

She hugged her arms around herself and shuddered. She had no idea where Nick was or what he was doing. He'd sent them all out here into the garden, and gone back inside. Sorting out beds?

There was a double in the room next to him in a jumble of other furniture, she knew that, and a pile of bed bits and two single mattresses in the next room, but the first of the bedrooms had all the boxes stacked in it and there was no way he could deal with those in a hurry. No matter. They could share one room, if necessary. They'd be fine. At least they'd be dry and safe.

She glanced at the bedroom windows but she couldn't see any sign of movement. What was he doing?

She could always go and investigate, but she couldn't let the children out of her sight, so she stayed there, hugging her arms and wondering if it was her punishment for spending the weekend with him instead of at home.

So much for her happy little bubble.

She was still shaking.

He'd seen her through the bedroom windows, and she'd looked cold and confused and—well, devastated wasn't too strong a word.

He gave the last duvet a tug, went into the kitchen and made her a hot drink and took it outside.

'Here,' he said softly. He perched beside her on the bench at a discreet distance and put the mug in her hands, and she wrapped her fingers round it and breathed in the steam. 'Is it tea?' she asked, her voice sounding far-away and worryingly unlike her.

'Yes. Here. I've brought you chocolate.'

He held it out, and she gave him a sideways look. 'Are you giving me first aid, by any chance?' she asked with a wry smile, and he smiled back.

'Rumbled. But you're in shock, Ellie,' he said gently. 'It's a lot to take in, but you don't need to worry about tonight, at least. I've made the beds. I thought you'd want Evie in with you, so I've pushed the double bed up against the wall so she can't fall out that side, and I've built the twin beds in the other bedroom for Maisie and Oscar, so they'll be together.'

'How have you even *got* so many beds?' she asked, totally unexpectedly, and he had to hide the smile.

'I told you. I have sisters with children. We had the beds in our house in Bath so I just brought them with me.' He waved the chocolate under her nose. 'Here. Eat it.'

She glanced down, then took it from him and ate it, her eyes on the children again as if she was checking to make sure they were still safe.

'They're OK, Ellie,' he said softly. 'Nothing happened to them.'

'But it might have done. If that ceiling had come down while they were sleeping—'

'But it didn't. Nobody was there, nobody was hurt.'

'That was just sheer luck. Nick, how am I going to clean it all up? How can I get the water out of the carpets? And I'll never get that filth out of their bedding—and the kitchen! All the things on the side—the kettle, the toaster, all the storage jars...'

He could almost hear her mind working, cataloguing the extent of the disaster, and as it sank in she turned her head and looked up at him, her eyes lost.

'Nick, what do I do now? Everything's going to need replacing—where on earth do I start?'

To hell with the discreet distance. He shifted closer, put his arm around her shoulders and hugged her up against his side. 'You contact the insurance company in the morning, you tell them what's happened, and you hand it over to them. You do have insurance, I take it?'

'Of course I do, but what will they do? Get a plumber, I suppose, and then what?'

'They'll clear the house of anything that's been damaged, put in dehumidifiers to dry out the structure and once it's all dry they'll repair it, redecorate and re-carpet it, replace the damaged furniture and light fittings, maybe refit the kitchen—'

'But...that'll take weeks!'

'It will. It'll be several weeks, maybe even months, but that's fine. You're all safe, you've got somewhere to live—don't worry. It'll all work out, Ellie.'

She shook her head and eased away from him, her face looking stunned as the enormity of it all sank in.

'We can't stay here that long. It's not fair, it's not reasonable, and it's the last thing you want.'

'No, it isn't,' he said, trying to sound convincing, but she was shaking her head again.

'Yes, it is! You told me you were ready for a quiet life. Believe me, there's nothing quiet about life with my children, and I can't live on eggshells in case they upset you—'

'Ellie, stop it,' he said gently, taking hold of her hands and stilling them before she slopped tea all over herself. 'It's fine,' he lied, as much to himself as to her. 'We'll be fine, and if you and they aren't happy here, then the insurance company will find you somewhere to go, but for now, at least, you don't need to worry. Let me do this for you, please.'

She stared at him as if he'd got two heads. 'Why? Why would you put yourself out like this?'

'Why wouldn't I? You'd do it for me, I know you would. You'd do it for anyone.' He gave a smile that felt a little crooked. 'You remember telling me why you liked general practice? Because you could make a difference to people's lives, and that's important. It's important for all of us, and it's so easy for me to do this for you, and if it makes your life easier now, then that makes me happy. And anyway, why wouldn't I want to have you around? In case you haven't noticed, I rather like your company.'

He saw something flicker in her eyes, and guessed what she was thinking before she even spoke.

'We can't…' She broke off, and he rolled his eyes and sighed, a little hurt that she could think so little of him.

'Ellie. Seriously? Your house is trashed, you and the children are homeless, and you think I'm worried about sex? I thought you were a better judge of character.'

She swallowed. 'I'm sorry. It's just—the situation's

never arisen before, but I made a decision long ago that there would be nobody sharing my bed while the children were around, and certainly not a man I've only known a few weeks. Even if they have been pretty significant weeks…'

He smiled and hugged her again. 'They have, but, honestly, I'm not stupid and I'm not selfish and I absolutely understand where you're coming from. I'm offering you somewhere safe to stay, no strings, and at the moment you're all out of options.'

'We could always stay with Liz and Steven once he's out of hospital.'

'I wouldn't have thought so, or not for a while. Steven's fracture is going to need surgery, and once he comes home he'll need help with all sorts of things, so I doubt you'll even be able to rely on Liz for a while, at least for the first week or so until he's over it and on the mend. It was a nasty break.'

She nodded slowly, and swallowed. 'Yes, I saw. I was wondering about that, just before I opened my front door.' She shook her head. 'I haven't even given him a thought since, and his problems are far worse than mine. What kind of a person does that make me?'

'Worried. Worried for your home and your children and their safety and security—and anyway, you knew he was being taken care of and there was nothing you could do to change things for him, so why would you think about him when he wasn't your top priority? You've had more pressing things to deal with, and he would understand that. And anyway, he's in the right place and I'm sure he'll be OK. Apparently he fainted, so they'll probably want to check that out as well. Liz said she'd let you know as soon as she had news.'

She nodded again, and finally leant back against the

bench and drank her tea, her eyes on the precious little people that were her life, and he sat with his arm behind her along the back of the bench and watched her watching over them while his heart ached for her.

He just hoped this situation didn't end up breaking any of their hearts or spoiling the fledgling relationship he had with Ellie, but that was the least of his worries, because it wasn't just about how he felt, or her, come to that, it was about the children.

And they, he reminded himself, were all that really mattered.

Her phone rang just as the children were sitting down to eat, and she pulled it out and sighed.

'Sorry, I have to get this, it's David,' she said, and walked into the kitchen.

He could hear snatches of what she was saying, giving him the gist of what had happened. Then he heard his name, and his ears pricked up. Whatever happened to keeping it secret? And what would David be making of it? Not that there was any way they could keep it from him. The children were bound to let it out.

'Hey, Oscar, don't feed Rufus,' he said softly, dragging himself back to the task in hand. 'People's food isn't good for dogs.'

'Why?'

He stifled the smile. His sisters' endless choruses of 'why?' had driven him nuts when they were this age, and his nephews and nieces had carried on the tradition. Apparently it was universal.

'It just isn't. Their tummies are different,' he explained, and waited for the inevitable reaction.

'Why?'

'They just are,' he said, and steered the conversation

away from the dog's digestion. 'He had fun with you in the garden.'

'I like him,' Maisie said. 'He always looks happy.'

'He is happy when you're here. He loves children. Have you all finished?'

Oscar pushed his plate away and looked hopeful. 'Can we have pudding?'

He scanned the fridge in his head. 'Would you like some yogurt?'

'Do you have ice cream?'

'No, Maisie, I don't, I'm afraid. I've got yogurt and blueberries, and I can cut up some banana. How about that?'

It seemed to appeal, so he cleared the plates and took the fruit and yogurt back to the table, giving Ellie a reassuring wink in passing.

She flashed him a smile, hung up a few moments later and followed him back.

'Sorry about that. He'd had a message from his mother but he couldn't get hold of her and he wanted to know what was going on.'

He sliced banana into the bowls and glanced at her. 'Is he coming back?'

She shook her head. 'No. He can't, he's at the airport. I've said I'll deal with it.'

'Did you tell him about the house?' he asked, dolloping yogurt on the fruit.

'Yes, and I told him we were staying with a friend so he didn't need to worry, but he wasn't, really, he was more worried about his father. He knew you'd helped Steven, and he seemed to know who you were. Guys, did you and Daddy walk past the house this weekend on your way to the beach, and did you tell him all about Nick and Rufus?'

They nodded, and she exchanged a speaking glance

with him before looking back at the children. 'I think you need help with that, Evie,' she said, and took the baby's spoon out of her hand, and he watched her feed the little one and wondered what else had been said.

It was another hour before the children were tucked up in bed, and half an hour after that before they were asleep. Even so, she sat for a good while longer on the double bed she'd be sharing with Evie, until she heard the soft sound of Nick's bare feet padding down the hall.

He paused at the door and raised an eyebrow in enquiry.

'OK?' he mouthed, and she nodded and got carefully off the bed, put the pillows in the way so Evie couldn't roll out and tiptoed across the room.

'What's wrong?' she asked in a quiet undertone.

'Nothing. It's just you've been ages, and I wondered if you were having difficulty settling them.'

She shook her head. 'No. I'm just worried they'll wake up, and it's a long way to the sitting room. I don't think I can leave them. They might wake up and not know where they are.'

'Fancy a coffee?'

She sighed with joy, and smiled at him. 'I'd *love* a coffee. I'll come with you and get it and bring it back here.'

He shook his head. 'I have a better idea. Go into my bedroom, and I'll bring it. We can sit on the bed and talk with the door open, and you'll hear if any of them stir.'

She hesitated, and he shook his head slowly and gave her a rueful smile. 'Ellie, I thought we'd had this conversation? Go on, go and get comfortable. I won't be long.'

She went up on tiptoe and kissed his cheek. 'You are such a star,' she murmured, and went into his bedroom to wait for him. The overhead light seemed too bright, so she put on the bedside lights and settled herself against the pillows she'd slept on only last night, wrapped in his arms.

It seemed a lifetime ago, and so much had happened in that time.

She heard his footsteps and he appeared with coffee and a heaped plate on a tray. She sat up straighter, suddenly aware that she was hungry.

'Are those sandwiches, or am I hallucinating?'

He grinned and shook his head. 'I made them a little while ago, because I wasn't sure if you'd be able to leave the children. I thought you could eat while you watch them, if necessary, but this is a much better idea.'

His smiled warmed her all the way to her toes, and she shuffled over and he settled himself beside her and handed her a mug, putting the plate down on the bed between them.

'I could get used to this,' she murmured contentedly.

'Feel free,' he said with a smile, and leant over and dropped a chaste, tender kiss on her lips. 'Now eat.'

She ate hungrily, then sat back with a sigh and sipped her coffee. 'Bliss. I was starving. Thank you so much—for everything. I don't know what we would have done without you.'

'Well, that's easy. You wouldn't have been in this mess without me, because you would have found the leak much earlier because you wouldn't have been here.'

'I might not have done. I might not have found it until the ceiling fell down on the children in the middle of the night. It's going to give me nightmares,' she said, and suppressed a shudder.

'No, it won't,' he said firmly, 'because it didn't happen and it's all fine—well, no, not fine, obviously, but at least everyone's OK. So what did David have to say about the house?'

She sighed and rolled her eyes. 'Oh, not a lot. He wanted to know if we were all right, but he was more worried about his father, naturally, and of course he couldn't come back to see him and make sure he was all right. He asked if he could leave me to deal with it. I pointed out he usually does.'

'I heard you mention my name.'

'Yes, he brought it up because he knew you'd been there helping. He said, "Is that the Nick who lives in Jacob's Lane?" so I imagine the children will have given him chapter and verse when they walked past. They don't normally hold back. He certainly knew you'd got a dog.'

'Does he know you're staying here?'

She shook her head. 'No, and I didn't tell him. I didn't want him jumping to conclusions. He wanted to know where I'd been, as I obviously hadn't been at home, and I just told him I was away for the weekend. I could hear the cogs turning, and I wouldn't be surprised if he puts two and two together and makes ten, but there you go, there's nothing I can do.'

'I wouldn't worry about it. You are divorced, aren't you? You're entitled to a life.'

She gave a little huff of laughter. 'Oh, yes. We're very definitely divorced, and I know he hasn't been a saint since we split up, but then it's different for him. He's not a mother.'

'It's not different!'

'It is, or sort of. He doesn't live with them, and they never see him in his other life. It's harder for me to have a relationship, and I don't know how he'd take it. Not that it's any of his business, but I'd still rather not discuss it with him. He wanted to know why we weren't going to stay with his parents. I had to point out that I don't have keys, she was at the hospital with his father, either waiting for him to go into Theatre or waiting while he was in there, and if he couldn't get hold of her then I couldn't, so how was I supposed to get the keys, and anyway she had quite enough to worry about without being bothered by my problems. I also told him not to tell her about the house, because I really don't want her worried. I'll tell her when I know Steven's OK.'

'Good plan. And in the meantime, stop worrying. It'll all sort itself out.'

She gave a short sigh. 'I don't think so. I think I'm going to have to sort it.' She dropped her head back and stared blankly at the wall opposite. 'Oh, what on earth am I going to do, Nick?' she said, feeling utterly defeated and so, so tired. 'I don't even know where to start.'

'Keep it simple. Lucy should be back by now. Phone her and tell her you need the day off tomorrow, and then call the insurance company first thing in the morning. Do you have the documents?' he asked, all practicality, but she hadn't even thought about that.

'Yes—but not on me. They're in the dining room, but at least it's dry in there so they should be OK. I can get them tomorrow.'

'I'll go and get them for you now. Where are they, exactly?'

'Oh—are you sure? You don't need to do that, Nick, I could go.'

'What, and leave the children with a virtual stranger? No. I'll go, Ellie. It's better for them, and I don't mind. So, how do I find these documents?'

She gave in, because of course he was right. 'In the dresser—far end, bottom shelf, in an expanding file full of all the important stuff. It's black, with a red handle, and my laptop's in there, too. That could be useful.'

'Anything else there that you want? Anything valuable? Bearing in mind that the alarm's not set because the power's off.'

She swallowed. 'Only my mother's jewellery.'

'Where is it?'

'In my bedroom, in the…' She gave a despairing laugh and started again, feeling colour creep into her cheeks. Ridiculous, considering what they'd done right here in this bed over the weekend. 'It's in the top right-hand drawer, under my underwear. It's at the back, under the stuff I never wear.'

'What colour is it?'

'What, my underwear, or the jewellery box?'

His mouth twitched. 'I think I pretty much know what colour your underwear is. I meant your jewellery box.'

She couldn't help smiling. 'Tan leather. It's the only thing in there apart from the undies. Actually you could bring me some clean stuff for tomorrow. That would be really nice.'

'OK. Is that all there is? Any other jewellery?'

She shook her head, fingering the ring she wore on her wedding finger. 'Only this. It was Mum's, too.'

He reached out and laid his hand over hers, giving them a gentle squeeze. 'I'm sorry, Ellie.'

She glanced at him, puzzled. 'Why should you be sorry? You didn't flood my house.'

'No. I meant your mum,' he said softly.

She swallowed hard, suddenly swamped with emotion, and for a moment she couldn't speak. Then she sucked in a breath and met his thoughtful, troubled gaze. 'Thank you.'

She leant over and kissed him, and then smiled at

him. 'David said his mother had called you a good Samaritan, and she was right, you are. I don't know what I would have done if you hadn't been around this afternoon to help with Steven and then this. I was so shocked, so scared for the kids, for what might have happened, and there you were, taking control, turning off the water, checking the electricity was off, sorting it out—if you hadn't been there…'

'But I was, and you're here now.'

'But only for one night.'

He shook his head slowly, his eyes intent and sincere. 'You don't have to go, you know. You can stay here for as long as you need to, as long as it takes.'

'Nick, it could be months, you said so yourself.'

'That's fine. Really. You're safe, the children are safe, and that's all that matters. Everything else can be dealt with, starting right now.'

He leant over and kissed her, a tender, lingering kiss, then got off the bed and walked towards the door, but she stopped him.

'Nick, wait, you need keys.'

'They're on the side in the kitchen, and don't worry, I'll make sure it's all secure before I leave. Phone Lucy,' he added, and then he went out and a few moments later she heard the front door shut and the crunch of gravel as he drove away.

She lifted her fingers to her lips, and could have cried at his thoughtfulness, his gentleness, his compassion. Instead she pulled out her phone, sucked in a deep breath and called Lucy.

Time to put on her big-girl pants.

Doing it all by torchlight didn't make things easier, but at least her directions were good.

He found the big black file and her laptop and put them in the hall, then went upstairs and looked in her underwear drawer for the jewellery box and some clean undies for her for tomorrow, but he had to struggle to keep his mind in order, especially when he found the bra he'd taken off her the first time. None of that in his immediate future, he thought with a sigh, and picked up a random selection of this and that, shut the drawer firmly and headed for the stairs.

Then he stopped and shone the torch into the ruined bedroom, and saw teddies.

Wet, soggy teddies, but much loved.

He picked his way carefully across the room, and felt the floor giving underneath his feet. The chipboard must have degraded with the wet. Well, just so long as it held his weight, but at least the carpet would stop him falling through into the kitchen. He hoped…

He tested the floor and found the position of a joist, and walked along it, grabbed the teddies off the children's sodden beds and made his way cautiously out again, went into Evie's room and picked up her teddy from her cot and went back downstairs, put everything he'd gathered together into the car and went back into the kitchen.

He'd brought his cool box, and he emptied the contents of her freezer drawers into it, decanted her fridge into carrier bags, put them in the car, and then hesitated, another thought occurring to him. They might be ruined, but on the other hand, they might not. Worth a try.

He went back into the kitchen, took the children's pictures off the fridge, put the magnets in his pocket, locked the house and drove back.

As he pulled up on the drive and got out, the front door opened. Ellie stood there, framed in the light, and

CHAPTER EIGHT

SHE'D BEEN WAITING in the kitchen for him, watching out of the window with one ear listening for the children, and as the car turned onto the drive and the lights swept across the window, she felt a little surge of—what? Relief? Joy?

She didn't wait to analyse it, just went to the door and opened it, and as he stepped inside he took her into his arms and the world seemed to right itself.

'I'm sorry I've been so long. Are you OK?'

His arms felt so good around her, and she rested her head against his chest and breathed him in. 'I am now. I'm sorry I was a bit hysterical earlier. Did you get everything?' she murmured.

'Mmm-hmm, and I brought a few other things,' he said, dropping his arms and easing back a little. 'I emptied the fridge-freezer, but mine's fairly empty so we should be OK. And I brought their teddies from their beds, too, but they're a bit soggy and dirty. They'll need a wash, but I thought they might want them. Oh, and there's something else. I hope they're all right, but it was hard to see by torchlight.'

He went back to the car, opened the back door and took something out, and as she saw what he'd brought her hand flew up to her mouth and she let out a little sob, overwhelmed that he'd thought of something so small and yet so significant.

'You brought their pictures?'

His grin was a bit crooked. 'Yeah. It seemed a shame to leave them, and my fridge is a bit bare. I thought it might help them feel at home. Here. Stick them up.'

He pulled the fridge magnets out of his pocket, piled them on the worktop and left her to deal with them while he brought in all the other things.

'I'll need to find you room in a chest of drawers, and make sure I remember to give you a set of keys,' he said, putting the stuff down.

'We're only here for the night,' she reminded him, and he rolled his eyes, but even as she'd said it, she knew it was a token protest, and she couldn't think of anywhere she'd rather be. She just hoped he didn't regret it in the morning, but she wouldn't say anything to the children yet about how long they'd stay, just in case he changed his mind.

They sat down at the dining table after she'd unpacked everything, and while they drank another coffee and ate the cake he'd found in her fridge, she tracked down her house insurance documents in the file.

'Well, that looks pretty straightforward,' she said after a quick scan through them. 'All I have to do is ring them and they send an assessor and it all goes from there.'

'Good. And Lucy was OK?'

She nodded. 'Yes, Lucy was wonderful, and said if I need anything just ask. I'm sure there will be a million things, but they'll crop up when I know I haven't got them. Oh, and Liz phoned. Steven's out of surgery, and he's OK, but he's staying in for a few days for investigations. They think he might have some kind of heart condition that caused the blackout, so they want to look into that.'

'Yeah, they will,' Nick murmured, frowning. 'I wonder what caused it? Arrhythmia? He said he felt hot and sweaty and a bit weird, and he was very pale.'

'Who knows. I just hope it's nothing too serious. So tomorrow, Lucy said you'll split all my patients between you, and if I can get this done early I'll come in and do what I can. I'm going to take the kids to nursery but I can't ask Liz to pick them up, at least not until they know more about why Steven fell.'

'No, of course not. Don't worry about it. We'll work it all out somehow.'

'Somehow' was right.

It was chaos, the usual Monday morning rush after the weekend compounded by the fact it was the Easter holidays and Dev was off.

He and Lucy and Brian divvied up the patients between them, diverted some to the nurse practitioners and took advantage of the ones who failed to turn up for their appointments by catching up a little with the backlog, and by lunchtime they were more or less there.

For the morning lists, at least.

And then as they sat signing repeat prescriptions and checking results in the staff room, Ellie appeared looking harassed and racked with guilt.

'I'm so, so sorry. Has it been hell?' she asked, and he got to his feet and put the kettle on.

'It's been fine. We've managed. How did you get on with the insurance company?'

'That's why I'm here. The assessor's coming at two thirty, so I've asked nursery to keep the children until five. If I get away early, I'll come and do my afternoon list, or as much of it as I can, but if not I don't know what to do.'

'You don't have to do anything,' Brian said firmly. 'You don't need to be here at all today. Go and sort out your house stuff and we'll see you tomorrow if you're able to come in, and if you're not, then we won't. Now sit down and have a coffee and relax for a minute.'

'That's not fair. Have you got any results I can look at, or repeats to sign?'

'No, they're done, but you might want to look at Jim Golding's PM report,' Nick said quietly, putting a mug of coffee down beside her. 'He had an undiagnosed aneurysm in the aortic arch. It ruptured.'

She scanned it, and her eyes widened. 'Really? Wow. Poor Jim. No wonder he was feeling peaky. It must have been brewing for days—weeks, maybe.'

'Mmm. Says it was catastrophic, so the DNAR was irrelevant. We couldn't have resuscitated him anyway.'

She nodded slowly, and he met her eyes over the top of the screen. They were sad, filled with regret, and he cut her off before she could say it.

'You didn't let him down. The other thing he said to me was, "I'm glad it's not Dr Kendal." I don't think he wanted you to be upset, and I have a feeling he knew he was going to die then. He's was ready, Ellie.'

She nodded. 'I know. He told me, when he asked for the DNAR. He said he didn't want anyone trying to save him if his time was up, because he was ready to go and join Kitty. He missed her so much—sorry…'

She swiped away a tear, and Lucy looked up and shook her head.

'There's no point at all in telling you not to get involved, is there?' she said with a wry smile, and Ellie gave an uneven little laugh.

'No, probably not. Right, I'd better go and meet my assessor and see what he makes of it.'

'Don't come back today,' Brian said firmly. 'You've had enough to deal with. We can cope.'

'But I—'

'But nothing. Look what you all did for me while I was off. What you're still doing. Go, Ellie. Do what you have to do. The world won't stop turning. It never does.'

She nodded and went, and Nick turned to him.

'Thanks. She's been so determined not to let anyone down, but—Brian, if you'd seen that house… And her father-in-law fell because he'd had a blackout, so that's now under investigation and she's bound to be worried about him, too. I think he's one of our patients.'

'He is. I'll look into it,' Brian said, and got stiffly to his feet. 'I'll be glad when the builders finish this week and we get our new staff room downstairs. My hip really doesn't like the stairs. Doesn't like anything much. I suppose I need to bite the bullet and get it done.' He gave them a crooked grin and limped out, and Nick met Lucy's eyes.

'He's needed a hip replacement for years,' she told him quietly, 'but he couldn't do it because of his wife, and since then—well, I don't think he feels he can take the time off.'

'That's crazy.'

'That's general practice, Nick. It's what it's like now. I can't tell you how glad we all are that you're here. And—Ellie. Tread carefully, Nick. She's been through a lot and this is the last thing she needed.'

'I know. Don't worry, Lucy, I'm looking after her—after all of them.'

She held his eyes. 'Don't break her heart.'

He frowned, and Lucy shook her head. 'Don't pretend

you don't know what I'm talking about, Nick. I've seen the way you look at each other. I'm not stupid.'

'Nor am I, and the last thing I want is to hurt her. I'm just offering her a roof over their heads and a safe place to be, for as long as it takes.'

'Good.' She put the signed prescription on the pile and stood up, letting the subject drop. 'Back to the grind, I suppose. Are you coming?'

He nodded and followed her, her words echoing in his head.

Been through a lot...last thing she needed...don't break her heart...

'How did it go?'

Ellie shrugged and tried to smile, but she knew it was a poor effort.

'OK, in a way. They'll fix everything, I just have to remove what I want to keep with me, and they'll put everything that isn't damaged in the rooms that are OK and fix the ones that are broken, then replace the damaged stuff.'

'Timeline?'

She shrugged again and put the knife down, abandoning the vegetables. 'Weeks? Maybe up to two months? The main problem is the chipboard flooring in the bedroom, and the kitchen units and worktop. It's swollen and disintegrating and it all needs to be replaced, and of course the wiring needs sorting and it'll need decorating and carpeting and—oh, it goes on and on.'

He nodded, his eyes searching hers. 'Do you get to choose the kitchen?'

'Within reason, apparently. If I want a better one I can pay the difference, and if I want to make changes to the house I can do that and pay the extra, so I could do that—put doors in between the sitting room and dining room so it's essentially one space, and refit the kitchen and reinstate the door to the garden, but…' She shrugged. 'I'm not sure. It still isn't big enough, the garden's too tiny for a proper extension, and it might make more sense to get it fixed and sell it as it is and buy something that works for us.'

He nodded, still studying her, and then he tipped his head on one side. 'You said "OK, in a way". So what's not OK?'

She gave a tiny huff of what should have been laughter if it wasn't so unfunny. 'I don't have temporary replacement accommodation insurance. It's an optional extra on that policy, and I obviously didn't tick the box.'

She swallowed, because he probably didn't want to hear the next bit, but he got in before her.

'Well, that's not an issue,' he said, before she could say the words. 'I've said you can stay here, and you can. You don't *have* to, obviously, but if you would like to, then I don't see the problem.'

She searched his eyes, and then they went all blurry and she had to blink.

'Thank you. That's very generous of you, so we will, please, for now. I'll see how Liz and Steven feel once he's better—'

'Ellie. It's fine. They're not young any more, and little children are wearing.'

'Well, then, you don't want them, either,' she said, racked with guilt again, but he shook his head.

'Nonsense. That's not what I'm saying. I just know that when my parents have one of my sisters over with their family for the weekend, by Sunday night they're exhausted and more than ready for them all to go home, much as they love having them. I would say they're pretty much the same age, both the children and the grandparents.'

'And how about you? What happens when you get sick of us and you're ready for us to go home? Because we can't, Nick, we don't have one any more—' She broke off, her voice cracking, and turned away, sucking in a deep breath and trying to get herself back under control.

She heard the soft sound of his footsteps, felt his hands cup her shoulders and draw her gently back against his chest.

'Ellie, stop it. Stop torturing yourself. Yes, it'll get noisy and frustrating at times, and we'll trip over each other a bit, but honestly, I love having you all here and all families go through that. There are times when my sisters could cheerfully rehome their children, but it usually lasts about ten minutes. We'll cope. I'll cope. It'll be fine. Now come here and have a hug and stop worrying.'

She turned in his arms, buried her face in his shoulder and let out a ragged little sigh.

'What have I done to deserve you?' she asked, and she felt a chuckle rumble through his chest.

'You don't really know me yet. I'll probably be getting on your nerves by the end of the week.'

'Why would you do that?'

She felt his shoulders lift in a little shrug. 'As I said, you don't know me. I'm sure there are all sorts of things that'll irritate you.'

She leant back a little and looked up at him. 'Well, you haven't so far.'

He grinned. 'Give it time. Talking of which, is that our supper you're getting, or something else?'

'That's our supper. The children have been in bed for ages, they were tired. I got the travel cot from Evie's bedroom cupboard. She didn't sleep too well last night, and nor did I with her wriggling around, so she's got her own bed now so I don't need to worry about her falling out, and I brought the baby monitor so I can relax in the sitting room without worrying, and I also brought them some toys.'

He nodded thoughtfully. 'I had an idea, I don't know if it appeals. I thought I could stack all those boxes from the other bedroom into the garage, and then you could have it as a playroom. There's a sofa bed in there, and we can turn it into a little sitting room for you.'

'We can keep out of your way, then,' she said, not sure if she felt relieved or rejected, but he just laughed.

'Ellie, that's not what I meant! But the sitting room is upstairs, and Evie could fall down them and hurt herself, which is the last thing you need. I need to get a stairgate, really, so she can't crawl up them.'

'I've got one at home. I could bring it.'

He nodded. 'Then we can keep her safe, and they can have somewhere to make a mess when they want to without you having to feel guilty—which I know you will, before you deny it. So, what's for supper?'

He moved the boxes after they'd eaten.

It took him over an hour, and by the end of it his hip was aching and he was more than ready to sit down, but at least the room was clear. It just needed a vacuum while the children weren't asleep, and maybe a little table and chairs for them to sit at to draw and paint, and it would be fine.

There was nothing they could do to the carpet that would do it any harm, anyway. It was worn and tired and needed replacing, but it could wait. It could all wait, and it would have to, because Ellie and her children were his priority now, not the house.

He put the last box of Samuel's things down on the stack in the garage, and rested a hand on it, closing his eyes and breathing in slowly.

'Miss you, Sam,' he murmured, and sucking in another breath, he walked out of the garage, locked the door and headed back inside.

He could hear water running. Ellie must be in the shower, and the longing to take his clothes off and walk in there and join her was overwhelming. Hell, it was going to be tough.

He went back to the kitchen and found it was all cleared up and the dishwasher was on. He boiled the kettle, made himself a mug of tea and was about to head up to the sitting room when she appeared, wrapped in a dressing gown with a towel round her head and looking way too good for his peace of mind.

Her smile was wry. 'I don't suppose you've got a hair-dryer?'

He shook his head. 'Sorry, no.'

'I need to write a list. There are loads of things I haven't got. I'll go back and get them tomorrow. And in the meantime we need to have a talk.'

He frowned at her. 'About?'

'Us being here and how we're going to manage it. If we're going to be here for weeks, we'll pay our way, obviously. A share of the electricity and gas bills, the food—all of it. Or we move,' she added as he opened his mouth, and he had a horrible feeling she meant it, so he shrugged and gave in.

'OK. I cleared the playroom.'

'I saw. Thank you so much. I'll move their toys and stuff into it tomorrow and we can keep out of your way then.'

'Ellie, you're not in my way,' he said, but she just shook her head reproachfully so he gave up.

'Whatever. Want a cup of tea?'

* * *

They fell into a sort of routine over the course of the next week.

He got breakfast for everyone on her work days, she cooked the evening meal most nights, and by the weekend she'd rounded up all the things she'd forgotten to bring from the house, and they were settling in nicely.

A bit too nicely, and she was worried that they were constantly underfoot, but when she tackled Nick about it again on Friday night he was adamant that they weren't. Nevertheless, the children spent a lot of time with him, more than was probably wise, if they weren't going to get too attached to him. And that went for her as well as the children.

'We'll keep out of your hair tomorrow,' she told him, and he rolled his eyes.

'You don't need to. I'm doing the Saturday morning surgery this weekend anyway, so I won't even be here.'

'But that's only until eleven. It's fine, they want to see their grandparents. We'll do that late morning.'

'Whatever, but you don't need to.'

'Yes, I do, Nick, because we're spending too much time together and it's going to make it difficult, especially with David.'

'How will he know?'

'Because the children will inevitably say something. All they ever talk about is you and Rufus, and while Oscar and Evie babble a lot and don't make much sense, Maisie is as clear as a bell and she's utterly besotted by you. It'll be Nick did this and Nick did that and he'll start asking awkward questions.'

His eyes went oddly blank, as if the shutters had come down. 'And that's an issue.'

'Not yet, but it could be.'

He nodded. 'OK. Well, you've got the other room now. Feel free to use it whenever you want and I'll try and keep out of your way.'

Did he sound hurt? Oh, lord, this was too difficult. Why on earth had she thought it would work?

'I didn't mean that, Nick. It's your house. We should be keeping out of your way, not the other way round.'

'Ellie, I'm done with this conversation. I know you don't want the kids getting attached to me, I get that, so I'll discourage it.' He picked up his laptop off the side and opened it at the table. 'Anyway, I've got work to do. Sorry.'

She got up from the table, clearly dismissed, and had to tell herself it was what she wanted. Wasn't it?

'That's fine. I've got a book to read. I'll see you tomorrow.'

She walked out without looking at him again, but she felt a little bit sick as she went into the playroom and closed the door, and try as she might, she couldn't concentrate on the book because the words kept blurring in front of her eyes.

Damn.

He hadn't meant to be like that, but she was right, he was spending too much time with the kids, with her, with the whole family thing, and he really hadn't expected it to be like this.

Well, he was at work in the morning, and he'd take himself and Rufus off later and go and do something else. Maybe go for a walk on the beach, but not here, because that was where they'd go, so he'd go further along towards the pier and keep out of their way.

He got out a wine glass, put it back and made some

tea and took it up to the sitting room with his laptop, but he could see the light on in the playroom, and he glanced down and saw her there, her head bent over her book.

He left the lights off and stood in the shadows and watched her for a moment, then gave a sharp sigh, sat down and turned on the table lamp. He was turning into a stalker, for heaven's sake, spying on her while she read her book. And besides that, he hadn't lied, he did have work to do, things to read up on, so he made himself do it just so he didn't add lying to the list of his failings.

At ten thirty she took the children out to see their grandparents, so Nick could come back to a quiet house. They might get some sandwiches from the kiosk and eat them on the beach as it was a nice day, and if Liz didn't feel up to giving them lunch.

Obviously not, she realised as soon as Liz opened the door. She'd left the children in their car seats for a moment so she could catch up, and she was glad she had because she was shocked at how tired and strained her mother-in-law looked.

She hugged her gently. 'We won't stay long, but the children really want to see you both. Maisie's been so worried about her grandad, and they've all asked to see you. Even Evie beamed when I said your names. She tried to say Grandma, but it didn't quite work.'

'Oh, bless her. No, you must bring them in, but just for a few minutes. He's so tired.'

'I'm sure. I'm sorry I haven't been to see him but it's been—difficult,' she said vaguely, not wanting to add the burden of her house woes to Liz's already heavy load. 'So, how has he been post-op?' she asked softly.

'His arm's been very painful,' Liz said, 'and we're both a bit worried about the blackouts.'

'Has he had more?'

She sighed. 'No, but he hasn't driven for weeks, just suggested I drive if we went anywhere and I should have smelt a rat, but of course being a man he didn't do anything about it, just waited for it to go away. He didn't mention it until Nick asked him about the fall, and it's a good job he did ask or who knows when he would have bothered to mention it. Anyway, he's had a whole raft of blood tests and he was on a monitor for a while. They think he might have some kind of heart condition which causes—oh, I can't remember what they called it. Some kind of lock, and they also said something to do with dropping, but they didn't think it was that.'

'Drop attack? That's a name for a certain type of blackout but that's neurological, not cardiovascular, which would be from a heart condition. They probably said TLoC?'

'Yes, that sounds like it. So what is it? I was so tired and so worried I didn't take it all in.'

'No, I can imagine. It's short for transient loss of consciousness, which covers all sorts of reasons for fainting or losing consciousness for a brief while. It can be caused by a disruption of the heart rhythm, and it sounds like they think he might have had that. So what happens next?'

'He's going to see the cardiologist again next week, but—oh, Ellie, you know him. He hates making a fuss, and he doesn't want to go, but I'm so worried about him…'

Ellie hugged her gently. 'He must go. I'll talk to him. And don't worry, they'll sort him out. He might need a pacemaker or drugs to settle it down.'

'Oh, he's on a new drug—ami-something?'

'Amiodarone? It's an anti-arrythmic, so that makes

sense. What's important is that he doesn't keep falling over, because as he's no doubt now realised, it can have consequences.' She headed back to the car. 'OK, guys, out you get, but remember, Grandad's quite sore so you need to be very quiet and gentle.'

She hoisted Evie into her arms and followed them in, and they found Steven in the sitting room, his arm propped up on a cushion, having a snooze.

He opened his eyes as they went in, and his face lit up at the sight of the children.

'Hello, my babies,' he said warmly, and Maisie wriggled up beside him and tucked herself under his good arm, and Ellie saw his eyes fill. 'Goodness, I've missed you all.'

'Are you all right, Grandad?' Maisie asked him worriedly, and he nodded and smiled down at her.

'I am now I'm having a cuddle with you.'

Oscar stood at his feet, eyeing the cast in fascination. 'What's that?' he asked, so Steven explained, and then came the inevitable, 'Why?'

'Because that's what happens when you break something. Here, why don't you play with this?' Ellie said, and handed him a car out of her bag. 'Play on the floor with Evie.'

He pulled a mulish little face. 'But I want a cuddle, too.'

'You can have a cuddle in a minute when it's your turn,' she said firmly.

'Promise?'

'I promise. I just need to talk to Grandad for a minute.'

'Then are we going home to Nick?' Maisie asked innocently, and she heard Liz suck in her breath.

'Yes, darling, we are,' she said, and then met Liz's eyes. 'I didn't want to worry you, but when I got back to my house last Sunday the tank in the loft had been leaking and the power had cut out, so until it's all sorted it isn't safe to live there and Nick was kind enough to offer us a roof over our heads until it's fixed.'

She knew she was being hugely frugal with the truth, but the alternative was to tell her she'd been away for the weekend, and she didn't want to do that. Not in front of the children.

'Heavens! Oh, Ellie, you should have come here!'

'No,' she said firmly. 'You two had enough to worry about, and Nick's just moved into a big empty house, and he was there, and he offered, so I accepted. I didn't really have a choice, but it's been fine, really, and it's only for a little while, and we're paying him rent.'

'Are you sure? You are having the house properly looked at?' Steven asked, and she nodded.

'Oh, yes. It's being done on the insurance. David knows.'

Not that they were living with Nick, but he would now. She sighed inwardly and turned her attention to Steven, moving the attention away from Nick and back to him.

They didn't stay much longer, just long enough for her to convince him that he wasn't making a fuss or wasting anyone's time and that he couldn't afford to ignore it, and then she rounded them all up and took them home.

Well, Nick's home. Not theirs. She had to remember that, because it would be too easy to get used to it and as she'd found out last night, even he had boundaries.

Even so, it felt like home, she thought as she turned onto the drive and parked next to his car. Certainly more like home than their own did at the moment. She'd rescued what she could from the wreckage, including a lot of toys, and she was so grateful to Nick for their little playroom because it gave them somewhere to go so they weren't always in his personal space. Even if it had felt like it last night.

She was so conscious of that—maybe too conscious of it, but he hadn't had to offer them a roof over their heads and she didn't want him to end up regretting it. And a little part of her wondered if he'd suggested giving them the playroom simply *because* he wanted them out of his way. He'd certainly been happy enough to get rid of her last night.

She hadn't spoken to him since, and she was a little wary of how he'd be with her, but she needn't have worried. He appeared at the sitting room door as they went in and smiled at them as he came down to the hall.

'Hello, all. Where have you been? Have you had fun?'

'We went to see Grandad. He's got a big fat bandage on his arm. He broke it,' Maisie said mournfully.

'Mmm. I know, I saw him when he did it.'

'I want a bandage like G'andad.'

'No, you don't,' he said to Oscar, his smile wry. 'Trust me. Broken bones aren't very comfy.'

'Why?' Oscar asked, tipping his head on one side in a gesture he'd picked up from Nick, and her heart squeezed in her chest. He would have been such a wonderful father…

'They just are. It's like if you cut yourself when you fall over, but much more sore.'

'Did you be broken?'

He nodded slowly. 'Yes, and it was very sore. It was a long time ago, though, so I'm OK now.'

Apart from the limp when he'd overdone it, and the fact that he'd never be the fantastic father he could have been if only Rachel hadn't freaked out at the thought of IVF. It must have broken his heart…

She swallowed the lump in her throat and smiled at him.

'So, how was your first Saturday morning surgery?'

'OK. No problems.' He searched her eyes. 'How's Steven? On the mend?'

'Slowly. He's seeing the cardiologist again next week. They seem to think it was syncope, probably from arrhythmia, so they got cardiology on board. I can't believe he didn't tell Liz.'

He rolled his eyes. 'I know. It's typical, we hear it all the time. Probably too scared of what he might be told. Have you had lunch?' he asked, and she shook her head.

'No. I thought we'd go to the beach and buy some sandwiches and eat them down there. It's a gorgeous day.'

'You could come, too,' Maisie said. 'And Rufus.'

Ellie held her breath as he hesitated for a moment, then he gave her a slightly crooked smile and passed the buck.

'Your call.'

The children bounced up and down, squeaking excitedly, and Rufus rushed around and barked with delight, and she laughed and gave up trying to keep her distance.

'I think that's a yes,' she said, and met his eyes and wondered when, and how, she'd done whatever it was to deserve this man.

Except he wasn't hers, and she'd do well to remember it.

CHAPTER NINE

THEY HAD A lovely time on the beach.

They called in at her house and rescued the windbreak and the buckets and spades from the back of the garage, and set off, armed with cheese sandwiches and bags of crisps, some fruit and a big bottle of water, and of course Rufus, who thought it was wonderful.

They built sandcastles, and dug a moat and tried to fill it with water, and then they got bored with that and dug a hole and tried to bury Nick.

And of course she had to help them, which would have been fine if it hadn't been for the way he was looking at her as she bent over him and piled sand on his chest and patted it into place.

'OK, you've got me where you want me now, what are you going to do with me?' he asked innocently, but there was nothing innocent about his eyes.

She sat back on her heels, scooped Evie onto her lap and studied him. 'I don't know. Kids, what do you think we should do to him?'

'Pour water all over him,' Maisie said, giggling, and before Ellie could stop her she picked up a bucket and ran towards the sea as she'd seen Nick do over and over again.

'Maisie, no, wait for me,' she called, but Maisie ignored her, which might have been all right if a huge wave hadn't come and knocked her off her feet.

'Maisie!'

She dumped Evie on the sand, but by the time she was on her feet Nick had pelted down the beach and into the water, but the receding wave had pulled Maisie under, and for a hideous moment Ellie was sure she was going to drown.

She didn't, but only because Nick threw himself into the surf and plucked her out of the sea. He stood up and waded out, Maisie clinging to him, and carried her gasping and sobbing up the beach to Ellie.

Speechless, she reached for her, and he put Maisie into her arms and stood there dripping, his face taut, chest heaving.

'Is she OK?'

She nodded. 'I think so. Thank you. Thank you so much. I thought…'

'I know. So did I, but she's fine.'

'Mu-Mu-Mummy,' Maisie was saying, over and over again, and Ellie held her tight and squeezed her eyes shut to stop the tears.

'Here, she's cold, aren't you, Maisie?' he said, and she felt him wrap a towel around her little girl and tuck it in. 'Come and sit down, Ellie. She'll be fine with a cuddle.'

Would she? Oh, she hoped so, because anything else was unthinkable. Her legs gave out and she sat down with a plonk on the edge of the prom and looked at the other two.

'Keep an eye on them, Nick. They move so fast.'

'I know. Don't worry, I won't let them out of my sight,' he said, with an edge to his voice that showed how worried he'd been. 'I'll pack our stuff up and we'll go home and warm up.'

She nodded, and bent and kissed her daughter's sodden hair, eyes squeezed shut against the tears of relief. She could hear Nick talking to the others, his voice cheerful and reassuring, and gradually she relaxed. Just a tiny bit.

She rocked Maisie until the shuddering stopped, and then she lifted her head and met his eyes.

'Where are the others?'

'Right behind you. We're ready to go. How is she?'

'Cold but otherwise OK, I think.'

'I can understand that. I'm freezing. I need a hot shower and I expect she does, too.' He crouched down so he was on Maisie's level and smiled at her.

'Are you OK now, poppet?'

She nodded. 'I'm—chilly,' she said, her breath still sobbing a little, and he grinned at her a bit lopsided.

'Yeah, me too. The end of April's a bit early for a dip in the sea. We might need to try again in the summer—or wear a wet suit.'

She looked at him and laughed, to Ellie's surprise. 'You're wearing a wet suit.'

He looked down and grinned at her again. 'Yes, I guess I am, sort of. Wet jeans and T-shirt, anyway. Still, it got the sand off.' He tipped his head on one side in that way of his. 'I tell you what we need to do. I think we need to go home and have a hot shower, and then make some nice rock buns and eat them while they're still warm from the oven. What do you think? Shall we go home?' he asked, holding out his hand to her, and she slipped her hand trustingly into his and slid off Ellie's lap.

He lifted her up onto the concrete walkway, picked up the bag of buckets and spades, tucked the windbreak under his arm and headed back towards the steps with Rufus at his heels, and Ellie plonked the baby on her hip and took Oscar by the hand and followed.

She watched him, the big, strong man holding her skinny little daughter's hand and smiling down at her as they walked, and her heart squeezed in her chest. It could all have been so different…

Maisie was fine after her hot shower, the incident all but forgotten, but not by Ellie.

They'd made rock buns and eaten them, played in the garden with Rufus and then gone to bed after an early supper, exhausted by the sea air and exercise.

Nick had cooked them both a meal while she'd put the children to bed and read their stories, and he was loading the dishwasher now while she wiped down the table and tried not to relive the afternoon again.

'How do you do it?' she asked, and he glanced over his shoulder at her with a puzzled frown.

'Do what?'

'Make it all seem so undramatic? One minute she's drowning, the next she wants to make rock buns.'

He smiled wryly. 'I thought she needed distracting, and I've never met a child who didn't like making and eating rock buns.'

'No, nor have I but I would never have thought of it. They were an inspired idea. Thank you—not just for that, but for saving her life. I can't thank you enough for that.' She felt her eyes fill, and blinked. 'I thought she was going to drown, Nick.'

'There were other people there on the beach, Ellie,' he said softly, 'and they were all running towards her. She wouldn't have drowned.'

'She could have done. It happens.'

'I know. But she didn't, just like the ceiling didn't fall on them. Come on, let's get a drink and go and lie down on the bed and chill for a while.'

'Not the sitting room?'

He gave her a rueful smile. 'I twanged my hip a bit leaping up, and the muscles are screaming now. I could do with a lie-down.'

She felt a wave of guilt at least as big as the wave that had knocked Maisie over. 'Oh, Nick, you should have said! You've been on your feet for hours since then, what with the baking and cooking supper and everything. Where does it hurt? Show me.'

'Oh, the usual place.'

He ran his hand down over his left buttock and thigh, and she studied him thoughtfully. He was slightly crooked, the muscles pulling him sideways a bit. They definitely needed freeing off.

'Want a massage?' she offered tentatively. 'I did a course once, when I was doing my orthopaedic rotation, and a physio showed me how. It might help.'

He gave a soft huff of laughter, and shrugged. 'You know what? That sounds amazing. I give in. Do your worst.'

Why? Why had he let her do this?

He turned back the duvet, lay face down on the bed in his jersey boxers and pushed them down as far as they'd go, then felt her hands on him, warm and firm and familiar, exploring his muscles, kneading his buttock gently, the flat of her palm running over his thigh.

And his body was revelling in it.

It had been a long, difficult week since they'd moved in, with her just *there* every time he turned round, sweetly scented and enticing, all mother earth and wholesome woman, and it was doing his head in. He hadn't had any respite from her at work, either, and he wanted her.

He wanted her so badly he could taste it, but he'd

gritted his teeth, kept his mouth shut and his thoughts to himself, and he did it now, lying there and letting her do her worst.

And she did exactly that, with all the skill of a consummate professional, and for a moment he regretted it, but it was worth it just to have her hands on him.

Well, mostly. He let out a grunt at one point, and she apologised and eased off, but he could feel it doing him good in a fairly hideous way.

'You OK?'

'I'll live,' he said through gritted teeth. 'Just be a little careful with the scar tissue.'

'Sorry.'

'Don't be. It needs doing. I just haven't found a physio up here yet. Looks like I don't need to. You're every bit as brutal.'

She chuckled and carried on, her thumbs finding all the knots with deadly accuracy, and gradually he felt the taut muscles relax and stretch out again.

'There. I think you'll do,' she said, and then she pressed her lips fleetingly against his skin as if she was kissing it better. 'Sorry about the torture. You can get up now.'

No way. The pain had settled his libido down, but it was over now, and since he'd felt the soft warmth of her mouth against his skin his need for her was back with a vengeance.

He hoisted his underwear back up but stayed where he was. 'I think I might just lie here like this for a bit,' he said casually.

He felt the bed shift as she got off it, then the light touch of her hand on his shoulder. 'Sure. Can I get you a drink?'

Bromide? Or maybe that malt whisky that he still hadn't found...

'Tea would be nice.'

And it would take her a few minutes, which might give him time to get his mind sorted out and his body back in line.

To her surprise he came into the kitchen as the kettle boiled, dressed in jeans and a T-shirt and bare feet.

'Oh! You're up. I thought you were going to stay there?'

'No, I changed my mind. I feel a lot better. Thank you.'

He smiled, touched a fleeting kiss to her cheek and reached for the last of the rock buns. 'Fancy sharing?'

She laughed and shook her head. 'No way. I ate my bodyweight in them this afternoon, and we've had supper. I don't know where you put it. Right, here we go. Sitting room?'

'Mmm. Why not?' he said, and headed out of the kitchen.

She followed him up the steps, and he lay down on one of the sofas, feet crossed at the ankle, and stared up at the timber ceiling.

'What do you think I should do with those pine boards?' he mumbled through a mouthful of rock bun.

She studied them thoughtfully from the other sofa, then lay down to get a better view. 'I don't know. They're a bit orange.'

'They are, but they're iconic. It's a tough one, and it's a one-way trip.'

'But if you don't like them…?'

'I know. But what else?'

'How about colour-washing them? You know, in a sort

of whitey grey wash to mute them down a bit? Sort of New England meets industrial chic?'

He chuckled, and studied them thoughtfully. 'That would work. It's a look I like. I'm going to paint the whole house white when I get round to it, and probably have neutral earthy grey carpet throughout.'

'Carpet, or wooden floors?'

'No, carpet. I don't really want wooden floors because Rufus slips on them, but apart from that I don't know what to do with it. It's early days, I suppose, and I'm still getting used to the house. Maybe I need to give it time to talk to me.'

'What, like mine, which has been shouting at me because it's so inadequate for the last four years?'

He turned his head and looked at her over his shoulder, his smile wry. 'Something like that. When do they start on yours?'

She sat up again so she could see him better. 'Monday, apparently. They pack everything and put it in storage, and it comes out when it's done, but I can get access to it if I need to. The trouble is, I need clothes for work and I haven't really got anywhere to put them, or the children's clothes. I wonder if they'd deliver my chest of drawers here? Would you mind?'

He turned his head again and looked at her as if she'd said something really weird. 'Why on earth would I mind? Of course I don't mind, but you don't need a chest of drawers, there's a spare one in the garage. We can get your stuff tomorrow if you like. I'm sure we'll find somewhere for it.'

'Are you sure? I just feel we're moving in wholesale.'

He laughed and looked away again. 'Don't be silly. Bring whatever you need. We can find room for it. The playroom's got lots of space.'

How easily he said that, as if it had always been a playroom, but she supposed it hadn't ever been anything in the three or four weeks he'd lived there before her housing crisis.

What on earth would she have done without him?

'Coffee?'

She glanced up from the repeat prescriptions and smiled at Nick. 'Mmm, please. You're a saviour. I haven't had time. It was a bit of a rush, what with meeting the builders on site before I started. Thank goodness nursery could take them for longer. Oh, I've got news about Judith Granger, by the way,' she told him.

'Oh. Bad news?'

She shook her head. 'No—well, a sort of guarded no. Polyps. She's on the waiting list for a colonoscopy. They're going to remove them and send samples for histology to see if any of them have turned cancerous, so at least it's being dealt with. I should hear a few days after she has it, but I don't know when that'll be.'

He put the coffee in front of her and sat down opposite.

'So what's wrong, then?' he asked softly.

How did he know? She looked up, and he tilted his head on one side and raised an eyebrow.

She glanced across at Dev and Brian, and shook her head. 'It's not important now. Thanks for the coffee. I might go back down—I've got a few letters to write.'

He nodded and stood up. 'Yes, so have I. See you, guys.'

They walked out together, and he followed her into her room and shut the door.

'Come on, then. What is it?'

She felt her shoulders sag. 'I heard from David. He's coming up this weekend to see his parents, and obviously he wants to see the children, but they don't feel ready to have them staying there. Steven's struggling with the arrhythmia and the pain, and Liz is exhausted, so—well, I wondered if it'd be all right if they stayed with you.'

'*They*?' He looked confused. 'Where will you be?'

'Well—at yours, of course. Where else? Assuming that's all right?'

He gave a tiny huff of laughter. 'Of course it's all right. So why would it be an issue if the children stay as well?'

'Because I just don't want to take you for granted. You do so much for us, and I thought you might have been looking forward to a weekend without them.' A weekend like the others they'd shared…

He smiled, his eyes tender and a little rueful. 'I was—but not because of them. It would just be nice to spend time alone with you. I've missed it.'

'Are you sure?'

His mouth quirked a little. 'That I've missed it, or that I don't mind?'

She chuckled. 'That you don't mind.'

'Absolutely. Honestly, it's not a problem.'

She felt relief wash over her, and she smiled at him. 'Thank you.'

'You say that a lot, you know.'

'Because I mean it. I don't know what we would have done without you.'

'You would have found a way.'

He cupped her shoulders in his hands and stared down into her eyes, and then he bent his head and kissed her.

Just lightly, just enough contact to reaffirm their relationship, and then he let her go. 'I'd better get on, and so had you. I'll see you later.'

On Friday David arrived in time to pick the children up from nursery and spend the afternoon and early evening with them, so she took advantage of that to check on the builders, see what progress had been made and then blitz Nick's house while she had the chance.

She was just loading the washing machine for the second time when Nick came home, and he propped himself up against the utility room doorframe and smiled at her.

'More washing?'

'Always. It's relentless. I hate to think what it's doing to your energy bills.'

He waved a hand dismissively. 'What time are they coming back?'

'I'm picking them up at seven.'

He glanced at his watch and raised an eyebrow. 'That's in ten minutes.'

'I know. It's fine, they'll still be eating if I know them. They have a flexible attitude to bedtime, which doesn't always work with Evie.'

'Are you driving?'

'Yes. They're always tired on a Friday after nursery.' She shut the washing machine door, pressed a button and straightened up. 'Right, time to go. Our supper's in the oven, I've cleaned the sitting room and kitchen, vacuumed the bedrooms and walked Rufus round the block.'

'You're a star. Thank you.'

'Just my side of the bargain,' she said with a wry smile, and squeezed past him. Or tried to, but he caught her shoulders, pulled her up against him and kissed her.

Not like he had this morning, but that had been at work. This kiss was lingering and full of promise, and he lifted his head and gave her a wry smile.

'You'd better go and get them,' he murmured, and she nodded and walked out of the door, her lips tingling and her whole body mourning the fact that they didn't have their weekend.

To her amazement the children had finished eating when she arrived at her mother-in-law's house, so she bundled them into the car and drove straight back to Nick's. As they stepped through the front door they were bubbling over with what they'd done with their father, including a walk past her house to see how the builders were getting on, apparently, which left her mildly irritated as it was none of David's business.

Nick just raised an eyebrow, and she shrugged and chivvied them along the hall to their bedroom, Evie on her hip.

By the time they were ready for bed there was a wonderful smell coming from the kitchen. He must have taken the casserole out of the oven and checked it. It had better be ready, she was starving…

'Anybody need a bedtime story?'

'Me, me, me!' Maisie shrieked, and Ellie turned and looked up at him, standing right behind her.

'Are you volunteering?'

'It looks like it.'

She laughed softly. 'You are such a sucker. I tell you what, why don't you read one to Maisie and Oscar, and I'll settle Evie, and then I'll read you two another story, OK?'

They nodded, delighted by the two-story promise, and as she scooped up the grizzling Evie from the floor and headed towards her room, she could hear the soft rumble of his voice and the shrill, piping clamour of their responses.

Then a laugh, and another bit of conversation, and then it all went quiet and he started to read.

'Come on, baby,' she said, picking up her bottle off the bedside table and settling down against her pillows. 'Let's read you a story, too. Shall we have this one?'

Evie snuggled down in her arms, the bottle in her mouth, but she was asleep before she was halfway down it, the story barely started.

'Poor tired baby. Have you had a busy day?' she murmured, and dropping a tender kiss on her smooth, soft brow, she eased the bottle out of her mouth and laid her carefully in her cot. She gave a tiny, sleepy cry of protest, rolled onto her front with her bottom in the air and was silent.

Ellie gave it a moment, listening to the soft sound of her breathing and the low rumble of Nick's voice from next door, and then he said, 'The end,' very softly.

Silence.

She tiptoed out and met him in the hall, his finger on his lips. He tipped his head on one side, hands together in the prayer position under his cheek, and she nodded and slipped past him, tucked them up, kissed them both goodnight and tiptoed out again, all without disturbing them.

'They're good sleepers,' he said when she joined him in the kitchen.

'They are. It's their saving grace. Thank you for doing that. It's always a juggling act at bedtime, and I usually end up having to read two because they always want different things.'

'I got away with it lightly, then. Must be the novelty. Supper's ready, by the way. Are you hungry?'

'Starving. Let's hope it lives up to the smell.'

'It does. I tested it—well, I had to,' he said with a grin. 'It might have needed seasoning or something.'

'Yeah, right. Come on, then, let's have it. My stomach's eating itself.'

They were up with the lark in the morning, and she prised herself out of bed and went into their room and shushed them, but she needn't have bothered. Nick was already there, and he turned to her and gave her a wry grin.

'They're bright-eyed and bushy-tailed today,' he said drily, and she muffled a laugh and apologised, then kissed them both good morning.

Maisie was kneeling up on her bed and bouncing excitedly. 'Daddy said we might go to the farm park today if it's a nice day,' she said, and Ellie felt a little flicker of relief. If they were doing that, there was no chance of them popping in here on the way to or from the beach, which meant they'd have privacy. She just hoped the weather played ball.

Nick obviously clocked that, too, and he opened the curtains and one of his eyebrows twitched. 'Well, it's a lovely day,' he said with a smile. 'What time are you dropping them off?'

'Nine o'clock. Why?'

'Perfect. We'll have time to walk Rufus round the block before you go. You like that, don't you, guys?'

'Can I hold his lead?' Maisie asked, and Oscar immediately said he wanted to, and if Nick hadn't calmly intervened there would have been a riot.

'You can take turns. And don't start arguing about who's going first, we'll toss a coin.'

'What's that mean?' Maisie asked.

'Get dressed nicely for Mummy, and I'll show you. I'm going to have a shower.'

Twenty minutes later they were gathered in the kitchen, and he was showing them a coin.

'OK, so that's the head, and that's the tail.'

'But it hasn't got a tail,' Maisie said, as if she suddenly didn't believe a word he said.

'Ah, well. Look at Rufus. What's at this end?' He swivelled the dog round so he was facing them.

'His head.'

He turned him back again. 'And this end?'

'That's his tail.'

'Exactly. The coin is the same. There's a head on one side, so the other side's called the tail.'

'But it doesn't *have* a tail,' Maisie said again, with that stubborn look on her face he was beginning to recognise, and out of the corner of his eye he could see Ellie, hand over her mouth, eyes creased with laughter.

'I know. Silly, isn't it? But it doesn't matter, because we know that, and so long as we can tell the difference that's all that matters.'

'But why does it matter?'

'Because,' he said, picking up the coin and flicking it into the air, 'when it lands, it's got to be one way up or the other, and if it's the one you chose, then you win.'

'Why?' they chorused, and he gave up.

'I tell you what,' he said, utterly exasperated, 'whoever's ready at the door first with their shoes on has the first go. Deal?'

Ellie dropped the children off promptly at nine, armed with sun cream, wellies and strict instructions to wash their hands after they touched any of the animals, and she went back, walked through the front door and straight into Nick's arms.

He gave her a hug, then lifted his head and looked down into her eyes.

'Well, we're alone. What now?'

She smiled wryly. 'Coffee? We should give them half an hour or so to realise they've forgotten something. And anyway, I could do with one. It's been a long old week.'

'Tell me about it. Cappuccino?'

'Perfect. We can drink it in the garden. It's gorgeous out there, it seems a shame not to soak it up.'

They went out with their coffees and sat on the bench in the sunshine, faces turned up to the sun.

'This is so nice' she sighed. 'I love this garden. There's always somewhere shady and somewhere sunny, no matter what time of day. I do envy you. Mine's in deep shade all morning and full sun all afternoon.'

'How's the building work coming on? You mentioned it last night but you didn't say a lot.'

'Oh, it's gutted, all the back half. I didn't really recognise it, but the site foreman was on the phone so I couldn't talk to him about timescales or anything, which was a bit frustrating, but they're certainly getting on with it. The skip was full of kitchen, I know that. We could take a wander round there later, have a closer look.'

'Have you decided what you're doing with it?'

'No. I think a quick fix and put it on the market, to be honest. It's just not big enough, and after being here, seeing how the children love to run around in the bigger garden, having the luxury of a playroom and a utility room instead of the washing machine in the garage—well, it's just pointed out all its failings, really, and they were bad enough before.'

'Can you afford to move?'

'Oh, yes. I don't have a mortgage, don't forget, so I should be able to upgrade if I don't go mad.'

'You'll lose your sea views.'

She laughed. 'Well, you know how much that bothers me,' she said, smiling up at him, and then she felt her smile fade as she read the look in his eyes.

'Come to bed,' he murmured softly.

'What, in broad daylight?' she teased, and he grinned.

'There's nothing in the rules that says it needs to be dark.' His smile faded, his eyes intent. 'I just need to hold you.'

She lifted a hand and cradled his jaw, feeling the prickle of stubble against her palm. 'That's a shame,' she murmured. 'I was hoping for rather more than that.'

He gave a soft huff of laughter and pulled her to her feet.

'I can't tell you how happy that makes me…'

CHAPTER TEN

THEY WENT FOR a walk later, to see her house.

It was the first time he'd seen it since it had been emptied, and now it was gutted it seemed small and cramped and sadder than ever. And noisy, with the roar of the industrial dehumidifiers in the background.

They went out to the garden so they could hear themselves think, and from out there he could see it wasn't possible to do all the things she'd said she'd like to do.

'There isn't really any way to make it work, is there? No easy way, and you'll never be able to make the garden bigger.'

'No. No, I won't. It isn't big enough to do anything significant with, but it'll do until I find somewhere better to go.'

Somewhere like his?

He felt an odd tug in his gut, a fierce longing, and suppressed it. 'Have you chosen the kitchen units?'

'No. I've got a brochure. I need to do it by Monday, I think.'

She looked dispirited, and he slung his arm around her shoulders and gave her a quick hug.

'Come on, let's go and get Rufus and take him somewhere nice for lunch, a pub with a garden. Got any suggestions?'

'There's a pub on the other side of the river that's supposed to be nice. I know the way.'

That day set the tone for the next two weekends when David came up.

Ellie kept the children overnight, he had them in the day, and she and Nick spent those precious days together in what she'd come to think of as their fantasy bubble.

And all the time her house was nearing completion.

So was work on the medical centre, and they moved into the new downstairs staff room with brand-new, comfy furniture and a decent coffee machine, which made Nick happy. She found out that Judith Granger didn't have cancer, to her relief and Ellie's, and she was less stressed about work because Liz was able to help again with the children from time to time as Steven's heart seemed stable on his new drug regime.

Not so hers.

Living with Nick, listening to him interacting with the children, listening to the children playing with Rufus in the garden, lying on the sofas at night and staring at the ceiling and talking about not a lot, not to mention the days they spent together when David was there for the weekend—it was like living out a dream, and when her house was finished she'd have to go home and stop playing Happy Families with a man who'd only taken them all on out of the kindness of his too-generous heart.

He never complained, but then he never had, to the point that he'd had to take drastic action to get his parents to notice that he was struggling, and the last thing she wanted was to put him in that position again, so as soon as her house was ready, they'd move back.

But for now they were where they were, so she still had a little more time, and she tried not to think about it.

And then, long before she was ready, the house was.

Or almost. It was David's last weekend before she moved back in, and she spent those two days unpacking all the things that had been put in storage and putting them away, making up the beds in readiness in bedrooms that smelt of fresh paint and new carpet. All that remained was plumbing in the sink and the new dishwasher and washing machine on Monday, and she could move in, so she went back to Nick's and started to sort out the things they had there.

She was packing up the toys in the 'playroom' that really wasn't, when he came in and sat down on the sofa, studying her thoughtfully.

'What time are you picking them up?'

'Five. Why?'

He looked at his watch. 'So we've got two hours. Come to bed with me, Ellie.'

She looked away, her throat working, unable to hold his eyes. 'I don't think we should.'

'Why? You've been avoiding me all weekend. I don't understand. Have I done something wrong?'

'No! No, of course not. It's just…' She shrugged helplessly. 'I'm not sure it's a good idea. Not now.'

'Why? Why should it suddenly not be a good idea?'

She looked back at him, feeling a little desperate.

Because every time we make love, I fall a little deeper in love with you, and it's killing me.

'Because we've invaded your space for weeks now, and I'm so conscious of taking advantage of your good nature, and I really don't want to do anything to make it any more difficult for us all when we move back out.'

'How will it make it more difficult?'

'Because I don't honestly know *what* I feel for you, and every time we make love, it confuses me even more. Yes, I care, but I also feel a huge amount of gratitude, and obviously sexual attraction, that goes without saying, but I don't know if it's more than that, and I don't know if you really want us or if you're only doing it because that's what you do, take on lame ducks and look after them. You've done it all your life, and here I am, another lame duck with a whole brood of baby ducklings all needing your help, and the closer we are to each other, the harder it is to know what's real and what's just wishful thinking.'

'Oh, Ellie. Come here.' He sighed and reached for her, getting to his feet, but she held up her hands.

'Please, Nick. Don't touch me. Don't make it impossible for me to do this. I have to do this my way. It's not that I don't want you…'

He dropped his hands and took a step back, and he looked confused but resigned.

'OK. If that's how you feel, then I respect that. And of course we don't have to do anything you don't want to do. The last thing I want is for you to stay with me out of *gratitude*.' He glanced at his watch, and opened the door. 'I need to walk Rufus. I'll see you later.'

He didn't understand.

Why would she feel like that? He could understand where she was coming from, but really? *Gratitude?* Surely to God it was more than that? He shook his head, not sure whether to feel rejected or not, but it nagged at him as he walked.

Was she right about him? About him taking lame ducks under his wing and looking after them? Was that all it was, him falling back into familiar habits? Because it didn't feel like that. Maybe she was right, maybe they were too close.

But he wanted to be close to her, and he was pretty damn sure she wanted to be close to him. Or she had.

What had changed?

And then Rufus sat down and refused to move, and he realised he'd been walking for two hours.

His ankle was killing him, his hip was aching, and there was no way on God's earth he was asking Ellie for a massage.

He looked around and realised he had no idea where he was, so he got his phone out and pulled up a map.

Three streets away, buried in the back of the housing development behind her house. He must have walked round in a circle. Just like his mind.

He hobbled slowly back with the reluctant dog, and she was just getting the children out of the car when he arrived home.

She gave him a sharp look and frowned.

'Are you OK? You've been ages.'

She sounded worried, so he dredged up a smile and tried not to limp.

'Of course I'm all right, I've been exploring.'

'You're limping.'

'Only a bit. I got a bit lost and overdid it.'

He looked away and smiled at the children as they ran towards him, little Evie taking a few tentative steps before sitting down with a plop.

'Hey, you're walking, clever girl!' he said, and scooped her up without thinking and carried her inside, and she snuggled into his neck and patted his face.

'Nick,' she said, as clear as day, and he had to swallow hard. God, he loved her. Loved them all. When had that happened? Ellie was right, it was going to be impossibly hard when they moved back into their house in the next few days, and he was going to miss them unbearably.

How did I let this happen?

'We went to Southwold and had too much ice cream

and Oscar was sick in Daddy's car,' Maisie told him, getting down on the floor in the hall and cuddling the exhausted Rufus, and he had to remind himself that what their father chose to feed them was none of his business. And anyway, who was he to criticise? He'd nearly walked the dog off his legs.

'I bet that didn't make him very happy,' he said, and Maisie giggled.

'He was very cross.'

'Well, it serves him right,' Ellie said. 'He shouldn't have given you so much ice cream. He knows Oscar gets carsick sometimes. Right, come on, time for supper and an early night. You've got nursery at eight tomorrow.'

She didn't know how she got through the evening.

Nick was obviously sore, but she didn't dare suggest giving him a massage, not after what she'd said, and as soon as they'd eaten in a rather strained silence she made the excuse of needing to pack a few more things and took herself off to give him space.

He seemed—well, she didn't know what he seemed.

Hurt? Angry? Confused?

All of the above, perhaps, and she felt awful, but she'd also felt that she was being sucked inexorably into a delusion of happiness that probably wasn't real. How could it be? She hardly knew him.

So she shut herself away in the playroom and sorted out more of their things, folded washing, had a shower and dried her hair and got everything ready for the morning.

She heard him go out with Rufus for the last time, and went into the kitchen, made herself a drink and took it to her room, closing the door firmly.

A few minutes later she heard him walk down the

corridor and pause by her room. She held her breath, her heart pounding, and then he went past and she heard the slight creak of his bedroom door, the click of a light switch, the sound of running water.

She let out her breath and felt the tension drain out of her. She felt sick. Sick that she'd destroyed the dream, taken it away from both of them, but it was only that, a dream.

Wasn't it?

So why did it hurt so much?

Please let the plumber come tomorrow. I need to go home...

They moved out the following day.

The plumber had been, she said, and so she left the children with Liz and went back to his house to get the last of their things.

She was there when he got back, ferrying stuff out to her car, and she put the things in the boot and closed the lid, then turned to him.

'I think that's everything,' she said, and her voice sounded tight and strained and maybe a little tearful. 'I'll just have a last check round.'

He followed her in and sat on the bottom of the stairs, Rufus at his feet having his ears fondled and watching her every move. He heard her go into the utility room, heard the sound of the tumble dryer start, and then she reappeared.

'I've put the bedding on to dry,' she said. 'I washed it this morning. I think I've got everything now, but if I haven't—'

'I'll take it to work.'

'Thank you.'

Her voice was small and sad, and he wanted to cry for her. For her, for him, for the children.

He got to his feet, his ankle still sore from yesterday, and for a moment they just stood there facing each other, neither of them sure what to do.

She broke first, and as she took a step towards him he reached for her, folding her against his chest and gritting his teeth. Don't go, he wanted to say, but he didn't, because he knew she would whatever he said, and he knew he had to let her go if that was what she really wanted. She needed to know how she felt, needed space to do that, and maybe he did, too.

'I'll miss you,' he told her gruffly, and she nodded.

'I'll miss you, too,' she said, her voice clogged with tears. 'Thank you so, so much for all you've done for us. I have no idea what we would have done without you.'

'You would have coped. You're strong, Ellie. You don't need me, or not for that. It just made it a little easier for you, that's all.' He dropped his arms and stepped away from her, and it felt as if he was tearing his heart out.

'You'd better go, it's getting late,' he said, his voice scratchy and rough, and she nodded and picked her bag up off the floor.

'Your keys,' she said, and held them out to him.

He took them carefully, without touching her fingers, because he knew if he touched her again he wouldn't be able to let her go, and then he stood back and watched as she got in her car and drove away.

Then he closed the door, went into the kitchen and the first thing he saw was the pictures plastered all over the fridge. He laid his hand over Evie's tiny handprint, and had to swallow hard.

No. He wasn't going to do this. He was *not* going to cry.

He wrenched open the fridge door, poured himself a glass of wine and took it into the playroom.

The playroom.

He looked around, hearing the children's voices in his head, their laughter, tears, squabbles, the shrill chatter, the endless 'Why's from Oscar. He heard Ellie's voice yesterday, begging him to let her do it her way.

He couldn't stay in there, so he went up to the sitting room and lay on the sofa, staring at the ceiling.

You could colourwash it... New England meets industrial chic...

He swore and sat up, turned on the television and ignored it, like he ignored the wine.

Rufus came and got on his lap, looking forlorn, and licked his face and barked softly.

'Oh, Rufus. Are you hungry?' he asked, and took him down and fed him, but the dog turned away from the bowl.

She'd probably fed him.

He opened the fridge again without looking at the pictures and stared at the contents without any real interest. He had to eat something. Cheese?

He made a cheese sandwich, and it reminded him instantly of the night she'd found the leak, lying on his bed with her eating sandwiches and listening for the sound of the children if they woke and were disorientated.

And the picnic on the beach, when Maisie had nearly drowned.

He went out into the garden, sitting in the twilight with his sandwich and the glass of wine, and he could hear the sound of the children again.

A dog barked in the distance, but Rufus ignored it, lying on his feet and looking forlorn. The dog had followed him everywhere he'd gone to try and escape the memories, but he couldn't, because their presence was everywhere, in every nook and cranny of the house.

So he gave up, the wine untouched, the sandwich half-eaten, and got into the bed where he'd made love to her so many times.

Not a huge improvement.

He stared up at the ceiling and wondered why a woman he hadn't even known three months ago could make him feel so lost and so alone. So rejected, for heaven's sake.

He thought back over all the things she'd said over the past few weeks, trying to work out when she'd changed. Or maybe she hadn't. Maybe he'd just ignored the signals.

She'd jumped at the idea of the playroom, and according to her it was always a question of keeping out of his hair and giving him his space, but was that simply because she herself had needed her own space? Saying it was for him, when really it was for her?

Maybe he *should* be feeling rejected. Maybe he'd taken too much for granted, assumed that they'd want him in their life as much as he'd finally realised he wanted them in his? Was she just protecting the children? He could understand that, but it didn't surely mean they couldn't still carry on as they had before? Did they have to lose everything they'd had in order to protect the children?

He had no idea, but he knew he couldn't solve this on his own. They should be talking. Properly talking, so they both knew where they were coming from.

Except not now. She needed time to find out how she really felt, something she obviously felt she hadn't been able to do while she was still living with him and had no easy options, and maybe he did, too, so now probably wasn't the best time to tackle it. No, if that was what she wanted, he'd go along with it and wait, give her the time she'd asked for.

It was hardly going to kill him.

It didn't feel like home.

It should, because nothing about it had really changed, but in a weird way it was completely different. It reminded her of when she'd gone home from uni and her father's wife—not her stepmother, she could never bring herself to think of her as that—had gone through the house from end to end and eradicated all that was familiar.

Which was ridiculous, because everything about the bits that had been changed—the carpets, the colour of the walls, the kitchen units and appliances—all of it had been her choice.

And yet it felt like a rental. An inadequate rental.

It didn't help that the children were so unhappy, either. She'd thought they'd be pleased, but Evie had taken ages to settle in her cot, and Maisie had cried herself to sleep because she missed Nick.

They'd had a special bond since he'd rescued her from the sea, and she'd wrenched them apart without giving the children time to say goodbye. That had probably been unfair, but she'd been unable to do it without breaking down, and anyway he'd gone to work that morning before she'd had the call from the plumber to say he was going in, so she hadn't really had a chance.

She got out of bed in the dark and stood at the open window, listening to the quiet sound of the sea, the barking of a dog, the hoot of an owl. Was it the one she'd heard from his house? Possibly. He wasn't far away. A car drove past slowly, and she wondered hopefully if it was Nick, but it wasn't.

She got back into bed and tried not to think about him, but it was impossible. She could feel his arms around her, his mouth on her, their bodies so in tune. Hear his voice so clearly as he'd reached out to her just yesterday afternoon.

Come to bed with me, Ellie...

And she'd turned him down, so it wouldn't hurt, and now she regretted it because they could have had that one last bitter-sweet time together before the dream was over.

Because it couldn't be real. She'd only met him at the end of March, and it was still only June. How *could* it be real? That sort of thing only happened in books.

No, it was gratitude, and honeymoon sex. A dangerous combination.

Time to get back to reality, however stark it was.

Nick stuck it out for two weeks before he cracked.

In that fortnight, he went through the house and cleaned it to within an inch of its life. Not that it needed it, because she'd pretty much kept it clean, but he pulled out all the furniture and found a toy and a T-shirt of Maisie's with unicorns on the front that made him want to cry.

She loved her unicorn T-shirt so much...

And then he went into the playroom, but it was too sad and empty, barren now without the clutter of multicoloured plastic toys that had filled it until so recently, so that weekend he found the shelving unit he'd brought from the house in Bath, rebuilt it in the playroom and then tackled the stack of boxes one by one, starting with the stuff from his old house, which he'd never had time to deal with.

He found a few things worth keeping, but all the rest he took to the dump or charity shops. Most of it meant nothing, or at least nothing he wanted to remember. He didn't need mementos of a broken marriage, and this was long overdue.

And then the following weekend he tackled Sam's possessions, and it tore him apart.

Or maybe he was already torn apart and it just set his emotions free.

He found all sorts of things—a postcard of the seaside town they'd visited the last time he and Sam had gone to the beach, with a photograph of him and Sam on the sand, and a half-eaten stick of peppermint rock, bright pink on the outside, white inside with the name of the town running down the core in bright pink letters. They'd had an amazing day. He'd lifted Sam out of his wheelchair and dug a hole in the sand and propped him up in it so he could be comfortable on the beach, and he'd buried his legs, just like the children had buried him in the sand.

And Sam had laughed until the tears had run down his face.

They'd stayed there until he was too cold, and then they'd gone and found a stall selling rock, and he'd unwrapped it for Sam and he'd sucked the end of it and said it was the best thing he'd ever tasted.

Sam had insisted on keeping it, smelling it every now and then to remind him of that day. Did it still smell?

He lifted it out of the box and unwrapped the end carefully, peeling the Cellophane away from the sticky sweet, and he sniffed it and smiled. It did. Only faintly now, but enough to remind him, and he closed the Cellophane wrapper and laid it gently back in the box next to the photograph and the postcard, and opened another box.

Photos in this one, lots of them, including a photo of them taken after his accident, in matching wheelchairs.

And the last photo of Sam, with Rufus lying by his side, shortly before he died.

The image blurred, and he blinked and swiped his cheeks with the back of his hand, laid the photo back in the box and closed the lid.

So many memories, so many happy times.

And they *had* been happy. It wasn't all about the sad stuff. He'd forgotten how good it was, how much fun they'd had. It had taken him all this time to realise it, but he'd been happy with Sam, and Sam had been happy, too, and despite all the problems he'd loved Sam with all his heart and wouldn't have changed a thing. Why had he never realised this before?

He packed it all away again. He'd go through it later with his family, when they were ready, because he knew it would be good for them to do it, but not yet. They weren't ready yet, but he had been, and he'd seen enough for now.

Enough to know that Ellie was wrong about him. It wasn't about lame ducks, it was about unconditional love, the love he'd felt for Sam, for his sisters, for his parents. The love he felt for her and her children, and he needed to tell her that.

He looked at his watch.

Midday. Would she be at home? He knew David was up this weekend, he'd heard her mention it in the staff room. Not that she'd told him. They were walking carefully round each other, treading on eggshells, and the atmosphere between them was strained to say the least.

Time to change that, to clear the air if nothing else.

He'd given her long enough.

She ought to make herself some lunch. She couldn't really be bothered, but it might make a change from moping around the house and wallowing in self-pity.

She went into her new kitchen and looked at the fridge. It was blank, because she'd left the pictures behind.

Had he thrown them out? He didn't need to, they weren't that precious. The children painted things at nursery all the time. She'd soon get more. But she could still see him laying his hand over Evie's handprint, see the look on his face, that touch of sorrow.

He should have been a father...

She pulled out cheese and butter, found a couple of slices of bread and made a cheese sandwich, but it reminded her of the beach, the day that Maisie had nearly drowned.

If he hadn't been there…

There was a knock on the door, and she put the sandwich down and went to open it.

'Nick?'

'Can we talk?'

She searched his eyes, serious but determined, and she shrugged and stepped back, letting him in.

'Coffee?'

'No. I want to take you somewhere. I've got something to show you, something that might solve your housing crisis.'

She studied him, but he was giving nothing away. 'Really? Because I went and looked at a house this morning and it was awful. So where is this house? Who's it on the market with?'

'It isn't at the moment, although it was. It's word of mouth.'

'Oh. Right.' Now she was intrigued, but only vaguely, because having him here in her house made her realise that all she needed was him, and she didn't know how to start that conversation.

'Shall we go?'

'Um—yes, OK. Is it far away? Are we driving?'

'No, I thought we could walk.'

'OK.' She picked up her keys, checked the windows were shut and set the alarm, closing the door behind her. 'So where are we going?'

'Just down here.'

They turned into Jacob's Lane, and her feet slowed to a halt.

'Nick…'

He turned to face her, his eyes more open and honest than she'd ever seen them.

'Hear me out, Ellie. We need to talk. There's so much we've left unsaid, so much we should have opened up about. You owe us that much. I owe us that much.'

She hesitated, but his gaze didn't waver, his eyes fixed on hers, so transparent now. She could read the love in them, read the hurt, read the willingness to listen. And so she nodded and went with him.

He opened the front door and ushered her in, closing it softly behind her, and Rufus ran to her, tail wiggling furiously.

'Hello, sweetie,' she said, crouching down and hugging him, but Nick was waiting.

'Come with me,' he said, and then he took her by the hand and led her through towards the playroom.

No, it wasn't the playroom, she couldn't call it that—and anyway, he went straight past it, down to the end, to his room. What was he doing?

'So, this is the master bedroom suite,' he said, and the penny dropped. 'It has plenty of storage, and a walk-in shower big enough for two.'

She remembered that only too well.

He opened the patio door and beckoned her out. 'It leads out into the garden, which I understand from a friend has sunshine and shade in some part or another all day long. It's totally enclosed, so it's child- and dog-friendly, it's got enough room for them to run about, corners for den building, and yet it's manageable. There's room over there for a new garage, so the existing garage could be turned into a playroom or games room. It needs a bigger paved area for family seating, but that could be done,' he added, and led her back inside.

'This is the second bedroom, with two more of very similar size, and a family bathroom here, which ideally could be refitted. And this is a very useful utility room with space for everything you might need, and a door to the garden.'

She shook her head and followed him, knowing exactly what he was up to but hearing him out because, as he'd pointed out, they owed each other that.

'Right, the kitchen. The proper dining table at the moment is in the hall, but there's room to extend the kitchen forward to make a bigger kitchen dining room, and then up here is the sitting room. It could do with updating. A good friend suggested New England meets industrial chic might work quite well.'

He turned and met her eyes as they got to the top of the stairs, and his smile was gentle.

'Am I a good friend?' she asked, a lump in her throat, and he nodded.

'I think so. Don't you?'

She looked up at the ceiling, blinking hard. 'Nick, what are you getting at? I need to know.'

'You do. Sit down. This could take a while.'

He reached for a box, a small cardboard box with a lid, and he sat beside her, took the lid off and handed her a photograph.

'Who's this?'

'Samuel. Here's another one of both of us, taken on the same day. It was the last time we ever went to the beach together. It must have been about five or six years ago. We had a wonderful day. We laughed the whole time, and I treasure that memory.'

She stared at the photo of him and his brother, so alike in many ways and yet so different.

'Here's another one. This is after my accident—I had a wheelchair for a while, so for that time we were the same, Sam and I. He teased me mercilessly about my incompetence with it, but his was electric so it was easier for him.'

He was smiling, his face an echo of happy memories, and he took the photos back from her and handed her another one, his smile fading. 'This was just before he died, about eighteen months ago, with Rufus.'

'Gosh, he looks so different.' She traced her finger over his face, ravaged by illness, his eyes vacant now, one hand lying over his faithful dog.

Her eyes welled with tears, and she handed it back and looked away, sucking in a breath.

'You don't need to cry for him, Ellie. It was a happy release, and we've all shed enough tears. Rufus cried for weeks, and so did we, me and my parents and my sisters, but that's over now. It's time to remember the good things, and there were so many.'

'I thought you resented him?'

He nodded. 'So did I. I've spent years thinking he was a burden, feeling resentful, but actually I just felt guilty because I was all right and he wasn't. Looking back on it, we were happy, Sam and I. We had a good childhood, although it was very different to what it would have been. But it didn't cost me my marriage. My marriage was a mistake, based on a whole lot of assumptions about how much I could ask of a woman who really had no idea what she was taking on.'

'In what way?'

He shrugged. 'My commitment to Sam, to my parents. My inability to give her the children she wanted without going through the process of IVF, which she really didn't want to do. It wasn't fair to expect Rachel to accept all that, but it did point up what was missing between us. We didn't love each other unconditionally. If we had, we might have made it, and I regret that, but it wasn't Sam's fault, it was mine.

'I thought I'd given up a lot to be with Sam, but actually I didn't give up anything worth having because my marriage was already broken. Sharing my time with him, caring for him, being with him taught me a lot about myself, gave me far more back than I gave him, and it hasn't held me back in any way. I've done what I wanted to, achieved what I set out to achieve, and I'm a good doctor, a fairly decent human being, I think, and I'm where I want to be. Or I was, until I met you, and then it all changed.'

'Changed?'

She searched his eyes, and he smiled tenderly.

'Yes, it changed. It was like opening a window on a part of me I hadn't known existed, and letting in the sunshine. I'd never dared to imagine living in a family, not after Rachel pulled the plug on our IVF plans. I'd put it all aside, and I thought I'd accepted it, but suddenly there you were with your beautiful little children, and I realised what I'd been missing. All that warmth and joy that I hadn't appreciated when I was young suddenly made sense.'

'So that was the draw?' she asked, feeling hollowed

out inside to know that it was only the children, but he shook his head fiercely.

'No! No, that wasn't the draw, you were. You, with your warmth and kindness and sense of mischief, your humour, your incredible sensuality—the kids were a drawback, Ellie. I didn't think I wanted to have anything to do with you because of them, but then you lost your home and I rashly opened the doors to you and in came the sunlight. Not a burden to be carried, but a joy.'

'Not always.'

'No, of course not, but they are a joy, and I love them. I love them dearly. I love you dearly, but I don't *need* you, any of you. I have a life I'm happy with, I'm reasonably self-sufficient—I can live without you, just as you can live without me. You're strong and clever and resourceful, you've made a home for your children that might not be perfect but that works perfectly well enough for now, and you're an excellent doctor, a caring and decent human being, and you've made a success of your life, just as I have.

'But it isn't what I *want*. What I *want* is you, Ellie. I love you. I love you so much, and I can't tell you how much I've missed you, but if you come back to me, then don't do it out of gratitude, don't do it because you feel sorry for me or guilty, do it because you love me, too, and you want to be with me for ever, unconditionally. Because this is the deal. If you come back to me, I want it to be as my wife, so don't do it if you can't buy into that, because I'd rather lose you now than down the line when it'll hurt all of us much, much more.'

Ellie stared at him, letting his words sink in, and she felt a bubble of something wonderful bursting in her chest.

'I do need you. I've missed you so much. I haven't

been able to eat, or sleep, or think—I thought, if I went home, I'd be able to see more clearly, but all I could see was that I was wrong, and I'm so, so sorry.'

She reached out and cradled his jaw in her hand, feeling the muscles jump beneath her thumb, and she smiled at him sadly.

'I love you, Nick. I love you so much. I didn't dare believe in it, I thought it was too quick to be real, but I was wrong, wasn't I? Because it is real, it isn't a dream. We did fall in love. I love you more than I ever thought I could love anyone. I just didn't know how to tell you, or if you'd want to hear it.'

'Is that a yes?'

She laughed, but it cracked in the middle and she reached for him at the same time as he reached for her.

'Yes, it's a yes,' she said, and he gathered her up against his chest and held her so tight she thought her ribs would crack.

'Thank you.'

She eased away and looked up at him again. 'Don't thank me, Nick. You've given me so much. You've given me back my faith in love, my ability to trust. I can't tell you how much that means to me. And—I've been thinking. You know how you talked about IVF, how it might be possible for you to have a baby that way?'

He looked away. 'I don't need a baby, Ellie. You've got three beautiful children, and I already love them. Why would I need more?'

'I don't know. Maybe because I do? Maybe because I want to carry your child, if I can?'

He looked back at her, his eyes bright. He blinked hard and sucked in a breath. 'You'd do that for me? It's not easy, Ellie. IVF is tough.'

'I know. But I've sailed through every pregnancy and

delivery, I think I can tolerate a little bit of tough for something so important.'

He shook his head, disbelief in his eyes, and maybe the dawning of hope? 'I'm nearly forty-one, Ellie. I've survived this long without my own children.'

'No. You've put away hope. You don't have to do that any more, not if you don't want to.'

'I can't believe you'd do that for me,' he said, his voice cracking, and she felt her eyes welling with tears.

'I love you, Nick. Why wouldn't I? And I'm only thirty-five. We've still got time. Let's see how it goes, eh? Just leave it there for now.'

'It's not a deal breaker?'

'Of course it's not a deal breaker. It's an offer, that's all. A part of my unconditional love for you.'

He was silent for an age, and then he nodded. 'OK. We'll think about it. And—more importantly, how about your children? How will they take this? Will they accept me?'

'Accept you?' She laughed softly, her eyes welling again. 'They haven't stopped begging to see you again since we moved out. Maisie cries herself to sleep, Oscar talks all the time about Rufus, and every time the doorbell rings they look hopeful.'

She took his hand. 'They miss you, Nick. I miss you. We just want to come home.'

EPILOGUE

THE APRIL SUN was warm on their faces as they sat in the garden, watching the children play.

They were running around on the grass with Rufus, their happy laughter filling the air, and Nick looked down at her and smiled.

'Happy?'

'Of course I'm happy. You?'

'What do you think? I reckon it's all going perfectly.'

It was. David had bought her old house as a base for his weekends now he was bringing his pilot girlfriend with him and wanted privacy, and they were planning to use the money on Nick's house. Especially now…

'So, how do you feel about starting that extension?' he asked. 'We'll need another bedroom soon, and the garage needs to be a playroom before the winter. Can you stand it?'

'I should think so. We can always ship the children out to David and Ava. She loves having them and he's so much more reasonable now. I never thought that would ever happen.'

He gave a chuckle, then lifted her hand to his lips, pressing a kiss to her wedding ring before laying his hand over the smooth curve of their baby. 'I never thought this would, either. I can't believe it.'

She laughed softly. 'I can. I'd forgotten about morning sickness, but at least it's over.'

He laughed and hugged her closer against his side, his arm around her shoulders.

'I'm so glad. I wonder what the children will make of him?'

'They'll be delighted. Maisie was thrilled when Evie was born, and Oscar will be so happy to have a brother.' She looked up at him. 'Can we call him Samuel?'

His eyes were suddenly bright, his smile a little crooked as he bent his head and kissed her.

'I think that would be wonderful…'

* * * * *

HEART SURGEON'S SECOND CHANCE

ALLIE KINCHELOE

MILLS & BOON

This book is dedicated to all those who have helped me along the way, my family, and those who have become like family—you know who you are.

And to Victoria Britton—without your belief in this story, this book wouldn't exist.

CHAPTER ONE

Rhiann

DREAD POOLED LOW in Rhiann's stomach as the door to the exam room opened with a slow and ominous creak. Broad shoulders in a white coat filled the space and her eyes roamed the doctor's familiar form, taking in the subtle changes time had wrought.

Three years ago he hadn't had those deep lines etched into his face. His dark hair had a little more silver at the temple than she remembered, but he was as lean and handsome as ever.

Dr. Patrick Scott stepped into the room, his eyes looking down at the screen of the silver laptop in his hand. His movements carried the spicy aroma of his cologne into the small room, the pleasing notes covering the harsh antiseptic and teasing a part of her that had gone dormant since her divorce.

But on top of the overtly masculine scent he brought with him a wave of sadness that hinted at tragedy.

"Hello, Mrs.... Masters...um..."

His deep gravelly voice trailed off and his sky-blue eyes jerked up to meet hers when he recognized her name. The slight fake smile he'd had on his lips when he'd opened the door faded fast. Judging from the ice that frosted over his gaze, the animosity he held for her hadn't eased since she'd last seen him.

The exam room door shut behind him with an audible click and the laptop clattered slightly as he set it roughly on the counter.

"What are you doing here?"

The uncharacteristic coldness in his tone sent a shiver coursing down her spine. Patrick's voice had always held such emotion, its rich timbre broadcasting his feelings with the simplest words. In all the years she'd known him Rhiann had never heard this distant tone.

Rhiann hugged the baby in her arms close to her chest, tears filling her eyes as she fought to keep her emotions from overwhelming her. She'd hoped the time since they'd last seen each other might have given Patrick clarity and smoothed the raw edges of his anger, but clearly not enough time had passed. Now she could only hope that he would be professional enough to put their personal grievances aside and focus on her child's best interests.

She needed to keep a clear head today, so she stuffed her feelings away as best she could. She had known coming here was a risk, but there was no other way or she'd have explored it already.

"I need your help. Well, he needs your help. This is my son Levi. He has a heart defect, and the cardiologist at St. Thomas' wants to do surgery to fix it. But if anyone is cutting my baby open I want it to be the best surgeon I can find." She paused to swallow down an oversized lump in her throat. "And that's you."

"You expect me to save someone you love. How ironic."

A single dark eyebrow raised as he stared down at her, his expression unreadable and as cold as marble. His eyes searched hers—for what, she didn't know.

Just as she was sure he was about to tell her to leave, to scream at her like he had the last time she'd seen him, his gaze flicked down to the baby in her arms and the ice in his eyes melted the tiniest bit.

"Please, Dr. Scott."

The formality felt stiff and awkward as it rolled off her tongue without the teasing tone she'd used each time she'd called him by his title in the past. Years ago they had been the closest of friends, sharing every secret with each other. They had even flirted with the idea of a relationship on an occasion or two.

But it no longer seemed appropriate to call him by his given name. Not when their friendship had crumbled on the back of accusations and misplaced blame. Their personal connection was more of a hindrance than a help in her quest to get her son the care he needed, so she kept things formal, hoping to appeal to his professional side.

His eyes snapped up to meet hers and that hint of softening was gone. "You ask too much."

The once happy-go-lucky Patrick had earned a reputation over the last couple years for taciturnity. His white-hot talent was tempered by his ice-cold bedside manner, but he was the best pediatric cardiac surgeon in the southeast, and that fact made people overlook his brusque manner.

He'd changed three years ago—just as she had.

Rhiann remembered the caring man he'd used to be, though, and she hoped there was enough of that man left deep inside for him to agree to help. Her son's life depended on it.

"Maybe I shouldn't have come here, but I had to try. I had to give my sweet baby every chance possible. Because he's just a baby."

She reached for any way to connect with the man

standing before her, sensing that rejection sat poised on his lips.

"Look at him. He's an innocent child who needs your assistance. Can you live with yourself if you don't at least try to help him?"

"I'll have my partner—"

"I didn't come here for your partner. And even though I know he's an excellent surgeon, I refuse to let you pass Levi off to Clay. Because I came here for the best surgeon I know. Not for second-best."

He muttered a curse, so low it was barely perceptible, and pinched the bridge of his nose. "You know if he needs surgery we'll be seeing each other a lot over the coming weeks and months? Do you know what seeing you that often is going to do to me?"

Clearly not a single thing had changed between them. He still hated her. But that fact changed nothing about her mission today.

Emotions threatened to clog her throat and Rhiann coughed a bit to clear it. She swiped at a hot tear that had leaked from her eye and run down her cheek. With a hard inhalation she tried to lock those feelings away, because she needed to keep a cool head. She had to convince Patrick to help Levi.

"Whatever you think I did or didn't do, that was in the past and between us. It has nothing to do with my son. I've run that day through my head no less than a thousand times, but there's nothing I could have done that would have changed anything. I can't change the past, but you can change Levi's future. You can *give* him a future."

His brows furrowed, Patrick pressed his lips together tightly, but her words must have touched something in the man she'd once known because he was pulling his stethoscope from around his neck.

"Let me take a look at him, run a few tests, and we'll go from there. His records from his previous doctors haven't been transferred yet, and I'd like to review those as well."

"That's all I ask."

Rhiann's heart thudded in her chest as Patrick sat on a rolling stool and pushed it over to listen to Levi's heart. His hand brushed hers, warm despite his cold manner, as he moved the stethoscope gently over her son's back. He sat close, his knee bumping into her thigh when he shifted to listen to Levi's chest.

She inhaled sharply at the touch and he looked up at the sound, their gazes meeting over Levi's head. The spark that fired up in his eyes brought back a time when distance between them hadn't existed and their lives had been far easier, and she wished they could return to the easy-going camaraderie of those days.

The exam room suddenly shrank in size as new strain filled the space and fire warred with the ice in Patrick's eyes.

The silence amped up the tension until finally he snapped back to the present enough to speak. "What tests has he had done? And how recently?"

"Most recently he's had chest X-rays and an EKG. Two weeks ago."

Rhiann swallowed hard. Her own medical training made this harder, because as a paramedic she knew enough to know that Levi's heart condition was really bad.

"They told me Levi had a heart murmur when he was born—but a lot of babies have murmurs, you know? So, I was watching it, but it only kept getting worse. Then he started turning blue, and I knew it was more than just a murmur. I pushed and pushed until we saw a specialist.

Six months ago he had a shunt put in that was supposed to help. But, as you can see from his coloring, it's not enough. I'm not even sure the shunt has helped at all."

"I'm not sure it has either."

Patrick rolled the stool over to his computer and Rhiann breathed deeply for the first time since she'd made the appointment to see him. The keys clicked and clacked beneath Patrick's nimble fingers as he made some notes on Levi's chart.

He spoke without looking at her. "You might want to have Pete with you for the tests, for emotional support. How's he handling all this, anyway?"

"I have no idea. Pete sent me divorce papers shortly after Levi was born. I haven't seen or heard from him since before Levi had his shunt put in. Last I heard he had moved back home to California and was living near his parents. Despite loving all the music here, you know he always hated Nashville. Not close enough to the water for him. And once he gave up on the idea of a music career—well, I'm afraid it's just me and Levi now."

Patrick spun on the stool and stared at her for a minute. "I didn't know," he finally acknowledged.

"Well, now you do."

Patrick had never liked Pete, so it would surely make him happy to hear that he'd been right when he'd warned her it would never last. The teensiest bit of joy flashed in his eyes and his lips curled up momentarily before he brought his emotions back under the icy veneer.

Her spine stiffened as she waited for the *I told you so* from her former friend.

"What happened?"

She sighed and let an abbreviated version of the story slip past her lips—a story she'd told more than once. "I had a hard time getting pregnant. We needed help from a donor. Pete never really connected with the thought of a baby that wasn't his biological child, and… Well, when the news came in that Levi wasn't absolutely perfect, that he had a heart problem, Pete just couldn't escape fast enough."

Levi was her family now. The only person in the world she had to love and to love her in return. She didn't need a man like Pete. She didn't need anyone at all except Levi. And for Levi she'd cross as many rivers and boundaries as she had to in order to get him the help he needed.

Right now Levi needed the surgeon sitting in front of her, and she was definitely crossing over the boundary lines he'd thrown up between them. Not just crossing them, but stomping on them and maybe setting them on fire for good measure.

Patrick snorted. "If only someone had told you that loser wasn't worth your time…"

Despite expecting the rebuke, the frigidness in his tone shocked her. Rhiann blinked away more tears. The man sitting before her bore little resemblance to the friend she'd once known. That man would never have spoken to her with such vehemence.

She hugged Levi closer, knowing she couldn't leave here without Patrick agreeing to help her son, and determined to take whatever Patrick felt he had to dish out in order to make that happen.

Very little in her life had come easily, and if there was one thing she knew it was how to stay strong and fight for what mattered. Levi was worth every fight she'd faced already, and he'd remain worth any fights there were to come.

The baby squeaked in protest as she unconsciously tightened her grip on him as she stiffened up her resolve.

She eased her hold and rested her cheek on the top of Levi's head, murmuring an apology.

She'd surprised Patrick, based on how his body stiffened beneath her hand when she reached over and put her hand on his white-cotton-clad forearm. His arm was warm beneath her fingers, which was surprising, since she'd almost expected his arm to feel like solid ice to match his demeanor.

"You can fix him, right?"

Patrick

Emotions rolled over Patrick. Waves of anger swirled around spikes of sympathy, and even a hint of something he didn't want to put a name to. He shut his feelings down and didn't allow himself the luxury of emotions.

No feelings meant no pain. And if anyone had ever perfected the art of depriving themselves of all emotion it was Patrick.

He pushed the stool back away from the teary-eyed blonde and her tiny son before the sweet scent of vanilla and apricots that wafted from her overwhelmed his sensibilities and made him do something stupid.

Like pull her into his arms and whisper reassurances about her son's future that he wasn't sure he could fulfill. Or kiss her to see if she still used the strawberry lip gloss he'd been so desperate to taste once upon a time.

He cleared his throat and pulled up the cold professionalism that had served him well these last few years. No matter how good Rhiann smelled, no matter how many sparks shot up from his arm at her simple touch, he would not allow himself to think of her that way—not her, not after what she'd done.

"I don't want to make any promises until I see exactly

what we're looking at. But I don't like what I'm hearing. You have to know that Levi's in poor condition."

From what he'd heard of the little guy's heart, surgery was almost a guarantee. But promises were wasted words when he was talking about a heart the size of a plum. And, with their past, if Rhiann had sought him out, surely she already knew things were bad.

"I can't lose him," she whispered, her lips feathering across the baby's forehead. The shadows in her eyes darkened as she processed his words. "He's all I have. Please, help him."

A mother's love visibly permeated her every move. It had brought her here today, despite knowing she'd have to face him again. That courage ripped open something deep in Patrick's chest, and he knew it would take more than a hastily slapped-on bandage to patch the gaping hole Rhiann's reappearance in his life had rent.

He stood abruptly, the stool rolling back into the wall with a rattling thud that echoed in the quiet stillness of the exam room. Fighting back the emotion that Rhiann kissing her child had triggered, he snapped out a quick response. "Levi needs an echo and a heart catherization. Once we get the results of those, we can go from there. I'll have my nurse schedule the tests."

Leaving the door to slam shut behind his rushed exit, Patrick strode down the hall to the nurses' station. He shoved the laptop across the counter. "Schedule these tests for Exam Three and get them out of here now."

He turned toward his office, heedless of the stares coming from his staff, but he didn't miss the muttered conversation behind him.

"I wonder what the mom in three said that turned the temp down on the Ice Castle? Geez..."

"Right? I didn't know he *could* get any colder."

He ignored their words and walked away.

Thankfully, Levi had been his last patient of the day. Shutting the door, Patrick leaned back against the smooth wood and closed his eyes, trying to shove all the pain back into the depths of his mind. He tugged at the tie around his neck, loosening the silk that threatened his air supply.

Nothing could have prepared him for Rhiann's return to his life.

Nothing.

Inhaling deeply, he focused on the abstract painting behind his desk. His late wife had painted the simple lines, with bold and contrasting colors, to help ground him when he found himself overwhelmed by the emotions and heartbreak that came with being a pediatric heart surgeon. Mallory had been deeply aware of his need to keep his environment outside the operating room calm. She'd known him better than he'd known himself at times.

He followed the lines across the canvas with his eyes, from light to dark, then back to light, while he took several slow, deep breaths.

He had to pull it together.

His nerve endings were twitching at the memories assaulting his consciousness, overpowering his present with painful reminders of the past.

Of all the people to walk into his practice today, it had had to be Rhiann—the one person he'd never wanted to see again. He'd wanted to rage at her and have her removed from his sight. He'd wanted to pull her into his arms and find out just what her perfectly pink lips tasted like.

There was just something about her… Something that had always fascinated him almost as much as it had angered him. Rhiann had been his first crush, his unattainable first love, but they'd never been on the same page when it came to a relationship. Then he'd met Mallory, and Rhiann's role as his best friend had been locked in.

At least until she'd betrayed his trust…

And now *she* had to be the first woman to catch his interest in three years.

The dark shadows under her eyes told him she wasn't sleeping, and he didn't have to wonder why. The way her clothes hung off a frame much thinner than he remembered had brought back protective instincts he would rather not have had reawakened.

Just for that he wanted to hate Rhiann.

Hate her for making him *feel*.

He'd tried not to notice how Levi's illness was affecting her. They weren't friends anymore and it shouldn't matter to him at all that she'd lost the dead weight from her life by divorcing that idiot Pete.

But it did matter.

Too much.

He'd almost told her to get out.

Almost.

But then he'd looked down at the little boy in her arms and found himself unable to banish her from his life once more. When he'd opened his mouth to tell her to go he'd heard himself say instead that they'd run some tests. Why? Because the blue tint to her tiny son's skin reminded him of who he was and why Rhiann had come back into his life. And, regardless of how Rhiann had betrayed him, he couldn't take all that resentment out on an innocent baby. Even if he wanted to hurt her like she'd hurt him, he couldn't bring himself to say no to Levi.

Instead of being a robust and active toddler, the frail eighteen-month-old Levi was the size of a nine-month-old. His little heart wasn't pumping right and his every breath seemed a struggle.

He hadn't got out of Rhiann's lap to run around the exam room. He hadn't crinkled the paper on the table with delighted giggles. He hadn't torn pages from the books and magazines. No, he'd only sat in Rhiann's arms and barely reacted to the exam.

Levi was a very sick little boy who urgently needed Patrick's help. And he'd help Levi. But not because he was Rhiann's son. He'd help Levi because it was the right thing to do, both as a physician and as a human being. He'd help Levi and then Rhiann could get out of his life once more, like he wanted.

Seeing Levi snuggle into Rhiann's embrace had triggered a heated assault on his emotions. The wall of ice surrounding Patrick's heart had thickened again, though, when he'd read Levi's birthdate on the chart. It was exactly two years later than his own daughter's due date.

But his sweet little Everly had never drawn a breath.

Everly would never snuggle into his embrace.

And the woman who had just begged him to save her son's life had been the one who'd cost him everything.

With a single angry gesture he swept everything from his desk into the floor. Files and stationery fluttered down without much sound, but the metal organizer tray clattered as it hit the floor and bounced.

A tentative knock preceded a soft, "Are you okay in there, Dr. Scott?"

"Leave me alone," he snarled in response.

The "Jerk..." his nurse muttered was only just audible.

He sank down onto the floor and leaned against the door. Taking some deep breaths, he stared at the platinum band on his left hand. His whispered words were too soft for anyone outside to hear.

“I miss you so much, Mallory. I don’t know how to go on without you.”

CHAPTER TWO

Rhiann

WITH THE WAY Patrick had run out of that exam room like someone had set his lab coat on fire, Rhiann wasn't entirely certain that she'd gotten through to him. Before he'd rushed out she'd been certain she'd glimpsed a crack in his frozen façade, but now, as the days passed without a word, worry crept in and set up shop.

If Patrick wouldn't help Levi she had to come up with a backup plan. She was all he had, and she refused to let him down.

On the fifth business day after Levi's appointment her patience ran out. When she stopped for lunch, she steeled her nerves to call his office and check in. Holding a finger against the twitch at the corner of her eye, Rhiann learned they had already scheduled Levi's echocardiogram.

And, of course, it was smack-dab in the middle of one of her shifts at work.

Before she could ask to reschedule, her partner shouted over that they had a call and she had to hang up quickly. She shoved the last of her sandwich into her mouth and ran over to Charlie and their rig.

In the three years she'd been a paramedic with County

Hospital, Charlie had been her partner. He'd been with County for seventeen years and, beyond having become one of her closest friends, the older man had quickly become her mentor and the nearest thing she had to a father figure.

She had never known her father—that deadbeat having left before she was born. Her mom had told everyone in town she had been widowed while pregnant—not that anyone had believed that. They'd lived in a small but immaculately clean trailer for the entirety of her childhood.

An only child of an only child, Rhiann had never had any other family. That had changed when she'd met Patrick.

Unlike her, Patrick had grown up in an affluent two-parent family. While his mom had never worked, his father had been an award-winning podiatrist. They'd been able to afford sports and extracurricular activities, private tutors, and anything else their son had needed. But, despite her being from a vastly different social class, his parents had always been kind to her, the poor girl from the outskirts of town.

Now her family circle had dwindled down to more of a triangle. She had Levi, and she had Charlie. And that had to be enough. Because she couldn't risk the damage to her heart if another man let her down.

Dispatch sent them out to a minor car accident, and after that to a nasty burn. Rhiann used the time between calls to tell Charlie about the upcoming tests and surgery.

"How much is all that gonna cost?" Charlie asked. "Sounds like a whole bucket of expensive to me."

He winced when Rhiann listed off the estimates that the calculator on the insurance website had given her. She'd flinched too when she'd seen the numbers.

"I'll figure it out somehow," Rhiann said, gnawing on her lower lip.

The tests and the surgery were going to break her already fragile financial equilibrium, but what choice did she have? Levi needed them, so she'd make it happen. She'd pick up as much overtime as she could, and she'd set up a payment plan with the hospital—like she'd done for his shunt surgery.

Next month, that would finally be paid off. She'd been looking forward to having a larger food budget again, but that was clearly not meant to be. Yet she knew she'd make it.

Charlie looked over from the driver's seat, a kind-hearted look on his age-lined face. "You always do, but it sure would be easier if you had some help."

Rhiann sighed, ignoring Charlie's last comment. Pete had no interest in helping support Levi. He had zero interest in being part of Levi's life. She'd only learned after her separation how little Charlie and the rest of her co-workers had thought of her now ex-husband. The station house had even had a running bet on just how long her marriage would last.

Charlie had won two hundred and thirty bucks for his guess. When she'd found out about it she'd made him take her out to dinner with some of the money before she'd forgiven him for betting on her marital status.

"So, this old doctor friend of yours is going to fix our boy up, right?"

"If anyone can, it's Patrick."

She might not have confidence in a lot of things, but she was confident in Patrick's abilities. Seeing him again, even if it had been hard, had felt good. They'd gotten that first awkward meeting over with now, and maybe someday they could work toward being friends again. He'd looked good, even with the uncharacteristic coldness of his personality, and that new touch of gray in his hair added a distinguished vibe she really liked too.

"What's that blush about? You hot under your uniform collar for a dude in a lab coat?"

"I am nothing of the sort!"

Rhiann slugged him on his shoulder and laughed. She and Charlie had an easy-going camaraderie that allowed for a lot of teasing. In some ways Charlie had filled a little of the void Patrick's absence had left in her life. But not entirely. No one could replace Patrick, after all.

He laughed. "That pink in your cheeks tells me enough—now tell me about your doc."

"He's not *mine*."

"So you've said." Charlie snorted. "But that pretty shade of embarrassment darkening up your cheeks tells me that you want him to be."

She looked away, staring out the window as they drove back to the station where both the paramedics and the firefighters for the county were based. She wanted to argue, but she didn't like to lie to Charlie. So she kept her mouth shut for the remainder of the drive.

They had only just pulled in to the station when Dispatch sent them straight back out.

"Couple of teens shooting things out over at the county line…" The voice on the radio crackled out the info and the address followed.

"I hate these calls," said Charlie, and turned the rig around with a sigh.

He flipped on the lights and sirens as they hurried toward the given address. They kept quiet as they headed to the scene, taking the time to mentally prepare themselves for what they might find. Kids and guns—it was never a good combination.

The address was a gas station just off I-24, and the lot was full as Charlie eased in, trying to find their patient through the crowd of people.

"There," Rhiann said, pointing to an older sedan with a shattered window near the air pump at the back corner of the lot.

A boy around thirteen, maybe fourteen, lay on the oily pavement next to the rusted car. Blood pooled around his right leg, and the bright red was a dismal sign, even as a young woman pressed what looked to be a jacket to the wound.

Rhiann hopped out of the rig and grabbed her kit.

"I think it hit a vein or an artery or something," the woman said.

Only a few years older than the boy lying on the pavement, the young woman was about three shades too pale. From experience, Rhiann knew that the shock of this was going to hit the woman hard once the adrenaline rush was over.

"Do you know his name?" Rhiann asked as she gloved up.

"Naw, I never seen him before today. I was just getting air in my tire when he came running up and some guy shot at him. I saw how he was bleeding—there was just so much blood—I took a first aid class and they said to put pressure on wounds, but I didn't have anything but my hoodie, and—" She finally ran out of air and stopped to take a shuddering breath.

Rhiann had some gauze pads ready. "Okay, you did really good. On the count of three, I want you to take your hoodie away and I'm going to take over, okay? One, two, *three*."

On three, the woman pulled the ruined hoodie away, and Rhiann got her first view of the kid's thigh. A large gaping hole exposed not only injured muscle, but a damaged femoral artery, and blood squirted out with every erratic pump of his heart.

"Charlie!" Rhiann shouted. "Nicked his femoral!"

She reached in and pinched the artery closed with her fingers. With her free hand, she fumbled through her bag.

"I can't find any clamps that will hold in the position of the damage. We need to get him to a surgeon and fast—before he bleeds out."

Charlie brought the gurney over and they carefully loaded the teen. Once they got him into the rig, Charlie got an IV started and hopped into the driver's seat.

"Dispatch, this is Rig Three. That kid you called us out to is in bad shape. Requesting permission to transport to Metro or Vanderbilt, because County's not going to be able to handle this. They need to have a surgeon meet us, because my partner's holding this kid's femoral artery in her hand and he's already lost a lot of blood."

Rhiann swallowed hard, feeling the nerves filling her when Dispatch gave Charlie the go-ahead to transport their patient to Metro. Every time a call took them to Metro she worried that Patrick would be in the Emergency Room when they rolled in. But only once had she caught a glimpse of him from a distance, and he hadn't seen her.

Shaking her head, she returned her full focus to the patient in front of her. "Charlie, you better be standing on that gas pedal, or this kid doesn't have much of a chance."

Patrick

"Dr. Scott, we have a three-year-old with a possible murmur. Would you mind taking a look?"

Dr. Dixon's grating nasally voice had called from behind him. Patrick stopped and spun toward the ER attending, who had stopped his escape from the hospital after rounds.

"Who's on call from Cardio?"

"Belcher. We've paged him three times, though, and he hasn't responded. I just don't want to discharge this kid if there's something serious and I—"

Holding a hand up, Patrick cut the younger doctor off mid-ramble. "I got it. You're trying to cover your own butt since Belcher isn't here to do it for you."

The attending's ears reddened at the accusation that Patrick had thrown at him, but he didn't deny it.

"Is that a no?" Dixon asked.

"I'll take a look. Where's the patient?"

The attending handed him a file, relief obvious on his face. "He's in Curtain Two."

"I'll find you when I'm done."

He strode to Curtain Two, where a cursory check told him the boy was fine. He heard no sign of a murmur at all. He'd just shoved the file back into the attending's hands when a trauma page came from overhead.

"Ready, Trauma Bay One. Ready, Trauma Bay One. Incoming. ETA: two minutes."

Nurses and doctors came from other rooms and started readying themselves for the incoming ambulance.

"What do we have?" asked, Dr. Abbott, head of trauma.

"Teen with a gunshot wound, possible femoral involvement," one of the nurses said, gloving up and putting a gown over her scrubs. "Probably going to be a messy one."

When he saw the rig that pulled in didn't have an MMH logo on the side Patrick's curiosity was piqued and he stayed to watch the trauma. But when the doors opened and Rhiann sat straddling the patient, her hand inside the gaping wound on the teenager's thigh, watching was no longer an option.

Shoving his hands into gloves and quickly donning a gown, he moved to support her as they lowered the gurney from the ambulance.

"I've got a young male, approximately thirteen years of age, name unknown. Large-caliber gunshot wound to the upper thigh. The bullet nicked the femoral artery and he lost probably a fourth of his volume at the scene. I couldn't get a clamp on the bleeder, due to the damage, so I'm currently providing manual pressure. He's been in and out of consciousness—mostly out."

Rhiann rattled off stats as they pushed her and the teen through the doors into the trauma bay.

Her face was pinched and the tension in her arm worried him. "Is your hand cramping?"

"Getting there." She looked up, their eyes meeting. "I'm tightening up, for sure."

He grabbed some lap pads and moved closer, trying to get a view of what they had to work with in the kid's thigh. "His thigh is trashed."

"I couldn't get a clamp on. The artery is almost shredded under my hand."

Patrick had an idea. "What if I clamp above and—?"

"Below? And that will let me get out of the way." She finished his sentence, nodding her agreement with his idea. "And hopefully that will hold until—"

"Until they can get him upstairs and into an OR." He returned the favor and finished her sentence.

A nurse held a clamp out to him and he took it. He nearly had to lay his head on Rhiann's shoulder in order to get close enough to get visibility and a good angle on the artery. He clamped it just above her hand.

"Clamp one is in."

He held his hand out for another clamp. Once the metal instrument was in his palm, he moved closer.

"I'm going beneath your hand now, Rhiann. I'm have to get in real close to be able to see." He bent down, his head wedged beneath her arm as he tried to see in the shadows.

"Can I get some more light?"

Someone angled one of the moveable overhead lamps.

"Thanks," he murmured.

His face was close enough to Rhiann's side that he could feel her breathing, her inhaled breaths bringing her uniform shirt into contact with his cheek. With the back of his wrist he nudged her arm, and she responded by moving it up slightly. It was just enough that he could get the clamp onto the artery, below where her fingers were pinched.

"Okay, I think you can let go now."

Rhiann eased her hand away from the open wound, and when the artery didn't spray blood the nurses in the room began to clap.

"That was amazing. It's like the two of you were sharing a brain," Dixon commented.

Patrick helped Rhiann off the gurney. As soon as she was clear the teenager was rolled out of the room, rushed straight for the OR, where surgeons would fix what Patrick and Rhiann had only temporarily patched.

Rhiann was flexing and relaxing her stiff hand. She turned away, taking her gloves off and dropping them into the bin.

He followed suit before spontaneously grabbing her hand. He massaged it to help loosen the stiffness. "How long were you holding that kid's life in your hands?"

"About five minutes?" She shrugged, sighing when

his fingers touched a particularly sensitive spot in her sore hand. "I'm not sure of any details right now except that your fingers are magic."

He ignored her words and focused on getting the last bit of tension out of her hand. "You saved that boy's life," he told her.

And she had. Her quick thinking in grabbing that artery with her hands had been the only thing standing between that kid and meeting his maker. Because of her this boy would leave the hospital—and not in a body bag.

"You helped." She grinned up at him, her eyes bright and full of accomplishment. "I thought my hand was about to fall off before you got that artery clamped."

Abbott slapped Patrick on the back. "Man, it was good to see the two of you working together again. As morbid as this sounds, I miss the days of you two being in my ER regularly, and seeing you work like a precisely calibrated machine to save a kid's life."

As Abbott's words sank in the fun of the save faded and Patrick remembered exactly why they didn't work together anymore. The recollection of why everything had changed flooded his mind. His chest tightened at the onslaught of painful memories.

He dropped Rhiann's hand as if she'd burned him and stepped away He glared at Abbott, who flinched under the scrutiny. "Those days are long past and you'd do well to forget them."

He left the trauma bay, hands fisted at his side, anger with himself tightening his muscles. He'd let himself get caught up in the adrenaline rush that a trauma could bring. Let himself enjoy the camaraderie and familiarity of working side by side with Rhiann again and let himself trust her every move.

But he couldn't trust her.

How could he have forgotten that?

CHAPTER THREE

Patrick

PATRICK AND CLAY were following a nurse's instructions to the staff lounge on the main floor at County. He hadn't spent enough time at this hospital to know his way around, despite having had surgical privileges there for years.

"Man, I hope there's some coffee in this place." Clay fidgeted with the strap of his bag and yawned loudly. "I'm getting too old for these early mornings."

Patrick raised a brow at his partner. "You aren't old yet. And it's not early—in fact, it's almost noon."

Clay grinned at him. "I didn't get home until after midnight, and when I was in bed I wasn't asleep for some time. I need coffee, but I'm not turning into a pumpkin just yet."

Rolling his eyes, Patrick pushed open the door marked *Employees Only*. "You go from Cinderella to the Wicked Witch when you haven't got enough sleep."

"My preferred comparison is Dr. Jekyll and Mr. Hyde, thank you very much."

Patrick walked into the small room and set his bag on a table along one side. "Oh, good—there's coffee."

A feminine voice from the corner stopped him just

as his hand closed on the handle. "I wouldn't do that if I were you."

He released the pot and spun around, because he knew that voice.

"Rhiann!" Clay had already stepped forward and was greeting Rhiann like an old friend. "I haven't seen you in so long. How are you?"

"Hi, Clay." She accepted Clay's outstretched hands and held them for a moment before looking in Patrick's direction. "I'm doing okay."

"How's Levi?" Patrick asked.

"We had the EKG this morning. They said they'd send his results over to you as soon as they're ready."

He nodded. "Okay…good."

"Who's Levi?" Clay asked, looking between Patrick and Rhiann.

"My son. He has something going on with his heart."

Her eyes met Patrick's and the certainty he saw there was humbling.

"But if anyone can fix him it's Patrick."

Parents came to him because of his reputation. They brought their babies to him because his record spoke for him. He got results. He saved more children than he lost. They trusted his medical skills even though they'd never met him.

This was different.

Rhiann trusted *him*. Not the world-renowned doctor with awards and plaques hanging on the walls of his state-of-the-art office. She didn't know or care about the number of articles he'd published in prestigious medical journals or his presentations at top conferences.

No. She trusted Patrick the man.

Despite barely speaking to him for three years, she

still trusted him. And that realization brought a lump to his throat that he didn't want to acknowledge.

"What are you doing here?" Clay asked, pulling Patrick away from his introspection as Rhiann broke eye contact.

"We're on the clock. Waiting on a transfer. The floor doesn't have her ready for us yet, so we thought we'd grab a coffee while we waited."

She waved a hand down at herself. The dark uniform suited her. Her hair was up in a professional-looking twist that left her neck bare…perfect for kissing.

He inhaled sharply. Where had *that* thought come from?

The older man in the corner cleared his throat. "You might have to grab a gurney and push me down to the ED after this." He held up a plastic cup filled with dark liquid. "That coffee's done put hair on my chest. I'm not sure how it hasn't eaten through this cup yet, but I'm pretty darn sure it's made its way through my esophagus."

The man wore a uniform that matched Rhiann's. He reclined back, legs outstretched, and faked a moan. "It's killed me, I tell you."

Rhiann rolled her eyes and snorted. "And that's my partner, Charlie. If there's drama to be found, Charlie's in it up to his ankles."

"Hey!" Charlie protested.

"Fine—up to his knees." She smiled indulgently at Charlie, her affection for the older man shining brightly in her eyes.

"Better," Charlie agreed, nodding his head in her direction before throwing the rest of the coffee back like it was a shot. "Gah! Who needs whiskey when you have County coffee? It burns all the same going down."

"Don't worry, old man, I have your antacids out in

the rig." Rhiann laughed at her partner's antics. Then she turned to Patrick with a smile on her face. "See why I warned you off that stuff?"

"Is there anywhere close where we can get some decent coffee?" Patrick jerked his head toward Clay. "That guy might implode if I don't get some caffeine in him soon."

Rhiann shook her head sadly. "Not in this hospital."

"Close by?"

She pursed her lips in disgust. "Not for miles. They like it strong enough that the spoon bends around here. Charlie still tries to drink it, but I've learned my lesson. I think it's probably too strong for your tastes too. But you might try the nurses' station up by the trauma ICU. They've been known to make a fresh pot for Charlie when he flirts a little. They might even wash the pot for you two."

Clay winked at her. "Thanks, doll. I always did like you. I'm gonna go see if I can sweet-talk a nurse into a coffee." He slapped Patrick on the shoulder. "I've got my cell—call me when they're ready for us."

"What are you guys doing all the way out here at County, anyway?" Rhiann asked. "Metro Memorial is your stomping ground."

Patrick shrugged. He leaned a hip against the counter. "Usually. But they don't have a pediatric cardiologist who has done a heart transplant on staff here at the moment, and I still have privileges, so when they needed a procurement team they gave me a call."

Her eyes teared up. "Someone's losing their kid today?"

"Several more are having their kids saved today."

He always tried to focus on the positives, because that was the only way he could get through the day when he had to do a transplant surgery. He focused on how many people each donor had saved, because otherwise he had to remember the pain that came with being a donor's family. Knowing that Mallory's last act on earth had been to give life to others had been the only thing that had got him through when he'd lost her.

"How many?" She grabbed a tissue and dabbed at her eyes.

He'd always loved her eyes, the bright green of new spring grass, and the tears in them now made the color even more vivid.

"I'm not sure." He thought back to all that he'd been told in the phone call. "I don't remember. I know the heart is going to a seven-year-old in Ohio. And the lungs to a nine-year-old in Pennsylvania."

"Small comfort, I suppose."

She smiled at him, but the sadness radiating from her eyes penetrated deep into his soul. She looked as if the world had just collapsed on her and she couldn't hold it up any longer.

Rhiann had always been so strong, but there was an air of fragility to her now.

He pushed away from the counter and laid a hand on her shoulder, trying unsuccessfully to ignore the frailness in her frame. "You okay?"

She nodded.

Charlie's radio crackled behind them, alerting them that their patient was now ready for transport.

"We need to go, Rhiann."

Patrick wanted to say more, but he didn't know where to begin or how to condense it down into a moment or two. His mouth opened and closed with no sound while Rhiann gazed up at him. Those big green eyes had been rendering him stupid for years, and it seemed they hadn't lost their power over him.

"I've got to go."

She gave him a quick hug and was gone again before he could return the gesture. Her arms around him had stunned him, and he couldn't process the feel of her softness pressed against him before she'd moved away and the entire moment was gone.

Clay came back in as Rhiann and Charlie rushed out.

"I come bearing gifts." He held out a cup of steaming coffee. "Rhiann was right—the nurses up there are incredibly friendly. I walked away with coffee for us both and three phone numbers."

Patrick took the coffee and sank down into a chair with a sigh.

"Wanna talk about that hug I just saw?" asked Clay.

He shook his head. There was no way he could talk about what he himself was struggling to understand. Having Rhiann's arms around him had him so mixed up it was like he had been thrown in a blender. How could he want to hug someone he had sworn to hate?

"No? How do you feel about Rhiann reappearing in your life?"

Patrick lowered his eyes to the coffee in his hand. "I don't want to talk about that either," he growled out.

"You haven't seen her in a long time. You have to be feeling *something* about her showing up after so long. She was your best friend for half your life." He paused. "Still don't wanna talk? Okay, I'll talk. You listen."

Clay moved a chair until he was sitting directly in front of Patrick.

"Your best friend there still wants to be a part of your life. You need to pull your head out of your nether regions long enough so that you can see that."

He took a sip of his coffee and stared at Patrick until the urge to squirm was almost more than he could bear. Clay had a gift for making anyone feel like a child with a simple raised brow.

"I can't trust her. She let—"

"I know what you *think* she did, and I still maintain that you're wrong—because Rhiann is a walking heart. She cares too much about everyone she meets. I know she would have done everything possible, even if you are too stubborn to see that." Clay plowed over Patrick's objections like an unsubtle bulldozer. "What if Rhiann has come back into your life for a reason?"

"What are you suggesting?"

"I'm not *suggesting* anything. I'm *saying* outright that you need to forgive her. And you need to forgive yourself for not being there when Mallory and Everly died. You couldn't have saved them, and you need to accept that Rhiann couldn't either."

"I didn't ask for your advice." Patrick stood up, intending to put some space between himself and his annoying partner.

Clay rose to his feet and blocked the only exit. "And yet I'm still offering it—and it's because you need to hear it. These last three years you've been grieving, and I gave you space to do that. But all this negativity is eating you alive, man. You have to stop just existing and move forward with your life. Do you think Mallory would be happy about how you've been living? About you being alone and shutting everyone out?"

"Clay—"

"Mallory would be heartbroken at the thought of you freezing out your best friend over her. She knew how much Rhiann meant to you." Clay got one more stab in. "I'm surprised that you've forgotten."

"Shut up, Clay."

But Clay continued, "I think that woman holds the key to your future happiness in the palm of her tiny little hand, and I think you are too smart to lose her twice."

Patrick's phone buzzed with the notification that their patient was ready for them. He glared at his partner and changed the subject. "We need to go scrub."

Clay tossed his cup into the trash and gave Patrick a somber look. "Once again, saved by the bell. One day you won't be so lucky. You'll have to face your past and learn to forgive."

Rhiann

Rhiann could tell by the number of glances that her partner kept sneaking in her direction that he had something to say. The older man was not known for subtlety, but he'd wait until they had a modicum of privacy before he unleashed his opinion on her.

Thankfully they had a patient who was not only awake, but chatty, so that should buy her a little time while she tried to figure out just what had happened in that break room with Patrick.

They were transporting an elderly woman back to her assisted living facility after a short hospital stay.

"Tell me something good," the lady said, reaching out to pat Rhiann's arm with her age-spotted hand. "I've got to go back to the home with all those old biddies who have nothing better to do than compare whose health is worse."

"I don't know much that's good right now. I'm not the one to ask." Rhiann laughed a wry, humorless laugh. "I can switch spots with Charlie and you can do a little flirting, though?"

"You'll do no such thing. I remember Charlie when he was hiding behind his mama's skirts. I can no sooner flirt with that child than I can run a marathon." She clucked her disapproval. "What kind of woman do you take me for? I'm no cradle-robber."

Rhiann met Charlie's gaze in the mirror, smiling at the hint of red she saw tingeing his cheeks. "Oh, really? Maybe you're the one who needs to tell *me* something good, then. You have any dirt on my partner that I might use to my advantage?"

"You could tell her about that pair of doctors you were getting friendly with while we waited on her to get ready," Charlie said loudly. "I'm sure she would rather hear about two handsome single doctors who got a little handsy with you in the break room than tell a story about me when I was a snot-nosed brat."

"Oh, yes? Are you being courted by two doctors?" Their patient's furrowed face lit with excitement. "Do tell me. I love a good romance."

Rhiann sighed, not wanting to disappoint the old woman. "There is no romance."

"You only say that because you didn't see the look in that man's eyes when he thought you weren't watching." Charlie snorted. "If I could show you what I saw…"

A wrinkly hand waved, urging Rhiann to spill her story. "If you don't tell me I'll get Charlie to—and, while I know his version will be quite entertaining, it will only contain a hint of the truth."

Rhiann pinched the bridge of her nose. "Fine. But there is no romance."

"Let me be the judge."

"The abbreviated version is that the two doctors are old friends of mine—Patrick and Clay. I met Patrick in high school, where we became best friends from day one.

He went off to med school while I stayed here locally, and when he came back it was with a wife and Clay. We were all friends for some time, and then something tragic happened. Patrick's wife and daughter..." She trailed off, unable to finish that part of the story. She wrapped up her tale in a no-nonsense, definitive tone. "Now we aren't friends anymore. See, I told you—no romance."

"Hmm..." the woman said. "That's quite a story you've told in only a few words there."

"You notice she only really told you about one of them. Right?" Charlie said.

Rhiann closed her eyes and sighed. "Charlie..." she warned.

"She only told you about one because she barely saw the other one. I was only teasing about her having the two of them after her. Even if poor Clay was interested he doesn't stand a chance—not standing next to Patrick."

"It sounds like there are a lot of strong emotions on both sides," the elderly lady said wisely.

"Hate is definitely a strong emotion," Rhiann agreed.

"Except hate is *not* what that man's feeling for you."

"Shut up, Charlie."

Charlie laughed from the front of the rig. "She got a little emotional and he nearly launched himself across the room to comfort her. Couldn't help himself—he just had to touch her. That's not how a man reacts to someone he can't stand. Even if he hasn't admitted to himself that he's got feelings for her, let me tell you, he's got them."

"My mama, God rest her soul, always used to say you couldn't have hate without love," said their patient. She shifted on the gurney. "I believe that's true. Maybe the boy had to hate you so he could see how much he loves you now."

Rhiann shook her head. "You're as bad as Charlie,

aren't you?" She ignored the hope that was trying to blossom in her heart like a stray flower in the crack of a city sidewalk. "I'm going to tell you what I tell him—and that's that I don't have time for romance. There's no room in my life for a bunch of hopes and dreams I have no control over. The only man I have room for in my life is my son, and I don't need anyone else."

"Pshaw! You're too young to be so jaded." She reached out and grasped Rhiann's hand.

"He shut me out entirely—told me to stay out of his life. Not only that, but he shook my faith in my own abilities. I gave up a job I loved to better be able to avoid him. If I'm jaded, there are plenty of reasons," Rhiann said quietly.

"Well, you met me, though, so that was fate," Charlie argued. "But I'm telling you true: that man might have some hate for you, but there's something far deeper peeking out when he looks at you."

"Listen to an old lady and don't let a chance at love pass you by. You might get burned—but what if you don't?"

Rhiann held the woman's hand, closing her eyes before tears made it to the surface. "I wouldn't even know where to start."

"You have his cell number, right?" Charlie asked.

"Yes…"

"Call him."

The old woman made a tsking sound. "That's a bit forward. Perhaps you could send him one of those little messages on his phone, though. Just something small."

"Oh, yeah, a text might be better," Charlie agreed. "Ask him how his surgery went. How many kids that donor saved. I bet he's found out since you mentioned it."

"I don't know about this…"

Rhiann swallowed hard. Patrick had made his position clear, and while he had shown hints of the friend she'd lost he was still ice-cold in most of their interactions. What if she pushed too far and he refused to help Levi as a result?

"Text him." Charlie's voice got gruff and his words came out like orders. "Go on."

"Yes, dear—go on." The elderly lady smiled at Rhiann. "I insist."

"Peer pressure doesn't end in high school, does it?"

Rhiann pulled her phone out and tapped in a message, asking if Patrick had found out how many lives the donor had saved. Surely such a simple follow-up question wouldn't be too upsetting?

She shoved the phone back into her pocket, her cheeks warming as she blushed. "There. Done. And when he ignores me I'm going to come over and tell you about it."

"I'd love to have you visit—even if it is just to say *I told you so*."

Rhiann's heart softened at the hope in her patient's voice. She squeezed the elderly woman's hand. "My son has some health issues that make taking him out much a little dangerous right now, so I can't make any promises. But I'll do my best to visit when I can."

Charlie volunteered to visit on occasion too, and they passed the rest of the ride in simple small talk that took some of the pressure off Rhiann.

They'd dropped the patient off and were sitting around at the station house when Patrick's response came.

Six lives saved. Heart, lungs, kidneys to two patients, liver, and pancreas.

She held the phone close to her heart and tried not to

tear up. Not just because six lives had changed for the better that day, but for the family whose world was now shattered.

"That your doc?" asked Charlie.

She wiped at her eyes. "I told you before—he's not mine."

"Yet." Charlie winked as he went to clock out. "Keep texting him and he might be."

CHAPTER FOUR

Patrick

PATRICK WAS MID-SHAVE when his phone buzzed. He finished quickly and wiped the last of the shaving cream from his face with a towel. As he was walking through to the bedroom, to get dressed for a long appointment-filled day at the office, he unlocked his phone and checked the incoming message.

He couldn't help but smile as he pulled up a picture of Levi, sleeping peacefully. The smile faded quickly when he read the accompanying caption.

He sleeps. I stay up and worry.

Patrick hit reply, concern for his former best friend bounding up over the ever-present animosity.

How long has it been since you have slept through the night?

He sat on the edge of his bed for several minutes, waiting for a reply that didn't come.

After several minutes had passed, with no response,

he finished dressing and packed his laptop and chargers into his bag.

His phone buzzed with Rhiann's reply as he was getting into his car.

Oh, probably not since his birth.

He needs you to take care of yourself properly and that means sleep.

Then fix him for me so I don't have to worry that he won't wake up.

Patrick sank into the leather seat and scrubbed a hand across his face. Even in a text message, her worry for that little boy came through loud and clear. And now he was worrying about *her*. While he'd tried not to see it, tried not to care, he'd noticed she looked like she wasn't sleeping, most likely not eating right either.

Rhiann was putting all her energy into caring for her son, but who was caring for her?

I'll do my best. Heading into the office now. You working today?

Patrick drove to his office, ignoring the buzzing of his phone while the car was moving. As soon as he'd put the car in "park," he snatched up the phone with a speed that would embarrass him when he thought back on it later.

Currently sitting at the station waiting on the guy filling in for Charlie, who is running late. I hate lateness. It's like my biggest pet peeve.

Patrick laughed as he stared down at the screen.

Says the girl who was late to first period at least three days a week in senior year?

You would know. You made me late most of those days.

Patrick grinned down at the phone, remembering back to high school. He had tried so hard to impress Rhiann back then, when he'd been all gangly teenage awkwardness and she had been the most beautiful girl he'd ever seen.

From the day he'd walked into third period Biology, after transferring his freshman year, and the teacher had assigned him to sit next to a tiny blonde with a wide smile that had sent his fourteen-year-old heart into orbit with his first real crush, Rhiann had been the most important person in his life. He had wanted her love almost as much as he'd wanted air to breathe.

It hadn't been meant to be. But their friendship had been his rock for so long. It had got him through his gawky years. It had kept him grounded when he'd finally matured into a frame that had drawn more female attention than he'd known how to handle.

Rhiann had been at his side, laughing at his sad attempts at flirting, turning him down gently when he'd occasionally worked up the courage to ask her out. Each time she'd hug him tight and whisper, "Losing you as my best friend would break me. I could never risk it."

Had the fracturing of their friendship contributed to her current fragile state?

He leaned back against the seat and closed his eyes. Was he partially to blame for the shadows under her eyes and the thinness of her frame?

Despite his mental determination not to care about what happened to her, his heart was not so hardened to her plight. And the fact that he was softening toward her was tearing him up inside. She'd cost him everything. Why couldn't he keep that focus at the front of his mind?

When he replied to her message he kept the tone light, away from the dark depths where his thoughts had gone.

If you were late because of me it's because you distracted me until I couldn't think, woman!

I would never distract anyone! I'm innocent! One hundred percent!

Lies, all lies! I gotta go examine sick kids now. Tell me something funny to distract me from the sad reality of my day.

What he'd told Rhiann was true. His job could be sad. Very sad. All those little ones with hearts that didn't pump properly. Hearts that had holes. Hearts that had just plain failed.

After losing his own daughter, he had put up walls that kept him from caring about another child. He couldn't risk the pain ever again. And he hated it that Levi and Rhiann were finding cracks in those walls.

But at the same time he couldn't bring himself to put the distance back between them. Despite Rhiann's objections, he could have passed Levi's case over to Clay. He *could* have. Perhaps even *should* have. But he hadn't.

He got out of the car and headed in. The receptionist and office staff were already in. They always got there before he did, to open the office and prep the exam rooms for the day. He waved distractedly at one of his nurses when she greeted him as he walked down the hall to his office. He dropped his bag on the table and went to the break room in search of coffee.

After pouring a cup, he was enjoying the dark brew when his phone buzzed again. He pulled it out of his pocket and nearly choked on the hot liquid when he read Rhiann's words.

Well, we just left the local elementary school, where we had to extract a little guy from a chair. Got a panic call from the teacher. Get there and the little dude is totally chilling, eating a snack one of the other kids got him, while the adults are running in circles around him.

How did he get stuck in a chair?

On his knees in the seat, apparently. Slipped through the hole in the back and couldn't come back through. His belly got stuck.

Wow. That's just...wow.

"And just who are you texting and smiling at so intently this early?" Clay asked, an all-knowing grin on his face.

"An old friend," Patrick said, refusing to give him the satisfaction of admitting that he was texting Rhiann. He shoved his phone in his pocket before Clay could come read over his shoulder.

"Rhiann?"

Patrick lifted one shoulder in what he hoped was a casual non-committal reply.

Clay's grin widened and Patrick tensed up for the teasing that was sure to come. But Clay only shot him a conspiratorial wink before turning his attention to the coffee pot.

Rhiann

Rhiann ran around her apartment, gathering up the items Levi might need at the hospital. The relief paramedic had been twenty minutes late, and now she was going to be cutting it a lot shorter that she'd have liked.

In her head, she checked off the list: Mr. Bunny, extra clothes, diapers, formula, sippy cup. She also tossed in a juice box and some applesauce in case he was hungry. She was hoping that after his surgery formula would be a distant memory, but for now he needed the extra nutrition it provided. The last thing she shoved into the now bulging diaper bag was her purse.

"Come on, little guy!" she said, trying to inject some fake excitement about the day into her exhausted tone. She picked Levi up out of his playpen, where he'd been sitting with some toy blocks and hugged him close. "We're going to visit Patrick again. I'm sad to say you haven't been able to get to know him yet, but I'm hoping that's gonna change. You see, not only is he your doctor, he has been Mommy's best friend for a very long time. We just had a timeout on our friendship. Long story… Maybe I'll tell you sometime."

Juggling Levi and the diaper bag, she managed to lock the apartment door without dropping anything. She slowly made her way down the steep, narrow stairs of her building and out to the parking lot. Tossing the diaper bag onto the backseat, she settled Levi in his car seat and buckled him in safely.

After digging her keys out of the pocket of her jeans, she sank into the driver's seat. When she turned the key in the ignition, though, all she heard was an odd whirring sound and some random clicks. Tears filled her eyes and she pressed her head against the steering wheel.

"Not today, please," she prayed aloud.

Not that any other day would be better. Another car repair was so far from being within her budget that it might as well be on Mars. But Levi couldn't miss this appointment.

"Come on, car. Please be good to me."

She tried the key again.

Nada. Not even the whirring this time.

She slapped her hand against the wheel in frustration, her thoughts churning with questions. Who could she call to get a ride quickly, so they didn't miss the appointment? How could she afford to repair the car? How could she afford *not* to repair the car?

Before she could think it out, she dug her purse out of the diaper bag and got her phone. She dialed Patrick's number, calling on him to rescue her like she'd done a hundred times in their nearly two decades of friendship.

"Hey, are you on your way to the hospital?" Patrick asked when he answered. "I should be there before long myself."

"Any way you could take a detour out to the suburbs?" She paused before explaining her dilemma. "I'm having a bit of car trouble. Okay, more than a bit. It refuses to start."

"Uh..."

He paused, and Rhiann's heart paused along with him. If he said no she'd have to pay for a cab or an Uber that would cost a fortune she didn't have.

"Yeah, I can come pick you up. Text me your address and I'll head that way now."

Rhiann hung up the phone and texted him her address.

Closing her eyes, she let frustrated tears fall for a moment, before wiping her face and taking a deep breath. This broken-down car was *not* going to break her. She'd been through far worse and come out the victor. So, after another minute of self-pity, she pulled herself together—because she would not become one of those weak women she hated, always blubbering and clinging to a man like she couldn't live without him.

She'd been flying solo with Levi for this long without having anyone to lean on. Staying strong was what she did. Her entire career had been built on her ability to stay cool under pressure, so she sure wasn't going to let a broken-down old car crumple her like a tissue.

Exhaling slowly, she pulled her emotions back under tentative control. "You've got this. You always do," she whispered to the red-eyed mommy in the rearview mirror, wishing she could truly believe that.

Her fingers touched on the simple necklace hidden beneath the collar of her shirt, seeking the comfort the little trinket always provided. While she wished someone else could give her the pep talk she desperately needed, as usual she was flying solo, so she had to fuss at her reflection herself.

"You've purged your tears, now Levi needs you to be strong again. You are all he has, and you can't let him down."

She called a mechanic friend who usually cut her a good deal. "Hey, TJ—it's Rhiann. My car is being a punk again. Could you look at it today?"

"Yeah, where's it at?"

"At my apartment."

"I can come get it in about an hour or so?"

"I'll leave the key under the mat."

"Sounds good. I'll see if I can get it going again—but you know that old clunker's not gonna limp along forever?"

"I know, but can you give it some crutches for now, please?"

"I'll try, babe. But it may be tomorrow before I can get it back to you."

"Thanks, TJ." She hung up the phone and leaned back against the headrest. If TJ couldn't fix the car, it couldn't be fixed. And if it couldn't be fixed, that opened up a whole new barrel of stress.

But didn't have time to start worrying about that now. Shaking her head, she fiddled with her keyring until she'd pulled her car key free of the rest. After glancing around the parking lot to see if anyone was watching, and then chastising herself for the silly thought that someone might steal her busted car, she tucked the key under the floor mat.

Unbuckling Levi from his car seat, she sat him on the backseat and gave him a toy to play with from the diaper bag.

"Here—Mommy has to take your seat out of the car so it can go in Patrick's car. I'm not sure what he drives now, but I promise it will be the nicest car you'll have ever ridden in."

Sadness washed over her at that thought. When she'd found out she was pregnant she'd had plans to give Levi the world. She'd failed. Her dreams had been brought down to the simple hope of giving him a future. Any future.

She unclipped the buckles holding his car seat and shook a few crumbs out of it. "There…now we won't mess up Patrick's car." Then she put the seat back in its place. Walking around the car, she climbed into the backseat, picking Levi up and giving him a kiss on the cheek.

Levi smiled, patting her face. "Do 'gain."

Rhiann laughed. "You want more kisses? My little kissy monster!" She gave him several kisses on his face, exaggerating the sounds. "Mwah! Mwah!"

A shiny black sedan pulled into the empty spot next to them. Rhiann knew without being able to see through the tinted windows that it was Patrick. No one else would be pulling in to this complex in a late-model luxury sedan.

She stepped out of her old clunker with Levi in her arms just as Patrick was getting out of his car.

"Hi. Thanks for this," she said awkwardly.

"You need a better car."

Wrapping Levi in a tight hug—the kind of hug she wished someone would give *her* at the moment—Rhiann responded tightly, "Yeah, well, I need a lot of things. But you know…priorities." Her words held a note of hurt she hoped wouldn't be audible to him, but from his wince she knew it had been.

"That didn't come out as I intended," he offered, his tone apologetic.

"Whatever." Rhiann pointed across the car. "His car seat is just sitting there on the seat. Can you put it in your car? Or would you rather hold him while I do it?"

Patrick glanced toward the seat. "I think it would be faster, and probably safer, if I take him and you put the seat in properly. I'm sure I can do it, but it will take me longer than it would you, for sure. And we're going to be pushing it to make our scheduled appointment time as it is."

He held his hands out to Levi.

"Hey, buddy. Do you remember me? Wanna come hang with me while Mommy gets your seat in my car?"

Levi dove toward Patrick's outstretched arms.

"I'm gonna take that as a yes," Patrick said with a laugh. "How are you this morning? I'm going to look at your heart today—did you know?"

When Patrick bent down to kiss the top of her son's head Rhiann couldn't help her sharp intake of breath. And as their eyes met over Levi's head Patrick smiled at her. Not just any smile—*the* smile. The one that had made many a girl swoon.

Rhiann learned she was far from immune herself as her heart fluttered in major awareness. She'd always found Patrick attractive. She was straight and had perfect vision, after all. And they had tentatively flirted with the idea of dating once upon a time. But they hadn't wanted to ruin their friendship. *She* hadn't wanted to ruin their friendship.

Then Patrick had gone away to medical school. By the time he'd finished he'd met Mallory and Rhiann had met Pete. Their friendship had continued, but any hopes of more had been firmly shelved since they'd both been married to other people.

Those days felt like a lifetime ago.

Now the very thought of anything else between them seemed impossible.

Even if her heart was shouting out *It's possible!* with each and every beat.

Patrick raised a single dark eyebrow and she noticed the mischievous interest in his eyes. His smile widened, and Rhiann's heart stumbled to a stop before jerking into a crazy rhythm that would have made the cardiologist currently in front of her concerned if he'd had her hooked up to an EKG.

"You okay there, Rhiann?" he asked, his low voice rumbling and doing things to her that a simple conversation shouldn't do.

"Fine." She jumped into action, installing the car seat quickly, listening to the one-sided conversation Patrick was having with Levi.

She couldn't help but smile at the tender way Patrick spoke to her son. He paused after his questions to give Levi a chance to answer, even used simple language to help the little one understand him.

The man was born to be a father.

CHAPTER FIVE

Patrick

HAVING RHIANN IN the car so close—close enough to touch—made thoughts run through Patrick's head. And those thoughts troubled him, given his history with Rhiann. But his anger from a few days ago had mellowed into an edgy awareness of her presence. Instead of wanting to ignore her and push her away, he wanted to pull her close and inhale the soft scent that surrounded her.

Merging onto the interstate, he brought the car up to speed quickly.

Rhiann made an appreciative noise from the passenger seat.

"Man, this car is a thing of beauty!" she said, with a wistful-sounding sigh. She ran a hand along the dashboard. "It's *so* much nicer than my plastic-covered non-starter."

Patrick chuckled. "It cost a fair bit more too."

She leaned back into the leather. "I don't think I've ever ridden in anything this fancy. It puts Ol' Betsy to shame."

When he'd turned sixteen Patrick's parents had bought him a base model sedan with absolutely zero frills, but good gas mileage and safety ratings. Rhiann had affectionately named the boring gray sedan Ol' Betsy, and the name had stuck.

"Ah, but remember the times we used to have in that old car? All the trouble we got into? Ol' Betsy was a solid companion for me all through high school, college, and med school." He changed lanes. "She was a good car. She had over three hundred thousand miles on her when I sold her off."

"If only my clunker was as reliable." She sighed again, and this time the sound was filled with worry, if he wasn't mistaken.

"You used to have a Mustang," he said. "You kept that candy-apple-red shining like a light. What happened to that?"

"Babies with broken hearts are expensive." She shrugged.

"Does your car break down often?"

She huffed out what sounded like an annoyed breath. "More than I care to admit to a man driving a car worth more than I make in a year."

Patrick let the conversation trail off for a moment while he tried to think of a response that wouldn't get her back up. Finally he decided to just change the subject.

"They put Levi's shunt in during a cath, right?"

"Yes."

"Okay—so you're familiar with the procedure, then."

"Somewhat. I know they'll put him to sleep and you'll go in through a vein or an artery in his groin. Last time he was so bruised that he didn't hardly move for days."

"Knowing he bruises easily, I'll do my best to be gentle."

"Okay."

Rhiann grew quiet and stared out the window as cars and the south side of the city flew past. Patrick didn't mind. He let the silence fill the car and drew in a few deep, calming breaths.

He had to get his mind straight for this procedure and not let himself be distracted by his patient's mother. Pushing Rhiann into that role would help him get the mental clarity he needed to treat Levi appropriately.

He pulled into the parking garage at the hospital and parked in the staff parking lot. When Rhiann mentioned being glad he was there so they could walk in together, Patrick realized he needed a little more space between them. He had to get this procedure right.

When they reached the sidewalk, he waved a hand toward the main entrance. "If you and Levi go through those doors, then continue down the hall to the second set of elevators. Take them up to the fifth floor and just follow the signs to the Children's Cardiology Admission Unit. They'll get him checked in and get him prepped."

"You aren't coming in with us?" Rhiann asked, nibbling on her lower lip like she did when she was nervous.

Patrick indicated the staff entrance. "I'll meet you up there. I gotta go this way and get my stuff prepped."

She looked a little teary-eyed for a moment, before squaring her shoulders and nodding at him. Taking Levi from him, she said, "We got this. Right, little guy?"

Unlike the naïve child in her arms, Patrick remained unconvinced. He wavered for a moment about going in with her, but in the end he kept his distance.

He stood on the sidewalk and watched them walk away. *Distance*, he reminded himself.

With a determined attitude, he strode toward the staff entrance and headed up to the CCAU to get prepped for Levi's procedure.

It didn't take him long to change into fresh scrubs and double-check the procedure room. His favorite anesthesiologist was working with him. He nodded at the older man, who was checking his own prep.

Satisfied that everything was to his liking, Patrick made his way out to the holding area, where Rhiann would be waiting with Levi.

She smiled when he walked in, but it didn't reach her eyes. The fear in them cut him deep and he had to force his emotions down again, become the Ice Castle, as the nurses referred to him.

"Has the anesthetist been out to talk to you?" he asked.

"Yes, a little while ago. Are you going to start soon?"

He nodded. "Just waiting on them to get him sedated, then we'll bring him in. I'll come out to talk to you when he's being moved to Recovery."

He turned to walk away, and had almost made a clean getaway when he heard her whisper, "Take care of him, please, Patrick."

He released a ragged breath and kept walking. If he turned around—if he saw the emotion her voice held portrayed on her face—he wasn't sure he would be able to do this procedure and Levi needed him.

The walls he'd built around his heart cracked. Ice shards as big as daggers stabbed into his chest.

A small voice inside his head whispered that Levi's mommy needed him too.

Walking into the scrub room, he leaned against the wall for a moment. Since Rhiann's return to his life his icy walls of self-protection had started melting away. Powerless to stop the avalanche of painful memories and the emotions they uncovered, Patrick buried his face in his hands.

He shouldn't care about Rhiann, or her emotional state. He shouldn't care how this was affecting her or anything outside of taking care of his patient. Because he'd sworn to hate Rhiann with every ounce of breath in him for the rest of his life.

Rhiann had always been a brilliant paramedic. The skill level she'd shown had often amazed him. He had seen her make saves that he wasn't sure a lot of doctors could have made. And that was why he had found her inaction when Mallory and Everly had needed her so unfathomable.

He could never forgive her for letting them die.

"You okay, there, Dr. Scott?" one of the scrub nurses asked.

He shook himself hard. "Is my patient ready?" he snapped, forcing himself to be the emotionless robot he'd been ever since he'd lost his family.

The hint of concern in the nurse's voice disappeared. "Wheeling him in now."

"I'll get scrubbed and be right in."

Rhiann

Despite knowing the procedure would take at least thirty minutes, at the fifteen-minute mark Rhiann could no longer sit in the stiff uncomfortable chair. She paced the small waiting room from one end to the other and back.

After she'd nearly worn a hole through the flooring, an older woman at one end smiled at her sadly. "First big procedure?"

"Unfortunately, no."

"Ah… I'd say it gets easier, but mine is fourteen, and this is his fourth, and it really doesn't."

"I'm sorry to hear that."

The door opened and Rhiann spun around.

"Patrick!" She rushed over to him, nearly losing her balance when she reached him. She grabbed the door frame to right herself. "Is Levi okay? How did it go? Did you get all the info you needed for his surgery? When can I see him?"

He held up a hand to slow the flood of questions. "Levi's in Recovery. If you'll just breathe for me, I'll try to answer you."

Rhiann forced herself to take a few deep breaths. Her voice was far calmer when she spoke again. "Okay—first, when can I see him?"

"Now, if you stay calm."

His gaze was questioning, but firm. Rhiann knew he'd never let her near his patient if she was going to upset him—even if said patient *was* her son.

She nodded.

"This way."

Patrick stepped back and motioned her into the hall. He directed her with his hand at the small of his back, like he'd done a thousand times before. His strength radiated out, and like a sponge she soaked up every bit that came her way.

Since her divorce Rhiann hadn't cared to date. She'd been asked out a few times, but her focus had always been entirely on Levi. She was determined never to rely on another man after losing the two she'd counted on within such a short space of time. Between Pete's total apathy and abandonment, and Patrick's animosity and anger, she'd decided men weren't worth the trouble. She couldn't count on them being there for her when she needed them. So she refused to need another man, period.

Now, maybe the loneliness was finally getting to her, but her body found being this close to Patrick something she was extremely aware of. And, while maybe she didn't *need* a man, she was certainly finding that parts of her might *want* Patrick. From her hands that itched to reach for him to the nape of her neck that desperately wanted his kiss, and all the way down to her toes that wanted him to make them curl.

"Let me swipe us through this door and we can save a few hundred steps," Patrick said, stopping at a set of double doors marked *Do Not Enter: Staff Only.*

He leaned across her to swipe his ID badge on the sensor. Her quick intake of breath caught his attention and his eyes focused on hers. She worried at her lower lip with her teeth and his gaze dropped to linger on her mouth.

The doors opened slowly and closed just as slowly. Neither of them moved.

Patrick leaned closer and she let her eyes flutter closed, thinking he might kiss her.

The doors creaked opened again, the mechanical sound jarring the intimacy from the moment. He murmured an apology as she opened her eyes.

He led her into a curtained area where Levi lay on a hospital bed, still asleep. A nurse sat on a wheeled stool at the computer next to the monitors at his head. She smiled, then turned her gaze back to the screen.

Rhiann sat gently on the edge of the bed and brushed Levi's hair back. The oxygen he was on had helped ease the blue tint of his lips and hands, but he still looked pale and so very small, lying there in that bed.

"I love you, sweet boy. Mommy's here when you're ready to wake up."

Patrick put a hand on her shoulder. "He should be awake soon. The anesthesia usually wears off in about half an hour, but sometimes it can take a little longer. We'll want him to stay here until he's fully awake and we've seen him drink clear liquids and keep them down."

"So everything went okay?"

"Perfectly. No issues with the procedure at all. I got all the images I needed and he did beautifully. Between the data we got today, and the results of his echo, I was able to confirm a diagnosis of Tetralogy of Fallot and get a better game plan in play for when we do surgery."

"What is that, exactly?"

"Did none of his previous doctors mention Tetralogy of Fallot?"

"No..." She racked her brain, replaying all the conversations she had with doctors, but she was sure she'd have remembered such a term.

"It's one of the most common cyanotic congenital heart diseases, but it's still pretty rare. In the simplest terms, it's four heart defects present at the same time."

"Oh, my—" She broke off, her eyes filling with tears. "Is it...? Can you fix it?"

"Surgery is a definite. That shunt they placed over at St. Thomas was just a stop-gap measure that's not doing nearly enough."

"And there's no chance of it self-correcting? Murmurs can self-correct, right?"

He shook his head at her, his expression softening. "No. It's far more serious than a murmur. Rhiann, he has *four* separate heart abnormalities. He has pulmonary valve stenosis that's reducing blood flow to his lungs. He has a ventricular septal defect reducing how much oxygenated blood his body's receiving. And his aorta is shifted. Those three are making his heart work overtime and thickening his right ventricle. I have to go in and do an intracardiac repair. We're looking at patching the hole between the ventricles and repairing the pulmonary valve, possibly replacing the valve."

Her throat felt tight. It took all she had to choke out a single word. "Prognosis?"

"If he makes it through surgery—excellent. But given Levi's precarious health situation surgery is risky." He squeezed her shoulder, as if to reassure her. "I'm afraid surgery isn't optional, though. If he doesn't have surgery his prognosis is not good at all. So I'll get my office manager to put the surgery approval request in to your insurance company and we'll get it scheduled from there."

"Okay..."

"Do you have any more questions about today or his upcoming surgery?"

She turned slightly, so that she could make eye contact with him. His hand dropped from her shoulder with the movement, making her wish she could rewind and keep the comfort of his touch.

"No. I think knowing all of the details will make it harder on me. I'll agonize over the minutiae and think of every single way something might go wrong and then drive us both crazy about it."

Patrick snorted and an impish grin lit his face. "Like homecoming sophomore year, when you psyched yourself out so badly that you left poor what's-his-face standing on your porch until I got there to calm you down? And then he wanted to fight me for stealing his girl and you punched him in the nose?"

"Shut up."

He laughed. "He told everyone I blacked his eye. Too ashamed to admit that *you'd* done it, I think."

The nurse by the bed tried to cover her snicker, but it didn't quite work. And when Rhiann looked over at her she saw the nurse's lips were turned up in a smile.

"What?" Rhiann asked her curiously.

"I'm sorry. It's just... I've worked in this department for over two years and I had no idea the Ice Castle knew how to smile, let alone laugh."

Rhiann narrowed her eyes at Patrick. "Ice Castle?"

He rolled his eyes. "I don't know what she's on about. I just come to work, do my job, and go home."

"You shut down, didn't you?"

He huffed, a pained expression crossing his face. "I'd lost everything that brought me joy in life. My job was the only thing left to hang on to."

She crossed her arms over her chest and stared him down. "You didn't answer my question."

"And I'm not going to!" he snapped, anger flashing in his eyes. "I'm going to go and check if the images are up. I want to review them one more time while everything is still fresh in my mind."

He hurried out of the curtained area like a pack of rabid dogs were on his heels.

She'd been so focused on what losing Patrick and then Pete had done to *her* life that she hadn't considered what the last few years had been like for Patrick. Yes, she'd lost the two people who'd meant the most to her, but they were both still alive and healthy. Patrick didn't have that comfort, small that it was.

Tears filled her eyes. Her heart hurt for the pain he must have been in. For the caring and loving man she'd once known to have forced all his emotions behind such a cold front, it had to have been bad. A protective measure, no doubt. She wondered how much force it would take to crack that ice, and if she'd ever see her devoted friend again.

"Oh, I didn't mean to upset him," the nurse said with an apologetic tone.

"You didn't. That was all me. Lord knows, I've had a lot of practice." Rhiann shrugged.

She stared out through the slightly open curtain for a moment, hoping Patrick would come back so she could apologize for inserting her foot so far into her mouth they might need to go down to the ED to have it extracted. They'd only just begun patching up the disaster that had once been a beautiful friendship and now she'd had to screw it up before they were remotely close to stable.

But as Levi started to stir, Rhiann shifted from concerned friend to worried mommy.

Once he was good and awake the nurse brought in a small cup of juice, and then stepped away to check on another patient. Rhiann fawned over her son, praising each sip of juice he took and every smile that crossed his lips.

"You'd think he'd just won the Nobel Peace Prize instead of drunk some juice from a sippy cup," a gruff masculine voice said from behind her.

"I think drinking juice should be a sport at the next Olympics," Rhiann said, a slight smile on her lips.

"I'm sure our Levi will take the gold, then."

Our Levi...

Rhiann's eyes teared up and she blinked them away quickly. She doubted Patrick had meant to claim Levi in the way her stupid, stubborn, hopeful heart had taken that statement. Levi's own father had even stopped referring to him as his son once the words "heart problem" had crossed that first doctor's lips.

Our Levi...

Those two little words made her want things.

Impossible things.

CHAPTER SIX

Patrick

UNSURE IF HE should apologize for overreacting, or just keep his mouth shut and pretend the little spat hadn't happened, Patrick stood just inside the recovery area nervously.

That was not a normal emotion for him.

Nervousness.

Scratching at his chin, he realized it wasn't just nervousness that wasn't normal for him. He'd hidden the hurt, hidden the pain, behind the venom in his voice and the frigid mask he donned each morning to block out all the emotions he couldn't bear, and he had been doing it for so long that all emotions felt foreign—too remote to be his own.

He couldn't remember the last time he'd felt anything but focused on his work prior to Rhiann showing up and ripping the stitches out of his hastily patched-up emotional state. Since her reappearance his internal monitors were going haywire. Not only had his blood pressure skyrocketed, but his heart sputtered and raced alternately, depending on her proximity. And he'd never considered himself an angry sort of man, prone to outbursts, but the anger he now hemorrhaged at the slightest provocation startled him.

He'd left and gone to change back into his street clothes to give himself time to cool off. When that hadn't been quite enough he'd gone to the staff break room for a while and stared out the window looking over the hospital parking garage. He'd watched people trekking in and out, in and out…

Like looking at the painting in his office, finding something to focus on had helped him calm himself. With time and space to breathe, he'd realized Rhiann's words had been uttered out of concern for him, not nosiness or anger. And he'd responded like a jerk.

That was becoming the norm for him when he was with her.

But he'd watched the gentle way she cared for her son and felt an intense longing rise up within him. The love she showed for her baby made Patrick's heart hurt.

He wanted to experience that.

The all-consuming love of a parent for their child.

The day Mallory had told him she was pregnant had been one of the best days of his life. He'd wanted Everly more than anything from the moment he'd known of her existence. He'd longed to be a dad.

But that opportunity had been ripped away from him. And he needed to remember whose fault that was. Why was he having such a hard time remembering that?

"Dr. Scott? I think we can go ahead and discharge this patient if you are ready to sign off?" A nurse interrupted his bumpy trip down bad memory lane.

"Yeah, absolutely."

He moved to the computer terminal and put in his log-on credentials. With a few clicks Levi's discharge orders were complete, ready for the nurse to implement.

"I'll be right back with his paperwork." The nurse left the little room, pulling the curtain closed behind her.

Patrick stood there silently, undecided on how to proceed. The rattle of a bed being rolled down the hall and the incoherent chatter of nurses and patients kept silence from overwhelming the small recovery area, but the only noise in Levi's room was the soft beep of the heart monitor and the occasional glug of juice from the sippy cup.

Rhiann and Levi both sat quietly.

"I'm sorry I pushed you too far earlier," Rhiann whispered.

The softness in her eyes spoke of sadness and regret and he was glad she'd spoken first.

"I may have overreacted." Patrick stepped close to her, taking her hand in his. "Truce?"

"Anytime."

The smile on her face sent his heart-rate up to a faster pace. He dropped her hand and stepped back, pretending to look at something on the computer he knew he'd already logged out of. Rhiann and Levi were getting under his skin and he couldn't allow that to happen.

He'd put some physical space between them and now he turned the conversation from emotional to logistical. "You ready to get this boy home?"

"Yes, please. But…um…" Rhiann winced as they made eye contact.

He lifted an eyebrow in question.

"Do you think we could stop by the grocery store on the way home? My car isn't going to be ready until tomorrow and I could really use some food."

More time with this woman who made him emotionally unstable and her sweet son who was slowly but surely cementing a place in his heart?

Why not? No way could that go wrong.

Saying no to letting her buy food coupled with the apologetic look on her face would move him into that class of men who kicked puppies for fun, so what else could he say but, "No problem."

The nurse came back with a few forms for Rhiann to sign and some discharge instructions. While they went over them Patrick played peek-a-boo with Levi, to give Rhiann time to take care of the paperwork.

The adorable baby clearly thought it was hilarious whenever Patrick reappeared, even if he'd only hidden behind his hands. And even though he was getting attached to Levi, and he knew that was a bad idea—boy, did he know—he couldn't resist the baby's sweet smile and rare giggle.

When the paperwork was finished, leaving them free to go, Rhiann picked Levi up and he immediately reached for Patrick instead.

Patrick caught him as he leaped from Rhiann's arms toward him. "You want me to carry you outta here?" He chuckled as Levi babbled at him. "I know—us guys have to stick together. Besides, there's a much better view from way up here, huh?" he teased, knowing Rhiann would take the bait.

"Are you calling me short?"

"Is your mommy short?" He tickled Levi's side. When Levi made a happy sound, Patrick pretended the baby had spoken. "No? Mommy's not short? She's just vertically challenged? Okay, maybe you're right."

"Ha-ha." Rhiann stalked out of the recovery room.

"Think we should tell her she's going the wrong way?"

Rhiann spun and headed back in their direction. "Lead the way, then, Dr. Thinks-He's-Funny."

Carrying Levi, Patrick walked toward the elevators. Rhiann followed along beside him.

Somehow it felt right having her at his side. Despite the past—or maybe even because of it—Rhiann just fit. But wasn't that just like history, to haunt a man with the memory of things he couldn't have, things he *shouldn't* have? It liked to jump in when least expected and parade out the memories. Then the heartache mixed with just enough of the good times tempted and teased him into wanting the impossible.

He tucked Levi into his car seat, making sure his restraints were buckled carefully. After climbing in to the driver's seat next to Rhiann, he finally made eye contact with her. And then he couldn't look away, even though he knew his eyes were probably giving all his thoughts away to this woman who'd watched him grow from awkward teen to confident doctor.

Her eyes widened as they stared at each other, not speaking…

Rhiann

A horn blared on the level above them, and Patrick jerked his eyes away from hers and threw the car in reverse. He maneuvered the sleek sedan out of the garage without glancing in her direction again.

Wariness filled her, and she was uncertain of his current mindset. Despite that, she would have sworn that he'd been about to kiss her. *Again*. Because she'd felt the same tension, seen the same look in his eyes, outside the recovery room earlier.

But learning how he kissed had been removed from today's agenda, it seemed. She sank back into the soft leather seat with a sigh of disappointment.

Patrick shifted at the sound, but didn't speak.

When they got off at the exit closest to her apartment,

she asked again, "Are you sure you don't mind if we stop at the grocery store?" She hated to push her luck with him when they were finally speaking again. But she really needed him to stop for groceries. "If not, my dinner options for the night will probably be plain ol' mac and powdered cheese."

Not her favorite, but that was about all that was left in the cabinets.

Patrick eased the car into a space at the grocery store. His shiny sedan looked out of place next to the dull faded red farm truck he'd parked next to.

He was unbuckling Levi before she could get her thoughts straight.

"You don't have to go in with me," she tried to offer. "You and Levi could wait here. I only need a few things."

She would prefer for them to wait in the car so that she could get the things on her list without the distraction the two of them combined would provide.

"Nah." Patrick smiled. "He and I could use a little exercise—right, buddy?"

Levi held his arms out to Patrick to be picked up.

Rhiann shook her head and walked into the store. She got a cart and tried to take Levi from Patrick, intending to put him in the seat. But Levi refused, clinging to Patrick like he might disappear forever.

"I don't mind carrying him." Patrick stepped past the line of carts with Levi in his arms. "Get what you need. We'll stay close."

Her little boy was soaking up all the positive male attention. It hurt her heart to think about how Levi would react when he wasn't seeing Patrick again, and she sincerely hoped that Patrick wouldn't push Levi away once he'd completed the surgery. If he did, Levi's physically broken heart might be emotionally broken.

She'd have to talk to Patrick. Maybe she could convince him to ease his way out of Levi's life after the surgery, rather than figuratively slamming a door in his face. Was asking him to take her to their appointments and shopping like this going to make it harder on Levi in the future?

She bit her lower lip and mulled that over. The Patrick she'd known and loved for years wouldn't have thought twice about helping out a friend, but he'd made it crystal-clear that they weren't friends and he wasn't that man anymore.

So why did he seem to be enjoying himself so much?

Deciding it might be best not to take up too much of Patrick's time, Rhiann tried to hurry through her shopping.

She grabbed a couple packages of meat that were on sale while Patrick made animal sounds at Levi, who tried his best to imitate him. The tiny little moos made her smile. Then she picked up some potatoes and a few other fresh veggies as Patrick touched Levi's hand to some of the produce, letting him feel the differences in texture and describing them to the very interested toddler.

Levi had never shown such interest in fruit and vegetables for her, and yet jealousy didn't factor in to her emotions at all as she watched how carefully Levi reached out and touched a kiwi.

When they moved on, and Patrick told Levi how awesome he was, and how he was way cuter than any of the babies pictured on the formula cans in front of them, Rhiann fought back tears at how amazing Patrick was being with her son.

Patrick and Levi trailed along behind her as she got in line and unloaded her items onto the belt. With heat flooding her cheeks, she dug a little stack of coupons out of her wallet and double-checked which ones she could use today. After matching them up, she tucked the others safely back into her wallet.

Her pride might be dinged by using her coupons in front of Patrick, but the five bucks she'd save would feed her and Levi for a day. When putting food on the table was a struggle, hunger beat pride any day.

She watched the screen as the teenaged cashier swiped each item across the scanner, wincing when the beeping stopped and the total glared at her in neon green glory. Even with coupons, and what little she had in her bank account right now, she was going to be hard-pressed to pay off the car repairs that she'd already authorized.

She sighed and thought about putting a few things back, but she and Levi had to eat.

"Rhiann, if you need—"

"Shh..." She waved a dismissive hand at Patrick.

She might have had to ask him for a ride, but she would *not* let him offer her money. The heat on her cheeks was enough to fry an egg, but she would not let him pay for her groceries. She still had a few tendrils of pride left unbroken in her.

She swiped her card and pushed in her pin number without making eye contact with the pimpled cashier or with Patrick. She bagged her purchases before the teenager could begin, placing them in the cart herself. Without a word, she hurried out to Patrick's car and waited for him and Levi to catch up so that she could load the groceries onto the backseat next to Levi.

She'd thought having to go to Patrick and beg him to help her son would be the hardest thing for her to do outside of actually letting her child be cut open, but having Patrick know just how far she'd fallen in a few short years might actually be worse.

She swiped at the hot tears leaking freely from her eyes while she waited.

The lock beeped and she grabbed for the door handle blindly. She had the few bags loaded and had returned the cart before Patrick had even gotten Levi buckled in. Sinking down into the passenger seat, she tried to wipe the remnants of her tears from her face before Patrick got into the car.

When he shut his door and looked at her, she cut him off before he could speak. “Things are just really tight with the car repairs and all Levi’s medical expenses. Okay? And that’s all I have to say about it.”

CHAPTER SEVEN

Patrick

Embarrassed tension rolled off Rhiann in palpable waves. She had always been a proud and independent person, and her financial situation had to be eating at her. He wanted to help, but wasn't sure she'd let him. She'd grown up with very little and had always been self-conscious about the fact. He couldn't imagine she had changed after being completely on her own for some time now.

After seeing what little groceries she'd bought, and how concerned she seemed over money, Patrick started to calculate potential ways to help her without it seeming like a handout or an insult.

He swung into the parking lot of a local restaurant. "I'm going to grab some dinner to go. What do you want?"

"I can't afford to eat here." Her words came out as a low whisper.

"Not what I asked."

"Just get yourself something. I'm all set."

She waved toward the three bags of groceries on the backseat, half of which were filled with food for Levi.

Her gaze dropped to her hands and she picked at a ragged cuticle rather than look at him.

"Suit yourself."

He left the car running and went inside to order some takeout. After a rushed glance at the menu, he ordered what he wanted and two more full meals of things he remembered that Rhiann had used to like, plus a trio of desserts as well. By ordering a third meal he could make sure she'd have a solid meal tonight and leftovers for the next day too.

When he returned to the car with the large bag of food she gave him a pained look. "Patrick—"

"I don't want to eat alone," he interrupted when he saw her pride stepping up to refuse the meal, playing it like she would be doing him a favor by eating with him.

It wasn't a total lie. He'd eaten alone for most of the last three years, and even though his determination was to keep people at arm's length he still got tired of his own company.

"Do you ever just miss having someone to sit across the table with while you eat? Or to sit on the other end of the couch while you watch TV?"

"Yes..." Again, her voice was barely more than a whisper.

"Me too. Let me eat dinner with you and Levi tonight. Please?"

From the silence in the car, he worried she might still refuse him, but finally she nodded and he released a cautiously held breath. Somehow getting a good meal inside her had become vital to his existence.

That realization disturbed him, though, and he spent the remainder of the drive to her apartment complex contemplating how he could care so much for her well-being when he was still determined never to forgive her.

A few minutes later, he pulled the car into the space where her car had sat that morning and turned the engine off. "If you want to take Levi, I think I can handle all the food," he suggested. "Then we only have to make the one trip."

"You would literally dislocate every bone in your arms before you'd make a second trip with groceries, wouldn't you?" she asked with the hint of a smile.

He winked at her, exaggerating the facial movement. "I'd have to turn in my man card if I didn't."

A small chuckle escaped her. "Fine. I suppose I'll carry my son—even though he has clearly decided that you are way cooler than I am."

"Well, we established years ago that I am, in fact, the coolest and you are just chopped liver." He grabbed up her groceries in one hand and the takeout he'd purchased in the other. "Now, lead the way before my arms actually fall off. I'm a surgeon, woman, I need these hands."

He followed her up a set of metal stairs in a breezeway that had more than a few patches of rust. With his gaze soaking up the general unkempt nature of the building he almost walked into her when she stopped at the top of the first flight to unlock a door.

"This is us."

Something in her tone told him to tread carefully.

She stepped inside and put Levi down in a playpen that sat along the back wall. "Home sweet home."

"It's…cozy."

Other words to describe the rundown apartment that wouldn't come across as an insult were few. *Cozy* had been the best he could come up with.

She wrapped her arms around herself and he could see her hackles rising in defense of the home she'd made since being on her own.

"It's warm and dry, and it provides everything we need."

"Did Pete take everything in the divorce?"

The question slipped past his lips before he could censor it. Emphasis on the *everything*.

He eyed the threadbare couch next to him. Besides that and a tiny television mounted on a small stand the living room was bare. In the small dining area a rickety-looking table was pushed back against the wall, with two mismatched chairs and a highchair off to one side. Only a few pictures of Levi in cheap frames decorated the beige blandness of the walls.

"He took all the things his family had bought us, and well…" Her words trailed off and she waved a hand around the apartment. "There wasn't a lot left."

"He got everything and you got Levi?"

A slight nod was her only answer. "You can put the food down on the table. I have to put the groceries away. Do you want plates or do you just want to eat out of the containers?"

"Containers is fine with me. No use in dirtying up extra dishes."

She put the meat and veggies she'd bought in the fridge while he watched over her shoulder. The kitchen held only a few cabinets, and he wondered if they were as sparsely filled as that refrigerator.

Her lips turned up in a shy, embarrassed sort of grimace that he thought was meant to be a smile.

"I'm afraid all I can offer you as far as drinks go is water or coffee. I wasn't prepared for guests."

She wasn't prepared for *guests*?

If he hadn't thought she'd boot him out the door, he'd argue that she wasn't prepared for *life* right now.

"Water's fine," was what he said instead.

She poured two glasses from a pitcher she pulled from

the fridge. "No ice maker, but this has been in the fridge all day so it should be nice and cold."

"Thanks." He took one of the glasses. "I got ribs, a steak, and some chicken tenders. Your choice."

Shaking her head, she argued, "You paid—your choice."

He raised an eyebrow at her and waited.

Finally she huffed, "Fine. If you don't mind, I'd really like the steak."

He pushed the container with the steak in her direction and took the ribs for himself, thinking the chicken tenders would reheat better for her the next day.

She put Levi in his highchair next to the table and gave him some of the mashed potatoes from her meal, along with a jar of diced chicken baby food that she'd warmed for him. The child picked at the food, barely eating.

Rhiann, however, devoured hers. She polished off the steak and both sides before Patrick had even eaten a third of his. He put some of his ribs and a baked sweet potato he had yet to touch onto her makeshift plate.

"I can't eat yours too," she argued, eyeing the ribs with interest.

"Please, go ahead. I'm not going to finish them," he lied, knowing he'd have to get himself something else later, or make a sandwich when he got home.

"If you're sure..." She picked up a rib and moaned at the first bite. "These are *so* good. How can you not want to eat them all?"

She had a smear of sauce next to her lip, and without thinking Patrick leaned forward to wipe it away. Her quick intake of breath and the way her eyes darted to his, sparkling with interest, told him everything he hadn't known he needed to know.

If he could get over the past he could finally get out of the friend zone with Rhiann.

Rhiann

Rhiann's heart pounded as Patrick rubbed his thumb along the corner of her mouth. For a moment she was transported back more than a decade, to a time when Patrick Scott had been her everything. It hadn't always been easy, but their friendship had been the most stable relationship she'd ever had in her life.

She'd told Patrick for years that she wasn't interested in dating him, but it had been a lie. It hadn't been a lack of interest. It had been the fear that she'd lose him. So she'd hidden her feelings behind jokes and even pushed him toward other girls—because having him as a friend was better than losing him if things went sideways.

But now every speck of interest she'd suppressed throughout the years was returning full-force. And while she knew she should look away, she seemed physically incapable of the task.

Levi slapped a hand in his mashed potatoes and white mush went everywhere. His peals of giggles and the now cold potatoes clinging to her nose jarred Rhiann out of her trance.

Rhiann moved away from Patrick's touch and grabbed a kitchen towel to wipe the potatoes from her face and then from Levi's fingers. "You think that's funny, do you?" she teased, wiping his little hands clean of the mess from his food experiment.

Levi had saved them from making a mistake. Even if she wanted Patrick to kiss her with every ounce of her being, she needed him to forgive her before they could consider any sort of relationship going forward. They were barely friends at the moment, and their platform was not stable enough to build any sort of future on.

"So...should I go?" Patrick tossed his empty takeout container in the trash before sticking the meal they hadn't touched in the fridge.

She smiled at him, glancing up at him through her lashes. Once she'd have boldly claimed the rest of his evening, but now an invisible hand squeezed her windpipe and her voice squeaked when she answered.

"I'd like it if you stayed. I've really missed my friend."

He shifted back a step, immediately throwing those walls back up between them. *One step forward, two steps back.* He visibly drew back into himself, like a turtle going into its shell.

Suddenly her heart began to race. Was she moving too far, too fast? She'd only just gotten Patrick back into her life, and their brief moments of contact highlighted how much her life had gone downhill since their falling out.

"It's okay if you don't want to stay," she added quickly. Not wanting to push. Not wanting to be rejected again.

She chewed her lower lip and hugged herself uncertainly. So her life hadn't gone exactly as she'd planned? Losing Patrick had certainly fractured her future plans, but she'd survived. Pete's leaving had been another blow. But she was a survivor. She didn't *need* Patrick in her life. Still, if she could prompt a reconciliation by taking things slow then she'd become a snail—because she missed him, and she really did *want* him in her life.

He rubbed the back of his neck. "No, I think I'd like to stay a while. Can I...?"

Waving a hand, he indicated that he wanted to get Levi out of his highchair.

"Go ahead. You can take him in to play and I'll get this cleaned up."

Rhiann took her time cleaning up the remnants of their meal, listening to Patrick's one-sided conversation with Levi. His light-hearted tone made her wistful for long-ago memories.

Leaning a hip against the counter, she smiled as she watched them simply enjoying each other's presence. Levi needed the attention as much as Patrick seemed to need to give it to him. That nurse today had called Patrick "Ice Castle", but there was not even a hint of the coldness it would take to earn such a nickname now, as he played with Levi.

Knowing how far he had shut down pulled the smile from her face. Her heart hurt at the realization that his grief had taken the loving, caring man she'd once known and turned him into a man whose coworkers found him emotionless. Patrick had always had the biggest heart. His capacity for love and compassion had never been surpassed by any other man she knew.

Things had got quiet in the apartment.

Heat flooded her face when she realized Patrick was staring at her.

"Lost in thought?" he teased, his blue eyes sparkling with mirth. "You've been staring a hole straight through the side of my head for the last ten minutes."

Her cheeks burned. "Sorry."

"Why don't you come hang out with us?" He tickled Levi and they both laughed. "I think this little guy might be getting tired of looking at me and would rather look at his pretty mama."

"I don't think he knows I exist when you're around." She moved to sit on the couch next to him and her words just tumbled out, almost by themselves. "Do you think he's getting too attached to you? I don't want him to get hurt when you're out of our lives again."

CHAPTER EIGHT

Patrick

"I'D NEVER HURT LEVI." Patrick bristled at her words. How could she think he'd ever hurt an innocent child?

She reached a hand out and touched his bare arm. The thought that he'd like her to touch more than his arm rose up from deep within him. But he squashed that down to focus on the more pressing concern that she thought he'd hurt Levi.

"I know you'd never *intentionally* hurt him." She let her hand trail down over his wrist to grasp his hand. Squeezing his fingers tightly, she continued, "Think about how he clings to you already. How do you think he's going to feel when you're gone from his life with no warning?"

"Why would I…? Oh."

She was going with the assumption that once he'd operated on Levi they would go back to never speaking again. He couldn't blame her for thinking that—not with how he'd treated her the last three years. And, honestly, he hadn't let himself think about what the future might hold for them.

He couldn't—wouldn't—look toward hopes and dreams anymore. Not after learning how badly it hurt to hit the bottom when those plans were yanked away in a moment.

"Who said I'm going anywhere?"

"Have you forgiven me, then?"

The hope in her eyes nearly did him in, and he saw it dashed when he didn't answer her immediately. An apology tugged at his lips but he refused to voice it. Even as they sat there, side by side, hands clasped, forgiveness wasn't something he was ready to consider.

"I see," she whispered, freeing her hand from his.

She stood and picked Levi up.

"It's getting late. I should put him to bed. And I think you should go."

"Rhiann, wait." He tugged her and Levi down next to him on the couch. "I don't want to go back to us not speaking. I don't want the hate that has been festering between us to return. I just—"

"You just still can't forgive me."

The smallness of her voice cut clear down to his soul.

"I'd say I understand, but I don't. Patrick, you're a doctor. You *know* that not everyone can be saved."

"Can we talk about something else?"

Anything else. Anything that didn't make him feel like a complete jerk for not being ready to forgive her. But Rhiann had been in the wrong. He was going above and beyond by even *being* here this evening and giving her a second chance at being in his life after her actions had cost him his wife and daughter.

"Someday we're going to have to talk about it. And we can't move forward until we do. Talk about losing Mallory and Everly."

"I can't talk about them with you. If you'd gotten them to the hospital faster they might have survived—or at least one of them might have survived." He blinked away what felt suspiciously like angry tears. "I just can't. Not now."

A muscle in his jaw twitched and she visibly tensed, waiting for his next words. He closed his eyes and took a deep breath, and he didn't open them until he was calmer.

"Please, let's change the subject. I'm not ready for that discussion. But I promise you I won't just disappear from Levi's life, okay?"

"Okay."

She stayed on the couch next to him, Levi in her arms. He knew not talking about Mallory and Everly was surely a bullet that they dodged today only to find that tomorrow's ricochet held twice the velocity, but he just wasn't ready to talk about them. Not to her.

"What do you want to talk about, then?"

He could hear the distance in her voice as she pushed him away, probably subconsciously. But if she could bring up the tough subjects, then so could he.

In for a penny...

"How long have you been struggling financially?"

"That's hardly your business." She glared at him, the glisten of tears bright behind the angry front. "We get by just fine."

An eyebrow raised. "Really?" He tapped the arm of the shabby couch. "We had a nicer couch in college. This tattered thing is worn out and probably older than we are."

She shrugged. "It was twenty bucks at a yard sale and better than having no couch."

"Pete really doesn't help you at all?"

Her gaze focused on a loose thread on the couch cushion, her slim fingers following to rub over the piece of string like it might answer for her.

"He signed over his parental rights and our settlement freed him of all obligations to Levi—financial or otherwise."

Every muscle in his body stiffened at her words.

"What?" Anger rumbled in his voice.

"You heard me." She gave him a sad little smile. "While he said he was on board with IVF, and then using a sperm donor, when it came down to it he really wasn't okay with the idea of raising a child that wasn't biologically his. He wanted a clean break from both of us, and I didn't have the energy for two fights. I chose the fight for my son and that meant letting Pete walk away."

With his fist balled up, Patrick brought his hand to his forehead. If Pete Blackwell had been in the room, he'd have rammed his fist down the loser's throat.

Anger coursed through his entire body.

He'd wanted nothing more than to be a father. *Nothing.* That opportunity had been stolen from him—ripped away in the space of minutes—and Rhiann's ex had thrown his child away like a used tissue.

"We sold the house. There was almost no equity, because we hadn't owned it long enough. I got Levi, my car, and the sadly low balance in our savings account. He got everything else."

"Doesn't sound fair."

She shook her head. "No, a baby with a messed-up heart isn't fair. Losing the most important person in my life because of factors out of my control—that's not fair either. Everything else is just reality. I grew up with nothing. We have what we need. I know how to survive on very little."

"Can you tell me what you ever saw in Pete?" He leaned back and studied her face. "I never understood. Was it the whole singer thing?"

Rhiann laughed a little, and looked lost in thought for

a moment. When she finally answered her words were measured and the answer seemed practiced, as if she'd justified her choice before.

"We had fun together once. The day I met him was the day after I found out my mom had stage four cancer. You were busy with med school and I was so stressed I could barely take a breath. My work partner at the time insisted I go out with her and some of her friends. We went to a bar where Pete and his band were playing. After his set, he seemed to make it his mission to put a smile on my face." She blinked away tears. "He made me laugh at a time when I desperately needed to."

"And after that?"

"I know you only saw the bad. All the concerts and festivals—all the weekends we went away when he got a gig somewhere that distanced you and me. You hated it when I went away with him, but it kept us connected. It probably kept my marriage together longer. And, to be honest, I didn't see his flaws until we started spending more time apart."

"You didn't see that he was a self-centered jerk who didn't care anything about you unless you were changing yourself to fit the image of what he saw as the perfect wife."

She shrugged. "Maybe I didn't want to see it? Did you ever think about that? No, you just sat there and judged my choices—you with your perfect marriage—while I did my best to ignore the cracks big enough to drive a semi through in mine."

"Rhiann—"

"And now it's my turn to say I don't want to talk about it."

Despite the hurt and pain they'd caused each other, and his deep-seated desire to rub it in by saying that he had warned her about Pete, he couldn't bear to add to her pain tonight by verbalizing his *I told you so.* So he grasped for another topic.

"Levi looks content."

The little one was cuddled up between them, sound asleep, tiny thumb just barely in his mouth.

"He does." She reached over and brushed a lock of hair away from Levi's face. "Sometimes I feel like I'm missing out with him. I spend so much time at work—just to keep a roof over our heads, to keep up my insurance payments so that I can get his medical needs handled."

"You shouldn't feel bad that you have to work."

"Tell that to my heart."

"Well, you know there's no way I'm going to be charging you for operating on Levi, don't you?"

"What?" She looked astounded. "But I can't accept—"

He cut her off. "I'm doing it for Levi. There will still be plenty of other hospital expenses to pay, so save your money for those."

They just kept on diving back into the deep end, despite his efforts to lighten things up. He decided another change of topic was in order.

"Do you have much of a commute now?"

It was a good forty-minute drive from her apartment to Metro Memorial Hospital. More than he'd want to drive each way on a daily basis. But it was only about twenty to County, where he'd seen her recently.

"Not really." She leaned her head back against the couch, exhaustion lining her features. "The station house I'm working out of is about three blocks east of here."

"When did you leave Metro?"

Pulling one of the throw pillows into her lap, she angled it between them and he recognized the gesture for what it was: a defensive gesture.

"Three years ago."

Guilt crept in—unbidden but somewhat deserved. Three years ago Rhiann had worked for Metro, widely known as having the best private ambulance service in the area. Taking a county job, particularly in a poorer county, had to have meant a cut in pay that she could ill afford to have taken.

But he'd thrown such a fit when Rhiann had showed up at Mallory and Everly's funeral. In the raw freshness of his grief he'd laid out all his accusations against Rhiann very publicly. In front of a lot of Metro Memorial employees he'd put the blame for his wife and daughter's deaths directly on her inaction that day.

Had his words gotten her fired? Or had she chosen to leave on her own from embarrassment?

He rubbed a hand over his face, angry at himself now for the part he'd played in her troubles. She hadn't done enough to save Mallory, but he shouldn't have humiliated her in front of all of their peers.

But in the time it took him to try to come up with some words that might somehow serve as an apology for that, without implying full forgiveness, Rhiann had fallen asleep.

She was curled up on the other side of the couch, and even in sleep her features remained troubled. She didn't have the peaceful look that followed most mothers into sleep. Even in slumber, she couldn't truly rest.

He picked Levi up and carried him into the only bedroom in the apartment, where he found a crib set up next to a full-sized bed and a changing table. Carefully, he laid the baby on the changing table and put a fresh diaper on him. Levi slept through the diaper-change. Then he placed the baby down into the crib without waking him, and covered him with the light blanket he found there.

Returning to the living room, he debated briefly on whether he should let Rhiann sleep there on the couch, but decided she'd rest better in her own bed.

He picked her up carefully, cradling her slight weight close to his chest, and walked back into the bedroom. Laying her gently on the bed, he eased the shoes from her feet and pulled the comforter over her. Bending down, he brushed a soft kiss against her cheek.

"Rest now," he murmured.

Leaving the bedroom, he walked to the kitchen, to make sure Rhiann had put the leftover food away and switched off the lights. Just as he was about to flick the switch, a stack of flyers caught his eye.

He picked up one of the brightly colored pages. The bold letters on the pink paper announced a spaghetti supper at the county station to help cover Levi's medical expenses.

She had to be hating the idea of a fundraiser for their benefit. That her pride was even allowing it told him more about her precarious situation than she'd ever admit…

Walking into his place a little while later, he sank into the plush leather couch and couldn't help but be struck by the differences in this couch and the one in Rhiann's apartment.

Feet propped up, head thrown back, Patrick grew angrier by the moment as he thought about how Pete had left Rhiann with nothing but a sick child and a growing pile of bills.

He moved to the desk and opened his laptop. With only a very small amount of digging, he found the jerk on social media. From his profile picture, it seemed Pete had moved on from Rhiann with a redhead who looked like she'd had more than a little work done.

With a few clicks he pulled up private messaging and

fired off a message to Pete, asking for a catch-up and leaving his number in a second message.

Almost immediately, his phone rang.

"What's up, Doc?"

Pete's annoying voice reached through the phone and prodded at Patrick's patience as surely as if he'd been there and poked him in the chest.

Agitated, Patrick paced the length of his house, trying to expel some of the anger.

"Never thought I'd hear from *you* again," Pete continued, without waiting for Patrick to say anything. "Wasn't like we were buddy-buddy on the best of days. So, tell me—why the sudden urge to reconnect?"

"I saw your son today."

Pete snorted. "You must be mistaken. I don't have a son."

"Levi." Patrick's hands fisted at his sides. He was already impatient dealing with this jerk. Man, he wished they were face to face so that he could punch Pete right in the jaw.

"Ah… You mean Rhiann's son."

"*Yours* and Rhiann's."

Pete made a noise of disbelief. "That's where you're wrong. Legally, that kid's not mine."

"How could you just walk out on your wife and kid like that?"

A wry laugh came across the line. "Don't know if you realized it or not, but things were never that good between me and her. D'you have *any* clue how many fights we had over you?"

Patrick ignored the jab. He'd heard jealousy more than once from Rhiann's ex. Pete had never been able to accept the friendship between his wife and Patrick.

"Do you know how much she's struggling right now?"

The line went so silent that Patrick held his phone away from his ear to see if the line had been disconnected.

When he saw it hadn't, he growled, "Hey, I'm talking to you. Do you have *any* idea how much she could use your support? How much Levi could use your support?"

"I told you. I don't have a son."

Patrick sank back down at his desk and picked up the flyer he'd taken from Rhiann's counter. "She's having a fundraiser just to pay his medical expenses. She's barely eating in order to keep your son fed."

"You know what you sound like right now?" said Pete.

The question hung unanswered, dangling between them like a live wire.

Patrick waited for Pete to continue.

The other man made him wait until Patrick was so on edge his knee was bouncing up and down with the effort of restraining himself.

"You sound like a man trying to offload a broken brat just to get between the mother's legs for a night. Trust me—she ain't worth it."

The anger that had been rising up within Patrick came to a boil. He slapped his hand down on the desk. "You listen here—"

"What's the matter, Doc? Can't handle the truth when it's thrown at you? Or did my words hit a little too close to home? You've been angling to get Rhiann beneath you for years—even when she was my wife. Don't think I didn't see the way you looked at her." He snorted. "If you want her now, you're gonna have to accept she comes as a package deal with that sick brat. You're a fancy cardiac surgeon, aren't you? Maybe she'll let you try to fix him? And if you're lucky the boy will die on the table."

Patrick vibrated with anger, knowing that if Pete

had been there in front of him he'd have had his hands wrapped around the loser's throat.

"I always knew you had the hots for her. Tell Rhiann *I told you so* from me."

Pete's derisive laughter lingered long after the line had gone dead.

Patrick knew he should have trusted Rhiann when she'd said there was no help to be had from Pete.

And he knew he should have denied always wanting her.

But it would have been a lie.

CHAPTER NINE

Rhiann

WHEN RHIANN LOOKED down at the screen and saw the California number displayed there she did a double-take. She'd taken Pete's number out of her phone, but she still remembered every digit.

"Hello?" she said with caution.

The last time she'd spoken to Pete he'd called to ream her out because the billing department at the hospital had left a message on his number instead of hers.

"I don't appreciate you having your boy-toy fuss at me about that sick little brat you tried to saddle me with," said Pete.

"I have no idea what you are on about."

At least he wasn't going to spend an hour jerking her around before he started in on her this time. Holding the phone against her shoulder, she waited for Pete to continue.

"Mmm-hmm. I bet you don't."

She heard the flick of a lighter and his deep inhale as he took his first drag off a cigarette.

"Your bestie hit me up last night. He's under the mistaken impression I owe you something."

"Who are you...? Wait, do you mean Patrick?"

Patrick had always been a point of contention between them. Pete had been jealous of their friendship from practically day one. If Patrick had contacted Pete, then there was little wonder Pete was upset.

"Who else, honey? I told you all along he was just biding his time and waiting for a chance to get in your pants. Tell Lover Boy to stay out of my face or he won't like the results."

The line went dead.

She closed her eyes and tried to think about what must have happened. Patrick had to have gone straight to call Pete after she'd fallen asleep. The man had some nerve. He really did.

An hour later Rhiann stalked around Metro Memorial, looking for Patrick. His partner, Clay, had told her she could find him doing rounds at the hospital when she'd stormed into his office looking for him.

The elevator slow-climbed up to the pediatric cardiology floor. The doors had barely opened when she shot through them, intent on finding her target. She started down the long beige hallway and spotted him talking to a couple doctors and nurses next to the family waiting area.

When she reached him, she grabbed his arm and turned him in her direction. "How *dare* you?" she growled out. "What were you *thinking*? No, you couldn't have been thinking or you wouldn't have done tit."

He blinked, confusion darkening his expression. "Uh...hi."

"What gave you the right to go behind my back to Pete like that?" The more she thought about it, the angrier she got. Her muscles were taut with adrenaline. Her fingers itched to slap his smug face. "I can't *believe* you would contact him. After everything I told you!"

Clarity lit his eyes. "I can explain."

"There is no explanation! I trusted you and you—"

Words failed her when Patrick pulled her in close to his chest. His arms wrapped around her waist. From thigh to shoulder they were pressed together, and his lips were on hers before she could push him away.

Warm, soft, teasing, his lips covered hers. He rocked his mouth over hers and his tongue licked along her lower lip until he coaxed a gasp from her. When her lips parted beneath his, he slipped his tongue between them and twisted it with hers.

The hand she'd put on his chest to push him back grabbed his lab coat instead, and crumpled it beneath her fingers as she pulled him closer.

A first kiss almost two decades in the making.

It was worth every minute of the delay. Delicious and tempting, making her want it never to end.

Kissing Patrick was awakening sensations that had been missing from her life for a while. She'd barely noticed men since everything in her life had fallen apart, but she was certainly noticing Patrick now.

She'd been so focused on Levi, on just surviving, that she'd barely managed to function. The only thing further from her mind than dating had been falling in love again. But the moment Patrick's lips touched hers she wanted things.

Like promises and forever.

Patrick eased back. When their lips parted they stared at each other, trying to process all the emotion and change that had come with a kiss of that magnitude. His stunned expression told her he was as shocked as she was. He probably hadn't expected everything that kiss had held either.

A snicker from his one of his colleagues startled her out of her reverie after that nearly perfect first kiss. Rhiann remembered not only where they were, but why she was there. The burn of embarrassment flooded into her face and she turned to walk away, mad at herself for responding to his kiss as she had.

"Don't go," said Patrick, his voice barely above a whisper.

He grabbed her hand and tugged her down the hall to an empty conference room. He ushered her inside and closed the door.

Rhiann tried to wrap her mind around what had just happened. Patrick hadn't been supposed to kiss her. That scenario had never come to her when she'd run through the possibilities for this conversation in her mind on the way over.

But when she turned to Patrick he hauled her in close for another kiss. Deeper, more intense than the previous kiss, it made her feel things she'd never felt before. The depth of emotion each of them poured into the embrace was intoxicating when combined. It took all her willpower to push him back.

"Stop—please." She pressed against his chest when he tried to recapture her mouth.

He released her and ran his hands through his hair. "I'm sorry about Pete. I overstepped."

"Yes, you did." Tears filled her eyes. "Then *and* now."

He winced. "I didn't mean—"

"What were you *thinking*? I told you how things were with Pete. I trusted you to leave well enough alone. But of course you always think you know best. And then, when I call you on it, your answer is to *kiss* me? You just told me last night you haven't forgiven me for Mallory and Everly."

"I thought I could convince Pete to step up."

"You thought wrong."

She wrapped her arms around herself, trying to shield herself from the pain that was sure to come. *This* was why she'd been determined to keep men at arm's length after Patrick and Pete had both walked out of her life. Men always hurt her, always let her down. And somehow she'd let Patrick get beneath her defenses and handed him the power to hurt her again.

"Why did you kiss me when you can't forgive me?"

"Rhiann…" He took a step toward her. His hand was gentle when he grasped her arm. "Please let me try to explain."

She moved away, pulling herself from his touch and putting the large conference table between them. "You can explain from over there."

"I'm so confused…" He raked his hands through his hair and looked at her like he expected her to give him some answers.

She had none. "You kissed me because you're confused? About what?"

"Us—this." He waved his hand between them. "One minute the past is all I can think about, and I hate everything about that day and the part you played in it, but then the next I can't imagine another minute without you and Levi in my life. I'm falling for you—not a teenage crush, like before, but the real kind of love that makes a man stupid—and I don't know how to stop it."

Rhiann stared at him for a moment, unsure how he could both insult her and tell her that he was falling for her in the same breath.

She shook her head. "How can you say you're falling in love with me and yet still hate me?"

"The line between hate and love is starting to blur."

With one hand on the doorknob, she turned to Patrick. "I don't have the time or the mental energy for this kind of confusion over another man who doesn't know what he wants. My life is about needs now. Levi's needs. And I need you to respect that. From now on I think it's best if we stick to the professional boundaries between a doctor and the parent of one of his patients."

Her eyes were blurred from tears as she made her way out of the hospital. Of all the outcomes possible today, the one thing she'd never considered was that Patrick would tell her he loved her and hated her at the same time.

He'd never forgive her for the loss of his family and she'd been stupid to think otherwise. There would be no promises from him, no genuine declarations of love.

And certainly no forever.

Patrick

Patrick was watching the video file of Levi's echo again when his mom burst into his office, the door slamming hard enough against the wall that all the framed awards and diplomas rattled. She held a sheet of hot pink paper in her manicured hand.

"Why didn't you tell me about this?"

She slapped the paper down on the desk in front of him, the ice in her tone rivaling anything he could have managed.

"Rhiann's son has a heart problem? That's bad enough. And they're having a fundraiser set up for him and you don't *tell* me? No, I had to hear it from Clay. *Clay!*"

He sighed and closed his computer, knowing this was not going to be a quick visit, after which he could get right back to work without losing his train of thought.

"Hello to you too, Mother."

"Don't you 'Mother' me. Why would you not tell me Rhiann needs help? You know how many groups I'm involved in. With only a few phone calls I can make sure this event is a success."

She sank down across from him with a huff. Her disappointment in him seeped from her very pores and filled his office with a cloud of *You should be ashamed of yourself.*

He shrugged. "I didn't think she'd want us there."

"*You* there. You didn't think she'd want *you* there." She raised an eyebrow at him. "The worst thing I've done is allow your grievances to keep me out of her life. I chose your side in the break-up, but I'm starting to think that was a dumb move."

"Excuse me?"

His mother waved a hand at him dismissively. "Now tell me the truth—how sick is her little boy and why is she having to hold a fundraiser?"

"HIPAA laws—"

"I'm not asking for his medical file. I understand you can't give me specifics. But are they raising money to take care of his needs or raising money to bury him?"

"Hopefully to take care of his needs," Patrick allowed himself to answer. He couldn't think of the alternative—not with Levi.

"And the fundraiser is because…?"

She let the question trail off, but he knew she wouldn't leave the topic until he gave her an answer that satisfied her.

"Pete left her high and dry. I don't have all the details. She'd probably be okay if Levi wasn't so seriously sick, but with all his medical bills, and everything associated with that, she's really struggling."

"I see."

His mom's face had tightened with anger. And that was an emotion he could relate to.

"Yeah, I talked to him the other night. He's even more useless than when they were together. I don't know what she ever saw in him."

"She wanted someone who wasn't *you*. She was trying to convince herself that you were not what she wanted. And when you came home from medical school with Mallory in tow, she clung to him, even though she knew he wasn't good for her. Probably tried to convince herself that she loved him too."

Patrick snorted. "I hardly think—"

"Well, I *know* you hardly think—or we wouldn't be sitting here having this discussion. And you've always been blind to that girl's feelings for you."

"She named her son after me. His name's Levi Patrick."

His mother's hand fluttered up to rest over her heart. "Even though you're a first-class doofus? If that doesn't tell you how much you mean to that girl you're a blind idiot—and I'm suing the hospital because you were clearly switched at birth. No son of mine can be that clueless."

"Mom!"

"So she's unattached, you're unattached…seems to me like there's a situation to be rectified there."

His mom's eyes twinkled and she reached over and poked his arm.

"We've had many conversations about that girl. I know you've had feelings for her since high school. And now it's time to put the blame away and move on."

"I think I'm falling in love with her." His voice was barely more than a whisper.

"I've been waiting for you to admit that for years. You sat on a stool at my kitchen island and told me all about that girl long before you even brought her around to meet me. I heard about every shade of blonde in her hair, how her green eyes sparkled, and even how perfect her dimples were. But that was puppy love—the kind no one expects to last."

"How can I love her when to do so tarnishes the memory of Mallory and Everly?"

"Oh, baby!"

His mother moved around the desk and pulled him into her arms. The scent of her perfume wrapped around him, comforting and familiar.

"Of course it doesn't tarnish their memories. You loved Mallory—and Everly too. I know what their deaths took out of you. But you've grieved their loss and now it's time to move on with your life. Mallory wouldn't want you to be alone forever. She loved you too much for that."

"But Rhiann—"

"So help me—if you try to shove the blame for their deaths on Rhiann again, I'm going to turn you over my knee like an errant toddler."

He swallowed back the protest he'd been about to voice.

She looked down at her watch. "Shoot—I'm going to be late. I don't have much time, so you listen to me and you listen good. That fundraiser is in three days. *You* are going to escort me there, because your father won't be back from his conference until Sunday morning. And I want you to spend the time between now and then in deep thought about the day we lost Mallory and Everly. Because you haven't been thinking clearly about what happened. Son, I love you, but you're letting your emotions overwhelm the facts. Rhiann loves you too much to have let your family die without doing everything she possibly could have done. And if you really think about it you'll know that I'm right."

She patted him on the cheek and left, her words weighing heavy on his heart.

He knew she was right that Mallory wouldn't have wanted him to be alone. Mallory had said as much once. But loving Rhiann felt like an insult to his late wife. Rhiann had been the last person to see Mallory alive—the last person she'd spoken with. His pregnant wife had bled out on Rhiann's watch and Rhiann hadn't done enough to save them.

When he'd lost Mallory and Everly he'd shut down his heart. And even if he could find it in himself to forgive Rhiann for not saving them, she had a son—Levi, with his dangerously damaged heart.

He wasn't sure he could risk loving and losing another child.

CHAPTER TEN

Rhiann

THE EVENING OF Levi's fundraiser arrived and not a moment too soon. The day's mail had come, bearing the medical bills for Levi's cardiac catherization, surgical and nursing costs, and the associated lab work. Her insurance only covered so much.

The bills were mounting and so was the stress.

Patrick had already told her he was waiving his fees, for which she could only be incredibly grateful, but the hospital wasn't being quite so generous.

Thinking of Patrick reminded her that he hadn't contacted her in the week since he'd kissed her. Despite telling him to leave her alone, and that she wanted to keep things between them professional, she'd secretly hoped he would call.

Nerves and all-out anxiety swept through Rhiann now, as she hurried around the station, straightening tablecloths and making sure every table had shakers of parmesan, salt and pepper. Specks of sweat dotted her forehead. She pressed a slightly damp palm against the green fabric covering her stomach and tried to calm the churning.

She sighed.

"Chin up, Mama. We got you. I put flyers on every

vertical structure between here and the interstate, And Jason covered from the station south, toward the next town."

Charlie pulled her into a big, comforting hug. Life would have been so much simpler if she could have fallen for a man like Charlie. Charlie was everything that Pete hadn't been. Stable, caring, and loyal.

But Charlie's touch made her feel none of the things Patrick's did. He was a good man, but he was missing the kind of connection with her that had the power to shatter her soul.

One of the guys from the ladder truck came in, distracting her from her thoughts.

He whistled. "Whoo-wee. That line goes all the way down the block. I hope y'all have a lot of pasta ready to go. These folks look *hungry*!"

"Down the block?"

"Oh, yeah—clear down to the stop sign." He smiled. "You didn't think no one would come, did you?"

She blinked away tears. "Of course not."

"We take care of our own." Charlie hugged her tight once more. "Now, go open that door and let's make you some money."

Rhiann picked Levi up and hurried over to the door. She propped it open and waved the first batch of people in. There was a donation bucket set just inside the door, with her coworker Jason manning it for safety.

"Thank you all for coming," she said over and over as people started filing in.

She watched as plates of spaghetti and crusty chunks of garlic bread were served and table after table filled up. Still the line continued.

It didn't take long before Jason waved the paramedic captain over to exchange the collection bucket for an empty one. He took it into his office for counting and safekeeping, squeezing her shoulder as he walked past.

Charlie came over to where she stood by the door. He had a wide grin on his face. “We’re gonna have to wait for this batch of people to head out before we can let more in. Apparently, we’re pushing the fire regulations.”

“I can’t believe this…” Rhiann said.

And she couldn’t. She’d hoped for a good turnout, but the amount of people filling the room was more than she could ever have imagined.

“I told you—we got you.”

Charlie winked at her and walked over to a small podium they’d set up.

“Hello, everybody!” His voice carried through the speakers. “To the folks still outside: we’ll be getting you in to get your spaghetti as soon as some of these tables free up. We’ve got more pasta cooking, more garlic bread getting toasted up and browned to absolute perfection, and we have more money to raise for that adorable little boy right there and his super-sweet mama.”

He pointed over to Rhiann and Levi.

The crowd broke into applause.

Charlie had to wait for them to simmer down a bit before he could finish his speech. “While most of you are still stuffing your face, maybe someone would like to come up here and tell the rest of us just how much Rhiann means to you personally. I’ve only known her for a few years myself, but already she’s wormed her way right into my heart and I’m not ashamed to say that she’s like family.”

Rhiann mouthed *I love you*, to her partner. Then she swallowed hard as a line of people made their way up to the podium next to him.

A young woman with an aura of fragility took the microphone. She waved at Rhiann.

"I met Rhiann when I had a car accident two summers ago." Her voice was soft, even with the microphone. "A kid on a skateboard rolled out in front of me over on Sycamore Street and I swerved to miss him and took on a tree instead. She held my hand while we waited for them to come cut me out of my car. I'll never forget her kindness that day. As you might imagine, I was a barrel of nerves, and she kept me from panicking. When I heard her little boy needed surgery, I thought, *This is my chance to come repay her, if only a little bit.*"

A hot tear slipped from Rhiann's eye, burning its way down her cheek. "Thank you…" she murmured, but doubted the woman could hear her over the crowd.

The next to take the podium was an elderly gentleman whose voice wavered when he spoke.

"I'm ashamed to say I wasn't very nice to that young woman over there on the day we met, but I hope she's forgiven me. My late wife had just passed away, and… well, I wasn't handling her loss very well. Losing your best friend after close to sixty years together changes your whole attitude. Anyway, Miss Rhiann came by my place to check on me, because my daughter had called and asked for someone to. But then she came back every night for a week, because she said I was a cantankerous old man and she found me entertaining. Our visits aren't every night anymore, and I don't need them to be, but she gave me a reason to get through the day during a time I had no other reason to. And I want to thank you."

He nodded over at Rhiann.

She blew him a kiss.

Two preteen boys stepped up to the mike next.

"Uh… Miss Rhiann saved us last year when we did

some things we shouldn't have." One nudged the other. "I *know*," said the one talking, with a glare at his silent friend. "She…uh…she literally saved our lives. We wouldn't be here if it wasn't for her."

She remembered them. They'd been playing with matches and had set something on fire in their closet. One of the boys' shirts had caught alight and she'd put him out before the fire truck had even arrived.

The tables emptied, new people trickled in, and the stories continued—car accidents, home injuries, elderly people who'd taken a fall. All of them had a story to tell. But the ones that touched her the most were those that told a story of despair and how she'd given them hope and brought them back to the light. How she'd bolstered them not just by fixing their physical ailments, but their emotional ones as well.

And, even if they didn't realize it, she knew that was what they were doing for her in return.

Patrick

Patrick and his mom slipped in while Rhiann had her back turned and was talking to someone else. His mom had dropped a folded check in the collection bucket, hiding the amount from easy view, but he was sure it was a nice amount.

He had the distinct impression that any check he put into the donation bin with his name on it would never be cashed, though, so he'd pulled out cash and made his contribution in five crisp hundreds.

The paramedic taking the money had widened his eyes at the amount, grinning when Patrick made the *shh* sign with his finger over his lips.

They grabbed their plates of spaghetti and he guided

his mother to a couple empty seats at a table in the back. By the time they'd settled down to eat, the circle of people around Rhiann had grown.

The dress she wore was in an ideal shade for her. Even from across the room he knew it was a perfect match for her emerald-green irises. Her smile was bright and wide, but a hint of tears sparkled in her eyes, visible even from across the large room.

Patrick wanted to take her in his arms and wipe all evidence of tears away. To tell her that a fundraiser wasn't necessary, because he was willing and able to provide for all of Levi's needs. Even if wanting to do that, wanting her and Levi, stabbed like a white-hot knife in betrayal to his wife and daughter.

When Rhiann turned in his direction he lowered his head and avoided her gaze. Twirling spaghetti with a plastic fork, he glanced up quickly to make sure Rhiann wasn't coming over to their table.

"You're trying to avoid her," his mother stated, accusation high in her voice. She swatted his arm and her glare could have boiled water. "John Patrick Scott—what have you done now?"

"Shh..." He took a bite of spaghetti and waved a hand toward the woman currently with the microphone. "I wanna hear this."

"We *will* talk about whatever stupid thing you've done this time."

He was glad he was surrounded by firefighters and paramedics in case his mother decided to act on the anger in her eyes. At least here, if she tried to kill him, someone should have the skill to bring him back.

He lowered his gaze again and pushed the pasta around on his paper plate. But he wasn't really seeing the food. His attention was focused on the outpouring of love surrounding Rhiann.

A steady chain of people were coming through the door, dropping money in the collection bucket and showing how much Rhiann meant to them with their presence. Men, women, even children were walking up to a makeshift podium and saying their piece. Each one shared a personal emotional story of just how much Rhiann had positively affected their very existence.

Rhiann wasn't just someone who flitted briefly into people's lives and then out on the next breeze. She made a difference to them. A life-changing difference.

Patrick listened to memory after memory crossing their lips as they recounted the day when she'd saved a life or rescued a loved one. They spoke of her bravery and compassion. Of her dedication to the job. All of which warred with his three-year belief in her wrongdoing when it came to his own family's tragedy.

Each time someone spoke of how she'd saved them, or their loved ones, his heart squeezed so tight he thought it would never beat again. His lungs couldn't draw air as a young couple showed off a chubby smiling baby whom Rhiann had rescued from choking.

She'd saved so many people in this community.

How could a woman who was so committed to saving strangers have allowed her close friend to die?

The angry burn of tears scorched his eyes. He pushed the rest of the pasta away. "I need to get out of here."

With one sculpted eyebrow raised, his mother looked him up and down. "Only if you're going to finally get out of your own way when it comes to this girl."

"Do you need a ride or not?" His voice was rough, and harsher than he normally used with her.

She waved him away. "I see several other people that I

know here—as you know, I invited several of my groups. And if I can't find a ride, then I'm fully capable of calling my driver. The question is, are *you* safe to drive?"

Standing, he pressed a kiss to the top of his mother's head. Then he did something that he'd rarely ever done in his life. He lied to his mother.

"I'm fine. Text me when you're home safe, please."

But he wasn't fine. Not even close.

Keeping to the edge of the room, he skirted around the crowd of people surrounding Rhiann. This was her night, and he didn't want his presence to spoil any of her fanfare. He stood by the door for a moment and watched as people fawned over her, over Levi.

The line of people coming in had finally tapered off. But the room was full of people who'd come just to show their support for Levi. And for Levi's mama and her contribution to their community.

Why hadn't she been the dedicated paramedic this crowd knew her to be when his wife and daughter had been dying?

His hand was on the door to exit when the paramedic captain stepped up to the podium.

"Since it seems like we're winding down here, I thought maybe you all would like to know how much we've raised tonight for little Levi."

The crowd shouted their agreement and the captain held up a hand, waiting for them to quiet.

"We've raised over ten grand for them tonight so far!"

Tears poured down Rhiann's face and Patrick shoved the door open and stepped out into the crisp night air, unable to stand seeing her tears. The cold seeped into his burning lungs and he fought back the urge to cry, to punch the brick station wall.

The drive home passed in a blur. He couldn't remember getting on or off the interstate, or taking the turns that had brought him home. All he could think about was the relief on Rhiann's face when the total had been announced.

He poured himself a drink and paced around his living room, trying to reconcile the Rhiann he remembered from the past with the Rhiann he blamed for letting his family die. Those stories tonight said she hadn't changed—that she was a consummate heroine who would have done all in her power to save a beloved friend, because she had done no less for hundreds of strangers.

Hating Rhiann for Mallory and Everly's deaths had been the easy part of losing them. He'd placed the culpability squarely on his best friend's petite shoulders, blinded by the rage of his grief.

The ER doc on call had told him that Rhiann and her partner had not gotten Mallory to the hospital in time to save them and he'd refused to hear any details beyond that—hadn't allowed Rhiann even to speak to him about that day, assuming her words would be filled with excuses and apologies.

Blaming her for the loss that had broken his heart into thousands of painful pieces meant he didn't have to blame himself for not being there for them.

The hours on the clock passed from late to early as he paced. Thoughts and emotions coursed through his veins. His heart still ached with the memory of Mallory and his sweet Everly. But when he blinked their faces were replaced in his mind with visions of Rhiann and Levi. And suddenly he needed to know exactly what had happened that day.

His office door slammed back against the wall as he shoved it open. Where had he put that file?

He dug through the desk before looking over to the

bookcase. The file from the day Mallory and Everly had died still sat unopened in its manila envelope, where he'd placed it the day he'd moved into this house. He'd taken it from the house he'd shared with Mallory, but had never had the courage to open it and read the medical reports.

When your heart was already shattered, why pick up a fresh shard and stab it through the pieces that remained?

His fingers slid along the back flap of the envelope and broke the seal.

CHAPTER ELEVEN

Patrick

THE TINY DROPS of blood that welled up as the paper sliced into his hand felt appropriate—right—given the pain that lay within this envelope. He deserved to bleed, to ache, as he read about the final moments of Mallory and Everly's lives.

Heart pounding, Patrick pulled the stack of paper out of the envelope and sank down into his desk chair.

A pale pink sticky note rested on the top, with a single sentence written in blue ink in Rhiann's familiar scrawl.

If you need to talk it out, call me.

Patrick took a fortifying breath and pulled the sticky note off. The top cluster of papers was Rhiann's incident report about the call. A form designed to keep emotions out of the mix, it needed facts, not opinions. But a few circular spots on the page where the ink had smeared looked like tear stains.

He swallowed hard at this evidence of Rhiann's emotions still lingering on the pages. Skimming over the boxes listing dates and times, he moved quickly to the second page, where Rhiann's messy handwriting gave details on his wife's last moments of life.

We were called to the scene of a collapsed pregnant woman with heavy bleeding at Opry Mills mall. Per Dispatch, the caller stated the woman said she felt light-headed and started swaying, then fell to the floor, with bleeding only noticed after she fell. The caller didn't specify the bleeding was vaginal.

As we arrived on scene I recognized the woman as Mallory Scott, whom I knew to be twenty-four weeks pregnant with her first child. Mallory was in and out of consciousness and only vaguely aware of her surroundings.

She struggled to remember my name, despite our long friendship. Cradling her stomach with her hands, she complained it felt like someone was tearing her uterus out. Beyond her description of the pain, she exhibited multiple signs of severe placental abruption and hypovolemia, for which our care directives recommend swift transport to Emergency Obstetrics at MMH.

We got her on the gurney and into the back of the rig. I put in a large-bore IV line and hung a bag of saline and started her on continuous high-flow oxygen while my partner radioed MMH to have OB and PICU on standby for our arrival. I also asked that they page Mallory's husband, Dr. Patrick Scott.

Monitors confirmed active labor contractions with almost no break in spacing. Uterus was tender and rigid upon exam. Visual vaginal inspection showed substantial bleeding. Fetal heartrate undetectable in the field even with multiple attempts.

I raised Mallory's feet and covered her with warming blankets for transport in an attempt to minimize shock.

A major accident on I-65 forced us to backtrack and take an alternative route that added ten minutes to our trip in.

Five minutes out from the hospital, Mallory coded. After lowering her to level I began CPR and continued compressions until we pulled in to MMH.

Hospital staff took over from there.

Notes: BP was one-seventy over one-ten—extremely high. Heart-rate tachycardic in the one-twenties upon pickup.

Patrick shoved the file across the desk, holding a hand over his mouth as he fought back a wave of nausea. Some of the pages flew off the edge and fluttered to the floor.

Three years ago, he hadn't wanted any details. Once he'd heard that doctor say the sentence "The paramedics didn't get here fast enough", he'd refused to listen to another word. He had taken the file, along with the day's medical notes, but had never opened the envelope.

He'd been wallowing not just in grief but in his own guilt.

He'd been away at a medical conference for nearly a week before they'd died. He'd flown in that morning and had gone straight to the office to see patients instead of going home to his pregnant wife. If he'd gone home that morning maybe he would have noticed something. Or at least if he'd been with them he could have used his medical training to stop the bleeding and save even one of them.

He waited until his stomach had calmed some before reaching for the on-call obstetrician's notes.

Patient came in via ambulance and presented with severe placental abruption.

No heartbeat detectable for mother or fetus upon arrival.

Caesarean section performed, but neither mother nor preterm child survived.

Apparent cause of death for mother: severe uterine hemorrhage leading to hypovolemia.

Apparent cause of death for fetus: placental abruption or result of maternal demise.

Patrick's chest shook with every ragged breath he took. A lone tear trekked down his cheek and fell with a plop, landing on the word "demise" and blurring the ink.

The chair beneath him squeaked as he leaned back away from the file. He sat there in silence, letting realizations and emotions roll through his every cell. With every word he'd read, his sorrow had grown. The only way Mallory or Everly would have had a chance at survival would have been if Mallory had collapsed at a hospital. Based on the timeline, though, even that might have been iffy.

Staggering out of his office, he wandered into his bedroom, where he sank onto the bed. For three years, he had held all his grief in, locking it behind a cold façade. He hadn't even seen what a toll that was taking on him until Rhiann had reappeared in his life and her sweet smile had chiseled a hole in his defense.

But now that she'd cracked the ice around his heart, those buried emotions hit Patrick full-force. The grief he'd hidden behind a mask of cold professionalism, the anger held contained by his clipped tone—all of it boiled up and ravaged him.

Waves of anger had him pounding his fists into the mattress, and the grief that followed shattered his heart like glass. But his grief wasn't for his lost wife and child, because time had already dulled that loss. No, this grief was deeper, because it had cut his best friend like a knife, wounding her, someone he'd loved for close to two decades.

All this time he had blamed Rhiann. He'd shut her out of his life and pushed her as far away as possible. But there had truly been nothing she could have done differently. She didn't have the training or the equipment to handle a severe placental abruption in the back of a moving ambulance.

After the way he'd treated her, the blame he'd shoveled onto her unnecessarily, how had she managed to forgive him? Because she had. He'd seen how she looked at him, the hope and the longing hidden behind her lashes and the soft expression on her face when he played with Levi.

And he might have ruined that.

He grabbed the picture of Mallory off the nightstand and started talking.

"You'd be ashamed of me. But it's been so hard without you here. I'm not even sure you'd recognize me now. Some days I look in the mirror and don't recognize myself. I shut out one of the few people who has always been there for me. I blamed Rhiann for taking you and Everly away from me. But I finally see the truth now."

Mallory would have kicked him in the shins for the way he'd treated Rhiann. Never once had she been jealous of the close relationship he and Rhiann had shared. She'd accepted it—no questions asked. And it was one of the reasons he had loved her so much.

Had loved...

The past tense on that thought brought tears to his eyes. But he could no longer live in the past, reminiscing over memories. He'd forgotten how to live when he'd lost his wife and child, but Rhiann had breathed new life into him and he had to move forward.

It was time for him to say goodbye and step into the hope of a future.

To fight for his future if need be.

And the first step in that plan meant he owed one woman an apology.

With one last look, he kissed Mallory's picture and then tucked it away in the drawer. With only the slightest hesitation, he pulled his wedding ring off his finger and placed it gently on top of the photo.

"I'll never stop loving you, Mallory, but I'm ready now to love someone else too. And I think you'd want it that way."

Rhiann

It was three minutes before the start of her shift when Rhiann parked outside the station. It wasn't like her to cut it this close when it came to work.

Charlie raised a brow as she ran past him to clock in. When she got back to the rig he was loading up to prepare for their day.

He gave her a worried glance and asked, "What's wrong with you this bright, shiny morning? Don't you see the colorful blue of the sky filled with white wisps of cloud floating by on the perfect amount of breeze?"

"Levi."

She grabbed her go-pack and started sorting through it to make sure it was stocked up for the day.

"I don't know if he's getting a cold or if his heart is getting worse. But he just clung to me this morning, and it nearly broke my heart to leave him at home with the babysitter. So, forgive me, but I didn't spend enough time looking at the sky to spout off any poetry about it."

Dread had pulled the sun from her sky and locked it away behind a wall of maternal anxiety. And the only breeze she'd felt had iced her limbs and sent a chill of foreboding down her spine.

"Poor kiddo…"

Charlie slapped a hand on her shoulder and squeezed. He'd lightened the intensity of his touch over the years, thankfully, and no longer made her feel like a nail he was pounding into the floor with his hammer-sized fists.

"We can go check on him on our lunch break if it would make you feel better? I'll let you out and circle around to grab some food while you go in and see him."

"You're the best, Charlie."

"I know." He made a face.

She smiled—her first real smile of the day.

"I met someone last night," Charlie said. "I don't know if it'll go anywhere, but she had me so tongue-tied it's a pure miracle I'm talking today."

Charlie let out a slow whistle. Rhiann knew what he was doing—changing the subject to distract her from worrying about Levi. His efforts were appreciated, even if they wouldn't likely be successful.

"One look had me thinking about futures and finding someone to grow old with."

Charlie was a serial monogamist. He fell in love as fast as most people changed their pants, and out of love again just as fast. He flitted from woman to woman, but somehow always left them with a smile—even when he'd dumped them. Whenever he finally fell for someone for real, she'd be a lucky girl.

"About time," Rhiann teased. "You were starting to look a little old, there all alone."

Charlie just chuckled at her teasing. "I've just told you I've met the potential love of my life—which you laughed at me about, by the way—so when are you going to tell me about what's going on with you and Dr. Silver Temples? Did you hook up last night?"

Rhiann gaped at him. "Why would you think that?"

"He was at the fundraiser, making moon eyes at you from the back of the room. I spent a good fifteen minutes talking to his mother. Lovely lady… I'm sure she made a nice donation."

Her hand froze, the gauze she'd been stuffing into her go-pack dangling in mid-air as she processed his words. Patrick had been there last night? She hadn't seen him. Or his mom.

She would have liked to have caught up with Marilyn. She hadn't seen her in years now. Understandably, Marilyn had sided with Patrick and stayed away after their falling out. But why hadn't they come up and greeted her? Or at least let her know they were there?

"Off in La-La Land, thinking about your dreamy doctor?" asked Charlie.

"More like Confusion County while I try to figure out why he'd come but not let me know he was there. But then again, the last time we spoke…" Rhiann trailed off.

Charlie made a noise of frustration and slammed a hand against the ambulance door. "You can't stop now. You're almost to the good part—I just know it!"

She laughed. Truly, though, she needed someone to confide in—someone who wouldn't be judgmental.

"After Levi's procedure, he drove us home and we hung out for a while."

Charlie waggled his brows at her.

"Not like *that*." She pinched his hand—a sharp, tight pinch to pull his mind out of the gutter. "Purely innocent…not so much as a kiss." She sighed. "But then he left my place determined to call Pete and make him do his share to help with Levi. Financially, if nothing else."

A huff escaped the older man. "Me and this doctor of yours are going to get along just fine. What have I been saying?"

"Shush."

She didn't want Charlie and Patrick to get it into their heads that they needed to gang up on Pete. She *liked* having him out of her life, and having them pull him back in was not something she had any interest in.

"So, anyway, Pete called me and cursed me out over it. And I went to find Patrick…"

Charlie leaned forward, eyes wide, eager for the next morsel of gossip she might drop for him. "And…?" He waved a hand for her to continue. "Gah—you should write for television, because you are *wicked* at the cliff-hangers. Woman, if you don't spill your guts right now, I might have to spill them for you!"

Her sigh was quiet, but weary with the weight of her confession. "He kissed me. Twice."

"Ha!" Charlie jumped up and pumped his fist in the air. "I *knew* it!"

Rhiann shook her head. "But then he told me that he doesn't know if he loves me or he hates me and that he's confused."

Charlie flopped dramatically onto the gurney with an exaggerated groan of dismay. "He's *confused*? Oh, geez…"

"Exactly." She brushed back a lock of hair that had

escaped her ponytail before asking, "And do you know who else is confused?"

Charlie propped himself up on one elbow and pointed a single finger at her.

"Got it in one," she said.

"I'm going to let you in on a little secret," said Charlie, and he crooked a finger at her, beckoning her closer. In a stage whisper, he told her, "We men are pathetic, stupid creatures who occasionally manage to hold it together long enough to get one of you lovely women to fall in love with us. If he mentioned the L-word, you aren't out of the game just yet."

"But was I ever really *in* it? I shouldn't even care, as long as he helps Levi, but so help me, I do."

The heaviness of caring for a man who was so ambivalent toward her settled over her like a thick fog, its weight bearing down on her and dulling her reactions. Between that and the crushing urgency of wanting to be with Levi, Rhiann was barely standing.

The radio beeped just then.

"Trust me, if he even *said* the L-word, he's thinking it. Don't give up hope just yet."

Charlie winked at her as he reached for the radio.

CHAPTER TWELVE

Patrick

TWO HOURS AFTER he woke up, his eyes crusted from the purge of tears and little sleep, he pulled his car to a stop in front of Rhiann's apartment. Her car wasn't in the lot, but for all he knew it could be broken down again. Hopefully she was upstairs, because the conversation they needed to have deserved privacy.

He couldn't be sure she wasn't working today though…

Anxious to see her, he got out and climbed the stairs to her apartment two at a time. His knock was firm, loud, echoing in the quiet of the mid-morning hour.

Shuffling noises came from inside. Someone was home, at least.

Unable to be still, he shifted from one foot to the other while he waited for her to come to the door.

At last the door creaked open.

"Rhiann, I—" He cut himself off abruptly.

Rhiann hadn't answered the door. An older woman peered out. Her hazel eyes narrowed suspiciously at him.

"Can I help you?"

Patrick looked at the door again—yes, it was the right apartment number. "I was looking for Rhiann Masters."

Her eyes traveled his length and calculated his value. Finally she deigned to answer him, once she'd deemed him worthy of an answer. "She's at work. You'll have to come back later."

A soft cry came from inside, and as she turned to look the door opened wider. Over her shoulder, Patrick could see Levi, lying on the couch. The baby's color was ashen and his breathing labored.

Concern washed over Patrick. "How long has Levi been like this?"

The woman stiffened up, clearly taking his words as an accusation. "He was ill when I got here. Rhiann knows that he's getting worse. I'm sure she'll be home soon. She's a good mother."

"I know that." Patrick shouldered past her and crouched down next to Levi. "Hey, little buddy. You look like you feel pretty bad."

Levi raised a hand toward Patrick, but it fell limply back to the couch. Only the faintest of smiles crossed his lips.

Patrick brushed his hand across the back of Levi's forehead, relieved to feel a normal temperature. He wasn't sure that he could handle the stress of Levi being ill. He tried to stay calm as he mentally calculated all the things that could be causing Levi's decline.

Had he picked up a virus while surrounded by all those people at the fundraiser? Had his tiny ticker reached its predetermined number of ticks?

"Now, see here—!" the older woman began.

Her bony hand dug into Patrick's shoulder like she might be able to physically remove him from the apartment. Patrick would have found it laughable if he hadn't been so worried about Levi.

"I'm his doctor," he said, without sparing her another glance.

Rubbing his hand over his jaw, he cursed himself silently for not bringing his medical bag with him. He'd never imagined he'd need it.

"What?" The woman's hand left his shoulder to flutter in front of her mouth, shaking. "I don't know you… How do I know you're telling me the truth? You could be a serial killer for all I know."

Brushing Levi's hair away from his face, Patrick stared at the baby again. He checked Levi's pulse with his fingertips and wasn't happy with the numbers. Without his equipment he could only go ahead based on visuals. Levi's breathing was ragged, and every breath seemed to be a struggle.

Patrick made a decision, scooping Levi into his arms. "Levi needs to go to the hospital *now*."

"I haven't called his mother yet."

"I understand that. But I also know that every minute we wait could put this baby's life at risk." He stared her down. "So, here's what you do. You call the station house and have Dispatch put you through to his mama. Tell her that I was here and that I've left with Levi to go to the hospital. If she thinks you need to call the cops, you can tell them to find me in the pediatric cardiology department of Metro Memorial Hospital."

"You can't just take him…" Disapproval and a smidgeon of fear darkened her face.

"I can and I will. Now, please gather his things and call his mother."

Patrick cradled Levi to him, the sound of the little one's ragged breathing sending a spike of fear chilling down his spine. The change in breathing when he raised him upright cemented for him the fact that Levi's illness was related to his heart.

He had planned the surgery for next week, but it wasn't going to be soon enough. Levi needed surgery yesterday. And Patrick could only hope that the baby was strong enough to survive it.

The babysitter stopped arguing and threw some diapers, a change of clothes and some formula packets into the diaper bag.

"Has he eaten today?"

She shook her head. "I couldn't even get him to drink any formula. Rhiann said he'd refused for her too."

"Is there a car seat here?"

She nodded. "I have one in my car that he uses on occasion. It's my grandbaby's, though."

"I'll make sure it gets back to you."

Pulling some keys out of a purse on the table, she walked to the door and leaned out of it. The faintest beep-beep came from the lot below.

"It's in the blue sedan. You'll need to install it yourself, because I haven't got a clue how these fancy new seats go in."

He nodded at her as he picked up the diaper bag. "Call the station and get them to call Rhiann. She needs to meet me at the hospital as soon as she can."

As he carried Levi out the door he heard her on the phone, asking the dispatcher to put her through to Rhiann because of an emergency with her son.

He talked to the baby as he walked down the stairs. "I hope that call doesn't panic your mama too much, because I think we're all about to have a rough day ahead of us. She needs you to get better. And I'm going to do everything I can to make sure you do."

It took a little maneuvering to get the car seat from the babysitter's car while juggling Levi in his other hand.

"This would be so much easier if you'd let me sit you down—you know that?" he asked Levi while he struggled with the car seat.

But Levi clung to him, and he didn't want to upset the baby when the little guy was already struggling to breathe.

"Here, let me hold him while you get it strapped in."

Patrick looked over his shoulder to see the babysitter, standing next to his car. She carried her purse and had put on a light sweater.

"If you're taking him to the hospital, then I'm going with you."

Levi let the older woman take him, but he whimpered in protest. More time had passed than Patrick was comfortable with while he fought to get the car seat installed correctly in his backseat. He thought about calling an ambulance, but now that he had the seat installed he could probably get him to the hospital just as fast.

He hoped.

While he settled Levi in the car seat, the babysitter got into the passenger seat. Clearly she'd meant it when she'd said she was coming along for the ride.

After finally getting Levi buckled in, he brushed his lips over the baby's pale forehead. His words were so low that only Levi could hear him. "You have to be okay. You hear me? I can't bear to lose another child."

Rhiann

Charlie had just pulled the rig away from the ED at County when the radio crackled. Rhiann sighed. That should have been their last call of the morning before they broke for lunch. She was itching to get home and check on Levi. She had a gnawing in her stomach, urging her to get home.

Charlie grabbed the radio after voicing a choice expletive. "What have you got for us, Dispatch?"

"Nothing for you, but I have an urgent message for Rhiann. Mrs. Bradley called to say that a man came by and has insisted on taking Levi. I'm afraid the call cut out after that. We're trying to reach her again and will pass on any info we get."

"Ah, crap…" Charlie fussed.

Rhiann's ability to breathe disappeared with the dispatcher's words. Tears started leaking down her face and she panted for air. *Someone had taken her baby?* The giant lump that rose up in her throat refused to be swallowed.

"Mark us as off the clock, will ya, Dispatch? I'm going to take her straight to her place. She's in no shape to drive." Charlie reached over and squeezed Rhiann's hand. "You all right?"

She shook her head. "Levi…" she managed to gasp on a strangled breath.

Her chest tightened until it felt like Charlie had backed over her chest with the ambulance. Lungs she'd used for years forgot how to breathe.

"I know—and I'm going to get you there as fast as safely possible." He flipped on the blue lights and pulled a U-turn at the intersection. The siren blared over the impossibly loud beat of her heart. "You let me worry about that."

Rhiann wiped the tears from her face, but more kept pouring down. Guilt welled up and threatened to choke her. She shouldn't have left him. She'd known he needed her and still she'd gone to work. What kind of mother left when her sick baby needed her?

In her brain, synapses fired and question after question filled her mind. What if he wasn't okay? What if the last time she saw him was to be him reaching for her and her denying him? Someone had her baby. Who knew what they might do to him? What if she never saw him again? Pete had said he didn't want him, but what if he'd changed his mind because of Patrick's pushing?

She gasped, fighting for air that refused to go into her lungs. "Charlie, I can't breathe. I can't..."

Charlie reached over and pushed her head down between her knees. "You gotta get it together. You are a strong, independent woman. We are about five minutes out and that's all the freaking-out time you get until you have the full details on what's happened. Do you hear me?"

Rhiann mumbled something that must have sounded like an agreement because Charlie continued with his tough love pep talk. Her adrenaline levels surged and her skin crawled with the need to do something, to find her baby. Sweat beaded on her face.

"Levi needs you. You have to be strong for him. Come on and breathe for me. Inhale. There you go. Now, let that breath out and get it to take some of that anxiety with it."

Rhiann kept her head down and focused on breathing and calming her emotions while Charlie drove them toward her apartment. Charlie kept on talking. She focused on the soothing, familiar sound of his voice, trying to keep panic and negative thoughts from taking over her mind and shutting down her body.

Her cell phone rang just then and she pulled it out. "Hello?"

"Hello, Mrs. Masters—this is Jeannine at MMH Pediatric Cardiology. Your son has been admitted here and Dr. Scott has asked if I'd keep trying to reach you. He said he tried to call you a couple times and sent you a few texts as well."

"I'll be there as soon as I can."

Rhiann hung up the phone and opened the missed texts. Patrick had texted her the same information.

"Levi is at Metro Memorial," she told Charlie. "Can you take me there instead?"

If Patrick had taken Levi from Mrs. Bradley and straight to the hospital, without waiting to talk to her first, Levi had to be in really bad shape.

Charlie drove on to Metro Memorial in the ambulance. Even though she knew there was a chance he could get into serious trouble for that, he never once said they should go back to the station for their personal vehicles.

He pulled up in front of the main entrance. "I'm afraid this is as far as I go. I've gotta get this rig back before they fire us both. But I'll check in on you as soon as I can. You're okay?"

She nodded at him and squeezed his hand. "As long as my boy is, I am."

Climbing out of the rig, she made her way into the hospital. She checked at the desk and was given a room number for Levi on the pediatric cardiology floor. The elevator slow-climbed up to the right floor, and it seemed that no matter how many steps she took toward Levi, she couldn't get there.

Finally she made it to the room. She swallowed down the massive lump in her throat and opened the door, beyond afraid of what she'd find on the other side.

The bed was surrounded by an all too familiar oxygen tent. Levi lay sleeping. A heart monitor and other monitors were attached to him, their green data constantly updating on the screens behind him. The beeps and bleeps reassured her that Levi was still alive.

"Rhiann!" Patrick called her name, relief evident in his voice.

"How…? How is he?" Her words stumbled past the sobs coming out of her mouth.

"Oh, Rhiann, my dear." Mrs. Bradley was talking. "I hope I did the right thing by letting this young man bring Levi here. I wanted to call you, but he wouldn't wait."

Rhiann stepped up to Levi's bedside, staring down at him, seeing how hard he fought for each breath.

"Of course you did the right thing. If Patrick says he needs to be here, then I trust his assessment."

Tears welled up in her eyes and she blinked hard. Angrily, she reminded herself that she'd had her breakdown in the rig and now she had to keep it together. Levi didn't need to wake up to find her flipping out at his bedside. He appeared to be having enough trouble without getting worked up over her being upset.

Patrick laid a hand on her shoulder. "He's struggling. That surgery can't wait. His heart condition has worsened and the time for waiting has passed. If you'll give the authorization, I'd like to do it immediately. As soon as I can get an OR."

All she could do was nod in agreement. It took all her self-control not to cling to Patrick and avail herself of his strength to help her through this.

The police officer in the corner of the room finally spoke up. He had clearly wanted to watch their dynamic and interactions before he decided to speak.

"We got a call from to say that this guy may or may not have abducted this child. What's your relationship to the child?"

"I'm his mother." Her eyes filled with tears as she

looked over at her sick baby. "And, no, Patrick didn't abduct him. He's his doctor and he's trying to save him with much-needed surgery." She looked up at Patrick. "Are you really going to do it now?"

Patrick stepped around the bed and pulled her into a hug. "I'll get set up and be back as soon as I have some news." Patrick brushed his lips against her forehead and squeezed her tight before stepping away. He paused at the door. "Now's not the time, but once we get through this crisis, you and I…we need to talk."

She raised a questioning eyebrow at him.

"Not now. First we have to take care of our boy."

He was out the door before she could think of how to respond to that.

"So, I don't think my services are needed here, are they?" The police officer grinned at her. "Finding out my child abduction case was just a doctor who cares too much for his patient has made my day."

Rhiann shook her head. "We're good. You can go."

"Have a good day, then, ma'am. And I'll pray for a full recovery for your little boy."

"If you don't need me to stay, I'll be going now too—if I can get a ride back to get my car." Mrs. Bradley patted Rhiann's arm and then shuffled out of the room without waiting for Rhiann's reply.

Sinking down into the chair at Levi's side, Rhiann started talking to Levi, even though she knew he was currently asleep. "Mommy is here now, sweetie. You are going to be just fine. Everything is going to be okay, I promise. I know it will be, because Patrick's going to take care of you. He's going to fix you right up so that you can grow up to be big and strong." She wiped a tear from her eye. "I have faith in him. And I have faith in you."

A short while later Patrick came back into the room.

He brought several people with him, including several nurses and, most surprisingly, his mother. "We've got an OR ready now. These nurses are going to get Levi prepped for surgery."

The nurses took the oxygen tent away from the bed and focused on getting Levi ready to move him to the operating room. The commotion woke Levi up and he fussed for a moment.

"Can I hold him for just a minute—please?" Rhiann begged.

At Patrick's nod, she picked Levi up for a brief cuddle. Knowing she had to let him go into surgery, and worried that he wouldn't come out, she knew she had to be prepared for the worst and yet not let him see. She blinked away tears as she eased him back down on the hospital bed.

"Mommy loves you so much. You have to go with Patrick now, but I'll be waiting for you when you get back."

Patrick grabbed her hand and held it briefly. "I'll update when I can."

CHAPTER THIRTEEN

Patrick

PATRICK RAN THROUGH the plan in his head, over and over. He controlled his breathing and brought his focus to this procedure only. Everyday stresses and concerns fell away as he breathed deeply. He inhaled and exhaled, clearing his mind as much as he could.

All the obstacles with Rhiann lingered.

Clay walked in, tying his scrub cap. "You know I'm supposed to have a date tonight? With a blonde who has legs that are longer than mine?" He faked a long-suffering sigh as he started scrubbing his hands at the sink next to Patrick. "*And* she's a gymnastics teacher. Do you have any clue how flexible she is?"

Knowing the type of woman Clay usually dated, Patrick had a pretty good idea. "I appreciate you postponing her for me."

"You're gonna owe me big-time for this. I think first stab at vacation time for the next full year and my next five on-call weekends."

"If that's what it takes," Patrick said dryly, picking up the antimicrobial soap and beginning his scrub.

The scent of the soap wafted up as he started sanitizing his hands.

"Today has been an emotional roller coaster for me," he told his partner. "Last night I finally read through the medical reports from the day Mallory and Everly died. Then I went to talk to Rhiann and found Levi in this condition. I'm already on edge, and this kid has managed to dig his way right through me. I don't know if I can take it if things go south."

Clay considered his words for a moment before speaking, and to Patrick's relief he didn't mention the medical reports and focused on the living child they could save.

"Well, you're probably too close to be one hundred percent objective. In fact, you might want to let me be the lead surgeon on this one. You know I've worked on several TOF cases."

Patrick shook his head. "No, I need to be the one to do this."

Determination filled him like never before. This surgery was something he couldn't pass off to Clay. He hadn't been around when Mallory and Everly had needed him. He'd let them down. But there was no way he was going to let Levi down. He had to do this himself.

Clay nudged him with his shoulder, taking care not to contaminate their scrubs. "And I need to be here to make sure you do. You know I got you, partner."

"Let's do this."

They moved into the surgical suite, where the scrub nurse helped them gown and glove. Levi was already on the table, intubated and still.

Patrick drew himself up momentarily. Seeing Levi spread out, unconscious, looking so tiny and frail, was almost too much. He sucked in a deep breath.

"I can do it," Clay offered again. "Let me help you."

"No." Patrick stepped up to the surgical table. "He's my patient and I've got this. Scalpel."

Patrick hesitated only briefly before slicing through the soft skin on Levi's chest. When he got him open, he found that the ventricular septal defect in Levi's heart was worse than the tests had shown.

"So…is it this little guy that's broken through the ice around your frozen heart or his hot mama that's got you thawing?"

"Shut up, Clay," Patrick growled as he prepared a synthetic patch.

He was getting through this surgery by pretending Levi was just another patient. He didn't need Clay to remind him that one mistake could cost him the child who had come to mean so much to him.

"Ah… I'll take that as both." Clay watched from Patrick's side, ready to step in at the first sign of trouble. "About time you got out of your own way a little bit."

"I mean it, Clay…"

Despite the defect being more difficult than he'd anticipated, and Clay's constant annoying chatter, Patrick was soon able to get the tiny patch in place and thus reroute the blood flow in Levi's heart over to the path that it should have taken from the start. Then he replaced the pulmonary valve that was too small and too delicate to be widened.

"Can someone send an update to his mother to say that things are going well so far?" he murmured, as he remembered what he'd promised Rhiann.

"I will, Dr. Scott." One of the nurses stepped away to make the update.

"You think we need to resect some of the tissue in the right ventricle?" Clay asked. "I think he's got a little too much to return to normal thickness on its own, don't you?"

Patrick nodded, and began the cut to remove the obstructive muscle tissue narrowing the pathway through Levi's right ventricle. After he'd finished that, and carefully checked that the blood would flow out from the left ventricle into the aorta, he closed, doing his best to match up the sides of the incision to minimize scarring.

Some scarring was unavoidable, but Patrick always did what he could to make sure he left as little a reminder as possible. Heart surgery kids had enough on their little plates without adding the self-esteem issues a giant scar might bring.

He took his time scrubbing down. Now that it was over, the emotions he'd suppressed during the lengthy, complex surgery were welling up, and he was struggling to keep his cool. The surgery had gone far more smoothly than he could have even hoped, but Levi still had a long recovery ahead of him.

The baby was weak, despite Patrick's careful management of blood loss, and it was going to be several long days before he could truly relax his guard.

But for now he had to give Rhiann the news that Levi had made it through surgery successfully, and that was something he could smile about.

And he'd go tell her about how well it had gone once he could get his hands to quit shaking…

"I guess you didn't need me after all." Clay looked at the clock.

"I guess not." Patrick dried his hands and leaned against the sink. "Thank you."

Clay shrugged. "That little one's mama is good for you. I'm starting to see hints of the old you peeking out behind the turrets on the ice castle."

With a snort, Patrick shook his head at his partner.

"I'm gonna head out now and see if I can catch a late dinner with Flexible Felicia."

Clay left, in a hurry to get away from the hospital and spend some time with his flavor of the evening. One day Clay might meet someone who would make him settle down, but Patrick had doubts that it would be the gymnast.

After a deep stretch, to try to loosen up the tight muscles in his back, Patrick walked out of the scrub room to find Rhiann.

Rhiann

Pacing from the door to the update board, Rhiann impatiently awaited news on Levi. Each time the board flickered as a case was updated Rhiann and the other anxiously waiting family members would hurry forward to check if it was their loved one with an update.

When the update wasn't for Levi, she continued her agitated strides from one side of the room to the other and back.

The update board listed each person as a case number—nothing identifiable. The assigned numbers sat there on their last update. Some said, "Surgery started" for forty minutes before updating to a "Going as expected." Others flashed more frequently, adding updates that the patient was "Doing well" or "Doing fine." The ones that switched over to "Closing, doing fine" or "In Recovery" earned a relieved gasp or a tearful hug.

When an update finally flashed up saying Levi's surgery was "Going well so far," Rhiann felt sick with relief.

"Honey, why don't you come sit down here with me for just a minute now you've had some news?" Marilyn Scott asked from her chair along the wall nearest the exterior doors. She patted the faded beige seat beside her.

The levels of anxiety building inside her, despite the

update, made that an almost impossible task, but nevertheless Rhiann found herself in the seat next to Patrick's mother. The low-backed chair put an instant ache in her back.

She looked around the room at the other seating options. Upright chairs and narrow couches made semicircles in various configurations around the large waiting room. Along the outer glass wall a series of backless benches rested, keeping the view of the valet stand and parking garage as unobstructed as possible. All were covered in shades of beige or gray. None were comfortable.

"I'm not sure why you're here, but thank you for waiting with me," Rhiann told the older woman.

Some patients had a group of family there, offering their support, taking up more than their share of the waiting room. Most of the pediatric patients had both parents, or a parent and a grandparent. Rhiann had thought she'd be the one sitting alone in a corner somewhere, holding a book she pretended to read. Or pacing back and forth, carrying all her things and the clear plastic drawstring bag full of Levi's clothes because she had no one to watch them if she left them sitting there.

"It's nice not being alone for once. But I'll understand if you need to go."

"I'm here because Patrick asked me to be. Precisely because he didn't think you should be alone." Marilyn patted her hand, shivering when the automatic doors whooshed open and let in a cold breeze.

"We should move away from these doors."

Rhiann didn't want the older woman to come down with a cold just because she'd been kind enough to keep her from being alone. She pointed to a spot under an arch, across from the surgery information desk. Marilyn nodded and they gathered their things to move over there.

"Why would Patrick do that?" asked Rhiann.

Marilyn settled down on the small couch and sighed when she felt the heat was on. She looked far more comfortable on this side of the room.

"Because you matter to him—don't you realize that?"

Rhiann's heart warmed at the knowledge that Patrick had not only thought of her needs, but acted on them to make sure she had everything. That was the Patrick who had earned the title of her best friend. That was the loving, caring friend she'd been broken-hearted to lose. It was nice to see him starting to be the man she knew him to be again.

Overhead, a creaky male voice announced over the PA system that they were conducting a test on their alert system and for everyone to ignore the incoming message. Despite that, when all the phones in the room rang, or buzzed, everyone looked at their screens hopefully.

A collective sigh echoed in the cavernous space when the words on the screen read, This is a test. Soon, the chatter of voices rose back to pre-announcement levels and settled into a loud and overwhelming din. Nothing distinct.

Returning to her conversation with Patrick's mother, Rhiann tried to rationalize his actions. "We were friends for years. I think having this contact over Levi has made him feel a bit responsible and want to help me. That's all."

Mrs. Scott made a tsking noise with her tongue. "I remember you, and your friendship with Patrick, and his asking me to be here has very little to do with that. This is entirely about my son falling for you and your little boy."

Rhiann blushed at the frankness in the older woman's words. "I'm sure you're mistaken. If Patrick has any emotion for me it's hatred, because I couldn't save his family."

She looked away and watched a window-cleaning

crew set up to clean the massive amounts of glass around the waiting room. The crew added a new layer of noise to the already loud room. The buckles on their harnesses clanked. Squeegees squeaked. But even the additional noise couldn't distract her from the uncomfortable encounter she found herself having with Patrick's mother.

Mrs. Scott laid a hand on Rhiann's knee, bringing her back to the conversation she was trying to avoid. "Hmm… I think I know my son better than that. For the record, I never blamed you for Mallory and Everly's deaths. And I told my son he was a moron for doing so."

Rhiann blinked away tears. She couldn't let herself start crying or she might not stop. "I could use some coffee. How about you?"

"I'm fine, dear."

Rhiann hopped up and hurried over to the busy coffee cart next to the surgery information desk. She ordered coffee and a pumpkin muffin, taking her time adding cream and sugar before she made her way back over to Patrick's mom.

She sipped at the coffee and pulled a face as she sat back down. "Ugh. This coffee is almost as bad as the station's sludge."

Mrs. Scott raised an eyebrow. "But they look so busy?"

"Location is everything. And most of their customers are probably patients' family, like me, and don't know any better." She shrugged, taking another sip. "At least the muffin is decent—if a little dry."

"I think my son is falling in love with you."

Heat flamed in Rhiann's cheeks and she dropped her head, wishing she'd taken her hair down from her normal work up-do simply so that she could hide behind its length.

Patrick's mom watched her reaction and smiled. Her

voice was softer now, kinder. "And if I'm not mistaken you are feeling the same way about him, aren't you?"

"I—" Rhiann's reply was interrupted by the buzz of the cell phone in her hand. She jumped up as soon as she read the words on the screen.

Please come to the pediatric surgery desk.

When she looked up Patrick stood just beyond the desk, a wide smile lighting his handsome face.

CHAPTER FOURTEEN

Patrick

WHEN HE MADE eye contact with Rhiann and smiled, her face went from anxious to relieved. Then she closed the last few steps between them and launched herself into his arms. Sobbing against his chest, she clung to him, barely staying upright.

"Levi's in Recovery," he said to the top of her head.

He held her close and murmured reassurances in her ear, telling her that the surgery had gone well and Levi was doing fine. The relief pouring off her was palpable, and seeped down deep into his soul. The tautness that had plagued his muscles since he'd walked into Rhiann's apartment so many hours ago and seen Levi in such distress dissipated in the warmth of her embrace.

As a surgeon, he didn't allow himself to dwell on losing his patients. Death was an unfortunate possibility in his line of work, but he didn't like to think about it. It wasn't that thinking of it made the likelihood increase, but there was no point tempting fate, right?

Some patients were harder to heal than others. The more damage he saw on the scans, the more his concern rose. Others he never once imagined he might lose. But each new patient was a fresh start—a chance to shake off any disastrous outcomes that had come before. Not that he had a lot of negative outcomes. He was one of the best pediatric cardiologists in the southeast, and that wasn't an ego thing. He had the success rate to back his claims.

With Levi, though, his nerves had been ragged from the start of surgery. Levi's wellbeing had become critically important to him. The churning in his stomach hadn't eased after closing. The lump in his throat that refused to be swallowed hadn't budged even once Levi had moved to recovery. Only now, when he had Rhiann in his arms, did any of that change.

Pulling her closer, he let his eyes drift shut as a sense of peace washed over him. Her height was perfect for him to rest his cheek on the top of her head. Having Rhiann in his arms shouldn't feel like coming home, like a balm for his discontented heart, but to say it didn't would be lying to himself.

As a teen, he'd wanted to be more than friends with Rhiann, but he couldn't remember ever feeling quite *this* way about her.

That seemed to be his normal lately. Finding new emotions where there had once just been ice. Contentment where there had been only apathy. Tendrils of want replacing sparks of anger. And he was learning to accept that change was inevitable—particularly when it came to his relationship with Rhiann.

His mother came up behind Rhiann, a hopeful smile on her face and questions filling her eyes. "How is he?" she asked.

Still holding Rhiann, because he couldn't seem to let her go, he answered, "Levi's in Recovery. The surgery went well. He's got a long way to go, but he made it through surgery like a champ. The next twenty-four to forty-eight hours will be the biggest mountain he has to climb."

His mother let out a shaky breath. "I'm sure he'll do great with the two of you at his bedside. If he's okay for now, then I'll be back in the morning to check on him. But you call me if you need anything." She reached out and tucked a loose lock of hair away from Rhiann's face with a gentle touch. "Either of you."

Patrick wrapped an arm around his mother and pulled her into a three-way hug with Rhiann. Having a mother like his made him a lucky man.

"Thank you for always coming when I call. I love you, Mom."

She pinched his cheek like he was five and he tried not to squirm. He loved her, despite her determination to make him die of embarrassment.

"That's what us moms do."

With Rhiann still tucked under his arm, he watched as his mother gathered up her things and bustled out of the waiting room with the grace he had always admired about her. She never got flustered, or angry, and he only wished he'd inherited more of her temperament than the more volatile disposition he got from his father.

"So," he said, looking down at the beautiful woman in his arms. He wiped the tears from her face with his thumbs. "Are you ready to see your son?"

Rhiann nodded.

"Then let's go."

Keeping a loose arm around her waist, Patrick led her through the hospital and past a few *Employees Only* signs. Finally he swiped his ID badge at the back door of the recovery room.

Nudging her into the bathroom along the right-hand

side, he said, "Go wash your face first. You don't want Levi to see you looking like that."

She brought a hand up to her face. "Is that a subtle way of saying I'm a hot mess?"

"A gorgeous mess." Even the teary streaks marring her cheeks couldn't take anything from her beauty. "I'll be right here."

A few minutes later Rhiann stepped out, her face freshly scrubbed and her hair now loose and tumbling in thick waves around her shoulders.

He pulled her close and brushed his lips against hers, finding comfort in her touch. But it was the wrong place, the wrong time, so he quickly moved away.

"He's right this way."

He engulfed her hand with his own, acutely aware of how much smaller her hand was compared to his. Following his lead, she moved with him through the recovery ward and down to Curtain Five.

"He's still intubated, and I'd like to keep him that way for about twenty-four hours. We don't want him moving too much just yet and undoing all the repairs I just so painstakingly made."

She reached out with a tentative hand and brushed back a lock of Levi's hair. "But he's doing okay?"

"He is doing as well as can be expected, considering how sick he was and how invasive the surgery was."

The last thing he wanted to do was give her false hope. Levi wasn't out of the woods yet. But he was hoping for a good outcome. More than hoping, really.

Because while losing Mallory and Everly had broken him, he knew losing Levi would shatter him beyond repair.

Rhiann

The twenty-four hours following Levi's surgery had passed in a blur. Bleary-eyed and exhausted, Rhiann dozed in the green misery the hospital referred to as "a recliner" in Levi's room. She refused to leave. How could she leave him there all alone?

Levi lay there, looking so small. She watched the machines that documented his bodily functions and could probably have recited each stat by heart. Her little fighter—he wouldn't give up. She wouldn't let him give up. *Couldn't* let him give up.

The nurses came in and out, their faces somber, and Rhiann couldn't help but wonder if they knew something she didn't. But they couldn't comprehend the pain she was suffering, watching Levi go through this ordeal.

The waiting was almost unbearable. Waiting for him to wake up. Waiting for a sign that he was getting better. But the monitors only showed the same numbers they'd shown all day.

When Patrick came in she practically pounced on him, begging him to be honest with her about Levi's condition, worried he was hiding something crucial from her.

He pulled her into his arms and held her close, comforting her with his physical presence. "Like I told you earlier, it's a waiting game now. We just have to wait and see if he's strong enough to pull through."

Patrick did his best to distract her and he even brought her some lunch. "Come on, Rhiann. You have to eat something."

He waved a chicken tender under her nose and she battled back a wave of nausea.

"The hospital food isn't great, but you need something in your stomach."

How could she eat? With her baby lying there in that hospital bed, tubes coming out of his tiny body?

Her stomach roiled with every nibble she took to placate Patrick.

"You'll feel better once you eat," he insisted. "I'll bring some real food in tonight, if you tell me what you want."

All she wanted was for Levi to get better. And Patrick couldn't do any more to help with that.

She ate enough of the chicken he'd brought to get him to hush, but she didn't really have the appetite for any of it. Seeing her eat seemed to chase a few shadows from Patrick's eyes, though, so she was glad she'd eaten if only for that reason.

He sank into a seated position at her feet. "I'm hoping that having him intubated for a day or so will give him time to gain a little strength. Maybe another twelve to twenty-four hours. I don't know yet."

"But the longer he's on the ventilator, the harder it will be for him to come off it, right?"

Patrick reached for her hand and she allowed the touch. "Yes. But don't give up hope. It's not time for that. I promise you, I feel good about his chances."

His fingers were warm on hers and the sensations created when his thumb moved back and forth over her palm provided a much-needed distraction.

"I've missed this," she said softly, not wanting to ruin the intimacy of the moment.

He raised an eyebrow. "Me sitting on the floor, looking up at you?"

"Of course—bow before your queen, peasant."

A snort came in reply.

"I meant us just hanging out together. I hate the locale and the circumstance, but I've missed *this*."

Leaning forward, he brushed his lips against her wrist. "You know, I think we spent half our free time in high school sitting like this. You perched on one of our beds and me on the floor below you, because if either of our mothers had caught us on a bed together—even fully clothed and obviously studying—they'd have lost their minds."

She laughed. "I know. Remember how my mom freaked out when we fell asleep on the couch, watching one of the *Halloween* movies?"

They spent the next few hours reminiscing, finding contentment in each other's presence.

When it came time for Patrick to leave, Rhiann noticed his hesitation.

"We'll still be here in the morning," she said, and gave him a quick hug.

This time he was quick enough to hug her back.

"I hate leaving you here alone." His arms tightened around her after his whispered admission and his breath ruffled her hair. They stayed like that until his cell phone buzzed with a message about another patient.

"You should go," she murmured against his chest, her cheeks heating at the affection she'd heard in his words.

He cupped her cheek with his hand, tipping her face up so that he could brush his lips over hers.

An uncomfortable laugh broke from her throat. "Are you leaving or not?"

"Not until you give me a proper goodbye." He nuzzled her neck. "When Levi's better, I want to take you on a proper date. Dinner, flowers, dancing—everything."

"Okay..." Rhiann said, her voice soft, barely above a whisper.

Her heart raced as his lips ghosted over hers once more, just teasing her with the promise of what would follow. His tongue licked at her lower lip, delving into her mouth as it opened. But he pulled back before things got too heated, and she sighed at the loss.

"I'll be back first thing in the morning," he promised.

CHAPTER FIFTEEN

Patrick

WHEN HE GOT to the hospital the next day, he was surprised to find that Rhiann wasn't in Levi's room. He checked the bathroom, and the small break room on the floor. The nurses usually let the parents who overnighted with their kids grab coffee there.

No Rhiann.

He stepped out to the nurses' station. "Do you know where Rhiann Masters is? The mother from Room 5102?" he asked the nurse behind the desk.

She jumped when he spoke, and looked up at him with weary eyes. "She said something about needing a shower and clothes that didn't smell like a hospital. I tried to tell her that anything she wears in here will smell like a hospital in about an hour, but she left anyways."

"Okay, thanks."

He resisted the urge to tell the nurse to grab a coffee. Some of them were just not cut out for the overnight shift.

He walked back down the hall and looked in on Levi, who was still intubated under his orders. He tousled Levi's curls gently, whispering to him, "I'm going to go check on my patients, but I'll be back to see you in a bit. I bet your mama beats me back, though."

But an hour later there was still no sign of Rhiann when he returned to Levi's room. "Where is your mama, huh?"

He washed his hands and moved on with his daily exam. Levi was still relying on the ventilator more than he'd have liked, but the baby had responded fairly well to having it turned down slightly. Patrick adjusted the notes to ask for the vent to be reduced a little more every few hours, so they could wean him off the machine—hopefully by the end of the day.

Exam done, he hung his stethoscope around his neck and reached out to touch Levi's tiny hand. "I always tell my patients' parents to talk to their little ones as if they can hear every word when their kids are lying in these beds, so I'm going to take my own advice and talk to you like you can hear me."

He traced his index finger up and down each of Levi's fingers and swallowed down the overwhelming desire to pick the toddler up. Levi needed time to heal, time to recover. Patrick knew the importance of that more than anyone, but he desperately wanted to feel Levi's slight weight against his chest again.

"I need you to listen up, buddy. I know you've had a rough start, what with your bum heart and your deadbeat father. But I'm going to make sure that the rest of your life goes better for you. I've already fixed your heart. You just have to get a little stronger so you can see that."

He took a deep breath and continued speaking earnestly. "And, it might be a little old-fashioned, but I'd like to ask your permission to date your mom. I know we have a past, and you've heard about some of that. But I swear I'll put it behind us."

Patrick paused to wipe a tear from his eye. He'd messed up a lot of things in the past. But he wasn't lying when he said he was putting it all behind him. Mallory and Everly's deaths had started a chain reaction of loss in his life and he was still recovering. But being here felt right.

For three years he'd only existed. He hadn't been living. Then Rhiann and Levi had come into his life. Now, he wanted to be everything for them. He wanted to truly live because of them. *For* them. *With* them.

He cleared his throat and returned to his one-sided conversation.

"But most of all I promise to be the man your mom needs. She won't have to work so hard, because she'll have me to help her with the bills. You'll have a place where you can't hear the neighbors cough because the walls are so thin, and your mom won't skip meals so that you don't go hungry. I'd even like to say she wouldn't have to work, but your mom loves her job and I don't think she'd give it up. I wouldn't ask her to."

He smiled down at Levi.

"And every night I'll help you with your homework. Your mom's rubbish at math, but I can help you with that. I'll be at all your Little League games, academic team meets, chorus concerts… Whatever extra-curriculars you get into I'll be there, because I want to be the dad you deserve."

A sound in the hall caught his attention and he spun around, expecting to see Rhiann standing behind him, listening to every word he'd just said to Levi, but the doorway was empty.

He released a held breath.

"So, you just get through these next few days, and I'll help with all the rest. I have a lot riding on this. Convincing your mama might take some effort, but I'm up for the challenge. What do you think? Do we have a deal?"

Levi couldn't answer, of course. But Patrick liked to think the little boy would be one hundred percent on board with his plans. He took a few deep breaths and a feeling of contentment washed over him now that he'd voiced his intentions.

When Levi clutched his thumb with his little hand, Patrick sighed. "It's all going to work out," he said. "I won't let you down."

Rhiann

Rhiann stood outside Levi's room with a hand over her mouth, trying to contain a sob. Patrick had obviously heard her gasp, but she'd moved to one side before he'd completely turned around.

Her heart had nearly melted when she'd heard his emotional outpouring to Levi. Okay, so Levi was unconscious, and may or may not be able to hear. But it had been a touching display, nonetheless.

Patrick's voice was low now, but it carried out into the hallway. "I won't let you down."

She closed her eyes and made a wish.

Rhiann had never been much for prayer. She put her belief into science and medicine. People. But she had hopes and wishes as much as anyone else. And right now her wish was simple.

She wanted to spend the rest of her life with the two current occupants of Metro Memorial Hospital's Room 5102.

With a shaky hand, she fished the dandelion necklace Patrick had given her in high school out of her collar and pressed her lips to the small orb for luck. He'd bought her the little trinket at a craft fair they'd attended one weekend on a lark. For sixteen-year-old kids, handmade crafts hadn't been a huge draw, but the shiny resin orb with a dandelion puff in it had caught his eye—because, as he'd said, she was always making wishes, and maybe she just needed a talisman for them to come true.

She'd worn it every day since.

"If you don't marry that man, I will."

Rhiann opened her eyes to see the nurse who'd been with Levi the day of his procedure standing in front of her. Tears had welled up in the other woman's eyes, on the verge of spilling over.

"All this time I thought that man was made of ice—but, oh, my gosh, he's a total softie!"

"Shh..." Rhiann urged. "He'll hear you!"

She grabbed the nurse by the arm and led her away from the open doorway. They went down the hall far enough that Rhiann was sure Patrick wouldn't overhear.

"It's so romantic! Old friends brought back together to save a small child!" The nurse faked a swoon. She even fluttered a hand over her eyes before straightening back up. "All you need is a villain to tear you apart just as he's about to propose and—"

"Hush with all that drama!" Rhiann sighed. "We haven't talked about the future, or what will become of us—if there *is* an us. I can't... My focus has to be on my son right now."

The nurse smiled at her and pulled her in for an impromptu hug. "Your son needs a happy mommy and a sexy new daddy." She waggled her eyebrows. "And if you can't see that man's sex appeal, I'm taking you down to the optical clinic for an eye exam."

Rhiann's cheeks heated and she looked away from the other woman. She wasn't blind. Of course she saw Patrick's appeal. Quite well, actually. Her priorities were just elsewhere at the moment.

"I *knew* you couldn't be oblivious to his charms."

Rhiann shook her head slightly. "My son deserves my undivided attention."

The nurse rolled her eyes. "He's sleeping. I promise you he will not notice if you're counting the tiles in that little room or stealing a kiss from his doctor. One's just a lot more fun."

A laugh escaped Rhiann, despite her intention to show less emotion.

"I need to get back to my son," she said.

It was both an excuse to escape the awkward conversation and the honest truth. She was itching to get back to Levi. To make sure the monitors all had the same readouts and his little heart was still beating. But she also really wanted this impromptu chat to be over.

"Really, I do."

"Okay, but think about what I said." The nurse gave Rhiann's arm a gentle squeeze. "For what it's worth, I'm glad to see someone crack through that ice around his heart."

Rhiann smiled and murmured something in reply, but she wasn't even sure what. She hurried up the hall to her son's room and made a bit more noise than she had earlier. She wanted Patrick to have the opportunity to tell her his feelings on his own terms—not because she'd forced his hand.

When she walked into Levi's room Patrick smiled at her a little sheepishly. She took pity on him and pretended she hadn't heard a word.

"How's Levi?" She moved over to the crib and touched her baby's soft skin. "I just had to get a shower and some clean clothes. I was smelling pretty rank."

He wrapped his arms around her, nuzzling her cheek

with his nose. "Mmm… Not a problem anymore. You smell amazing to me."

"Patrick…"

"Levi's okay. I think he should be able to come off the vent by tomorrow morning. I've put in orders for them to wean him off it. So long as there aren't any hang-ups along the way, the goal is tomorrow morning."

His breath was warm in her ear and the heat from his hand splayed on her stomach was delicious.

A tap on the door behind them sent Patrick jerking away from her. Another of the nurses stood there, her face as pink as the cartoon characters on her scrub top.

"Um… Sorry… Dr. Scott, could you take a look at Dr. Whitehurst's patient in 5116? I've got a call out to Dr. Whitehurst but he hasn't called me back yet. One of the other nurses said you were in here, but I…uh… I didn't mean to interrupt."

She spoke to the floor about three feet in front of Patrick's shoes.

"It's fine, Carrie. I'll be there in one second."

She nodded and left in a hurry, without making eye contact.

Rhiann laughed. "Well, look who just got caught making out beneath the bleachers."

Patrick pulled her to him briefly. His lips barely touched her forehead.

"I'd better go check on this kid. Then I'll be back, and we'll see how Levi does after turning that vent down."

CHAPTER SIXTEEN

Rhiann

SEEING LEVI WITHOUT the vent had sent a wave of relief over Rhiann. Finally, she let herself relax a little—let herself think that everything might be okay. She brushed his hair away from his face, tears in her eyes as she watched him.

"The sedation should wear off soon. We've had to keep him sedated because of the vent, but now that he's off it we can let him wake up. He may be pretty fussy, because his chest's going to hurt. But that's to be expected."

"Thanks, Patrick," she said, without looking up.

"He isn't out of the woods yet, but his numbers are looking good so far."

He stepped up close to her and she could feel his body heat along the length of her spine.

"You're looking pretty good too…"

She elbowed him in the stomach lightly. "Nice try, Doc, but your sweet-talking isn't going to work on me today. I could pass for an extra in a zombie movie, and we both know it."

"Looking tired doesn't make you any less beautiful."

"Hush!"

She sighed. Patrick was saying all the right things,

even doing all the right things. He'd been attentive to both her and Levi. He'd worried about her well-being and made sure she ate, even when she hadn't wanted to think about food. But the timing just wasn't right.

"I need to focus on Levi right now. Can you just hold those thoughts until he's doing better?"

He wrapped his arms around her and rested his head on hers. "I suppose..."

She gave a small sigh.

"Were you alone when Levi was born?" Patrick asked, his entreaty soft and tentative.

She blinked away tears. "I wasn't alone the entire time. Charlie showed up to check on me, and when he realized I was all alone he refused to leave. He ended up holding my hand and seeing far more of me than a partner should, but he stayed by my side. He's the closest thing to a grandparent that Levi has."

Patrick's voice sounded taut when he replied, "I'm glad he was there for you."

"Me too." She turned to face him. "But it made me stronger. It taught me that I didn't really need anyone else. When you don't rely on anyone, no one can let you down or hurt you."

He winced. "That's a pretty hard-hearted take on life."

"That's reality." She shrugged. "Everyone lets you down sooner or later. It doesn't shock or surprise me anymore because it's happened so often. Now it just makes me mad if I let myself get into that position in the first place."

"Rhiann—"

"You know, it's the people who make promises of forever that hurt the most. Pete promised me for better or worse, in sickness and in health, and he took off as soon as we found out Levi was sick."

Pete had hurt her, for sure, but the hurt of her broken marriage was something she could get past. Marriages sometimes ended. Relationships sometimes didn't work out.

Losing her best friend of so many years had caused far more damage to her ability to trust.

She tilted her head and bit her lip for a moment, wondering if she should voice that truth before saying, "And you… I'd say it was ironic, how fast you cut me out of your life for things that were out of my control, but there was no irony in it. Only shattered trust and the affirmation that I shouldn't expect even friendship to last forever."

He took her hand and she could see the struggle on his face as he tried to find words.

"Rhiann, I was broken. Losing Mallory…" he paused to swallow "…and Everly totally broke me. I lashed out at you because you were the one person I *could* blame. I was so…just so angry with life. Angry with myself for not being there for them, with you for not saving them, with Mallory for leaving me. I could barely function. Taking it out on you was not how I should have handled it, I know. But at the time I couldn't see that. Until very recently I couldn't see that."

She pulled her hand away to swipe at a tear running down her cheek. "The past is the past, right?"

"I owe you an apology for all that transpired. I know I can't ever make amends for the hurt that I've caused you."

She waved a hand in the direction of the crib, where her son was starting to stir. "Fixing his heart is enough for me. I don't know what it's like to lose a child, and I hope I never have to find out. I know what it's like to watch your child grow sicker and sicker, though. And this is the healthiest that Levi has looked in months. I would forgive anyone anything if it would make him better."

Patrick

His heart pounded in his chest as her words washed over him. She'd forgive anyone anything if it made Levi better.

Including him?

Taking a step back, Patrick inhaled a deep breath. Rhiann hadn't truly forgiven him, and maybe he didn't deserve her forgiveness.

Swallowing hard, he wished he could punch away the little voice screaming in his head that he *needed* her forgiveness. This was exactly why he didn't want anyone else getting close to him. People got close and then they had the ability to hurt him.

He blinked back what felt suspiciously like tears and strode from the room before he let it slip that her every word was slicing at his heart with a dull scalpel, leaving the type of ragged edges surgeons hated to stitch.

His hand shook as he punched the elevator button. When the elevator took too long he headed for the stairs, jogging down them and wishing that the physical exertion would help him expel the nerves and agitation saturating his body.

When his phone buzzed in his pocket he pulled it out to check the message—from Levi's nurse, who was worried about him. He took the stairs back up two at a time and was nearly out of breath when he made it to the pediatric cardiology floor.

Levi's room was filled with nurses. The charge nurse met his eyes and shook her head. "Dr. Scott, I don't think he was ready to come off the vent."

He squeezed the bridge of his nose. "Let's intubate him again."

Rhiann stepped up to him, hands fisted at her sides. "Can't you give him some more time? Maybe he just has to get used to not having help?"

He reached for her hand, and when she pulled away his soul felt her rejection. "His O2 levels are dropping and his heart-rate is fluctuating because he's having trouble breathing. He needs to be intubated to take some of the strain off his heart."

Moving to the sink, he washed his hands. As he was drying them, Rhiann spun him to face her. Her eyes were filled with tears and she snapped at him.

"Are you doing this because of what I said earlier? That's petty—even for you."

Shoulders back, posture rigid, Patrick towered over her and narrowed his eyes as he spoke.

"If you think that's the kind of man I am we have nothing left to say to each other beyond discussing Levi's care. You may be his mother, but I am his doctor. And I say he needs to be intubated. That has absolutely nothing to do with you and is one hundred percent because he needs it. Now, back away so that we can take care of Levi or I will have you escorted from this building."

She backed into the corner, her hand over her mouth, and he turned his attention from her to the little one struggling to breathe in front of him.

"Give me an ET tube."

CHAPTER SEVENTEEN

Patrick

FORTY-EIGHT HOURS passed before he was willing to take Levi off the vent again.

Time was a funny thing. That same forty-eight-hour stretch would pass all too quickly for someone enjoying a few days off work, but it would be excruciatingly long to a parent watching over a sick child.

Patrick found himself thinking it might have been the longest two days in his life. Longer even than when he'd lost his wife and daughter.

But it had to be even worse for Rhiann, he thought as he headed in after another night with little sleep.

He'd left the hospital at the end of visiting hours and now he was back early for rounds. He could probably push and stay later, but he had to work with those nurses regularly and he didn't want to get on their bad sides.

He didn't want to think about what they might be saying about him after he'd got caught with Rhiann in his arms and then got into a fight with her in a room full of nurses only a few hours later.

Rhiann was barely speaking to him. Every word was rationed, and their conversations were stilted, perfunctory, and only about Levi.

He stepped into the elevator and punched the number five. The doors had almost closed when he heard Clay call out, "Hold the elevator!"

Reaching out, he jabbed at the "open doors" button. The doors shuddered before opening wide once more.

"Thanks, man," Clay said with a bit of a huff as he joined Patrick in the elevator car. "I'm dragging this morning. Got rounds before a long day of appointments."

"I was going to check in on your Tricuspid Atresia kid this morning."

Clay leaned into the corner and sighed. "I'm worried about that one. The repairs look good. On the ultrasound everything looks like it should. But he's just not recovering like I'd hoped."

"I hear that." Patrick exhaled loudly, his cheeks puffing with the effort. "I'm going to try to extubate Levi again this morning. But I gotta tell ya I'm worried."

The elevator dinged and the doors opened on the fifth floor.

"Grab some coffee with me and we'll go round together. You look like you could use a friend this morning." Clay jerked his head toward the break room. "My treat."

Patrick shook his head impatiently. "Coffee's free here, moron."

"Why do you think I offered to pay for it?" Clay smirked. "Come on. Please?"

With a shrug, Patrick fell into step with Clay and they moved down the hall together. "How late were you out last night?" he asked his partner.

Clay opened the door to the staff lounge. He stopped halfway in the door to look at Patrick. "You always assume I was out. I'll have you know last night I was in by ten p.m."

"Date didn't go well?"

He shrugged. "Reached a point in the relationship where I needed more than a flexible pair of legs and she just didn't have anything to offer."

Patrick couldn't really relate to Clay's constant dating, the endless search for the perfect woman. He'd found two women in his life he'd been able to see himself having a future with and had been tempted very little beyond that.

Clay poured two coffees and held one out to Patrick. When he saw his partner's eyes light up with amusement, Patrick's back went up in preparation.

"You wanna hear the rumors circulating around this place?"

Busying himself with adding cream and sugar to his coffee, Patrick replied, "Probably not, but I'm sure you're going to tell me anyways."

Clay grinned. "I hear tell of how a pretty little paramedic and her tiny son have melted the Ice Castle into a slushy puddle of goo."

Patrick shook his head. "You should know better than to listen to gossip."

"Oh, I have it on good authority that you've not only been caught kissing a patient's mama at said patient's bedside, but that you've made promises to that sweet baby that have had ovaries bursting all over this floor. There's gonna be a mess of babies born in nine months that *you* are directly responsible for." He clapped Patrick on the shoulder with a laugh.

Sinking down onto one of the couches, Patrick hung his head a bit. Someone had heard his bedside confessional? *Damn.* Now it would be spreading around the hospital like a wildfire. Hopefully the rumors wouldn't reach Rhiann before he got her speaking to him again.

Clay kicked at his shoe and Patrick grunted before looking up at him.

"Dude, you and Rhiann have always been the end game. I know you loved Mallory, but Rhiann's your soul mate."

"I know."

"So the rumors *are* true!" Clay's smile was so wide you could drive a semi through it. "Good."

Patrick ignored his partner and stared down into his cup full of coffee. He'd never thought of it in terms of Rhiann being his soul mate. He'd had a massive crush on her for years, of course. From the day they'd met up until the day he met Mallory, to be exact. Surprisingly, the terminology didn't feel wrong, though.

"You know they've stopped calling you Ice Castle, right?"

"Never asked them to call me that to start with," Patrick replied gruffly.

Clay stole a brownie out of a box on the table. "Now they're calling you Fudge Brownie, because you're all gooey where it counts."

Patrick leaned back and rubbed his eyes. Sometimes he hated this place, and the gossip culture that seemed forged into its very structure. Every hospital was the same, though. The staff thrived on whatever juicy tidbit they could pass along, whatever rumor they could spread at the change of shift.

He hated being the center of that kind of chatter.

Fudge Brownie. He'd never live the indignity of that one down. At least Ice Castle had earned him some respect.

Tossing the now lukewarm coffee, he followed Clay out the door. "What do you think they'll call me if she never speaks to me again?"

Rhiann

Once Levi had been extubated for the second time, and for two solid days had shown not only no regression but strong improvement, Rhiann let herself relax the slightest bit while Levi slept. The worried vibe in her gut had finally begun to ease.

She stared out the narrow window, with its soulless view of the hospital roof and the side of the adult hospital next door. If she pressed her face to the frigid glass, the corner of the parking garage came into view.

At least this room had some natural light. Often they hadn't been that lucky.

While she gazed down at the layer of tiny brown pebbles covering the roof, she let her thoughts drift away to a future she wanted but dared not speak of. A future where Patrick played a big role in her life as well as Levi's.

The only upside to this hellish week was that Patrick had been close by, to break up the monotony of the days. Well, besides the obvious fact that Levi was still alive.

Of course spending so much time with Patrick also had a downside…

Namely, she had dug herself into a hole she'd never get out of by falling in love with him. It didn't matter that their friendship had been on the rocks for a while. It didn't matter that she should be focused solely on Levi. When Patrick was around she found herself distracted by the gorgeous cardiac surgeon with the heart-stopping grin.

She had no defense against the way her heart reacted to the sight of him holding her son. And now it looked like she'd ruined that by speaking before she thought.

"Knock-knock," a soft voice called from the open door behind her.

She spun around to see Marilyn Scott in the doorway, with a small toy bear in her hands.

"I saw this little guy and couldn't help but get him for Levi."

"Thanks, but you really don't have to keep bringing him things."

It was the fourth little gift she'd brought for Levi this week. He had a stuffed dragon made of red and orange corduroy, a wooden firetruck, and a colorful new storybook as her earlier offerings.

Marilyn sat the bear in the crib next to Levi and ran a hand over his hair. "Of course I do. I'm behind on spoiling him."

Since Levi's surgery Patrick's mother had made her intention of stepping in as Levi's grandmother crystal-clear. She doted on him when he was awake, celebrating his every tiny accomplishment nearly as much as Rhiann herself. And when the baby was asleep Marilyn prayed over him with a fervor that made Rhiann wistful.

She'd lost her own mother several years back, and with Pete's parents out of the picture too Levi had never known the love of a grandmother. The closest thing he had to extended family was Charlie, who was more about tickles and fart noises than prayers and gentle caresses.

And, of course, Marilyn had made her opinion on Rhiann and Patrick tiptoeing around each other just as clear. She was enthusiastically cheering them on, her hints as unsubtle as permanent marker on white paper.

Rhiann's instinct was to deny any feelings on either side, her pulse racing each time. But her heart tended to skip beats, and every inch of her was very aware when Patrick was near. Her heated blushes most likely gave her away, but she still maintained they were merely friends.

Although these last few days, she wasn't even sure she could truthfully call them that.

"How's our little man doing today?" Marilyn asked.

"Patrick said he might get to go home tomorrow, actually," Rhiann told her with a genuine smile. "He's doing great. He's still sleeping a lot, but he stood up this morning, and even took a few steps around the edge of the crib. He's getting upset about the IV, though, so we've had to start watching him like a hawk when he's awake to keep him from pulling it out."

Marilyn snorted. "The boy has to make up for all the mischief he's missed out on while he's been sick. He'll be climbing walls before you know it."

Rhiann closed her eyes briefly on a prayer. "I'll never complain about his activity level—and that's a promise."

"Ah, but I bet you might have a word or two to say about the mischief he'll make. Lord only knows how much Patrick got into as a child. I wish some days for a little of that mischief to return. Now he's grown up on me. Sometimes I think I should have had a dozen kids, so that I wouldn't have so much free time now." She sighed—a long, sad sound. "But wishes aren't worth the paper they're written on, are they?"

Rhiann smiled sadly in commiseration. She'd always wanted to have several children, but she wasn't sure that would happen now, given her current relationship status. "I don't know if Levi will ever have a sibling, but maybe someday."

Marilyn winked at her. "I have faith."

She hugged the older woman. "Thank you. For your faith and for being here this week."

"Where else would I be?"

A tap on the doorframe brought Rhiann's head around.

"Charlie!" She moved away from Marilyn to pull her

partner in for a hug. "I wondered when you'd get around to showing your ugly mug."

"Some of us have jobs," he teased, tugging at a lock of Rhiann's hair. "You know, I don't think I've ever seen you with your hair down…"

"It's good to see you again, Charlie." Marilyn nodded at him.

Charlie smiled a mega-watt smile at the older woman. "Trust me, Mrs. Scott, it's my pleasure."

Patrick's mom returned his smile with one of her own. "I've been meaning to ask…how did the fundraiser turn out? There was quite a crowd, so I imagine it went well."

Charlie nodded, and Rhiann felt her eyes welling up in memory of the community's kindness.

"Better than I even expected. It was enough to pay off Levi's old medical bills and make a start on the new ones."

"That's wonderful news!" Marilyn clapped her hands in exclamation and then sent a worried look over to the crib, to make sure she hadn't woken Levi. When the baby didn't flinch she continued, her voice softer, "I'm so glad to hear it."

"I couldn't believe the turnout." Rhiann sighed, still overwhelmed at the amount of people who'd come out to show their support.

"I can," Charlie said, as he propped a shoulder against the narrow window, blocking most of the natural light. "You do so much for others that you shouldn't really be surprised when they return the favor in your hour of need."

Rhiann shook her head, feeling heat rising into her face as she blushed at Charlie's praise. "I only do my job…"

Charlie snorted. "That job means the world to a lot

of people, and they were more than happy to show you just how much."

"Do you know how much I cried that night?" Rhiann tucked a long strand of hair behind her ear. "Each and every person who came up to me made me cry, I think."

"You should be proud of the impact you've had in their lives. I know I'm certainly proud of you and all that you've accomplished." Marilyn hugged her close. "Now, I have a meeting to get to, but I'll see you tomorrow. Kiss Levi for me when he wakes."

Marilyn waved as she left.

Rhiann turned to Charlie. "What brings you by today?"

"Can't a man come see his favorite girl without his motives being suspect?"

Rhiann was shaking her head at him, smiling widely, when movement in the doorway caught her eye.

CHAPTER EIGHTEEN

Patrick

HE'D GOTTEN INTO the habit of ending his rounds with Levi. Most days Rhiann was alone. A couple times his mom had been there. Once the babysitter had been visiting, but she'd left quickly after stuttering out a mumbled apology.

Finding another man in the room was *not* something he had expected. And seeing her smile at that man stabbed him right in the gut and twisted him up in knots a sailor would have been proud of.

He swallowed down the ball of envy lodged in his throat and tried to plaster a smile on his face when Rhiann looked up and they made eye contact. He wanted her to look at *him* with a smile on her face. He wanted to see those little dimples that only came out when she laughed showing up at *his* dark and sarcastic humor.

"Patrick!"

He moved quickly to Levi's side. "How's he been today?"

She followed him over to the crib and watched as he listened to Levi's heart and lungs.

Patrick closed his eyes and shut out Rhiann and the emotions of the moment. Once he'd calmed himself, he listened to the satisfying sounds coming from the baby's chest. Finally he was willing to call the surgery a success, because everything sounded perfect. Levi's coloring looked good, and he'd lost the blue tint to his lips and hands.

"He's been good. Still sleeping a lot, but he's eaten better than he *ever* has at all his meals today. He even toddled around the edge of the crib some."

With a gentle touch, he ran his hand over Levi's hair. His arms ached to pick the little one up and let him snuggle into his chest again.

"Good. As long as he doesn't have a setback tonight, I think we can get him out of here in the morning."

Even as he said it, he wanted to take it back. As long as Levi was in the hospital he had easy access to him—and to Rhiann. Once she took Levi home, though, he wouldn't have any reason to see them every day. But he couldn't hold Levi's progress back for personal reasons.

"That's great news!" the other man in the room said, drawing Patrick and Rhiann's attention back to him. "I know you're ready to get home."

Patrick's grip tightened around his stethoscope. He didn't like the familiarity in the other man's tone. Or how comfortable he looked in Rhiann's presence. He didn't like it because he felt excluded. Rhiann clearly considered Charlie family now, and he'd once been counted in that rank. Until a few days ago he had thought he might be again...

Rhiann smiled at Charlie like he'd just said the most brilliant thing in the world. "I still won't be back to work for a while, though, if I can swing the finances."

"Right. But a man can hope. I'd just about kill to get a steady partner again. I'm getting too old for this new-partner-each-day nonsense, you know."

"I'll be back when I'm back, Charlie," she said with a smirk.

And Patrick saw her eyes light with mischief. The type of mischief that she'd used to aim at *him*.

"Besides, getting me back isn't going to change the fact that you're getting old," she teased.

"Ain't that the truth?" The older man snorted. "Well, I'm going to take my old self home for the night. Four a.m. will be here all too soon."

"Thank you for coming by," Rhiann told him softly. Then she stepped into his arms and allowed him to pull her close for a goodbye hug.

Patrick tried not to watch. He didn't need to torture himself with seeing Rhiann in the other man's arms. But he couldn't tear his eyes away. There was nothing sexual about it—nothing that even hinted at anything beyond a close friendship—but it still hurt that he'd lost that closeness with her.

Charlie stepped over and stuck his hand out to shake Patrick's. "I want to thank you for taking care of Rhiann and her little man. It means a lot to me."

Patrick shook his hand. "They mean a lot to me too."

Charlie smiled widely at him, understanding the meaning behind Patrick's declaration. He nodded at him. "Good. Y'all have a good night."

With Charlie gone, the silence stretched between him and Rhiann, hanging awkwardly while he tried to find words that might ease the awkwardness.

"Do you really think he can go home tomorrow?" she asked.

"That's my hope." He tapped his fingers against his thigh. "And pretty soon you won't have to see me again. You won't have to pretend to forgive me, or act as though you like me, when inside you're cringing at my touch."

She stared at him, an incredulous look on her face. "Is that what you think I want?"

"I have no idea what you really want. Every time I think things are on track between us suddenly—*bam!*—we're hemorrhaging emotions and I can't find the bleeder." He ran a hand through his hair. "I know what *I* want, but I'm not sure it's compatible with this new-found desperation of yours to be on your own."

He swallowed hard.

"Somehow you and Levi broke through my defenses, and despite my vow never to let anyone close enough to hurt me again, here I stand, my heart racing like a teenage boy's, telling the girl he's crushing on that he likes her and praying she doesn't laugh in his face."

Arms wrapped around herself, she said, "Do I look like I'm laughing? Does the idea of being with me sound like a joke to you?"

The tiniest tendril of hope wrapped around his heart.

He stepped forward and laid a hand on her shoulder, but she pulled away.

Rhiann

Going to stand by the window, Rhiann stared out over the small section of roof, wishing there was a better view. Wishing there was somewhere she could go in this tiny room that would allow her to put a little distance between them at that moment.

When Patrick touched her she had problems thinking clearly. And she needed to think clearly if they were to move forward with any sort of relationship.

"Rhiann, no." He moved up behind her, his hands skimming up her arms from wrist to bicep. "Look at it from my perspective. I thought we were moving forward.

We were getting along again. The chemistry between us could start fires. And yet… And yet there's a gap between us that you won't let me breach."

"I don't want to get hurt again."

Patrick kissed the side of her throat. "I know that."

His lips hovered over her pulse and she arched her neck to allow him better access.

"Please," she begged him, not even certain herself if she was asking him for more or to stop.

When his mouth suckled gently at the pulse-point in her throat all her thoughts were scrambled into a nonsensical mess. His touch turned her from a level-headed paramedic, a strong single mother, into a fangirl who had just met her favorite celebrity.

But all too soon he pulled away.

"This isn't the place or the time," he said, by way of apology for ending something that had such exquisite potential.

He was right, of course. And they had a lot to talk about before they took things further.

But before she could bring that up Levi started to stir.

"Levi's waking up," she said, pushing away from the window and moving to her son's side, switching her focus from Patrick to Levi. "Hello, sleepyhead, did you have a good nap?"

She brushed his shaggy hair out of his eyes. Once he was feeling a little better she'd have to take him in for his first haircut—a milestone she hadn't been sure he'd reach. But every day his color improved, and all hint of blue was gone from his lips and fingertips now. Levi was growing stronger by the minute, and the new potential for him filled her with such hope.

He raised his little arms to her, wanting a cuddle.

She lowered the rail on the crib and picked him up

carefully, so as not to irritate his incision. He snuggled into her chest and went to pop a thumb into his mouth, frowning when his eyes landed on the IV in his hand. He reached for it with his other hand.

"Not quite yet, little guy," Patrick said, with a hint of amusement in his voice as he blocked Levi's access to the IV. "I'll get a nurse to go ahead and take that out for you, though, since it's bothering you so much.

"You can't do it?" Rhiann asked.

He tickled Levi's side gently. "I don't want him to connect me with anything painful, so I'd rather not."

She raised an eyebrow at him. "You did his surgery."

"Yeah, and he was sound asleep, with no idea that I was the one holding the scalpel that sliced through his precious skin. He's awake now. Completely different situation."

"You big softie."

She squeezed Patrick's hand. His gentleness with Levi made her fall for him a little more each time she saw the two of them together. Each smile he bestowed upon her son found one more chink in the armor around her heart.

"Only when it comes to you two." He winked at her. "I'll be back."

She watched Patrick leave before turning her attention back to Levi. "You need to leave that IV alone, baby. You wanna play? Look at this bear!" She grabbed the little brown teddy that Patrick's mom had brought by earlier. "Look at this guy. He's convinced someone that he needs to come live with you—can you believe that?"

She paused, and Levi babbled a bit.

"Of *course* you can believe that. Why *wouldn't* he want to come live with you? I know. Mommy's silly for even thinking that was unbelievable."

She made the bear dance in front of Levi. He kept his

eyes on the bear with a smile on his face, and the occasional laugh snuck out. It kept him distracted from the IV for the moment too.

Rhiann couldn't have kept the smile off her face if she'd tried. Love for Levi filled her to overflowing, and his happiness made her so joyous it could hardly be contained.

When Patrick came back in with a nurse, Levi beamed a radiant smile at him. He reached out for Patrick to pick him up, and Patrick did so without hesitation.

"Someone woke up in a good mood," Patrick said, hugging Levi close.

Levi chattered at him in a string of unintelligible noises.

Patrick treated the conversation seriously. "Your bear is a crazy dancer, you say? Has your mommy been giving him lessons? She's one of the most enthusiastically bad dancers I know. I'll have to tell you a story about our senior prom. It involves a wardrobe malfunction, five stitches, and a set of lost car keys—but that's a story for another time."

The nurse snorted and then tried unsuccessfully to cover the sound. She kept her head down while she got the bandage and supplies ready to remove Levi's IV.

"All right, Mr. Levi, you ready to get that IV out?" the nurse asked him.

Levi loved it when the nurses came in and talked to him. He couldn't get enough attention—particularly from the younger nurses. He giggled and waved at her.

"I'm gonna take that as a yes." She turned to Patrick. "You wanna sit down here with him, so you can hold him still?"

Patrick sank down into the avocado-colored recliner and the nurse made quick work of taking the IV out. In less than a minute it was gone, and Levi had a brightly colored *Sesame Street* bandage in its place. The few tears he'd thought about crying had soon dried up when he'd been handed a pink popsicle.

The nurse cleaned up and then removed her gloves with a snap. "I'll be in later to check on him."

Levi relaxed against Patrick, happily slurping on the popsicle in his hand, the very picture of contentment. And Rhiann had to admit Patrick looked quite content too.

"He looks happy there with you."

Patrick grinned up at her, his eyes bright. "I'm pretty happy here with him too."

While she meant every syllable of what she'd said, the next phrase that came out of her mouth surprised them both.

"I love you."

CHAPTER NINETEEN

Rhiann

THE NIGHT PASSED fitfully for Rhiann. Levi slept through without a peep, but she tossed and turned on the lumpy reclining chair without much rest. Her mind would not shut off long enough to let her sleep. Patrick's sudden departure the night before had her worrying she'd pushed too far, too fast, even though her rational mind knew that he'd been called to see another patient.

She'd already lost too many people in her life. With her own mom long gone, and no dad to speak of, Levi, Patrick and Charlie were all she had.

Besides Levi, Patrick was the most important person in her life. She couldn't bear to lose him again.

Clearly Patrick had not expected her to blurt out an admission of love. She hadn't exactly expected it herself.

Oh, she'd always loved him as her best friend. But now she loved him with the heart of a woman who had known loss. Loved him as the man she wanted to spend her life with.

When residents and doctors started coming down the hall Rhiann finally gave up on trying to sleep and got dressed for the day. Patrick had said Levi could go home this morning, and she was more than ready to get out of the hospital. Maybe in her own bed tonight she'd actually sleep.

She packed all Levi's things while she waited for him to wake up, tucking all the stuffed animals that Patrick's mom had brought him into the diaper bag.

When Levi woke, Rhiann changed his diaper and put a fresh shirt on him.

"Mommy will get you a proper bath once we get home," she promised him. "Between me and you, I don't really want to take you back to that dingy old apartment—but it's home, I guess. Sometime soon Mommy will get you a better place to live. Somehow..."

She looked up to find Patrick leaning against the doorframe. Heat flooded her face as she wondered how much of her little confession he'd heard, but she held her head high. Not having the funds for a nicer place was something out of her control at the moment, but maybe with Levi finally healthy she could start saving toward a better apartment.

"You ready to bust out of this prison?"

"Beyond ready."

He rolled his eyes and strode forward. "I was talking to Levi."

"I think I can speak for him on this matter."

Patrick handed her some papers. "His release paperwork. The nurse will be in in a moment to go over it with you—hospital rules."

Rhiann flipped through the sheets. Diet, exercise, wound care... Standard stuff. Nothing concerning. She laid the paperwork on top of Levi's bag.

Patrick stood next to the crib, tickling Levi and making faces at him. Levi laughed and didn't even have a coughing fit. He was truly on his way to being healthy, thanks to Patrick, which was giving her one more reason to fall for the man.

If Patrick Scott looked over at her and they made eye contact there was no way he wouldn't see the love that must surely be shining from her eyes like a lighthouse, beckoning him to her, and that might send him running again. So she busied herself double-checking that she'd packed all Levi's things.

With focused determination she scanned every inch of the hospital room, looking for any item that might have escaped her initial perusal.

"You okay?" Patrick asked, wrapping his arms around her from behind.

"Mmm-hmm." She tried not to melt into his arms—really, she did. But her body had other plans and she found herself leaning into the delicious warmth of his touch. "Just ready to take Levi home."

"You wouldn't be trying to get away from me, would you?"

She shook her head, unable to put her voice to words for fear that her true feelings would come tumbling out with no stopping them.

"Good. I have a surprise for you when we leave here."

Curiosity got the best of her and she looked up at him and made eye contact, despite her concerns.

"I'm not telling you what. You'll just have to wait."

He flashed her a grin that made her heart do crazy things. But the nurse came in to go over the discharge instructions before Rhiann could question Patrick about what he had planned.

Within a few minutes Levi was officially discharged, and he was tucked safely into the back of Patrick's car only a short while after that.

"I don't know why you wouldn't let me drive myself

home. You'll have to take me back to the hospital to get my car at some point."

Patrick hadn't got on the interstate to head toward her apartment, she noticed. Instead, he drove out past Vanderbilt and toward Green Hills. She watched the houses and businesses go by.

"Where are you taking us?" she asked finally.

"You'll see." Patrick reached over and took her hand in his. "You trust me, right?"

"Yes…" she said, dragging the single syllable out to the length of three.

But she sank back into the seat and tried to ignore the sweet sensation of his thumb grazing over the palm of her hand.

Lush vegetation nearly hid the driveway Patrick turned in to. Rhiann sat up straighter and examined their surroundings. The narrow lane opened to a small yard and then the most adorable little cottage, with trim that looked like gingerbread.

"Where are we?"

"Home."

"You moved?"

He nodded. "That modern half-glass monstrosity downtown was all Mallory. I never did like it. And with her and Everly gone all those reflective surfaces did was show me how alone I was. This is as far I as I could get from that."

Traditional architecture had always held sway over Rhiann. She'd take a stately old Victorian over a high-rise condo any day. Or, in this case, a cozy cottage over crazy modern angles. With the addition of a few chairs or rockers she could picture spending a lot of time sitting on that porch, watching Levi play. And with just a little work the already secluded yard could be transformed into the perfect oasis away from the stresses of working in the medical field.

"I love it."

Grinning at her, he opened the car door. "I was hoping you'd say that. Now, let's get our boy inside."

Our boy.

Like before, hearing Patrick claim Levi sent Rhiann's heart into a frenzy.

If only…

Patrick

With Levi in his arms, Patrick led Rhiann up the steps and into the little cottage he'd bought after losing Mallory and Everly. His realtor had hit a game-winning home run with this place. He'd told the guy he wanted something the complete opposite of the modern house he'd lived in with his late wife and this had been the first house he'd been shown.

He loved the character of the little house. It had a welcoming charm that was missing from the sleek lines and crisp angles of modern architecture. The crown moldings and wide windows added a homey touch that had whispered *This is home* from his first step inside the front door.

Over the last three years he'd spent hours upon hours on the porch, just soaking up the healing silence he found here. The small acreage had proved to be the perfect buffer to drown out the hustle and bustle of the city around him.

Until today, his parents and Clay had been the only people he'd allowed to invade the sanctuary he'd created here. But with Rhiann, it didn't feel like she was invading—more like she was enhancing his space.

He watched her face, hoping she'd love the coziness as much as he did.

"This place..." she said. "Wow. Somehow you've found a house that's the architectural version of you."

He snorted. "What does *that* mean?"

She shrugged. "The view is nice from the outside, but the look maybe doesn't appeal to everyone. This house looks like it has frosting on the eaves, and you have frost in your eyes, but once you get past the frosty exterior you find a warm and welcoming heart that feels just a bit lonely. Strong bones, but empty without a family."

Patrick's breath caught. Every word she'd said fit like a glove, but he was hoping to change that last bit...

"Look again." He managed to get out the words, surprised when his voice didn't crack under the pressure.

"Hmm...?" She looked around, her eyes scanning for something she might have missed.

"Go down the hall a bit. Maybe try the first door on the left."

Confusion filled her eyes, but she did as he suggested. Patrick followed her with Levi in his arms. She opened the door cautiously—and then gasped as she peeked inside.

"Patrick!" She looked back at him, fat tears welling up in her eyes.

"Levi? You wanna play in your room while I talk to your mommy?"

His heart raced as he set Levi gently on the colorful rug just inside the door. He'd barely slept this week, trying to make the perfect bedroom for the little boy, filling it with cars and trucks and all the things a boy needed.

"You set up a room for Levi here?"

Her voice shook. The emotion in her eyes gave him hope that by the end of the day his house and his heart would no longer be missing a family.

"Of course I did. I want him to spend a lot of time here." He took one of her hands in his and tugged her into the room across the hall. "This is my office. We'll leave the door open so we can hear Levi, but there's a bit more privacy. I have a lot to say, and a nursery's not the ideal spot for it."

"Okay…"

"Sit."

He gently nudged her toward one of the wingback leather chairs. Once she'd sunk down onto the edge of the seat, he kneeled in front of her.

"Rhiann, I don't deserve your forgiveness, but I'm asking for it. I know that Mallory and Everly's deaths were not your fault. I know that—and maybe deep down I always did. But I blamed you for years because I needed a scapegoat. Because if I didn't blame you for their deaths then I'd have to look inward and take my share of the guilt. I've never admitted this to anyone before, but I was away at a conference the entire week before they died. I was supposed to come in the night before, but my flight got bumped. Rather than cancel or reschedule my appointments, I went straight to my office instead of going home to them."

"Patrick—"

"Let me finish." He took a deep breath. "When they called me to the ER, while Mallory was still in surgery, a doctor told me that if the paramedics had gotten her there sooner they'd have had a chance. I latched onto that phrase like it was the gospel. I used his words as reinforcement that *you* were to blame and not me. You, because you were there and couldn't save them—not me, because I should have been there. I thought that as a surgeon I would have seen the signs…"

She put her fingers over his mouth to stop him from

talking. "You can't do that to yourself. No one was at fault. There was a bad wreck on the interstate that day. We had to go back and circle around through a neighborhood. It took us longer than was ideal to get to the hospital, yes, but the only way either of them could have been saved would have been if the obstetrician had caught the issues with the placenta before that day. Maybe—and this is a big maybe—maybe if it had happened at the hospital, where they could have been taken to the OR immediately, with the blood bank on standby… I tried—Patrick, you have to believe that I did everything I could that day—but I just couldn't save them. You couldn't have either."

He kissed her fingers before pulling them away from his mouth. "I know that now. And I know that there was absolutely nothing you could have done to change the outcome for Mallory or Everly. I am so ashamed that I ever believed you hadn't done everything within your power to save them. You would have done everything for a stranger. Knowing they were my family and you couldn't save them had to have broken your heart. And then I pushed you away too."

"Of course I would have." She teared up. The raw pain in her eyes spoke of her sincerity. "I loved them too, you know. I was looking forward to being Auntie Rhiann to your daughter. I grieved their loss like I grieved for losing my best friend."

"Can you forgive me for the last three years?"

He held his breath as he waited for her reply.

Rhiann

"There's nothing to forgive. I knew from the start you were just lashing out due to grief. I always hoped you'd come around—I was just trying to give you the space you needed to mourn."

She cupped his cheek with a shaking hand. Knowing she truly had her best friend back filled her heart with an overwhelming joy.

"There is a lot to be forgiven, actually, and I don't deserve a friend like you," said Patrick, and the storm in his blue eyes reflected the depth of his regret. His solemn expression added to the seriousness of his speech.

She teased him a bit, trying to lighten the somber mood. "I'm willing to put the past behind us so long as you promise never to be so stupid again."

"I'll try." He chuckled. "I'm gonna take a peek at Levi."

He walked to the doorway and looked across the hall. Rhiann wondered if he was seriously concerned with Levi's well-being at that moment or if he just needed a break from the serious conversation they were having.

Rhiann leaned back in the chair and watched him look in on Levi. "Is he okay?"

He looked over his shoulder and grinned. "He's sitting in the middle of the rug surrounded by alphabet blocks. We might have a future writer on our hands."

"You keep saying 'we' and 'our.'" She laughed, trying to not let her hopes grow too high. "You trying to lay claim to my son?"

"It's impossible not to love that little guy. I've fallen in love with him *and* with the idea of being his dad." He walked back over to her. "I'm pretty over the moon for his mommy too..."

"Patrick—"

He sank down on one knee in front of her. "Rhiann Masters, I am head over heels in love with you. I know all too well how short life can be, and I don't want to wait another day to start our lives together."

His right hand fumbled in his pocket for a second before bringing out a small black box.

"Will you allow me the honor of being your husband and Levi's dad?"

"Yes." She leaned forward and sealed her answer with a kiss.

Their lips met and Rhiann would have sworn their souls entwined. When she'd walked into his office that day only a short time ago, scared but determined, she had only asked for Patrick to give her son a future. She'd had no idea how much bringing Patrick back into her life would change everything—and not just for Levi.

After Pete had raked her heart and soul over the scorching coals of heartbreak she'd sworn off men. Focused entirely on Levi, she'd dropped back from truly living into barely surviving without realizing.

Patrick's presence had opened her eyes to that.

Patrick had healed Levi's heart and somehow patched hers up along the way.

Patrick broke the kiss to slip a ring on her finger. "You haven't even looked at this ring. I could have put costume jewelry on your finger."

"I love you. What you put on my finger means nothing compared to the love you've put in my heart."

"Sap," he teased, before brushing his lips across her forehead. "I love you. So, can I go play with my son now?"

"Go ahead."

Rhiann stood and watched as the man she loved gently picked up her son and tickled his sides. The love in his eyes matched the love in her heart.

She looked down at the beautiful ring on her finger and smiled.

Sometimes wishes did come true.

EPILOGUE

Three years later
Patrick

PATRICK SANK DOWN onto the grass and wiped a few blades of cut grass from the engraved marble.

"Hi, Mallory, Everly… I've brought someone for you guys to meet. Everly, this is your baby sister Arden. She's only a few days old, so I can't keep her out here long."

He shifted into a more comfortable position with Arden in his lap.

"I'll always miss you girls. And don't worry—I'll make sure to tell Arden all about you when she's old enough to understand."

"Daddy!"

He looked up to see Levi running full-force toward him. The four-year-old had made a complete recovery. Without seeing the scars on his chest, it was impossible to tell he'd ever had a heart problem.

"Hey, buddy."

Levi plopped down on the grass next to him. "I beat Mommy racing over here. But I think she let me win. She said we need to let you talk to the girls. But I think you don't want to be outnumbered." Levi gave him a little side-eyed grin. "Mommy doesn't know how boys think, does she?"

Patrick put an arm around his son and hugged him close, trying really hard not to laugh. "I'll always be happy to see you."

Levi reached over and tickled Arden. "Why doesn't she laugh yet?"

"She's too little."

He sighed. "She needs to hurry up and grow, because I need someone to play with."

Rhiann laughed as she walked up, catching only Levi's last statement. "I tried to keep him over by the car, but he's a little faster than I am at the moment. I didn't want him to disturb you. He was just antsy in the car."

"He's fine." He tousled Levi's blond hair. "Levi, do you think you can walk slowly back to the car with Mommy? Don't make her run, though, okay? Mommy needs to take it easy, like we talked about. I'll be right there."

When Rhiann held her hand out Levi took it reluctantly. He looked over his shoulder at Patrick. "Okay, Daddy…but only 'cause you asked me."

Rhiann smiled softly at him before she walked Levi back to the car.

He put a hand on the headstone. "The first few years without you both I barely survived. I shut out the possibility of love. But then Rhiann and Levi came into my life and forced their way into my heart."

He looked across the carefully mown grass to where his beautiful wife was walking with his son. And then down to the baby sleeping in his lap.

"And now we have Arden."

The breeze picked up and carried to him a soft note of gardenia. He closed his eyes and inhaled deeply. The scent reminded him of the perfume Mallory used to wear, and he thought maybe it was a sign that she approved of how he'd moved on.

"I love you both. Goodbye."

When he reached the car, Rhiann asked, "Did you have a good chat?"

"Thank you."

"For what?" she asked, taking Arden from him for a quick cuddle before she buckled the baby into her car seat.

"For being you."

His arms surrounded her before she could move away from the open car door.

"For being my wife and understanding that my love for them doesn't mean I love you any less."

He leaned down.

Seconds before his lips touched hers he was interrupted.

"Are you guys gonna kiss *again*? Grandma says you-all kiss too much and that's where Arden came from. Can you go for a brother this time? Because I don't want another sister..."

"I'm game if you are," Patrick told her. "Or at least I'm up for a little practice."

"You wish!"

The contagious happy laugh that escaped from his wife was a joyous sound he wouldn't mind hearing every day of his life.

She laid her head on his shoulder and he kissed the top of her head.

"Every day."

* * * * *

MILLS & BOON

Coming next month

UNLOCKING THE EX-ARMY DOC'S HEART
Juliette Hyland

Rafe's phone continued to ding. Apparently, a late-night ice cream post was popular. He ignored it, but the world invaded their private heaven with each buzz.

—I also want you. The real Rafe. The swing dancer, who has a midnight sweet tooth and gets cold easily. Not the persona that makes an algorithm happy. Annie swallowed the words as she spun her pint to him and grabbed his. "My turn for the chocolate."

A smile pulled at Rafe's lips. Lifting his spoon, he laughed, "I don't want cookie dough. *En garde*, Annie."

Giggling, she defended the chocolate from the swipes of his spoon as he dove for the pint. This was belonging. Laughing over ice cream, late at night, with no audience. How could she make him understand?

Finally, she pushed it to the middle of the table. "Guess I can share." The bottom of the pint appeared too quickly, and Annie waved away Rafe's offer to let her have the final bite. Looking at the clock, she reluctantly pushed away from the table. *If she didn't leave now...* "Thanks for keeping me company. We have a full schedule tomorrow. I think we both need some sleep."

Annie's fingers brushed his as they reached for the empty ice cream containers at the same time. Lightning flashed between them, and Annie didn't care about the buzz of the phone, or anything else. She just wanted, needed, to know how he kissed.

"Rafe," ignoring the tension racing through her belly,

she leaned forward. He tasted of chocolate, heat and summer. Her heart gasped at the tender way his mouth shifted under hers, accepting her exploration. If she took his hand, he'd come with her to bed. The thought excited her before panic rushed into its place.

Stepping away she stared at him, "I—"

Rafe placed a finger against her lips. "Don't apologize. Please."

Pursing her lips, she grabbed the containers, holding them before her, an empty sugar wall between her and temptation. "I wasn't going to apologize." Annie held her breath, wishing she had the courage to ask him to follow her, and hating the uncertainty that kept the words buried.

Rafe soft lips brushed her cheek, "I'll see you tomorrow."

His words held a promise and an escape.

Continue reading
UNLOCKING THE EX-ARMY DOC'S HEART
Juliette Hyland

Available next month
www.millsandboon.co.uk